Dedicated to every reader who turned to books to escape this crazy time in history. Thank you for reading our stories.

Introduction
by Mandy Haynes

The idea for this anthology came to me after receiving a message from a reader on social media. Even though we've never met in person, we've become friends through emails, posts, and messages. She's an avid reader and I enjoy talking with her about authors and books we both love. When Covid raised its ugly head, she knew all the plans I'd made to promote my new book were put on hold.

She started checking in on me to make sure I was doing okay, getting enough sleep, and eating my vegetables. Basically, she's become my second mom. Writing can be a lonely job, but her messages remind me that writers are never alone as long as we have readers. She always asks how my writing is going and ended the most recent message with, "If you're working on anything new and want to share, know I'd love to read it!"

I woke up the next morning with the idea for *Work In Progress.*

I don't know if you remember the Breck Shampoo commercial where the image of the girl with that head full of shiny hair keeps multiplying on the screen as she says, "*…and they'll tell two friends, and they'll tell two friends, and so on and so on…*" but that's what came to mind. If a reader picked up a copy of *Work In Progress* to read one excerpt, they would have *at least* ten new authors to follow by the time they put it down.

As soon as I finished my first cup of coffee, I sent an email out my fellow Pulpwood Queen and Timber Guy Authors to see if they would like to participate. By the time I finished my third cup, fifteen authors had sent in their submissions. On the day of the deadline, I'd received over sixty submissions.

Some of the authors that shared their stories are multi-award winning, best-selling authors who have lots of readers anxiously waiting for their next publication. Some of them are debut authors just getting started who don't have quite as many readers (yet). Some of them have been members of The International Pulpwood Queen and Timber Guy Book Club Reading Nation for years, and some of them are just finding out what it means to be a Pulpwood Queen and Timber Guy. But every one of them are authors I'm proud to know, and I'm excited to share their stories! So you can share them with friends, and *they'll share with friends, and so on, and so on....*

Thank you, dear readers, for your support! We'd be lost without you!

Forward

Why do I love the International Pulpwood Queens & Timber Guys Book Club? Let me count the ways…. Sixteen years. Five Girlfriend Weekends. A family of readers and writers too numerous to count. And then, there's Queen Kathy…

When I first discovered Beauty and the Book in 2007, the hot pink website matched the new paint on my sad single-mom-trying-to-be-sexy bedroom walls. I already had a tiara and pink feathered boa, required by a friend who dragged me to my first post-divorce New Year's Eve party. I also had a new novel, *Wife Goes On*, about how friends make all the difference. So I read *The Pulpwood Queens Tiara-Wearing, Book-Sharing Guide to Life,* emailed Kathy L. Murphy, and joined the club. It was a match made in book heaven.

Riding the rollercoaster of being a writer through the ups and downs of agents, publishers, divorce, motherhood, remarriage, cancer, and Covid, there is one thing that helped me hang on: my tiara. By 2009, we had emailed 68 times. (That's how many I saved, anyway.) We traded personal stories of mothers & daughters and professional tales of business & books. I felt special. So, I saved up and treated myself to the bundled birthday present of a flight from California to Louisiana, a rental car to drive to Texas, and an adorable room with a four-poster bed at the Delta Inn B&B – all to attend my first Girlfriends Weekend in the tiny town of Jefferson. There, I learned that it wasn't just me who felt special. That weekend - the first time I saw crocodile on a restaurant menu - I met authors River Jordan, Melanie Benjamin, Barbara Claypool White, Karin Gillespie, Hank Philippi

Ryan, and so many more who *all* felt special. And it wasn't just the authors…

When I arrived at Girlfriends Weekend, our sparkly craft-store tiaras made us all royalty, readers and writers alike. Jane Porter shared her sweet social media person, who helped me for years. Kaya McLaren stopped to visit me in LA while on a road trip and taught me about eating organic. Local Pulpwood members started meeting every month for lunch. So many new friends! And oh, so many good books to read and recommend!

I couldn't resist encouraging Caroline Leavitt, a hardcore vegetarian New Yorker, to brave this crazy southern weekend soon after… and she loved it. After that, I was sick for a few years. When I started going to conferences in a wig to promote my new novel, What A Mother Knows, I met Marci Nault. We became roommates at the Girlfriend Weekend in 2014, dressed as bobby-soxers to serve the traditional Friday night dinner for book club members. With a head covered in chemo curls, I had a blast playing Audrey Hepburn to Jamie Ford's Hunter Thompson at the Saturday night Gala. From the Elvis impersonator to the book club costume contest, the theme was always: fun.

The mood remained long after unpacking my tiara. When North Carolinian Denise Kiernan was in LA unexpectedly, I wasn't able to see her. But I gave her my home office for the afternoon. This is the level of trust between Girlfriends. I have dinner with Becky Aikman whenever she's in town. Julie Cantrell and I share a lifesaving personal connection despite the distance between us. Pulpwood Queens are friends you can count on.

When A Boob's Life: How America's Obsession Shaped Me… And You got a publishing deal on the eve of the Covid-19 lockdown, I had mixed feelings. I'd spent five long years on this book, switched agents and publishers, and was now attracting attention from producer Salma Hayek for HBO Max! Yet there was no longer any chance of a book tour, public speaking, or traditional promotion. There were far more serious problems at hand. So, I put on my tiara and contacted my Pulpwood pals. And of course, I called Kathy.

Sure enough, our Queen was up to the challenge of celebrating life and literacy during lockdown. She created a Zoom Slumber Party for the International Pulpwood Queens and Timber Guys Girlfriends

Weekend that opened the doors to readers around the world. But she didn't stop there. She created the daily blog The Pulpwood Queen Presents, a Book & Film Club, a Youtube Channel, and a weekly Zoom Conversations With Authors.

Let's just agree that Kathy L. Murphy is a gift to readers. She is proof that one person can make a difference. The importance of literacy cannot be understated – it spreads entertainment, education, and empathy. And now... drum roll please... she's asked Mandy Haynes to join her as the new executive director. Mandy was up to the challenge. She created *Reading Nation Magazine* and WORKS IN PROGRESS with Kathy's mission in mind.

Mandy Haynes is more than an editor. She's a Southern writer whose stories are known to be as smooth as Tennessee whiskey. When she offers a taste of what our tiara-wearing authors are working on, you know it's going to be delicious.

In these pages, you'll have over fifty flavors of mystery, romance, memoir, historical fiction, Southern gothic, even suspense. I dare you to see the titles and resist reading one or two right now. Sure enough, you'll discover new authors and new titles to add to your Must-Read List.

Thank you, Kathy, Mandy, and all the brave authors contributing to this exciting new Pulpwood Queens anthology, *Works in Progress*. Now excuse me, I have some reading to do.

Grab a tiara and join me!

XO
Leslie Lehr

Table of Contents

On Shinbone   21
  Laura McHale Holland

Johnnie Come Lately: a novel   25
  Kathleen M. Rodgers

Papa Jewel's Chosen One   29
  Mandy Haynes

The Insistence of Memory   35
  Tom Shachtman

News on a Sunday Afternoon   41
  Kathryn Brown Ramsperger

Dallas Aftermath   51
  Jeannette Brown

Boop   55
  Mary Helen Sheriff

Through an Autumn Window   63
  Claire Fullerton

Story 18   69
  Susan Wingate

The Sign   77
  Julia Carol Folsom

The Codger and the Sparrow   83
  Scott Semegran

Through the Peephole   95
  Linda Rosen

How Audrey Became an Academic   99
  Suzanne Kamata

Touched   105
  Carolyn Haines

From Pangaea, a Novel   121
  Debra Thomas

Buried Beneath   133
  Debbie Baldwin

The Black Sheep   141
  Johnnie Bernhard

Guesthouse for Ganesha   147
  Judith Teitelman

Of Locusts and Wild Honey   159
  Joe Palmer

Samuel's Wife   165
  Brenda Sutton Rose

Those Colorful Streets   177
  Nancy J. Martin

Ferry to Freedom   183
  Eileen Harrison Sanchez

Lacewood   191
  Jessica James

Champagne Widows   205
  Rebecca Rosenberg

The Art of Traveling Strangers   211
  Zoe Disigny

Five Will Die   225
    Trace Conger

Hepburn's Necklace   239
    Jan Moran

A Coffee Stain   249
    Anju Gattani

They Killed Papa!   263
    J. Lawrence Matthews

The Poisoning   271
    James Garrison

The Old Lady   279
    T. K. Thorne

Murder at the Thunderbird Inn   289
    Rebecca Barret

Lulu   297
    Jodie Cain Smith

Simone and the Sweetness of Sound   305
    Patricia Sands

This Time Around   317
    Kimberly Packard

The Bridge   331
    Debra Bowling

Spandex and Leg Warmers   343
    Susan Cushman

Before He Heard Her   359
    Carol Van Den Hende

The Trip   367
  Laura Davis

Meet Me in Mumbai   375
  Lovelace Cook

Mamma Mia! Here We Come Again...   381
  Stephanie Chance

Encounter   389
  Francine Rodriguez

Slice of Suburbia   405
  Joanne Kukanza Easley

The Book Of Fairfax   413
  E. V. Svetova

Those Who Live by the Sword Should   425
Die by the Sword
  Mickey Dubrow

Immortalizing Hudson   435
  Joe Formichella

Hiding out with Holden Caulfield   439
  Suzanne Hudson

In That Quiet Earth   449
  Robert Gwaltney

A Hollow Light   463
  Heather Frese

They Walk Among Us: A Mini-Memoir   471
  Grace Sammon

Gowns and Crowns   477
  Beverly Willett

The Orphans   485
  Susan Tanner

The Solace of a True Center   497
  Linda Carrillo

In Less Than A Year   509
  Barbara Conrey

Aucilla Hall Wilderness School   513
  Claire Matturro and Penny Koepsel

Me and my Shadow   525
  Ruthie Landis

In the Sanctuary of Hell   533
  Janet Oakley

The Pulpwood Queen's Work in   537
Progress
  Kathy L. Murphy

On Shinbone

Laura McHale Holland

I returned to Shinbone last week, but like countless nooks and crannies in the world, the lane isn't what it used to be. The attic apartment I rented—bartered for, actually—was gussied up and turned into a condominium, walled off from the rest of the house and on sale for $1.2 million, all 475 square feet of it. I don't even want to know how much per square foot that is.

My landlady, Mary, took me in, no written application or references required, in the spring of 1974. She's long gone now, bless her beautiful soul, and whoever buys that attic will be credit checked and underwritten for longer than old Rumplestiltskin's nap, that is unless they pay cash, which hard as it is for us 99 percenters to fathom, is a thing.

It's hard to say what drew me to Shinbone after all these years—just an urge that kept pestering like a hungry cat, I suppose. I stayed at Eloise's place near the foot of the hill where Shinbone ends. Eloise's former place, I should say.

There's a sign where Shinbone meets 29th Street now that says NO OUTLET. Back in 1974, folks were more flexible about the meaning of "outlet." Members of Shinbone Friends, formed because no neighborhood nearby would claim Shinbone as its own, would never have let such a sign stand. Most everyone who lived along the two-and-a-half blocks of unpaved freedom belonged to that group—old timers, young families, misfits and transients, some more active than others.

Eloise's cottage is now an Airbnb that cost me a pretty penny for a two-night stay. The interior is all hard lines in black and white with chrome accents. I doubt it looked anything like that when Eloise lived there. I can't say for sure because Eloise never invited me inside, perhaps because she, a former prima ballerina turned dance teacher, could tell from the get-go that I had no talent for graceful contortions. I was more of an arts and crafts person, dilettante might be the right word for it, teaching myself calligraphy from an instruction book I picked up at one of Dot's sidewalk sales. You could say Dot, all auburn curls and wiry energy, was an entrepreneur before anybody used that word.

Now, Eloise might not have been fond of me, but she was gracious in the way divas have as she walked her miniature poodle, Coco, up and down the lane, asking anyone and everyone—stranger and friend alike—if they had seen her runaway daughter. It didn't matter how many times she'd asked before; if she managed to corner you, she'd ask again, "Have you seen my Julianna?" while pulling out a crinkled photo of a beauty with thick chestnut hair and grey eyes, just like Eloise's.

She pestered everyone. Except for Mary, my landlady. Whenever they encountered one another—which was often since only the remains of a farmstead converted into a community center buffeted the ill will flowing between them— Eloise looked up as though admiring clouds passing above, and Mary peered at her feet, which were clad in those black lace-up boots women born at the tail end of the 19th century used to wear.

I asked Captain about this. A band-tailed pigeon with one natural and one wire foot, Captain lived high up in an oak tree behind Jeb Waller's Victorian at 3346 Shinbone Lane, situated directly across from my attic window at Mary's. Captain spent most of his time in Jeb's garage workshop. While Jeb fixed old toasters, bicycles, radios, basically anything and everything, a lost art nowadays, their conversations ranged from jazz greats like Betty Carter appearing at Keystone Corner to lowering of the U.S. maximum speed limit to 55 mph, to the Dada art movement in 1920s Paris, to heiress Patricia

Hearst standing guard with an M1 carbine rifle while her kidnappers robbed a bank. And to my eternal wonder they let me, a newcomer, join their conversations. This took a little getting used to because Captain's voice, gravelly like the songwriter Tom Waits, bypassed the ears and came straight into the mind.

I never could grasp the logic behind what Captain chose to divulge. He would, for example, detail ongoing feuds between neighbors over tree pruning and placement of garbage cans, but when I asked what went down between Mary and Eloise, he plugged that line of inquiry with, "If they wanted you to know, they would tell you."

How could I argue with that?

Even now, I question nothing from that time, for I left far more than my heart on the Shinbone Lane of yore.

I excerpted *"On Shinbone"* from a novel in progress that centers on Shinbone Lane, a fictional street in San Francisco. I lived in that city for twenty-nine years, many of them just a heartbeat away from the 29th Street hill, which is mighty steep, and I situated Shinbone at the top. The story begins in the mid-1970s, a time when I landed in San Francisco, but beyond that, the story doesn't follow my life experiences. I like to put characters together, figure out why I care about them, and then let imagination and heart take the lead. In weaving fiction, I mix the ordinary and the fabulous. I can't say why. That just seems to be my bent. When I started the book, I mentioned to my husband I was locating the story on a fictional lane and was trying to think of a good name for it. "Shinbone," he quipped. "Call it Shinbone!" I was leaning toward something like Parsnip or Buckeye, but the more I thought about Shinbone, the more I liked it. Plus it gave me an intriguing challenge: coming up with a tale about how the lane got that name. I'm still working that out.

Laura McHale Holland has loved the musicality of language since she was a tot. It is this lifelong passion for words carefully crafted to enchant, evoke and entertain that drives her creative work. As a proud member of the independent-author revolution, Laura writes stories true and untrue in multiple forms—from flash fiction to novels, memoirs to short plays—and in all of her work she looks for hope in unlikely places. She has won gold medals in the National Indie Excellence Awards and Next Generation Indie Book Awards, and was a finalist for INDIES Book of the Year. In addition, four of her short plays have been produced in Northern California, where she lives with her husband and two goofy little mutts.

www.lauramchaleholland.com.

Johnnie Come Lately: a novel
Kathleen M. Rodgers

Johnnie's Journal
December, 1979
Portion, Texas

Dear Mama, I'm up here at Soldiers Park, hoping you might come swaying by with the breeze. Most of the leaves have dropped and it's getting cold. I asked the old soldier, the one you talk to from time to time, if you'd happened by here lately, but he just stands high on his pedestal, armed and ready, and gives me the silent treatment.

He's not about to give up your secrets—the secrets you pour into him from this bench. Dark things hidden behind bronze eyes that only seem to come alive for you. He won't tell me what you two talk about, or why you up and left in the middle of Thanksgiving dinner. One minute Aunt Beryl was talking about it being the sixteenth anniversary of President Kennedy's death, the next you were out the door so fast you knocked over your iced tea. When you didn't come back, me and Grandpa Grubbs drove here to the war memorial, thinking we might find you talking to your statue. By the time we got home, Aunt Beryl had already packed up and left for Salt Flat.

This is the longest you've been gone in a while. It's been three weeks now. Tonight, I thought if I put my words on paper, somehow they would find their way to you. Like when I was little and wrote letters to Santa. Somehow I knew when Grandpa and I mailed them at the post office, they would find their way to the North Pole.

Something's wrong with me. I tried to tell you at Thanksgiving, but you twisted off. Granny Opal keeps asking why her cakes disappear. Don't I know her business could suffer if she can't fill her customers' orders? How can I tell her that sometimes I cram down a whole cake at one time and then stick my finger down my throat? I've been doing this since Clovis died last summer … when I got so sick on those donuts. None of my friends know. I keep it hidden from everyone. Like you, I'm good at keeping secrets.

Today, after school, I ate all the leftover stew Granny saved for supper. I lied and told her I fed it to a stray dog that came by the house while she was out.

She winked and said, "Maybe that stray dog has a sweet tooth, too?" I about died. We ended up eating cornbread and beans. Then I grabbed my notebook and jogged to the park. I may be fifteen, but I still need you. And I need you to tell me why you said such hateful things when I was younger. One time you called me sausage legs, and I hid in the playhouse and wished I could disappear. I cried so much, my throat hurt for days. But I'm skinny now, Mama, just like you, and my legs don't rub together when I walk. It's starting to get dark, so I better head back to the house before Granny sends out a search party. Before I forget ….

This past Sunday after church, Grandpa and I hiked down the path to the lake to hang the old Christmas wreath. The ribbon is so faded it's pink. A cardinal was perched on the dock, singing his heart out.

Grandpa Grubbs stopped dead in his tracks and said, "Looky there, young lady. It's your Uncle Johnny. He's come back to sing you a Christmas carol."

I hear it might snow.
Johnnie

PS: In case you're lost, we still live at 8 Lakeside Drive.

The novel opens with a journal entry penned by protagonist Johnnie Kitchen when she was a teenager. I've always loved reading novels that include entries from diaries and letters. While the majority of the novel is told in third person, single viewpoint, the journal entries sprinkled throughout the narrative give the reader insight into Johnnie's mind and heart. While Chapter One opens years later when Johnnie is in her early forties, the reader never forgets that first journal entry that helps drive the narrative in her quest to know what happened to her mama. A male cardinal plays a role throughout the story and adds an element of magical realism to the tale.

Would life have been different for Johnnie if she'd been named after a woman rather than her dead uncle? Or if her mama hadn't been quite so beautiful or flighty? The grandparents who raised her were loving, but they didn't understand the turmoil roiling within her. And they had so many, many secrets. Why did her mama leave? Would she ever return? How did her Uncle Johnny really die? Who was her father?

Now Johnnie Kitchen is a 43-year-old woman with three beautiful children, two of them grown.

She has a handsome, hardworking husband who adores her, and they live in the historic North Texas town of Portion in a charming bungalow. But she never finished college and her only creative outlet is a journal of letters addressed to both the living and the dead. Although she has conquered the bulimia that almost killed her, Johnnie can never let down her guard, lest the old demons return. Or perhaps they never went away to begin with. For Johnnie has secrets of her own, and her worst fear is that the life she's always wanted—the one where she gets to pursue her own dreams—will never begin. Not until her ghosts, both living and dead, reveal themselves.

Kathleen M. Rodgers is a novelist whose work has appeared in *Family Circle Magazine, Military Times*, and in several anthologies. A professional writer for more than forty- five years, her novels have garnered many awards and favorable reviews from readers. She's been featured in *USA Today, The Associated Press*, and *Military Times*. The *Flying Cutterbucks* is her fourth novel and is the April 2021 Book of the Month for The International Pulpwood Queens and Timber Guys Reading Nation. It released June 2020 from Wyatt-MacKenzie and is represented by Diane Nine, President of Nine Speakers, Inc.

Johnnie Come Lately can be found in hardcover large print in libraries across the United States, Canada, Australia, and New Zealand. The audio edition is narrated by Grammy® Award-winning vocalist and Broadway acStory behind this excerpt .

Papa Jewel's Chosen One

Mandy Haynes

I was peeling potatoes when Cherie came running through the back door into my kitchen, slamming the slab of solid oak into the counter in the process. The loud thud made me jump and almost reconsider my refusal to use a vegetable peeler - but just for a second. Even if I had cut my thumb off I wouldn't be caught dead using one. Vernie Robicheaux had given me the handcrafted knife in exchange for homegrown tomatoes out of my garden. He kept it sharp as a razor with a wet stone he carried in his pocket, using the blade as an excuse to visit ever since his sweet wife, Fern, died just three days shy of her eighty-ninth birthday.

The panicked look in Cherie's eyes could only mean one thing. Her great-aunt wasn't where she thought she should be. *Poor Lil,* I sighed, thinking about how much she missed her privacy. She'd probably decided to take a walk to the market, which she was perfectly capable of doing without an escort.

"Thank god you're home!" Cherie gasped, grabbing onto the edge of the antique pie safe that came with the house, one of several pieces of old furniture I'd grown to love, but didn't use for their intended purpose. The pie safe hid old CD's and a few cassettes, the buffet in the dining room held bottles of liquor and wine, and the beautiful vanity in the spare bedroom served as a desk.

The curio cabinet was my favorite re-purposed piece. I'd turned it into an indoor bird house for Poe, a curmudgeonly old crow who'd lost a wing in the war against my neighbor's cats.

I put down the knife and took a jelly jar from the shelf above the sink. "How long has she been gone?" I asked.

Cherie bent over double trying to catch her breath as I poured her a glass of tap water.

"Well, I stayed with her until late last night. It was after midnight, and she was sound asleep, so probably not too long." She took the glass from my hand and gulped down a big swallow. We both checked the time displayed on the microwave, it was nine o'clock on the dot. The sun was shining, the birds were chirping. It was a beautiful Friday, and I was making a dish for St. Anne's fundraiser. I couldn't believe there was anything bad going on.

"Well, that's good, right?" I smiled at my friend. Cherie could be a little over-the-top at times, especially when it came to her great-aunt, but her excitability was one of the things I loved about her.

She shook her head. "Wren, listen, it's bad. She's been off her medication for about two weeks …"

"You know what I think about that," I shrugged and fought to keep the sarcasm out of my voice. Keeping Lil on mind-numbing pills had more to do with everyone else's comfort than it had to do with Lil's mental health, if not something worse.

"And she's been listening to that damn Tom Waits CD nonstop."

Well, crap. That was never good.

I, for one, disagreed the new medications that had been prescribed to Lil. It was true that she'd been a little forgetful lately, but she was somewhere in her eighties after all. As far as I could see she hadn't changed in any other way – she was completely self-sufficient if not a tad bit more scatterbrained than when I first met her. Lil had always been different, shoot I was a spaz and I hadn't hit my thirties yet. Marie, Cherie's mother, tried to make it sound like Lil was senile. I had my own thoughts on why Marie wanted everyone to think her aunt was batty, and it had less to do with the safety of her aunt, and more to do with deed to Papa Jewel's property in Houma. Property that was worth a lot of money. Papa Jewel, Marie's great-grandfather, had left everything to Lil.

I tried to stay out of Lil's business, but when she's obsessing over

Tom Waits that meant something was brewing.

I put the stopper in the sink and filled it with cold water. "Just give me a minute, Cher, and we'll go find her."

I put the peeled potatoes into the water and washed my hands. My potato salad would have to wait. Last time Lil up and disappeared we found her buck naked—well, not completely naked if you counted the turquoise jewelry around her neck, fingers, and wrists—standing in all her glory on the courthouse steps. Reciting a poem I'd never heard before or since, looking like a character from a Shakespearean play or a boozy dream.

Luckily it had been three a.m. on a Tuesday, so no one was around to witness the event.

Lil swore up and down that she knew exactly what she was doing and if anyone saw her and got offended that was *their* problem. She couldn't understand why her niece had been so upset. And even though I'd been shocked at the sight of her standing there naked as a baby bird, after we got Lil back home and dressed, I realized that she wasn't out of her mind. She was just having fun – something that was hard for her to do since she'd been moved from her cabin in the swamp to the big house once owned by her parents in the Garden District.

So what if Lil wanted to run around in her birthday suit like a pagan moon goddess at three in the morning. But right now, it was late morning and sunny. There would be an audience and Marie would never live it down. She would make Lil's life miserable.

Cherie must've known what I was thinking because she grabbed my wrist and said, "Lil's bra wasn't hanging on the back of her bedroom door, so that's a plus." We both laughed in spite of ourselves.

"Did you check the closet?" I asked.

"I couldn't bring myself to. The minute I saw her prescription bottles still in the bag from the pharmacy and heard *2:19* playing on the stereo, set to repeat, I came to get you."

"Well, let me grab my keys and we'll go look in the closet together."

If the old top hat with the hawk and owl feathers stuck in the snake-skin band wasn't sitting on the shelf in Lil's closet, it meant Lil probably wasn't out reciting poetry to the trees.

There was something about Tom Waits playing on repeat that could bring out a little … extra in Lil. If the hat wasn't there someone was going to be airing their dirty laundry and letting loose the skeletons from their closets. Getting an unexpected visit from Lil wearing Papa Jewel's hat, the hat of one of Louisiana's most renowned Vodoun Priests, had that effect on people. They spilled their guts. Things they'd never dare tell the Catholic Priest in confession, they'd offer up to Lil even though she didn't ask. She just stood there. Stock still and staring, on front porches or front lawns, scaring the truth out of whoever happened to get a visit.

She was, after all, Papa Jewel's chosen one for a reason.

There were too many people living in this parish with secrets that were better off not being known. If Lil didn't watch out, they'd have her locked up in a loony bin.

"Let's go," I said as I pushed Cherie towards the door. "Hopefully, she'll be back home by the time we get there, if not maybe we'll find some clues and get to her before someone calls the law."

The memory of Dickie Pickle, handcuffed and and crying for Lil's forgiveness after he confessed to robbing his own liquor store and framing his brother-in-law, almost made me laugh. But then I remembered I was talking about someone calling the law on Lil, and by *law* I meant the men with straight jackets. The thought caused the laugh to turn into a lump in my throat so big I could hardly swallow.

I wasn't related to Lil by blood, but she was the closest thing to family I'd had in a long time and I couldn't let that happen to her.

Papa Jewel's Chosen One sort of found me. I was driving to one of the new Vanderbilt satellite clinics where I worked as a pediatric cardiac sonographer. I spent my time divided between the big house and three of our satellite clinics, so I had lots of hours on the interstate. I didn't mind – I loved listening to Tom Waites or John Prine first thing in the morning and thinking up stories. One morning a line from a song I'd heard a hundred times grabbed hold of me and I was standing on the front porch of a little cabin out in the swamps of Louisiana. The funny thing is the song had NOTHING to do with the swamps, or a cabin anywhere for that matter. It was like Tom Waites hypnotized me and handed me a gift. Eulalie, otherwise known as Lil, was born by the time I pulled into the parking lot of our Franklin clinic.

Six years ago I took the first couple of chapters of *Papa Jewel's Chosen One* to New Orleans with me over Halloween and had it blessed by an honest to god Voodoo Priest while we danced on Dumaine and drank liquor straight from the bottles as they were passed around. The pages still smell like clean sweat, gin, tequila, rum, and the sweet scent of Florida Water.

Mandy Haynes has spent hours on barstools and riding in vans listening to outrageous tales from some of the best songwriters and storytellers in Nashville, Tennessee. She traded a stressful career as a pediatric cardiac sonographer for a the life of a beach bum and now lives on Amelia Island with her three dogs, one turtle, and a grateful liver. She is a freelance writer for *Amelia Islander Magazine,* Editor-in-Chief of *Reading Nation Magazine,* Executive Director of The International Pulpwood Queen and Timber Guy Book Club, and author of two short story collections. *Walking the Wrong Way Home* was a finalist for the Tartt Fiction Award, and *Sharp as a Serpent's Tooth - Eva and Other Stories.*

www.mandyhaynes.com
www.threedogswritepress.com
www.readingnationmagazine.com
www.thepulpwoodqueens.com

The Insistence of Memory

Tom Shachtman

Sue-Ellen Blair McNaughton lay on the cracked leather sofa in her apartment-share in Brooklyn, trying to will her iPhone to beep with an incoming message from Jake, her boyfriend of thirty-one months. From him in the last thirteen days Ell had not had a single beep, ping, ring, or musical trill.

His ghosting throbbed through her like a hangover.

The phone pinged, jarring her. A text, and not from Jake, since it was in Spanish. From her dear great-grandfather Popo; to communicate better with him she had taken Spanish in college and spent her junior year in Barcelona. "Poco, ahora, por favor," was his message. She was Poco to his Popo.

You do not slough off a summons from a ninety-six-year-old who is one of the few people in your life—belay that, the only one!—who never criticizes you. His VA nursing home was only a half hour away on the B local. She could get to Atlantic Bay Terraces at the perfect time, an hour before dinner started; the interim would allow a leisurely but not too lengthy visit.

The third floor was for residents able to do some self-care but not enough to live independently. That was Popo! But the nameplate on Apartment 343 now read 'Pedro Villahermosa.'

"Popo, you changed your name?" She kissed his leathery cheek.

"I'm born Villahermosa, y'know," he said in the Mexican Spanish of his childhood, laced with American slang. "My father make it Herman when we go to Florida, and I go from Pedro to Peter. Now I change it back, so I'll die with my right name on."

"You're not planning on dying any time soon, are you?"

"No, little one. Still here and still OK."

He liked to say so, despite his left arm not moving much, and his left eye not seeing much from behind the sunglasses. The room's main decoration was still the framed poster of Salvador Dali's *La Persistencia de la Memoria* that she had bought for him at the Dali museum in Figueres. He often called it "The Insistence of Memory," a title that also appealed to her. Its melting clocks, scorched landscape, inverted human body parts, and surreal quality spoke to them both: an image that once seen could not be unseen.

Dali's dreamscape was not, however, that of Ell's own persistent/insistent dream, the one so distinct and often- repeated that to her it was The Dream. Hers was more frighteningly lifelike. Just the thought of it made her shudder.

"Still chasing the aides?" she asked.

"They like it when I sing to them."

"I'll bet. Popo, you worry me with this 'getting ready to die' stuff. Is that why you wanted me to come?"

"No, I think maybe *you* have a problem. I follow Jake on Twitter, and for a couple weeks now he don't say 'we did this' or 'we did that.' So I wonder what's up."

Ell shook her head, bemused that her older-than-old Popo would be so with it as to follow her boyfriend on Twitter and so sensitive as to infer trouble for her from Jake's lack of coupledom references.

"This why you never bring this Jake to see me?" Popo asked.

"You're right, I never brought him. Maybe I was telling myself – well, belay that, it doesn't matter what I told myself — I think I've been dumped."

"Not hundred percent sure?"

"Yeah, after thirteen days, I'm sure—I just don't like admitting it."

"Say it. Say, 'I've been dumped!' So what? Happened to my sister when she's your age. Bawled her eyes out. She's so down, my mother says, 'Men are like busses — you miss one, just wait, because another'll be along in a few minutes.' You're twenty-five, my little one. Not too thin, not too fat. You got the blue eyes, and the sunlight hair, and the really good brain, and you know how to laugh—there'll be plenty of busses."

"What a flatterer! No wonder the ladies like you."

"I'm gonna live to be a hundred and dance at your wedding." Indicating that she should close the door to the hall, he fetched a bottle of tequila from inside the bedside cabinet.

After pouring some into two very small paper cups, of the sort used to deliver daily doses of pills, he whispered, "Arriba!

Abajo! El centro!"

"Y pa'dentro!"

They drained the cups. She then flushed them down the toilet.

"How you doing with that kids book? I make everybody here read it," he said, reaching into the cabinet to fetch out his inscribed copy of *Dog-GONE-It!*.

An illustrated alphabet book for young children, its entries were spelled to accentuate their pronunciation and were accompanied by humorous definitions, such as two that were cited admiringly by reviewers, 'G is for GROV-eh-LING' and 'T is for TUMM-ee that likes to be scratched.' Published by Berlucci Imprints, a small press, it had been politely reviewed as "gently hilarious." Ell was happy to have it in print but considered it a minor opus. It had done little for her bank account, or for her confidence in being able to make a career of writing.

"Everybody here likes it, so I have to explain to them you use the pen-name Sukie Blair— "

"That was Jake's idea. He thought it wasn't a serious enough project for my grown-up name."

"Maybe you change it back later. My grandpa would be proud of you—he did some writing too, y'know. I remember when we went back to Mexico to visit ... Belay that! – You doing a second book?"

"A follow-up. About cats. *CAT-Ah-Log!* Pitched it to the publisher, and ... still waiting for an answer. And I don't have a clue what it'll say."

"Cats, y'see ... Well dogs, they want to be like us, like humans; but cats, they just want to be cats. To them, they're perfect."

"I'm stealing that idea, Popo."

"You will put in big cats? Lions, jaguars?"

"Like the one that mauled you?"

"Oh, Nama didn't mean to—she was my baby."

"Maybe it's time you told me that whole story," Ell said, the tequila's buzz emboldening her. "I know only parts of it from Mom."

"Fifty years ago, plus! I run this pet supply store, y'see, and I'm stocking some exotic animals—I know what they need, they know what I need. Kept some in the backyard in Rockaway; y'know the whole yard was cages – your great-grandmother, my Nancy, she hated that."

"I'll bet."

"We were near the airport – y'know, Idlewild that became JFK— and it's handy when they catch animals being smuggled—iguanas and spider monkeys and all—and they call me to take'em off their hands. I'm selling'em to zoos and collectors, but those deals take time, y'see, so I put'em in the back yard. Nama, she's maybe six months. We like each other. Can't find a buyer, so she just grows, y'see, but to me she's still my baby, and one day – well, she just takes a swipe at me with that claw. And, y'know, it was pretty bad."

"You're saying it was your fault?"

"Sure. After that, the Feds came and took her away, and the rest of the exotics. I go down to Mexico to heal inside and out—a curandera can do that, y'see. I get better, except for the eye."

"And the arm."

"Well, no, the arm was from the war, that torpedo in Okinawa. Anyways, after I come back from Mexico, Nancy says 'No more of this or I'm outta here.' I say 'Sure,' and Nancy stays. We have plenty of business at the pet store.

Twenty years on, I turn seventy-five and I sell the business and the building. Then Nancy takes sick and I bring her here—they take spouses, not just vets, 'y'know—that's many years ago now."

"Thank you for telling me. I wondered about it. But how did you get into dealing exotic animals in the first place?"

"I was always good with animals. My dreams told me I should do it—dreams wouldn't let me alone."

That notion hit her in the gut, since The Dream would not leave her alone.

"I bet you got dreams, too—all writers got dreams, right?"

"Sure. But just now my dreams have me confused."

"Scary and terrific, huh? All at the same time?"

"How do you know this?"

"Your Popo, he's lived a little, Poco. Maybe you're not listening enough to your dreams. They're telling you something – don't be deaf to your dreams!"

He laughed at his joke, a jest Ell did not quite comprehend, laughed so forcefully that he began to cough, alarming her. He motioned for her not to panic, and shortly his coughing fit did subside. He then looked quite tired, which they both took as reason for her to say adios.

This novel-in-progress is about a young woman writer, recently dumped by her long-term boyfriend, and with her writing projects stalled, as she investigates both a terrifying dream that haunts her, and her family's past, which includes a remarkable female ancestor and that ancestor's dream, which resonates with Ell's own.

Tom Shachtman has written or co-authored forty books, mostly non-fiction, including a trilogy about the Revolutionary War, the third volume of which, *THE FOUNDING FORTUNES*, was published in 2020 (St. Martin's Press), as was his satiric novel, *THE MEMOIR OF THE MINOTAUR* (Madville Publishing). His earlier books include a trilogy of short novels about sea lions, published in English, French, and German; a groundbreaking sociological study, *RUMSPRINGA: TO BE OR NOT TO BE AMISH*; and the award-winning science history, *ABSOLUTE ZERO AND THE CONQUEST OF COLD*, which became a two-part Nova documentary. He has also written documentaries for ABC, CBS, NBC, PBS, and for British and French television.

News on a Sunday Afternoon

Kathryn Brown Ramsperger

"Have you heard the shocking news, Cecely?" asked the old woman. She sat lapping up her strawberry ice milk. Her granddaughter sat at the opposite end of the oblong kitchen table. She did not look up from her dish.

"Mr. Gibson is coming," the woman continued, then hesitated, as though she were expecting an answer, or at least a reaction, from Cecely. It did not come, and Mrs. Amelia Bishop clicked her tongue against the few remaining teeth in her mouth.

"Don't you remember who he is? Cecely? Cecely? Answer me, girl!"

Cecely ventured to look up, then began playing with the orange worry beads in her lap. Her brown oxfords grated the chair rail. "No, Granny. I most certainly don't remember."

Amelia Bishop clicked her tongue again, twice. She rolled her eyes. "Cecely, child, who lives next door?"

Cecely put down the worry beads and looked up at her grandmother with focus now. "Which side?"

"Young lady, I do believe as the Lord made me, your mama brings you over here to perplex me. Little golden-haired girl that you are, people would believe you to be easy to care for . . . to please. But here you sit, spiting me with those big blue eyes, puckering that cute little bow mouth, not taking a smidgeon of interest in your old granny. You aren't listening to me, even though you know I'm the one with the experience, the one with the know-how that I can transfer on to you. This that I'm telling you can be of great importance to you later in life. Now, think, girl, on which side does Lorelei Gibson reside?"

Cecely picked up the worry beads again and placed them around her hair like a halo. "The left?" she asked. She rose and managed to take the china to the sink without spilling any ice milk, and her grandmother followed close behind her with the spoons and napkins. She glanced over her shoulder at her grandmother. "Am I right?"

"I should hope so, Cecely Martin," her grandmother said. "I also hope you will stay away from that old house when you visit me. Now be careful with pieces of the family china. You being my only granddaughter, you'll inherit it all someday. You take my advice, and you'll be a better safer person."

"So what if I inherit the china?" Cecely gazed around the kitchen. The refrigerator rumbled in its accustomed corner; the everyday glasses on top clattered against each other. The room was a cream color now; the once yellow walls had been grease-washed, and fingerprints covered the area around the table. The linoleum revealed exposed pieces of dark wood beneath. The room was large, and Cecely shivered as she walked back into the parlor. The parlor was colder than the kitchen. Even with gas heating, the old house harbored cold, claiming it for its own.

She sat on the love seat to wait for her grandmother to follow. She did not come. The girl heard banging from the kitchen, which meant her grandmother was angry. She began to wonder who the notorious Mr. Gibson could be. Perhaps he was a blackmailer, or maybe even a radio personality. Her grandmother had told her what radio rogues those people were, only she called them disc jockeys. They were hooligans with lots of members of the opposite sex hanging around to catch a glimpse of their sunglassed faces and leather jackets.

Cecely fingered the worry beads, arranging them in different designs on the red velveteen of her seat. A cat face. A bunny that looked more like a fox. A ballet slipper. How she wished they had money for ballet lessons. After a time, she lay down. Sounds of plates and silverware made her sleepy. She hung the worry beads on the stem of the marigolds on the mahogany coffee table. The orange of the beads almost matched their burnished flower petals. If they didn't match that exact orange, they most certainly blended with the mahogany of the table.

She slept. She dreamed of the circus. She was talking to a clown when her grandmother woke her. "You shouldn't have been sleeping with the screen unlatched on the porch door, Cecely! You never know what might enter an innocent home these days. You lazy little thing, it's time for your mother to come."

"It's four o'clock?" Cecely straightened her dress and put the headband back on her head. "You never told me about Mr. Gibson."

"Never you mind if you don't remember. Just don't go near that house." Her grandmother sucked her little finger and reached up to scratch her permed hair with her other hand. "I thought you'd like to hear about the time I killed the snake when I was a little girl barely older than yourself."

Cecely braided and unbraided her hair. "I think I'll take a walk."

"No!" Her grandmother jumped to grab her wrist with a rapidity Cecely had never witnessed in her. "Your mama'll be here in no time, and'll be blaming me if you go off on one of your endless jaunts. Listen to my story.

"I got my very first pony when I was twelve," Mrs. Bishop displayed her dentureless grin and put her legs over one side of the armed chair. "Mabel wanted that pony, but it was mine. I called her Dorcas. She was a white mare, and Daddy sprayed her bridle with gold so I could pretend to be a princess. It was fun to have her as my playmate in the summer. When winter came, I rode her in to town. We were trudging the third mile to town to get groceries on the twenty-third of October. I talked to Dorcas all the way about the apples I would pick when I got home that day. Daddy allowed me to keep ten apples every day I picked in his orchard. Nine for me. One for Dorcas.

"Dorcas was a good horse; she never bucked. So I knew something was wrong when she got all skiddish. She reared up with all her might. She did it to protect me, but I fell right off because she surprised me. Dorcas attempted to smash the rattler between her hooves, but she only hit its tail. The thing was still alive, and it was advancing toward me. I stepped mighty quick, let me tell you. I picked up a sharp rock beside me. As I stepped to pick it up, the snake slithered closer, and I dashed its ugly head just as it coiled to strike.

"Have you ever seen how quick a snake can coil to bite? I got it, though. Just at the right minute, do you hear? But when I went home instead of going straight to town, Daddy got the belt after me because I hadn't brought the eggs and milk. He didn't let me keep the apples I picked for a week, and he . . . Look, there's you mother . . .

"Anyway, he took the gold bridle. Dorcas died the next year."

Cecely wanted to know why Dorcas had died, but Amelia Martin was walking bow-legged up the stepping stones to the porch. She wore her Sunday dress with grey speckled designs on a rose background. The color was splashed onto her otherwise colorless body. She did not smile as she walked into the room. She shivered, then collapsed on the seat beside Cecely. The air around her seemed to suck the breath from her throat; she fumbled in her purse for another cough drop so she could speak without her usual rasp. When she spoke, Cecely had to lean close to catch her words.

"Guess you'll be coming with me, Cecely." She grasped her daughter's hand, and they began walking toward the screen door, heels clicking in time, together.

"You could at least say 'so long!'" Mrs. Bishop cried. "I've kept the little one all day long. Let me tell you, it hasn't been easy. She almost went down the street, and you know Old Man Gibson's returning today."

"Mr. Gibson?" Amelia straightened, and her bow legs came closer together. "Why didn't you tell me before?"

"I just now told you, Amelia. Besides, you weren't the person taking care of Cecely today."

"Why'd he come back?"

"He's come back to his wife. After all this time. After all he's done." Mrs. Bishop turned on the television. The voice of a television evangelist blared out, making their dialogue more difficult. "You don't know the worst of what he did. He not only threw things at her that night, he ran off with that young thing—a common—prostitute. You should have seen her in that purple dress as short as a shirt. She had bleached hair and a New York accent. Now ten years later, he's come back to Mrs. Gibson, and she's taking him back. She's even telling her neighbors. She's ruined the neighborhood. It's not safe to take a walk in now." Mrs. Bishop leaned her head back then brought it forward in a knowing nod, then turned it toward the television screen. The conversation was over as far as she was concerned.

"Sounds like the typical dirty old man story to me," Amelia said and turned her eyes toward the ceiling.

"Go on home," Mrs. Bishop said. "There's more, but I can't tell you in front of the child."

Cecely braided and unbraided her hair, following her mother's gaze toward the ceiling. It had soft drink stains in one corner. Her mother grabbed her hand and took her to the dusty, brown two-door car, which she'd parked with one tire jutting over the curb on the semi-residential street.

Mrs. Bishop continued to watch the television screen. As the car sped away, she did not look up.

***

After the program ended, she sauntered to the kitchen. She took the silver service, which she had gotten from the cabinet earlier to polish and placed it on the coffee table in the living room. She made coffee in the pot her son had given her for Christmas years before, and carefully placed china and silver tea spoons beside the silver. She touched her face, feeling for the wrinkles on her forehead.

In her bedroom, she snatched off her apron and her soiled dress that did not quite button at the waist. She scrubbed her body until the skin began to peel, then covered it with cocoa butter and honeysuckle talc. She put in her dentures. She looked in the small mirror above her dresser and put on lipstick and blush, then one dark line on each eye lid. Then she touched her face again, as though making sure it was still there. The wrinkles stayed, resolute and deep. Adorning her best dress and her pearls, a gift from her late husband the day they were wed, she turned, pivoted, twirled as best she could in front of the mirror. But the light was dimming. She couldn't see anything but the form of a woman, her belly sticking out a bit too far, in a flared dress. She shouldn't have given her girdle to the Goodwill people.

Patting her hair in place, Mrs. Bishop walked to the screen door and opened it with precision. She glanced next door. The porch light was on. Fireflies and moths dotted the misty light it spread and fell on the tint in Mrs. Bishop's new perm. Her eyes glistened as she saw the man and woman come down the porch steps. She noticed they were not holding hands. She moved right quick to sit on her love seat. She fingered the beads at her throat.

When the knock came, she started as if in surprise. She limped to the door. "Well, look who you've brought. It's been a long time." She fingered her beads and looked past the two in front of her across the street.

"Come on in and sit down," she grinned. "That's the same dress you wore last year about this time, Lorelei. It surely does bring back memories . . . Mr. Gibson, how have you been? How have you done?"

Mr. Gibson cleared his throat and cracked his knuckles. "Oh, a little of most things. I haven't had much time for anything but work. I've collected a few butterflies, and I make my own apple cider. Most of the time, I'm working. I was a postal clerk in St. Louis, you know. That's all over. I've officially retired. Come back home."

Lorilei Gibson smiled and put her hand on her husband's knee. Mrs. Bishop touched his other knee with her own. "Tell me what a postal clerk does. My word, he must keep awful busy." Her attempt at another grin looked more like a smirk.

"No, not really. It's just those long hours with nothing to come home to but a butterfly collection. It gets tiresome."

"Oh my, I'm sure it does. Well, Lorilei, are you glad to have him home, or is he still restricting your freedoms?"

Mrs. Gibson opened and closed the latch on her handbag. "Oh, it's different now. We're older. Mr. Gibson will have more time for me, and I shall try to be more understanding." She picked up the worry beads, then set them back on a flimsy marigold stem. They fell to the coffee table.

"Well, I have coffee here I've made especially for you," Mrs. Bishop said. She poured coffee into the delicate china cups. "Black for you, Lorilei, and I remember you take only cream, Mr. Gibson. I've also made some shortbread cookies for our little welcome home party. I hope you'll like them, Mr. Gibson. They are an old family recipe." She put her little finger in her mouth and bit the nail to the quick.

"Before I join you both, I believe I'll go wash my hands," Mrs. Gibson said. She walked with an unbalanced gait to the bathroom shutting the door behind her.

Mrs. Bishop and Mr. Gibson were silent. Mrs. Bishop rose and walked around the room, adjusting her dress, then the mirror framed in antique glass over the cold, blackened fireplace. She returned to the coffee table and put her right hand over the silver coffee pot with a loving touch.

"Won't you have some more? You've already finished, and she's not back yet."

Ken Gibson shifted before saying, "No thank you. A bit too hot for coffee today. It's been a long time."

"I could make a pitcher of tea."

He was silent, gazing out the window at the coming dusk.

"What good is it your coming back at this late stage, Ken? After we're all completely worthless?" Mrs. Bishop moved closer all the same.

"Mighty fine coffee, Mrs. Bishop. I'd forgotten what fine coffee you make," he said in reply.

"Then you'll have some more, Ken. You'll have some more." Mrs. Bishop poured the coffee and picked up the cream pitcher, giving a hasty glance at the bathroom door. She moved closer to Mr. Gibson, trying to put the pitcher down without turning away from him.

It happened in an instant. Cream was everywhere, spilling over the coffee table, the worry beads, the marigolds, and Mr. Gibson's blazer.

"Oh, I am so sorry, so sorry!" Mrs. Bishop cried. But it was too late.

"I do regret this has happened," sputtered Mr. Gibson. "I do so regret it . . . my only blazer. You must get a washrag, so it won't ruin the mahogany of your table." He walked in a panicked gait to the bathroom to join his wife.

She'd mopped it all up by the time they returned. By that time, any coffee left was cold.

The Gibsons did not stay more than another quarter of an hour. They said their farewells in haste.

That night, Mrs. Bishop wept, polishing her silver service, her table, throwing the marigolds away. The worry beads remained. They blended with the antique mahogany, which had a cream-colored stain that could not be removed.

I grew up all over, but my voice comes from my people in South Carolina. They told me my first stories, sitting on one of two front porch swings, sipping sweet tea my Grandmothers Benfield and Brown poured from sweaty cutglass pitchers. We used the front porch for story, the back porch for visitors.

Everybody came around to the back door except strangers and salesmen.

I wrote this story in my 20s because so much of what I heard from visitors was gossip. I wanted to take their low-tone whispers one rung lower, deep into what was really going on, to feel into it with the mind of a child. The emotion of it all. I pulled this story from my rejection pile when I read Mandy Haynes' collection of stories. The voice and tone reminded me of hers. It's a Southern story, written before I'd traveled much beyond the South.

I revised the Southern colloquial language at the suggestion of an editor, who never got around to publishing it. I tell writers to save every scrap of paper they write on, or at least take a picture of it. Where would we be without the bits and bobs left by writers like Hemingway, Steinbeck, Welty, and E.B. White, that now sit in their homes turned into museums. I'm sad I didn't save the bits and bobs of this story. I didn't take my own advice.

It makes me happy that my story has found its proper home. I'm pleased as punch to be a Pulpwood Queen.

Kathryn Brown Ramsperger is an award-winning author and book coach. She began her writing career with *National Geographic* and *Kiplinger*. She also directed the publications department for the International Red Cross and Red Crescent in Geneva, Switzerland. Her debut novel *The Shores of Our Souls* received awards from Foreword Indies and America's Best Book Awards, and it's a 5-Star Reader's Favorite. Her work-in- progress, *A Thousand Flying Things*, was a Faulkner-Wisdom Literary finalist, and Kathryn's also received The Hollins University Fiction Award from her alma mater. Most of her stories are about love, war, and the breach of judgment between the two— how our connections of love can heal if we let them. She's worked in Europe, Africa, and the Middle East, and is the mother of two. She now lives in Maryland with her husband and their furry friend Rhapsicle.

For more about Kathryn, visit www.shoresofoursouls.com or www.groundonecoaching.com.

Dallas Aftermath

Jeannette Brown

Sunday, November 24, 1963

Becky has the television on, but she's only half-listening as she rummages around in the cabinet to find a snack.

Theoretically, she's waiting to see Lee Harvey Oswald transferred from the basement of the Dallas city jail to the county jail, although the event keeps being postponed. Now they say the transport car is on its way, but they've said that before.

Becky's head is still spinning from the events of the past two days. On Friday, Oswald shot President Kennedy as his motorcade drove through the streets of Dallas. The authorities aren't totally sure that Oswald was the assassin, or that he worked alone, but he's all they've got. They have his rifle and fingerprints. They've pinpointed which window of the Texas Schoolbook Depository the shot came from.

The announcement had come over the loudspeaker around noon at the high school in Libertyville, Texas where Becky is a senior. Of course, everything stopped. Miss Johnson's hand was posed midway to the blackboard. Outside, the marching band was silenced. The students looked at each other blankly to see whether anyone could explain how a U.S. President could be shot while riding in a motorcade through one of the largest cities in Texas. Or better, explain that the announcement was a test, a joke, and that the President was alive and, at this moment, giving a speech at the Dallas Trade Mart.

Becky had waited for the announcement that the football banquet, scheduled for Saturday night, had been called off.

That would be fine with her. Next week was Thanksgiving and then Christmas and then 1964, then spring, and finally, graduation and her escape to Dallas. She was practically holding her breath.

But an hour later, the principal came over the loudspeaker saying that the President "would have wanted us to go ahead and celebrate."

Becky's boyfriend, Jerry, played back or end or something on the team. Becky borrowed an "after five" dress. She and Jerry made it through the banquet, but then had another argument about her continuing status as a virgin. She came home early.

So here she is again, waiting for something to happen in the "City of Hate" as one announcer described Dallas. Becky finds a bag of chips and settles in front of the television as the camera shows a line of men just hanging around. Lee Harvey Oswald is easy to spot: a slight young man, his hair hanging across his forehead, looking a bit dazed. A large man on the left wears a white Stetson. A guy on the right peers off camera, maybe hoping for the long-lost transport car.

Suddenly, Oswald looks startled. His body straightens. A man walks right up to Oswald and points a gun at his chest. Pop. Oswald collapses. He's dead.

After some confusion and shuffling, the TV announcer says the shooter is Jack Ruby, owner of the Carousel Club and a frequenter of the city courthouse. All the cops know him, which is why they hadn't kept him away from the basement. "He's harmless."

Once again, no one can believe what just happened, that a man was murdered on live television.

Becky turns off the TV, weary from trying to believe the unbelievable.

Dallas Aftermath is set in Dallas, Texas, a few months after the assassination of President Kennedy. It's the story of Becky, who arrives in Dallas from a small town, trying to escape the gossip surrounding her mother's death and her father's alienation. Upon her arrival at the bus station, she meets a private detective who has been fired from the police force because of his actions during the transfer of Lee Harvey Oswald which resulted in Oswald's death. Becky also meets a young woman who will lead her down a glamorous but dangerous path.

Dallas Aftermath describes Becky's attempts to find her new identity as well as the City of Dallas trying to shed its recent identity.

The novel, by Jeannette Brown, is complete at 72,000 words and ready to find a publisher.

Jeannette Brown's novel, *The Illusion of Leaving*, was recently published by Texas Review Press. It was voted one of the "Top Ten Texas Books for 2020" and is an October Bonus Book for the Pulpwood Queens Book Club.

Her work has been published in *Bellevue Literary Review, Southwestern American Literature, New Millennium Writings, Descant, Steel Toe Review,* and other publications. She is the co-editor of *Literary Lunch,* a food anthology. She has enjoyed residencies at the Sewanee Writers' Conference, Rivendell Writers' Colony and Hedgebrook/India. A Texan, she now lives in Knoxville, Tennessee.

Boop

Mary Helen Sheriff

I felt luckier than an outhouse rat to have Eve at school so close she could (and did) drop by on a whim. Of course luck didn't have anything to do with it, since her Mama had said she could either live at home during college or choose a school near me in Florida. A month in and all seemed a-okay, I thought as I watched her sitting under the shade of my garden umbrella.

"Let me water those roses for you." Eve leaned forward as if to get up.

"Nothing doing."

Eve didn't argue, not like her mama would've. I loved that about Eve, how she took me for my word. I know I'm old, but I don't gotta act like it.

What a scorcher! I wiped my forehead with the monogrammed handkerchief I always kept stuffed in my back pocket, relic of days past. Eve must be hotter than a nanny goat in a pepper patch. "Honey, you gotta stop wearing blue jeans in this heat."

"I like them."

Maybe so, but I suspected Eve's modesty prohibited her from displaying her beautiful long legs. I'm all for modesty, but this one wears a baggy old t-shirt over her bathing suit. Eve's a beauty, no doubt about it, but try telling her that. "You young people got the sense of a fence post."

Eve stuck her tongue out at me.

Not about to be outdone, I flashed mine back, basking in the rare glimpse of Eve's sassy side. "Talked to your mama last night. She told me all about her exciting holiday plans."

"What?"

"Didn't Justine ring you after she hung up with me?" Me and my big mouth. Darned if the petunias didn't need pinching back. Seemed like I did it just last week.

"She did, but I...wasn't home." Eve nibbled at her fingernail.

I smiled at her fib. Couldn't say I blamed her for dodging Justine's call. I needed to see about getting that caller I.D. doohickey hooked up here. "Mmm. Now you be sure to call her back tonight, you hear?"

Eve rolled up her blue jeans. "C'mon Boop, you might as well fill me in. You know you want to."

Oh and I did too. "Justine'll flay me."

"It'll be our little secret." Eve tilted her head to the side and batted her eyelashes.

Couldn't resist. "Alrighty, you didn't hear it from me, but—" My eyes darted around the garden checking for eavesdroppers, as if it mattered whether or not anyone could overhear. Who's the fence post now? "Justine's gotten ten days off for the holidays. Said she needed some warm sun. Never met a person more in need of a vacation. Wants to spend it with us."

"For real?" Eve's eyes sparkled like they had the first time I took her to Chuck E Cheese.

I felt a twinge of guilt for stealing Justine's thunder. "That's right, so she's coming to good old Pineapple Beach for Christmas. I wasn't looking forward to our trip back to Virginia what with the cold and my arthritis and flying in an airplane."

Eve's face fell flat like a flapjack. "You look tore up. What's wrong?"

"It's just—" A knock on the front door interrupted her answer. We returned to the air-conditioned bliss of my condo, and I answered the door.

My nutty neighbor Shirley in that dingy bathrobe of hers stood there again holding a measuring cup in her bejeweled hand.

"Afternoon, Boop. Do you have any sugar I can borrow?" Shirley flashed her crooked yellow teeth in what I reckon she thought an enticing smile. Suppose it could've been 100 years ago.

"Sure do. C'mon in. My granddaughter is visiting for a spell. Eve, this is Miss Shirley." They shook hands like men do. Times they are a changing.

With a groan, Shirley collapsed on the wing chair closest to the door. "Oh, I didn't mean to intrude."

So you say. Looking awfully cozy now, ain't you? "No trouble." I caught a glimpse of Eve as she sat down on the sofa. She appeared to have regained her composure. Darn it, the longer Shirley loitered, the more Eve'd clam up.

I had the sugar ready in a jiffy.

But instead of making for the door, Shirley set the cup on the table next to her.

"Let me help you up." I offered my hand, only Shirley ignored it.

I needed to shoo Shirley out of here so I could get to the bottom of Eve's mysterious disappointment. And though my mama would have whipped me for my lack of Southern hospitality, I opened the door. "So nice seeing you doing so good."

As soon as the words were free, I wanted to suck them back. Never, ever imply a hypochondriac is doing good.

"That's just it, my toe's been hurting. I'm worried I have gout."

My turn to groan. She must've taken it for a sympathetic groan because she didn't pay it no mind.

"Why don't you take a look? Tell me what you think?' Without waiting for an answer, she slid off her bedroom slipper and bent to remove her compression sock.

Eve leaned over the edge of the sofa to watch with a mixture of what I took to be curiosity, disgust, and pity racing across her features.

Not that Shirley noticed.

Other than the fact that Shirley was in dire need of a pedicure, I didn't see anything wrong with her old lady toes. "Oh-whee, Shirley. You got yourself a case of Hycomfloocus."

"I thought so."

Eve's attempts to contain her amusement made it hard to keep a straight face.

"Nothing a rest and a good soaking won't fix right up. Should be all better in a day or two. You hightail it to the doc, if it's not, you

57

hear."

Shirley nodded, dressed her naked foot, and at last pushed down on the arms of the chair to stand. "Rumor has it you have an empty seat in your bridge game. Maybe I— "

Oh my heavens! "Curses. We filled that seat. Sorry."

"Who?"

Holy Moly. No one. Nora and Maggie would go on strike if Shirley joined our crew. Hell, I'd go on strike. I coughed in a pathetic attempt to stall. The gift of gab had abandoned me in a crucial time of need.

"Me," Eve said.

I sure do love that blessed child.

"Oh, right," Shirley said.

I prayed my face didn't look as dumbstruck as Shirley's. "Thanks for the sugar," she said.

No sooner had the door shut behind her, than Eve snorted and set me off into cackles. I said, "Bless your pea picking little heart. You really want to be our fourth?"

"I thought you were going to have a stroke right then and there. It just popped out of my mouth. I've never played bridge a day in my life."

Who was I to argue with serendipity? "Want to learn?"

Eve stared at the door. "You sure nothing's wrong with her feet?"

"Sure as God made little green apples. C'mon, bridge would be a hoot. I'll coach you. Try it a few times, and if you don't like it..."

Eve's lips formed the start of a 'no.' "Please. Don't leave me at Shirley's mercy."

"Alright."

Ain't that the berries!

"What's Shirley's deal anyway?" Eve asked.

"Crazy old bat. I don't reckon Shirley even bakes at all. I suspect her kitchen's brimming with sacks of my sugar."

"Must be lonely." Eve hugged my throw pillow to her chest and rocked.

"Suspect so. Now what were you going to say about your mama's visit?"

"Oh, nothing."

"Didn't seem like nothing."

58

"It sounds great. Really." She checked her watch. "Isn't it time for Days of Our Lives?"

I've watched Days for almost sixty years. Some might call me an addict, but I preferred to consider the characters my friends, in which case I was merely catching up with the girls every afternoon. "Time's got a way of sneaking by."

I pressed the power button on my television. Eve shook her head in a silent judgment over my lack of a remote control. I appreciated her silence on the matter as I'd already heard enough on the subject. I had cable and color, which were modern enough for me. She and her mama acted as if walking across the room to flip a channel was a death march.

"*Like sands through the hourglass, these are the days of our lives,*" a sexy deep voice from the television intoned.

Course I'd never admit it to Justine or Eve, but some boy at the electronic store had talked me into purchasing a universal remote. I don't have an inkling how to make the thing work, so I hid it.

Soap opera storylines are so slow, it doesn't take much to follow them. Good thing since I spent the first fifteen minutes racking my brain trying to read Eve's mind.

And then it hit me like a pie in the face. "You coming down with a case of homesickness?"

"I'm fine." She was a lying no legged dog. Wasn't very good at it either. Too busy destroying her fingernails.

"I bet you want to go home and visit with your girlfriends, sleep in your own bed."

"It's fine." Eve made a show of concentrating on the Tide commercial.

She couldn't throw me off the scent so easily. "If you want to go home, your mama would probably understand. You want me to have a go at her?"

"No. It's fine. Mom works hard. She deserves a vacation." Eve lifted the corners of her mouth.

"You sure?" Days kicked back on, making a serious conversation difficult.

"Positive." Eve glanced at her watch. "Is it 1:21 already? I've gotta run. I haven't even started my paper, and it's due in the morning."

"Oh. What's your paper on?"

Eve flushed. "Um. Good question. Guess I need to figure that out."

And the fibs kept coming. I suppose this meant she wasn't okay about not going home. I watched as she gathered her flip flops and keys and considered running interference for her. If I told Justine though, she might fret. I couldn't go running to her with every little concern, or she might decide I can't handle Eve. It wasn't as though Eve was even admitting there was a problem. And if I told Justine without Eve's leave, then Eve might not trust me no more. And so it was that I concluded that keeping my own counsel was the best course of action, rather than a dereliction of my watcher duty.

At the door I asked, "We still on for breakfast Thursday?"

She was practically a grown-up. I needed to let her work this out herself.

"Always." Eve kissed me on the cheek and disappeared.

The previous story is a cut scene from *Boop and Eve's Road Trip.*

For context, Boop is Eve's eighty-year old grandma.

I really loved the character of kooky Shirley in the following scene and didn't want to cut the scene because of her. Finally, I realized she wasn't important to the story and the scene didn't really move the plot forward. If I wanted to hit the road sooner in the novel, then the scene had to go.

Also, you might notice that the scene is in the first person; whereas, the final version of the novel is in third. I made the switch because an agent told me it would be more marketable in third person. At first, I balked at making the change, but decided to try it for a chapter and the writing was much stronger in third person. The third person also benefited from the first person draft in terms of character development. Tons of work but worth it.

Mary Helen Sheriff is the author of the award-winning southern women's fiction, *Boop and Eve's Road Trip.* She serves as the CEO of Bookish Road Trip and a blogger at "...the gift of story." After 14 years teaching elementary school, middle school, college, and professionals, Mary has taken a break from the classroom to focus on writing. She has an MFA from Hollins University, an MA from Old Dominion University, and a BA from UVA. She lives in Henrico County, Virginia with her two children, two cats, and one husband.

Through an Autumn Window

Claire Fullerton

There's only one downside to being a transplanted southerner
living in Pacific Grove, California: to fly home, which is what I'll
always call Memphis, I leave the Monterey Peninsula and either drive
seventy-five miles to San Jose, or one hundred and five to San
Francisco. Either way, it's a hassle, especially when the trip is
unplanned. On automatic pilot, I followed my husband through what
seemed like blind paces from San Francisco to a layover in Charlotte,
where we got in another plane and landed in Memphis. One foot in
front of the other into Memphis International Airport, and I realized I
was walking into the valley of the shadow of death because my mother
wasn't waiting at the gate to catch me. It was the first time in my life
when she hadn't been at the arrival gate, jockeying for position to spot
me, jumpy as a golden retriever to have me back home.

Daphne Goodwyn had a knack for leaving indelible memories in
the most mundane of affairs. Airports were a big deal to my mother,
whether I was coming or going. She'd suit up her size eight figure in
loud colors, as if needing something eye-catching to draw attention to
herself, which, of course, she didn't. The good Lord saw to that, when
He colored all five feet seven of my mother with ivory skin, deep
auburn hair, and green oval eyes. She had an hourglass shape, a
stallion stride, and walked with her chin in the air. She had a

gregarious personality, a memorable laugh, and a manner that never meant maybe. I was just fifteen, flying alone for the first time on my way to a friend's vacation home in Florida, when I realized the full extent of my mother's attraction. Rushing through the Delta terminal to the departure gate with her hand on my wrist, she'd clipped through the crowd with such purpose that strangers got out of our way. Hurtling toward us from the opposing direction, an airport employee driving a six-wheel baggage cart sported a nametag embroidered William. One look at the sprinting, high-heeled Daphne packed into her Lily Pulitzer, and he screeched to a halt, angled a U-turn, and offered us a lift. The long and the short of it is my mother's crowd-parting looks were traffic-stopping, and I happen to know that she knew it. I, on the other hand, am small boned, dark haired, and flat-chested. Whereas my mother cornered the universe, through most of my stumbling childhood, you had to look twice to notice I was in the room.

I feel a little guilty saying it, but my mother cast a shadow I had difficulty getting out from under. I don't think it was intentional, she loved me dearly, but in a way, she made me feel eclipsed. I was conflicted throughout adolescence, but it was a subtle unease, rich with subtext, deep below the surface. I rationalized my discomfort by subscribing to the notion that I am artistic in nature, introspective in a way so different from my sparkling mother that my fear was I'd never measure up to her. I spent years at variance with how I was wired, but my tug-of-war was an internal one. My mother's aspiration had been to turn me into her replica, but I wanted to forge a different life, a life of my own beyond the confines of Memphis. Because I never wanted to create discord between us, I blended seamlessly in my mother's world, until I grew up and moved away. Because the truth is I'm a terrific actress. I am Daphne Goodwyn's daughter. I'm Southern to the core, after all.

My best friend from childhood was gifted at birth with the name Margaret Ambrose. She waited curbside in her navy, Ford Explorer, when the sliding glass doors by baggage claim swished open. Although illegally parked, she got out of her car, gave me a hug, and said, "Cate, I'm so sorry about your mother." My husband, Eric, who hails from Boston, hauled both our suitcases into the hatchback then unzipped his own to retrieve his leather jacket.

"I thought you said it doesn't get cold down here," he said, looking at me, baffled. Though Eric and I had been married four years, he'd only been down to Memphis once, and that was in the summer.

"It's anybody's guess how it'll be in the fall," I explained, "that's why I suggested you bring two coats down here. What I meant was for you to pack two different weights so you could be prepared for anything. Sorry about that, Eric, I should have clarified. At this time of year in Memphis, you have to play it day by day."

"More like minute by minute," Margaret said. "Y'all just missed a big storm. The lights are all out in east Memphis. It's supposed to rain all week."

I've never minded the rain. Autumn has always been my favorite time of year in the South. I've missed its stark changes since I moved to California. I still wait for it with fevered expectancy. In California, I look for any hint of fall in the air, and almost will it into being. The temperature drops, and that's me in the slightest of breeze, putting on a knee-length coat and wearing autumn colors in shades of Khaki, maroon and green.

Californians look at me as if I've lost my mind, but I don't care. I'm a forty-year old transplanted southerner, I have cart blanche to be as off-beat as I want. But I don't have to wait for the fall in Memphis. It creeps up slowly and gives me a sense of anticipation, knowing, as I do, that Halloween dangles like a carrot before a horse at the end of October. I'm more compatible with the fall than any other season. I look forward to Halloween more than any other date on the calendar.

Everything about it offers something that intrigues me: wind and mist and all things unseen. I've always liked the idea of that which lies beneath the surface. Even my way of God-fearing has a blend of mystic magic. There's something about fall's hesitant introspection that speaks to the core of my being. Everything on earth takes a big exhale, before winter comes barreling through to freeze it. I'm not saying there's a good time of year to bury your mother, but if I were given the choice, I'd want to do it in the fall. Something about the bleak, languishing season is compatible with the notion of endings.

I looked out the car window as we drove from the airport in mid-October's seven o'clock hour and thought how fitting it was: the trees burnt rust, the sun down low, rings like halos over the tops of streetlamps, everything sullen and quiet and still. There was scarcely any traffic out Union Extended Avenue. We were on our way to "view" my mother. Margaret had called Griffin Funeral Home earlier, for such is the personal wiring of Memphis that you can call a place like Griffin Funeral Home and ask them to keep the doors open even after they close.

"I told them you'd just flown in and wanted to see your mother," Margaret said, meeting my eyes in the rear-view mirror. From the backseat, I saw her forehead crease beneath her dark curls, her brown eyes darting askance. "You still want to do this, right?"

"I guess so," I answered. "I've always heard that you should for closure. I might be sorry I didn't later. I don't know. I'm on the fence."

Eric turned around from the passenger seat. "I'll support whatever you what to do, Cate, but if it were me, I wouldn't want to live with that vision in my head. You might want to remember your mother the way she was."

"The way she was?" I said without thinking, "My mother was so larger than life, I don't believe she's dead."

A Southern girl returns home for her mother's funeral.

Claire Fullerton is the multiple award-winning author of four, traditionally published novels and one novella. Her work has appeared in numerous magazines including *Celtic Life International, Women in Writing,* and *The Dead Mule School of Southern Literature*. She lives in Malibu, California.

Story 18

Susan Wingate

They blamed a Great Horned Owl: Owls the size of a Great
Horned can sweep in and snatch up a small dog so why not a baby?
Quiet too. Don't even know when they fly an inch above your head!
That's how they get their food. Good thing your head's not to the owl's
liking, Rupert.

Ah, hush, Sam.

Your head's not a good fit for nothing.

Things like that.

The earth shifted. The beige sand compacted and split.

Fissures appeared like veins on an old man's nose under the
weight of Charlie's enormous bare feet. And although he was not quite
sixteen months old, he towered over the beachfront wading in and out
of the water, like a dog dashing from waves, testing the coldness,
stumbling around, sometimes falling into a sitting position learning to
walk on his new baby legs. He pulled kites out of the air, disrupting
older kids who biked to the beach for playtime, who wanted to torment
Charlie. He was a lost child. His photos up on telephone poles, taped
to the window of the post office and grocery store, up on social media
pages: LOST CHILD: CHARLIE KETTERING, SIXTEEN MONTHS
OLD, WAS WEARING A DIAPER. A round face and baby-skin
smooth with a shag of blond hair defining his forehead, lovebird blue

eyes, bubble gum lips. His shoulders soft and delicate, satiny. The parents wanted to describe him more, how he gurgled in the tub and slapped at the water. How he smelled when she lifted him from his nap into her neck.

How he banged on metal pans and loved Cheerios out of the box and all over the tray of his highchair. How he was trying to say, "Mama," but couldn't get it exactly right. How each parent hoped for his first words would be for one and not the other.

How the father said, "What if he says, caca?" During one heated game of tickle me on the floor.

How the mother laughed and said, "Or doodoo."

They set their expectations high, walking him through the obstacles of life, expecting so much, demanding little: a spoonful of strained peas, some peaches, "Try this bean burrito, Charlie. Mmm. Good." Hoping he'd excel in school and sports and math, to become an astrophysicist (that was the father's hope), or a doctor (that was the mother's).

To the parents, Charlie represented everything perfect in the world. He was a hope and a future.

They loved him so much and maybe more in his absence. They were like all other proud parents, showing him off, talking on and on about how smart he was. Talking in percentiles, "and for his age too!"

Charlie had been overly large at birth, pudgy and beet-skinned, wet dark hair, blinding blue eyes that would end up changing to hazel but only after the abduction and only if he didn't turn up dead.

At birth, he weighed in at ten pounds, three ounces. Was twenty inches long. Took twenty-two hours to make his entrance into the world. He nursed immediately then slept on his mother's chest before they cut the umbilical cord.

But now, the father avoided the mother. He couldn't stand her eyes. They were vacuous and frightened all at the same time. Like a criminal's blank eyes who just died and while life pooled out around him—a river of ants scurrying away from their hill before a wildfire, spreading, dispersing until nothing is left inside the nest.

He avoided her by returning to work three days after the abduction, before he had time to grieve. Leaving her in the company of a scotch bottle and her tears. Leaving their upstairs apartment by the beach alone to meander through each room—there were only six—

drunk and thinking she might have simply misplaced the child. And doctors were afraid of medicating her. They were afraid of suicide, but suicide is a thing of lost causes when you believe there's nothing left, there's no hope. That the child is dead. For her, the child was missing, like a misplaced credit card or a favorite sock.

Gossip across their small island turned like this: the mother went into post-partum depression and killed the child. She was never quite right anyway; they'd say in defense of their suspicions. Seemed a little high-strung, some said. Couldn't hold a job, said others. And that's what the town people wanted to believe, that she'd killed her own son. Anything less wouldn't fulfill their need to accuse and convict her, to blame her for misplacing her own child. Because, who does that?

The disappearance occurred before the baby could utter his first word; before he could burble out momma or poppa.

"Can you describe what he was wearing?"

"He was wearing his diapers." He was twenty-four inches. Details. Details. "He's a baby for fuck's sake."

Rumors of baby sightings started. Sightings called into the sheriff's department by people who wanted to keep the child alive, who hadn't given up hope but who also weren't willing to pull off the road and chase down the baby. They were people who call in things like this to authorities, people living in small towns who witness things happening in the sky—eagles conjoining, falling stars, random satellites pulsing across moonless nights. People who watch for hover craft of UFO. People who secretly hope they get beamed up—the thin-lipped priest with bugged out eyes and elephant ears; the deli chef with a nose that blends into her face so much that one facial feature ends where the other begins; and a landscaper, the owner of the town dog, a dog who goes from store to store begging for treats with a head so large the dog often tips forward and walks on its front paws, the owner who swears the dog is so smart, he can say, "I love you," back to him. No one argued his claims because a dog with a head that great, you'd have to believe his brain was great too making him unusually intelligent as well.

The first rumblings of baby sightings took on momentum and after only a week, the sightings were happening everywhere and were specific; sightings of some poor mother's twenty-foot baby toddling about. That's what people in town called him. They'd say, so-and-so saw "The Twenty-foot Baby walking along South Beach this morning at seven. He was chasing gulls and picking at rocks, still wearing a diaper like when he went missing."

Because they knew this one detail: that's all he had on when he was secreted away like an owl on a rat.

Or they'd say, someone saw him crawling over the hill on all fours toward Mt. Finlayson in dirty diapers. His knees covered in trees and pieces of granite the size of a two-man rock, and a few dead rabbits, to boot.

Or the baby was splashing off Eagle Cove slapping at sea gulls flying by. In fact, he caught one just the other day, caught it for an eagle passing by. Held it up and the eagle snatched the gull right out of the baby's fingers.

Or the baby was seen stuffing things into his mouth, anything and everything, the way babies do—sand, rocks but also squirmy tentacled squid and a full crab!

People were keeping the baby alive. Because what other option was there?

And the diaper! Well, it spread six-feet-wide and hung a loose five-feet-long and was often dirty until the baby dashed into and out of the tides allowing saltwater to wash it clean.

The parents called him by his name, Charlie, the name typed onto his birth certificate—a document showing all pertinent information: that the birth was a live birth, the date of his birth: March 2, 2020; the father and mother's names; and the sex, weight, length of the child. Nowhere on the certificate was there a field for an abduction date.

The mother could have shown better judgment. Life might be different today had she. But in small towns, bad things don't happen to children. The size of town provides a sense of self-governance. There, no one bothered to lock their doors. People considered the island to be a demi-utopia, set in lush countryside amid rolling grasslands, wooded swaths, craggy bluffs. The island, from tip to toe, abutted water all around. It was an Alcatraz of freedom rather than punishment where no one desired escape.

At first, the parents considered their first apartment a launching pad, a shot to the moon. But now, it was their jail cell, a lifer's sentence in every memory: Oh look! Charlie's layette in front of the TV. Oh look, the blue secondhand highchair. Oh look, his binkie and favorite stuffed toy, a green and yellow turtle with an orange felt baseball cap on its head.

The apartment was meant to be a place where a family would thrive, but now it turned seedy and dry—an open field of tumbleweed snagging its thorns on everything it touched inside the small apartment and ripping everything to shreds.

Within their short five years of marriage, the wave of their life had already crested and ebbed.

The official reason why they divorced stated: irreconcilable differences. They didn't get along.

But how do people get along after the disappearance of a child? Or, God forbid, the child's death? The unofficial reason was a bag of ugly. Of raging then bouts of silence. Of sleeping in separate rooms and eating alone. Of her drinking and him overeating. Of him blaming her. Of her hatred of him.

So, by the time authorities gave up on trying to convict the mother, all that remained was a year-long disembowelment of their relationship.

By then, people turned their eyes onto several folks they believed who could've been guilty of the crime. The old man with dementia, the drunk who walked the streets, the leader of a drug ring (or someone connected with the drug ring), and even Charlie's father. Still, no one came close to knowing what happened. How the owl swept into the window that afternoon, after their weekly trip to the grocery store, and how its talons latched onto Charlie's neck whisking it outside into the air away, away, and away.

People liked to talk about things they knew nothing about, enjoyed sticking their noses into places they had no business sticking their noses.

Charlie wasn't an easy child. Doctors called him slow, then they diagnosed him with autism. He needed care on the minute, every minute. The parents tried their best, but they grew weary and, only four months after his first birthday, Charlie vanished.

The mother, we'll call her Emma, had wanted a family all her life. Dreamed of what her husband might be like—kind, thoughtful, a great sense of humor, honest, hard-working, dependable. Emma felt she'd found that in the father, we'll call him Jesse. He even matched several of the physical traits she admired: not too tall but not short, strong shoulders, blonde not like her hair, blue eyes—again—not like hers, not the color of mud. She longed to be a stay-at-home mom and knew how abstract that was in their high tech, equal rights world. Emma had been in only one relationship that ended up crumbling immediately after she decided he would be her first sexual encounter. No sooner did she pull up her panties did he bolt. It reminded her of how her mother would warn, "Why buy the cow when you can get the milk for free." She had admired her mother for working so hard as a single mom but always longed for more time with her. And Emma knew she wanted children and believed that to be a profoundly good mother, a mother needed to be there for them during the day and night. Full-time employment for Emma meant a part-time mother for her child.

Jesse's desires for a future together were compatible with Emma's. They weren't perfectly the same, but they never butted heads. He'd been involved in one other longish term relationship. The woman, a gal who lived on the island, was someone who unfortunately had difficulty with him ending the relationship. She'd had issues with drugs and alcohol and, oddly, continually bumped into him when he was alone.

Susan Wingate is a #1 Amazon bestselling and award-winning author. She is currently writing her eighteenth book.

Her book, *How the Deer Moon Hungers,* has won seven book awards, including a First Prize in the CIBA Somerset Literary Award, a Silver Award in the 2021 eLit Book Awards, the 2020 SABA Book Awards for the Judge's Selection "Best Fiction Author," Best Fiction in the 2020 Pacific Book Award, a Silver Award in the 2020 Moonbeam Children's Book Award, and July 2020 Book Cover in the Book Cover of the Month Awards.

Wingate writes about big trouble in small towns and lives with her husband on an island off the coast of Washington State where she tends to wildlife in her backyard wildlife sanctuary.

Susan writes across fiction genres often setting her stories in the Pacific Northwest where she and her husband, Bob live. Susan's writing has been published in journals such as the Virginia Quarterly Review, the Superstition Review, and Suspense Magazine, and several others.

FACTOIDS ABOUT SUSAN

If you want to know what makes me tick, it can be summed up with this one quote from *A Sand County Almanac*, "There are some who can live without wild things, and some who cannot." —Aldo Leopold.

Honestly, I cannot live without wild things, be they flora or fauna. In a nutshell, that's why I moved away from Phoenix and to an island. There, I would spot a rare wayward doe or buck in the earliest morning or later in the evening. Deer tend to be shy when they don't know you. After time, however, while gardening or landscaping or simply hanging outside, more deer would show—to eat trimmings, nibble on branches, or even newly-planted foliage. I remember once after planting two young cherry trees and went inside, I glanced out a window to gaze upon my handiwork. At that moment, a buck reared up and, balancing on his back legs, ate the tenderest of cherry limbs near the top of this small, new tree. I said, "Well, that's an expensive lunch."

Susan's Memberships Include: PENAmerica, the International Thriller Writers, the Mystery Writers of America, the Women's Fiction Writers Association, and the Pacific Northwest Writers Association.

www.susanwingate.com

The Sign

Julia Carol Folsom

The fat blonde cow chewed and shifted her weight, tail snapping at flies, as Frankie squirted milk into a metal bucket. The smell of hay and manure and sweet cow had started Frankie's day ever since she'd married Roy, almost fifty years ago.

It was June in Georgia, and dawn would be the only cool moment this day. Frankie latched the barn door and picked her way across the pasture, dodging cow pies, careful not to slosh the milk. Roy's tractor already buzzed in the distance. "Mornin, Lord," Frankie said, admiring the pink and gold streaked sunrise. "You sure know how to paint a picture."

In the kitchen she poured the milk through a cheesecloth and set the jar in the fridge, then went outside, wrung a chicken's neck, plucked the feathers, boiled the carcass, and carved it up. She had a few minutes to spare before frying the bird. Just time enough to tidy up that mess Roy had made in the carport.

She drug the ladder across the concrete floor to the upright freezer, where Roy kept his catfish and deer meat. Wet rag in hand, Frankie climbed up and swiped a thick layer of dust off the freezer top. And that was when she saw it—a large rust spot in the exact shape of Our Lord and Savior washing Simon Peter's feet. The Lord was bending over a basin and Peter had his arm stretched out. Frankie could almost hear old Peter hollering, "Whoa now, this ain't right."

By the time Roy came in for lunch, his deer stand, two tackle boxes, seven fishing poles and a pair of hip boots circled the mimosa tree in the side yard like boy scouts around a campfire. And Frankie, all four-foot-ten, eighty-five pounds of her, had somehow worked the upright freezer from the wall to dead center of the carport. She sat beside it in a folding chair, hunched over her King James, while a floor fan stirred hairs loose from her bun.

"What's all this?" Roy said. As usual, he was in overalls without a shirt on, sweat trickling down his sunburned cheeks.

Frankie looked up, her gray-blue eyes shining. "I seen me a sign, Roy. A sign from the Lord. I got to find out what it means."

"Means your husband's got an empty stomach." Roy said, checking the soles of his boots.

"You won't be joking once you look on top of that freezer."

"Married a goldurn lunatic," Roy muttered, climbing the ladder. "Dang it all, them bug spray cans rusted the top out. I told you we shouldn't keep 'em there. I need to sand it down and put a new coat of paint so-"

Frankie jumped up liked she'd been electrified, her Bible thudding to the concrete floor. "Don't you dare, Roy Henry Wilkerson. A sign's as sacred as the burning bush. Sometimes I think you are dumb as a chicken."

Roy cocked his head sideways, one way, then the other. "Looks like two dogs going at it to me."

"I bet the Lord don't think that's one bit funny," Frankie said, heading inside to fry up lunch.

Next day Frankie had an appointment at the Beauty School. While the beautician combed and snipped, Frankie told her all about the sign. The Bell sisters, Beulah and Eula, were getting perms and overheard the conversation.

Next week the sisters' old Chevy rolled down Frankie's long, unpaved driveway. First Beulah, then Eula, climbed the ladder. They each looked hard at the sign, and both came down with watery eyes.

"Frankie, you been chosen by God," Beulah said, dabbing at her nose with a wadded Kleenex. "Mind saying a prayer for our poor old daddy? He's down bad with the shingles, all upside his head. Don't nothin give him peace."

"Well." Frankie hesitated. "I ain't a preacher. But I reckon I can pray as good as the next one," she said, taking the sisters' hands.

Word of the sign spread like a leaky bucket. Eventually most of the folks from The Holy Gospel Church showed up in Roy's carport. Frankie kept coffee perking all day because some folks got to shaking after they looked at the sign and had to sit a while to calm down. Frankie was asked to pray a lot: for gall bladder operations, nephews in jail, husbands on the bottle, rain for the crops. Folks took to calling her "Sister Frankie."

The only one wasn't happy was Roy. "I've about had it with you and your holy-moly rust spot," he announced. "I want my wife back wifing and my freezer back freezing."

"But Roy," Frankie pleaded. "People count on me. They think I got the gift. I'll do better from now on, I promise."

And she did. After that day Roy's bacon, eggs and biscuits were on a plate before daylight. By sunrise Frankie'd finished her chores and was entertaining visitors in the carport. Some days cars lined the driveway like boxcars on a train. Neighbors rode mules, and some arrived on foot, hot and thirsty, after walking the dusty road.

Each morning Frankie eased up the ladder to check on the sign. One day when she reached the top, she screamed, stepped off mid-air, and fell smack on the concrete. Her left ankle snapped and crumbled like rotten wood.

Roy didn't find her until he came in from the fields for lunch. She was still lying on the carport floor, moaning. "Good God, what happened?" he said. "Your foot's plumb sideways."

"Why'd you sand out the sign, Roy?" she whispered, her face pale and tight with pain.

He didn't answer. Instead he scooped her into his arms and carried her across the yard to his pickup. They sped twenty bumpy miles to the county hospital. By the time they got there, Frankie was out cold.

She opened her eyes in a hospital room, the morning sun glaring through a crack in the blinds. Roy sat in a chair beside her bed, still in his work overalls, thumbing through the Georgia Fisherman's Guide. She tried to raise her head but quickly sank back onto the pillow, woozy with pain and medicine. "Roy," she said. "Somebody got to milk the cow."

He scrambled to his feet, the magazine dropping to the floor, and grabbed her calloused hand. "Now, look here, honeybunch." He cleared his throat, glanced at the ceiling, then back at her. "I got something to tell you and you ain't gonna like it. Them doctors—" His voice cracked. "They had to cut your foot off. It was eat up with cancer. Wasn't no choice about it."

"Oh," she whispered, closed her eyes again. "I misread the sign, Roy."

"I done heard a bellyful about that sign. Don't talk no more crazy." Roy held a glass of water to her chest, guided the bent straw to her mouth.

She turned her head away. "The sign, it meant get ready. My foot, the Lord washing a foot."

"Ready for what?"

"To dance them golden streets."

Roy made a huffing sound. "Don't mean no such a thing."

Frankie wouldn't hear of radiation or chemo. "If the Lord wants to take me," she told her doctor. "Ain't nothing can stand in His way."

Every night Roy drew a pan of warm water, gently washed Frankie's stub and changed the bandage the way the nurse had taught him.

Frankie grew thin as a corn stalk. Her graying hair turned white. Roy moved a La-Z-Boy out to the shed and Frankie spent her days there, Bible in hand, crutches at her side.

One day the Bell sisters dropped by.

"Sign's gone." Frankie called out as the ladies approached.

Her face was a map of pain, her eyes, dull as dishwater. "Didn't mean what I thought anyway."

Eula froze at the edge of the carport. "What?" she said. "Why?"

Frankie waved a bony hand in the air. "Roy fixed it. Nothin but a rust spot anyways."

"Oh." Eula cast a worried glance at her sister, then turned back to Frankie. "Well, we brought you a ham. And potato salad. Our mama's recipe. Figured Roy might not be much of a cook."

"Mighty kind of you," Frankie said, pushing out each word.

"But Sister Frankie," Beulah blurted out. "Our daddy got well.

Wasn't two days after you prayed for him, them shingles disappeared like a bad dream."

"Just one of them things," Frankie said. "Nothing to do with the sign."

Eula trudged back to the car to fetch the food but Beulah stayed in the carport, holding her pocketbook with both hands. She looked at the freezer, now just an ordinary upright fridge shoved against an ordinary wall. Then she said, her voice trembling, "I sure needed the sign today. I needed it like I never did before." She started crying, dabbing her eyes with her chubby hands. "Oh, Sister Frankie," she said, "my daughter lost her kids yesterday. The Social Services took 'em on account of that man she's with. I'm so upset I don't know what to do."

Quick as a butterfly Frankie grabbed her crutches and raised herself to a stand, her blue-gray eyes glistening like pearls. She half-hopped, half-drug her slight, one-footed self to Beulah's side. "Tell Sister Frankie about all it, sweetheart," she said, her blue-veined, nearly transparent hand on Beulah's shoulder. "I got nothin' but time."

When a farm wife discovers a rust spot on top of her husband's freezer, her life, and that of her husband and neighbors, are changed forever.

I grew up in Georgia and lately find myself writing about the generation of my grandparents, their neighbors and friends, and life in the rural south. This story pokes a little fun but is meant in a most loving way. After all, these are my people.

Julia Carol Folsom is a writer and attorney, born and raised in Georgia. She holds M.A. and J.D. degrees from the University of North Carolina and served in the U.S. Navy JAG Corps prior to entering private law practice. Her poetry and short fiction have appeared in three anthologies and numerous online journals. Her first novel, *Nice Girl,* was published in 2019. Her work, like her life, is southern to the core.

The Codger and the Sparrow
Scott Semegran

A wise, old woman once told Hank, "The only two women who should ever bear witness to your pecker are your mother— when you're a baby—and your wife—when you're married. Anyone else is just asking for trouble." This was, of course, Hank's grandmother who told him this, although he could never think of the reason *why* she told him this. He often thought of this nugget of wisdom—more so now that he was becoming as old as dirt, day by day—whenever he had thoughts of other women besides his mother or his wife. Both were gone now—his mother and his wife—as well as his grandmother. But whenever he thought about a woman, he thought of what his Irish grandmother told him.

Trouble? he wondered. He rolled the question around in his mouth along with the last swig of Whiskey Old Fashioned. *Hogwash,* he concluded.

Hank sat at the bar of his favorite neighborhood hangout, Home Runs—cigarette smoke in the air, one barstool occupied down the bar from him, karaoke singers serenading strangers in another room out of sight, yellowed ceiling tiles sagging. Like a gargoyle, Hank slumped on his stool, his fists like boulders on either side of his empty lowball glass, tufts of white hair on his weathered knuckles. Jack the bartender wiped bar glasses with a dish rag. He was at least half Hank's age, twice as tall with twice as much hair, but that didn't bother Hank. He liked the guy despite his youth and nice head of hair. When Jack was a teenager, his hair was long and shiny and all the girls at his high school swooned over his hair. When Hank was in high school, all the girls swooned over the hair of the four lads from Liverpool, the Beatles, which was nothing like Hank's military-style buzz cut.

"Want another?" Jack said to him.

Hank nodded. "Yup."

"Coming up," Jack said, grabbing a bottle of top-shelf whiskey from behind him, then beginning his ritual of concocting Hank's preferred recipe for Whiskey Old Fashioned: fresh simple syrup stirred with an ounce and a half of whiskey and a dash of orange bitters in a stirring glass, orange peel rubbed along the rim of the drinking glass, one amarena cherry with a dribble of syrup, and a single, large ice cube in it. There was only one problem: Jack's jar of amarena cherries was empty and he knew Hank despised maraschino cherries, a lowly replacement for the preferred darker berry.

Hatred wasn't a strong enough word for Hank's ill feelings toward maraschino cherries. "I've got to get a new jar from the back," he told Hank, thumbing toward the storeroom. "And I've something to ask you when I get back. Okay?"

Hank nodded. Jack quickly vanished to the back.

But Hank wasn't alone. At the other end of the bar sat Ernie, a drunk that Hank rarely conversed with, but saw regularly at Home Runs, one of about a dozen familiar faces that Hank recognized in his favorite hangout. Ernie's facial features were undeniable—bent, crumpled, and bashed like the wreckage of an auto accident. He glared at Hank as if he knew Hank's deepest, darkest secret, and that secret had something to do with Hank's involvement in a plot to overthrow the U.S. federal government. Or possibly Hank putting the moves on Ernie's wife or his ugly sister—the other half of the familial wreckage. It was hard to say. Ernie grunted something about the state of the evening. Hank shrugged. A woman pretending to be Donna Summers squealed from the other room, working extra hard for her money. Ernie's face burned red. Jack the bartender returned, placing the new jar of dark, Italian cherries on the bar, then continued with his concoction.

"The last time you were here," Jack began, opening the jar of cherries, then smiling at Hank. "You were telling me about reconnecting with an old flame. Is that right?" He spooned out a cherry and a bit of burgundy syrup, dropping it in the lowball glass. Hank's hands merged within interlacing fingers. He was jonesing to hold that next cocktail.

"Yup," Hank said, then snorted. "High school sweetheart."

"Is that right? That's wild." Jack stirred the whiskey, bitters, and simple syrup, then poured it into Hank's glass. He set the cocktail in front of Hank on a black, bar napkin.

Hank toasted Jack, then took a slurp of his cocktail.

Satisfied, he set the glass back on the napkin.

"She lives in Sugar Land. Found her online a few months ago. She seems to still be fond of me. At least I think so."

Jack's face lit up with astonishment. "Really?!"

"Yup."

A grin slid across Jack's face. "You sly son of a—"

Suddenly, Ernie cleared his throat, a harsh sound like an envelope being ripped open by a careless recipient. "You gonna tell her how your wife and kid *died*?" Ernie blurted, then smirked, the lame attempt at a smile appearing on his mangled mug like a gash in a potato.

Hank turned to Ernie, angrier than a trapped raccoon.

Now, *that* was Hank's deepest, darkest secret, not overthrowing the U.S. government or boinking Ernie's wife or ugly sister.

Had he said it aloud at Home Runs once after drinking one too many Whiskey Old Fashioned cocktails? Had he drunkenly confessed his darkest hours, days, and weeks after his loved ones untimely and unfortunate deaths to anyone who would listen at the bar, and simply forgotten? Hank couldn't remember how Ernie knew this about his lovely wife or his beautiful daughter, but he wasn't in the mood to engage with Ernie either. He wanted to punch Ernie's smug face, but he knew better. He could destroy him with one, decisive punch. He knew that much. Just knowing that satisfied him, but he wasn't going to let this slight on Ernie's part go unremedied.

"Suck a donkey dingle," Hank pronounced, then turned back to his Whiskey Old Fashioned, placing his protective fists on either side of his sweating glass.

Jack bellowed. "Burn! You hear that, Ernie?" He placed his hands over his gut, quelling his laughter. "Oh my god. That's the best."

Hank's propensity to not curse—no matter the circumstances—was legendary by this point and his colorful replacements to the run-of-the-mill vulgarities offered whoever was listening a humorous respite to profanity. Ernie's face burned red again—a hotter and more malicious shade than before—then he abruptly left the building without finishing his light beer or paying Jack for his tab. He scurried away like a raccoon besieged by the probing beam of a night watchman's flashlight.

Hank slurped some more of his cocktail with a carefree tilt of his glass.

Jack chuckled. "I can't believe you just told Ernie to suck a donkey dick."

"Dingle. I don't cuss."

"Dick. Dingle. Whatever. That was awesome. Your next drink is on me!"

"Put it on my tab. I've got to go after I finish this one," he said, taking another sip.

"You got it," Jack said, scribbling Hank's request on a pad of paper. "You going home?"

"Yup."

"See you next time, then."

Hank nodded, finished his drink, carefully set his glass on the bar napkin, then lumbered out the door.

It was late, the tarp of night having already laid over the strip mall where Home Runs resided right outside his neighborhood, Wells Port. The sordid, nightlife business of Home Runs occupied the left end and stayed open long past the other family businesses of the strip mall on the right side had closed. Hank's lugubrious march to his car accompanied the jangle of his keys in his pants pocket. He wondered how he got his large, meaty hand in his cramped pocket in the first place as he struggled to pull it out. He stopped to concentrate when he heard a familiar voice call to him.

"Hey!" the voice hollered, the tail end of the declaration cracking.

With his hand still trapped in his pocket, Hank looked up to discover Ernie standing a few feet away—his stiff arms by his sides, a knife in his right hand, his left hand clenched in a taut fist, and the mostly empty parking lot spreading out behind him. The four-inch blade twinkled like a distant star. No one else seemed to be around except for a black car parked at the convenience store at the other end of the strip mall. Besides that, only the hum of the interstate not too far away gave the night any signs of life. The air was still and humid. Cicadas chirped from the surrounding oak and ash trees. Hank's hand came out of his pocket—finally—without a struggle, rolling into an angry fist. He planted his feet like he was trained long ago to do.

"You embarrassed me..." Ernie said, adjusting the handle of the knife in his shaky hand.

Hank didn't move. He examined Ernie's stance—the wobble in his knees, his fidgety hands, and the way his bloodshot eyes darted away and back at him. What Hank didn't know was that this wasn't Ernie's first fight. He'd been in a few. Ernie's first fight was with an elementary school bully.

Young Ernie beat him over the head with a tennis racket. The bully left him alone after that. What old Ernie didn't know was that Hank had been in a thousand fights and would be in many, many more.

Ernie continued. "...in front of everybody."

"Just Jack," Hank said.

"That's *everybody,*" Ernie said, then he lunged.

In a split second, Hank landed a swift, decisive punch into Ernie's bulbous nose, sending him backward, his arms flailing, his feet dancing an uncoordinated two-step, the knife clanking on the asphalt a few feet away, twinkling across the black top like a falling star. Seconds after Ernie's body hit the ground, red and blue lights flashed from the grill of the black car parked at the convenience store. The unmarked car chirped a couple of times, then approached the street fighters. Once parked next to them, the car chirped once more. A man popped out, a silver badge attached to the front of his shirt, a neatly trimmed moustache above his slit of mouth.

"All right, turn around. Put your hands behind you," the officer in plain clothes said.

Hank, a man who respected authority, complied. He sighed. "I was only protecting myself. He attacked me."

"We'll let the court see the dash-cam video, but I've got to take you downtown nonetheless," the officer said, cuffing Hank's thick wrists. "Jesus, these cuffs barely fit."

"Yup," Hank replied.

The officer placed a hand on Hank's head as he pushed him in the back of the unmarked police car.

"We'll wait until EMS comes for your friend, then I'll drive you downtown."

Hank sighed again. "He's not my friend."

He sat in the backseat and watched through the tinted window until the ambulance came and took stinky Ernie away. He then watched out the window as the police car drove south on I-35, past parts of Austin he hadn't seen in a while: the 183 flyover, Airport Boulevard, Darrell K. Royal Texas Memorial Stadium, the University of Texas Tower, the Texas Capitol, the changing skyline of downtown, all of which sailed by within reflections of orange, pink, and yellow neon. The whiskey Hank consumed that night penetrated every artery, vein, and capillary in his body, stretching time into nonexistence. He wasn't aware of how long it took to get downtown, or how long it took to get through jail processing. He answered when he was asked questions, things like his name and where he lived, any other declarations they requested. He was fingerprinted and photographed. An officer asked him to take off his clothes, bend over, and spread his butt cheeks. When he stood back up, he could see his lumpy, pasty reflection in the officer's glasses. From a distance, he looked like The Thing— the deformed, orange, rocky strongman from the superhero group the *Fantastic Four.* His torso was short and stocky like an oak tree trunk, his hands and feet massive and bulbous with craggy knuckles, and his silver hair sticking straight up as if electrically shocked. As a child, his mother had to custom order his shoes as his feet were massive even then. He preferred sneakers to loafers, even now. He looked down at his shriveled pecker and wondered if the wisdom his grandmother imparted on him included a curious police officer witnessing his wilted carrot in a holding cell. He blinked, then found himself in a pink jumpsuit and rubber flip-flops, being escorted— handcuffed again by the way—to where he would spend the night. A cell door opened. His cuffs were removed. He was asked to step inside, then the door slammed closed behind him.

Hank quickly discovered the small, cinder block room's bunk beds were already occupied—the lower one by a motionless lump, the upper one by a wheezing monster—so he sat on the concrete floor, his back against the cold wall, his legs splayed out in front of him.

This isn't how I imagined this night would end, he thought.

Hogwash.

He closed his eyes and tried to sleep.

When the sun's orange glow illuminated the cell through a tiny, grimy window, a small opening appeared in the middle of the cell door and three brown paper bags were shoved through, plopping on the floor. Hank grabbed one and opened it, finding a peanut butter sandwich, a bruised apple, and a carton of two- percent milk inside. But he wasn't hungry, nor cared to try the offerings from the jail guards. He set the bag on the floor and waited for someone to get him. It took a couple of hours, but they eventually came for him.

Hank was handcuffed to five other criminals and led down a concrete hallway to a large service elevator. They descended to the second floor—accompanied by a tall and lanky White police officer—and led down another hallway to court room number two, the place where Hank might find justice or punishment; it could go either way, really. On his left was a sweaty, young Latino man with halitosis, a scraggly beard, and a cleft lip, who muttered in Spanish. On his right was a Black man who Hank surmised was about the same age as he was, the man's hair mostly white, his eyes yellowed with disdain for the police, and his white mustache fidgeting under his nose.

"This is some bullshit," the Black man declared.

"Yup," Hank agreed.

They didn't wait long before being led into court room number two. The six men sat in a pew to themselves. Hank looked around and most of the other pews were also occupied by a similar group of miscreants, all colors and creeds, and all men, not a single woman amongst them. It was like a church for the condemned; a chapel for male convicts. Hank didn't think he was a convict, but that title wasn't up to him.

A door at the back of the courtroom opened and the court reporter quickly stood up, the bailiff ordering the convicts to rise for the judge, an elderly woman so short and slight that she appeared to levitate to the judge's bench.

"Please be seated," Judge Richards ordered them, her name etched in gold letters on a block of dark, lacquered wood. Her black hair perched on her head like a raven, mad with irascible discontent. A streak of white ran the length of her crown. Gold glasses daintily sat on her pointy nose. The courtroom deputy, a young man who looked like a teenager, handed Judge Richards a stack of papers. She sighed, then called out, "Malarkey!"

Hank chuckled. She peered in his direction, but didn't know its origin.

Judge Richards cleared her throat. "This is how it's going down on this beautiful morning. I'll call out a name and you will stand. I'll read your charge and you will declare your plea: guilty or not guilty. If you plead guilty, then I will sentence you accordingly. If you plead *not* guilty—"

The room erupted with hoots and hollers. Judge Richards smacked her gavel against the sound block on her desk.

"Be quiet, you knuckleheads!" she said, then sighed. "Happens every time. Any who. If you plead not guilty, then a court date will be set for your trial. Understood?"

The knuckleheads hummed an acknowledgement. Judge Richards shuffled the papers on her desk, then lifted one. "Jackson, Melvin," she called out.

The Black man on Hank's right stood up, his left hand cuffed to Hank's right. He smelled of farts, menthol cigarettes, and WD-40. As a kid, he smelled of farts, bubblegum, and WD-40. He had never done anything in his life that would've gotten him in trouble with the law. Ever. He was as good as a person can be, except he had atrocious luck. And he was a Black man.

Judge Richards continued. "Mr. Jackson, you've been accused of stealing loaves of bread at a bakery. How do you plead?"

"Ma'am, I didn't steal no loaves of bread. The police are always accusing me of wrongdoing when there was no wrongdoing."

"Mr. Jackson—"

"Ma'am, I thought I paid for all the bread. Honest to God!"

"Mr. Jackson!" she cried out, then sighed.

"Yes, ma'am. Sorry ma'am."

"Mr. Jackson, how do you plead?" "Not guilty, your honor."

"Fine. Your court date is September twelfth. If you can make bail, then you can go."

"Thank you, ma'am," Melvin said, then sat back down next to Hank. He shook his head.

Judge Richards cleared her throat. "O'Sullivan, Henry."

Hank stood up, Melvin's hand rising with him. "Hank, ma'am. I prefer to be called Hank."

The judge stared at Hank, then read the sheet of paper aloud. "Mr. O'Sullivan, you've been charged with assault and disorderly conduct. How do you plead?"

"Well, your honor, I am guilty of punching Ernie, but he deserved it. Besides, he had a knife, so it was self-defense."

The knuckleheads hummed in agreement.

Judge Richards looked up from the piece of paper while the court deputy returned with a sheet of paper in hand. He gave the paper to the judge, who then read it. After considering what was on the piece of paper, she said, "There's a statement from the arresting police officer corroborating that the other perpetrator had a knife."

"Yup."

"But you're still pleading guilty?"

"Well, I did punch him. That's true." The knuckleheads chuckled.

The judge picked up the other sheet of paper and read it. "And it appears you have a clean record."

"That's right," Hank agreed.

"But in the end, the guilty must pay. So I sentence you to forty hours of community service. Do you have anything else to say?"

"No ma'am," Hank said.

"All righty then," she said, then handed the sheets of paper concerning Henry "Hank" O'Sullivan to the court deputy. "Next up: Salazar, Marco."

The sweaty, young Latino man to Hank's left stood up, lifting Hank's left hand with him. "*Sí*," he answered.

On Hank's right, Melvin elbowed him, then leaned in. "I told you. This is some bullshit," Melvin whispered.

"Yup," Hank agreed.

Then they listened to Judge Richards tell the court how Marco Salazar showed his pecker to the cleaning lady at the warehouse where he worked as a forklift driver. Hank wondered if Marco's grandmother would be disappointed.

From the award-winning writer of *To Squeeze a Prairie Dog* and *The Benevolent Lords of Sometimes Island*, Scott Semegran's latest book, *The Codger and the Sparrow,* is a comical yet moving novel about a widower's unlikely friendship with a young troublemaker.

Hank O'Sullivan can't catch a break. The 65-year old widower lives a routine life, and nurses his loneliness with cocktails at his favorite local bar in Austin, Texas. A brawl with an acerbic barfly lands him in jail. The judge pities the old codger and sentences him to do community service, picking up trash beside the interstate highway.

Luis Delgado lives with his stern, single father in a small apartment. The 16-year old troublemaker has remarkable artistic abilities, but his penchant for sneaking out and trespassing onto rooftops late at night also lands him in community service.

These outcasts form an unlikely friendship in an inhospitable setting. When Hank tells Luis about his desire to drive to Houston, Texas and reconnect with an old flame, Luis asks to tag along. Luis' estranged mother also lives in Houston and he has been saving money for a trip, dreaming of reconnecting with her. Hank agrees, setting in motion a raucous road trip in a hot pink 1970 Plymouth Barracuda. Neither Hank nor Luis find what they are looking for, but something altogether different and unexpected happens.

With humor and a bit of grace, *The Codger and the Sparrow* is a rambunctious story about an unusual friendship stretching across the generations.

Scott Semegran is an award-winning writer of nine books. BlueInk Review described him best as "a gifted writer, with a wry sense of humor." His latest novel, *The Codger and the Sparrow*, is a comical yet moving story about a 65-year old widower's unlikely friendship with a 16-year old troublemaker. His previous novel, *The Benevolent Lords of Sometimes Island*, is about four middle school friends who sneak away to an abandoned lake house to evade the wrath of high school bullies, only to become stranded on the lake's desolate island. It was a quarter finalist in the 2020 BookLife Prize and shortlisted in the 2021 U.S. Selfies Book Awards. His novel, *To Squeeze a Prairie Dog*, was the 2019 Readers' Favorite International Book Award Winner: Silver Medal for Fiction - Humor/Comedy, the 2019 Texas Author Project Winner for Adult Fiction, and the 2020

IBPA Benjamin Franklin Award Gold Medal Winner for Humor. Other books by Scott Semegran include *Sammie & Budgie, BOYS, The Spectacular Simon Burchwood, The Meteoric Rise of Simon Burchwood, Modicum,* and *Mr. Grieves*. He lives in Austin, Texas with his wife, four kids, two cats, and a dog. He graduated from the University of Texas at Austin with a degree in English.

Scott Semegran is one of the hosts of the web series Austin Liti Limits along with fellow award-winning writer Larry Brill.

www.scottsemegran.com

Through the Peephole

Linda Rosen

Pungent odors fester in my nose: cigarettes, armpits, tobacco, sweat.

For years that stench jumped out at me unannounced, just as he did that Thursday, long ago. I'd left the office to have lunch at home. Alone. Something I had never done before.

There was a knock on my door. I put the tuna sandwich down and looked through the peephole. A tall, thin man wearing a Yankees cap peered back at me.

"Can I help you?" I asked.

"We've got water dripping from our ceiling downstairs," he said, his voice as deep as the onyx of his skin. "Can I come in and look under your kitchen sink, see if it's leaking?"

"I'll go check," I said, and left the door safely closed just like my father advised when I told him I was moving into the city. I was still his little girl, even if I'd just graduated from college, from the womb of dormitory life. He warned me Manhattan wasn't the same as the suburbs with its trees and grass and doors we never locked.

With two steps I was in my kitchen. It was a small studio apartment. I opened the metal cabinet and peered under the sink, just in case he was legit.

"Sorry, sir," I called through the tightly bolted door. "The leak isn't coming from here. Everything's dry under my sink." I actually said "sir." Just in case.

Tuna sandwich consumed, dishes washed and left to dry in the green plastic basket, I unhooked the chain on top of the door, turned the deadbolt and heard the click. Never thought to look out the peephole. Never thought to make sure it was safe.

Like a cat pouncing on a tiny sparrow he jumped inside, shoved me aside, flipped me around, grabbed me from behind and slapped his hand across my mouth stifling my screams.

"Shut up! Or I'll have to hurt you."

It was that same deep voice from an hour ago, when I did peek out.

My heart hammered, nearly exploded my chest. I gulped down breaths. Tried to stay quiet. Ugly images popped in my head: rape, switchblade, gun, a beating.

With his hand clamped over my mouth, he pulled my head sideways. It felt like I was crushed in a vise. He pushed me into the kitchen.

"Give me a rag," he commanded, his voice full of gravel.

I squatted. Opened the cabinet. It wasn't easy moving around with his arm wrenching my neck, practically turning my head a full one-eighty. I managed to reach in and grab a piece of paper towel. Nothing big. Nothing large enough to tie me up, stuff my mouth, bind my wrists.

With a strong grip on my skull, he led me into the living room. And I didn't fight.

"Sit down and face the wall." He shoved me into a chair. "Don't turn around." Then he growled, "You're the wrong girl. I thought you were someone else."

My breath came hard and fast. My carotid pulsed. Frozen as Minnesota in February, I sat staring at the wall. I heard him moving around my apartment, my home. He was in the kitchen. At the door. Was he leaving? Damn. All I heard was the rough squeak of Bounty wiping the brass doorknob. It took forever; he must have wiped down the entire door. No fingerprints. Nothing to show he'd been there. Nothing but the putrid smell he left behind permeating my furniture, my clothes, my hair.

His footsteps came closer. I didn't dare turn my head. He was behind me. What now? He's going to rape me, slice my throat, strangle me with his bare hands. No. He dumped my wallet in my lap and hissed, "Give me five dollars for a taxi."

"Please, take all of it; just leave me alone." I stared straight ahead.

"No! I only want cab-fare. I told you, I have the wrong girl."

My hands shook like I had full blown Parkinson's. I managed to pull out five singles and lifted my arm over my shoulder, my eyes still fixed on the yellow paint on the opposite wall. He grabbed the money.

The bare wooden floor creaked as he walked across the room. I heard the door open. Then he barked, "Don't get up. Sit there. Don't move for the next five minutes."

I sat. Erect. Staring straight ahead. His fetid odor burrowed in my nose, my memory. I didn't budge. I wouldn't. He might find out and come back.

Through the Peephole is creative non-fiction. It is the story of an event that actually happened to me in the winter of 1971, fresh out of college, living in New York City. It was previously published in *The Dying Goose*, a digital magazine, in 2013.

Linda Rosen's books are set in the "not-too-distant past" and examine how women reinvent themselves despite obstacles thrown their way. A central theme is that blood is not all that makes a family– and they always feature a piece of jewelry!

Her debut novel, *The Disharmony of Silence*, released in March 2020 and her sophomore novel, *Sisters of the Vine*, one year later, from Black Rose Writing. Linda was a contributor to Women in the Literary Landscape: A WNBA Centennial Publication for the Women's National Book Association and has had stories published in online magazines and print anthologies. She is a member of the Women's Fiction Writers Association and the Women's National Book Association where she is Selections Coordinator of the Great Group Reads committee which curates a list, published annually, of novels and memoirs perfect for book clubs.

www.linda-rosen.com

How Audrey Became an Academic
Suzanne Kamata

It had been Eva's idea that Audrey apply for the job. The three of them – Audrey, Eva, and Isabel – had been having lunch at Aqulier in order to celebrate the publication of Audrey's latest book, a collection of short stories set in Japan that had already won two awards. Eva and Isabel, both associate professors, were on their lunch breaks. Audrey, who pieced together an income by teaching part-time at six different schools, including three universities, a private high school, a kindergarten, and an English conversation school, had fortunately already finished her two gigs of the day. They'd toasted Audrey's book with mineral water, and polished off the first course, a salad made of hydroponically grown micro-greens and were now digging into their handmade pasta, which was flecked with indigo leaves.

"There's going to be an opening at my uni," Eva said in a low voice, even though none of the neighboring diners were likely to be able to understand English. As she leaned forward, her shiny auburn curls caught the light.

Audrey knew from hanging out with her two Australian friends for all these years that "uni" meant "university." Eva taught linguistics at a public institution. Audrey wound a few strands of pasta around her fork and lifted them to her mouth, idly admiring Eva's dangly earrings.

"It's a post for an American literature instructor," Eva went on. "I think you should toss your name into the hat."

"I don't know," Audrey demurred. A strand of blonde hair had fallen across her face. She used her index finger to hook it behind her ear. "I kind of like teaching part-time." Her current schedule made it possible for her to pick up her daughter from the School for the Deaf and allowed her plenty of writing time. Plus, she didn't have to ask for days off in the summer to go visit her parents in the United States, or to jaunt off to a writer's conference in China, say, or Macau. She knew that her husband, Akihito, was hoping that she would get a full-time job, but she was reluctant to give up her relative freedom.

"You could make three times as much money as you're making now," Isabel added. "And you'd have fewer classes." Single mom Isabel was in the process of building a house. She had her suits custom-made in Hong Kong. Obviously, she was doing well for herself at the private women's college where she worked.

"Yeah, but the meetings." Eva and Isabel were always complaining about the hours-long meetings that ate up so much of their days – colleagues arguing for half an hour about which font to use in a newsletter, or whether the term "glocal" was preferable to "global."

"Also," Audrey continued, "I don't have a PhD." Her mind flashed to Dieter, Eva's volatile German colleague, who had hired Audrey to conduct a creative writing club in the English Resource Room. Dieter was desperate for tenure. He would probably want that job.

"But you have publications," Eva insisted. "You've published eight books. And your first novel is in the library at Harvard University. Just work that into the job interview somehow. They're always impressed by the mention of Harvard or Oxford."

"Hmmm," Audrey said. "Maybe."

"I'll send you the link to the job advertisement," Eva said. "Promise me you'll give it some thought."

The next morning, Audrey went to her kindergarten class, which would be followed by a quick lunch, a change of clothes, and the creative writing workshop at the university.

She found kindergarteners exhausting, but the teaching gig was only twice a month, and it paid well. Plus, she knew that if she decided to quit, she would be expected to introduce her successor, and she didn't have anyone in mind.

"Good morning, Audrey-sensei!" the head teacher said in her overly peppy kindergarten teacher voice.

"Good morning." Audrey could hear the pound of feet from the second floor as the children ran around. Their shrieks and giggles filled her ears.

"What have you got planned for today?" the teacher asked.

Audrey thought of the picture book she'd tucked into her tote bag – the English translation of the popular Everyone Poops! By Taro Gomi. After reading that, she'd teach them Duck, Duck, Goose. It probably wasn't what the *kyoiku mamas*, the educationally minded mothers who sent their kids to this expensive private preschool, would have wanted. They were probably expecting flash cards and grammar lessons, but Audrey knew what would work best.

"We'll work on the imperative form today," Audrey said. The head teacher nodded approvingly.

Audrey marched up the steps to the playroom where she usually taught. The four-year-olds were running in circles, driving themselves into a frenzy, while their homeroom teacher, a middle-aged woman in an apron appliqued with Pokemon characters, stood by, waiting for Audrey to take over.

"Okay, everyone," Audrey shouted. "Let's make a circle!"

The Japanese teacher immediately translated her words into Japanese, although Audrey was quite sure that after a year of hearing the phrase, the kids knew what it meant. Audrey started each lesson with everyone sitting in a circle on the hardwood floor, rolling a ball from one to another, and greeting each other.

There was always one kid who, when asked "how are you?" couldn't decide whether he was "fine" or "hungry" or "sleepy." And there was that one overactive boy who, instead of gently rolling the ball, felt compelled to throw it with full force to the far corner of the room. The Japanese teacher translated every utterance in English into Japanese, and did nothing when the children misbehaved, as if to prove the pointlessness of Audrey's presence, and the ineptness of her disciplinary techniques. No one in this room cared that she had an MFA from a prestigious university and eight published books to her name. Coming here was a semi-monthly exercise in humility.

They made it through greetings, and the picture book reading, with a minimum of heckling. And then she explained how to play the game.

"I'll go first," she said. Her hand landed lightly on each black-haired head as she went around the circle, which was quickly becoming an amorphous blob shape.

"Duck, duck...goose!"

Thus tagged, the little girl with the Hello Kitty sweatshirt sprang into motion, diving at Audrey's knees, and bringing her down to the hardwood floor. *Damn. That hurt.* Tears sprang to Audrey's eyes. "You got me," she managed to say. She touched her elbow, wondering if it was broken. "Who wants to go next?"

It had been twenty years since Audrey had filled out a job application. She had endured an intensive interview, before a panel of three grim-faced Japanese men, in order to get her first job in Shikoku as an assistant English teacher. After that, every job she had gotten in the country had been through referrals.

Instead of interviews, she'd had brief conversations over cups of green tea or coffee, in which they'd hammered out details. Audrey wasn't even sure she was up to a proper interview, but maybe she should just do it for the experience. She could put it into one of her novels or short stories, even if, or especially if, it turned out to be a disaster. And anyway, there was no guarantee that she would be called for an interview. First, she had to fill out the tedious Excel sheets, and write essays about her professional goals and her teaching philosophy, and then have Akihito translate everything into Japanese.

She announced her intentions that evening as they lay side by side on their futons.

"It's about time," Akihito huffed. When they'd first married, she had made more money than he did. He had, no doubt, anticipated an upper middle-class lifestyle with a golf club membership and foreign vacations, but then their twins had been born prematurely, and she had had to give up her full-time job to take care of their medically fragile infants. When their daughter's disabilities had become evident, going back to work full-time had become an impossibility. But now the twins were in junior high school, and they didn't need Audrey so much. The problem now was that there were rarely any openings for full-time native speaker English teachers due to the declining student population and the poor economy.

"Oh, and today I had a short story accepted for publication," she added.

"How much money will they pay you?" he asked. "None," Audrey said. She would be paid in copies. It was a prestigious journal, and she was feeling very proud of herself, but writing literature wasn't going to make her rich. It probably wouldn't even help her get a job, because all Japanese universities cared about were academic publications, and SCOPUS rankings. She would put it on her resume anyway.

In spite of her earlier reservations, she was starting to get excited about the prospect of teaching American literature. She would convey her love of *The Great Gatsby* to those bespectacled boys in their plaid flannel shirts, those girls with their Hello Kitty phones and acrylic nails. She would teach them, via *Moby Dick*, that whaling was not a unique part of Japanese culture. And she might introduce some more contemporary writers, like Kyoko Mori – see kids, it is possible for a Japanese-born person to master writing in English! By morning, she had practically completed a syllabus, at least in her head.

Several years ago, a couple of my expat friends, who were university instructors, convinced me to complete a master's degree and enter academia myself. Once I had gained a full-time position at a university in Japan, I discovered that the behind-the-scenes machinations were worthy of fiction. I initially conceived of a Japanese version of Mary McCarthy's *The Groves of Academe*, which I would entitle *Bamboo Groves*. For now, however, I have enfolded it into another work-in-progress, as the backstory for one of the characters of a multicultural beach novel which I am calling *Cinnamon Beach*. Stay tuned!

Suzanne Kamata is an American, most recently from South Carolina, who has been living in Japan for over thirty years.

She is the author or editor of going-on fifteen books, including *The Baseball Widow* (Wyatt-Mackenzie Publishing, 2021), a multicultural family drama in the vein of Celeste Ng's *Everything I Never Told You*, and the award-winning middle grade novel *Pop Flies, Robo-pets, and Other Disasters* (One Elm Books, 2020), now available as an audiobook and a paperback. Having raised two children, she lives on the island of Shikoku with her husband and two cats. She earned a BA in English from the University of South Carolina and an MFA in Creative Writing from the University of British Columbia. She is now an associate professor at Naruto University of Education.

Touched

Carolyn Haines

Acts 28: 3-6

3: And when Paul had gathered a bundle of sticks and laid them on the fire, there came a viper out of the heat, and fastened on his hand.

4: And when the barbarians saw the venomous beast hang on his hand, they said among themselves, No doubt this man is a murderer...

5: And he shook off the beast into the fire, and felt no harm.

6: Howbeit they looked when he should have swollen, or fallen down dead suddenly: but after they had looked a great while and saw no harm come to him, they changed their minds, and said that he was a god.

Chapter 1

In that airless zone of southeast Mississippi, July is only the promise of things to come. The last comfort of June's cool nights is gone, and August is building, building slowly in the shimmer of the sun. The days grow long and hot with no relief in sight. Mosquitoes and copperheads lurk in the coolest shade of the piney woods. It is only dawn and dusk that are bearable.

I can still feel the touch of a July morning on my skin, when the grass is soaked in silver pellets of dew and the first slanted white rays of the sun burn the green pine horizon into a dark, grainy day. Even now, some twenty years later, I remember exactly.

The date was July 1, 1926. By midday the sun was riding high in a sky bleached as pale as old lace. The air was as much water as gas. Standing in my kitchen, I could hardly draw a breath.

I folded the box of taffy closed and tied it with the red string Elikah had brought me from the barbershop. From his seat at the kitchen table, he watched. He'd finished his lunch and pushed the plate back, satisfied with the zipper peas and okra and the cornbread I'd made. In a week of marriage, he'd found no fault with my cooking.

"Tell Miss Annabelle I said 'Happy Birthday,'" he said as he pulled up his suspenders, snapped them into place on his muscled chest, and reached for his coat.

"You look nice." I was shy with him, still trying to find where I fit in his life. He was the handsomest man I'd ever seen. It hurt to look at him, and I couldn't bear it for more than a few seconds running.

"Go on." He nodded toward the door. "It's time."

Dressed in my hot, gray flannel dress, I stepped off the porch and into the heat of the one o'clock sun. It was a birthday party for Annabelle Lee Leatherwood, a nine-year-old chinless wonder who had the misfortune to take after her mother in physical appearance and personal conduct.

July 1, 1926. It was a new month. A new life for me, and I was late for the birthday party. Chas Leatherwood, a man of influence, ran the Jexville Feed and Seed. An invitation to his daughter's party was a summons, and Elikah had made it perfectly clear that I would attend, properly dressed and with a gift.

The sun was blinding, but the afternoon storm clouds had already begun to mount in the distant west. They came disguised as castles and dragons of fleecy white, but they were edged in angry gray. I knew they'd build, their deceptive masses catching colliding winds to crash and mingle, until, after a half hour or so of magnificent late-afternoon collisions, the rain would fall down in a straight sheet. But I figured I had at least three hours of swelter to endure before the momentary relief of the rain. And I was late.

I had made taffy for a present, but it hadn't set up properly, and I could feel it beginning to ooze through the pretty papers and the box as

I hurried to the Leatherwood house. The stickiness of the box was disgusting. Warm. Like blood.

The clouds to the west were building quickly, a wall of fanciful shapes. They were almost motionless, trapped by the heat, waiting for the wind. Just before the storm broke, there would be the blessed relief of a breeze. But that was still hours away.

Two mockingbirds argued and shrilled in the big magnolia tree in Jeb Fairley's front yard, and I stopped to listen and to give my burning feet a rest. Some folks didn't care for the birds, but I liked them. In the spring when their young are in jeopardy, they're bold, even aggressive. Once a mockingbird had come out of a crepe myrtle tree, where she had three fledglings in her nest, and pecked my stepfather smack in the forehead. The bird didn't live to tell about it. Jojo Edwards wasn't a man who let even a bird get anything over on him. He killed the mother and the babies and chopped the tree down for good measure.

That's an image I carry in my head, and not even the long passage of time can dull it. I see Jojo's angry, sweating face. Hatred sparks spew from the eye slits in his fat. I can hear the ax blade biting into the smooth, barkless skin of the crepe myrtle. The sound is punishment. The blade doesn't grab in the way it does on a tree with bark. I see the raw chunk when the blade comes away, the useless flutter of leaves dropping to mingle with the feathers of the dead birds.

The memory made me hotter, afraid, and I started to run. As I turned the corner of Canaan onto Paradise Street, I heard the music. Tinny, wobbling, it seemed to come from a long way away. From all I've learned of Jexville in my five days there as the wife of Elikah Mills, the music more likely came from the moon. The forbidden sound entered my ears and went straight to my blood. Who in Jexville owned a gramophone? Who dared to play one on the afternoon of Annabelle Lee Leatherwood's birthday party? The sticky plight of the candy and Jojo's cruel eyes were forgotten as I started to run toward the music.

The red dust spurted up around my black shoes and coated the hem of my dress, but I didn't care. A fine red grit was settling over the bottom of the taffy-soaked box. At the white picket fence of Elmer Hinton's yard, I ran out of breath and slowed. It was unseemly for a married woman to be seen running in the streets, but the music made me want to run more. I didn't know the song, but it was fast and naughty.

Forbidden.

With each step, the music grew louder, and when I turned right on Revelation Road, I saw her, a nine-year-old flapper who was dancing with abandon. Duncan McVay.

I would have recognized her anywhere.

Standing out on that hot street with that sticky candy, I was struck dumb by my first sight of her. She was wearing a yellow sleeveless dress that hung straight from her shoulders to her narrow hips, which were banded by a wide yellow ribbon.

From there, a short skirt barely covered possible. She was tall for her age, and her long, thin legs were a blur of motion.

She was riveting as she stepped forward, then back, eyes rolling for effect and then crinkling shut with laughter. She danced alone, aware of everyone staring at her but not the least put out. Around her sat a dozen other children. Some looked terrified, others jealous. No matter what their reaction, none of them ignored her. Duncan McVay was the center of everyone's attention, including the women who stood in a disapproving group beside the back steps. They watched, too, unable to stop themselves from looking even as they disapproved.

One other woman stood at the handle of the gramophone, cranking it tight so the record spun fast and the little girl danced all the harder. Although she tried not to, this woman smiled. She glanced from the dancing girl to the knot of unhappy women, and her smile widened slightly, her own blue eyes crinkling in just the same way as the girl's.

With a cry of delight the child finished the dance and threw her hands up in the air. Her black patent leather shoes were covered orange with the dust she'd stirred dancing in the only grassless patch of ground in the Leatherwoods' backyard. She'd virtually wallowed out a hole in the ground.

"Doesn't anybody want to Charleston?" Duncan looked at a tall, skinny boy. He looked down at the grass and plucked a handful.

"Robert? Do you want to dance?" Duncan persisted. "It's fun. And easy. Mama can start the record over and I can show you."

Robert kept looking at the grass. The other children were silent, until one girl giggled.

Without turning around, Robert stood up. He shot a quick look at

Duncan and saw that she was still waiting, but this time with some impatience.

"I can't," Robert whispered. "We're not allowed to dance." He turned and walked away, going right past me with his face a flaming red.

I still held the dust-soaked taffy box, which was getting soggier by the minute. My shoulders and the top of my head were beginning to bake in the relentless afternoon sun, but I didn't want to step into the yard. I'd heard enough about JoHanna and her daughter to know who they were. To be honest, I'd expected something else—horns, at the very least.

"I think it's time for ice cream," Agnes Leatherwood announced loudly. Only one child responded, a portly little girl whose unfortunate face slid into her neck without benefit of a chin. She directed an angry look at the girl in yellow.

"I want my ice cream," the plump girl said, her voice a challenge for anyone to contradict her wishes. When none of the other children got up, she put her hands on her hips. "If y'all don't come in the house now, you won't get any ice cream."

Two of the girls got up and went to stand beside her. They waited, just as their mothers waited at the steps. Agnes, a skinny version of her daughter, looked at Duncan as if she might cry.

"Put on another record, please, Mama." Duncan put one hand on her little hip and looked out. "Anyone here not a fraidy-cat?"

Two other girls got up and went to stand beside Agnes and Annabelle Lee and the mothers. Then two boys followed, then another.

The music spun out across the yard, a lively tune that set Duncan's feet flying. JoHanna McVay leaned one hand on the gramophone and watched her daughter dance. The women, transfixed, failed to go inside until the song ended.

Duncan was sweating and her black hair, cut in a sleek bob that framed her face and made her dark eyes more noticeable, was damp with sweat.

"One more song, then come inside and have some ice cream," JoHanna said, cranking the machine and putting on a slower record. By her tone and actions, JoHanna McVay acted as if nothing unusual had happened in the yard. If the other women and children had intended to exclude her and Duncan, she didn't appear to notice the slight. She adjusted the needle on the record and turned away to go inside. It wasn't until she moved that I took real notice of her. She was defined by movement. Her steps were long, a contradiction of the mincing feminine steps I'd been warned to execute, yet they marked her as a woman.

In contrast to the white blouses and drab skirts of the other women, JoHanna wore a soft coppery dress with golden flowers mingled as if the colors had bled slightly. Her pale arms were daringly bare. There wasn't a collar to her dress, but a loose gathering of material that fell in a soft fold across a generous bosom. Her entire neck and a portion of her chest were revealed by the loose construction. The skirt hung straight to her calves and was dangerously slit to allow for those long strides. I had the fancy that she was some force of nature.

Wind. The cool, teasing breeze of dusk or evening. Her hair, a reddish chestnut, was piled on her head in a mass that hinted at disarray. It captured the light in a dance all its own.

At the edge of the steps she caught sight of me, still standing at the corner of the yard. Several dribbles of melted taffy had oozed out of the box and drawn the interest of some passing ants. The small insects were gathering rapidly, as tantalized by the taffy as I had been by the sight of Duncan dancing.

"You must be Elikah Mills's new bride." JoHanna came forward, her hand extended. "I'm JoHanna McVay. Welcome to Jexville."

Her blue eyes assessed me, but I didn't feel judged, as I had by the other women. She saw the places where my gray dress had been let out. It had belonged to my younger sister Callie, and I'd had to take it for traveling down to Jexville for my wedding. It still didn't fit exactly right, binding me around my chest and arms.

"I see you made taffy for Annabelle. That was thoughtful." She noticed the sticky drizzle that fell at my feet. "If you don't move fast, those ants are going to be all over you."

She took my arm and edged me toward the house.

"How is it possible that no one in town mentioned that you were mute?" She looked me directly in the eye as she asked.

I smiled, then grinned. "I'm not mute."

She nodded. "I didn't think so. A tidbit like that would be gnawed and licked over to the point that even I would have heard about it."

I looked over at the child who was still dancing. A fine sheen of sweat now covered her face and arms, but she had no intention of stopping. She'd forgotten where she was or who was with her; she was taken with the pleasure of the music and executing the intricate steps.

"My daughter, Duncan," JoHanna said as she led me toward the steps. "I'm sure you've heard about us. Just believe about a tenth of what you hear and then sift through that with a malice comb. What you'll be left with is some very boring facts."

I cast a look at her, noticing for the first time that she was older than I'd thought. The fine lines around her eyes were visible only when she stopped smiling. Her chestnut hair was livened with reddish highlights, but there was also silver there, especially at the temples. I looked back at Duncan.

"She's nine and I'm forty-eight." JoHanna spoke without turning around. "I was sinfully old when I conceived and tragically old when she was born. The biggest disappointment in town was that my old body didn't give out and allow me to die in childbirth."

She was smiling, but there was a strange energy behind her words. "You look fit enough." The words popped out of my mouth before I thought them through. Speaking before thinking was a habit that had gotten me in trouble more than once. I'd vowed to curb it, but so far had only dulled it back some.

JoHanna put her hands on my shoulders and laughed. "Fit enough for what?" she asked. "Getting pregnant or having the baby?"

I could feel the blush move up my face, and I could see that only delighted JoHanna the more. Still laughing, she shook her head and pointed me toward the kitchen, where Agnes Leatherwood was pulling the dasher out of the gallon of ice cream she'd made.

"Mrs. Mills has brought a gift," JoHanna said, ushering me into the room.

Agnes took one look at the ruined box and dropped the ice cream dasher. "Thank you, Mattie." She took the box and put it in the sink. "That was very thoughtful of you." Out of the corner of her eye she glanced at JoHanna.

"The taffy didn't set too well." I realized I should have thrown the box away. All of the women were staring at me, at the dribble of taffy on the floor where I'd held the box away from me.

"Too humid for candy to set, but it was a sweet thing to think of."

JoHanna went to the sink and got the dishcloth. In a moment she had the sticky candy off the floor.

When she looked up, she saw that all of the women were still staring at me. She tossed the dishcloth across the room into the sink. "You know, Agnes, it's a shame that you won't let Annabelle dance. The girl is fat. Some exercise might do her good."

I saw the glint of humor in JoHanna's face as she winked at me, then turned to face the fury of Annabelle Lee's mama. "Annabelle is not fat. She's highly sensitive. And dancing is a sin."

"So is gluttony, but that hasn't stopped a good number of people in Jexville." JoHanna looked completely innocent, not as if she wasn't pointing out that half the women in the room were on the portly side.

"You are a scandal, JoHanna McVay. You're going to be the ruination of Will's good name and his business." The woman who spoke was big, and her face had gotten red.

"I dare say Will can take care of his own reputation and his own business." JoHanna went to the sink. "Now are we going to serve up this ice cream or not?"

Outside the gramophone had wound down. There was the scratch of the needle across the record, and then the sound of Duncan winding the handle. The record got off to a slow, dragging start, then picked up speed and was soon racing at a fast clip.

"Serve the ice cream," Agnes said. She was still angry, but she didn't have the courage to confront JoHanna directly.

JoHanna dipped the big spoon into the metal container and lifted out the ice cream, complete with big chunks of peaches. "This looks delicious, Agnes." She transferred it to a bowl, then handed it to me.

"Duncan looks hot. I'll take this to her." I didn't wait to see the reaction to my words. I walked out into the hot sun letting the screen door slam behind me. I should have taken the bowl to one of the children waiting in the next room, but JoHanna had stood up for me.

Duncan waved but didn't break her dancing.

I held up the ice cream, the condensation on the bowl leaking over my fingers and dripping twice into the dust.

Duncan grinned at me, and I signaled her to come into the shade and get the ice cream. She was so hot. Dust had begun to stick to her legs.

The sun was still shining in that white-hot way of July, which meant no storms were immediate. The air was perfectly still, so still that the scratches in the record were suddenly magnified. The song was a ragtime. I don't remember which one, but I held the bowl, glad to be out of the company of those women and fascinated by the intricate steps Duncan was only too pleased to perform for me.

There was no warning. The bolt of lightning came out of the hazy blue sky. It was a double fork. One prong hit the pine tree and the other Duncan. A blue-white light flared over the entire yard, and a ball of fire ran down the pine tree and exploded against the side of the house.

When I looked back at Duncan, she was on the ground with smoke coming off her and big holes burned in the yellow dress.

The bowl of ice cream fell to the ground, but my fingers were still bent in the shape of holding it. I remember that I thought I couldn't inhale. The dress was already too tight, and the air was suddenly sucked dry of oxygen. It seemed like an hour that I stood there, trying to run toward Duncan, trying to breathe, trying to scream.

JoHanna came out the back door not even bothering with the steps. She ran like a gazelle, her skirt flying up over her legs. She fell to her knees beside Duncan and lifted her into her arms.

Duncan's head flopped back, and I could see her eyes were rolled up in her head. Smoke came from her hair, which had fallen out in great clumps. I could smell the burning hair and cloth and flesh, and I felt the tears sliding over my face.

Some of the other women had come outside, and the children were peeping through the screen door. No one made a sound. There was just the music, and finally the needle made its way to the end of the record and set to shushing against the label.

"Get a doctor." I spoke but didn't believe I had. When I turned and no one had moved I pointed to the boy named Robert. "Run and get the doctor."

He took off fast, his eyes too large for his pale face.

JoHanna sat in the dirt, Duncan crushed against her, and she rocked back and forth. Small sounds came from her, murmurings that I couldn't understand.

No one went to her, so I did. It was impossible to look into Duncan's rolled up eyes and not know that she was gone. The bolt had knocked the life out of her in one powerful blast.

I was standing just at JoHanna's shoulder, wondering what to do, when the clouds began to roll out of the west. They were the same clouds that had been hovering on the horizon since noon, growing darker and angrier with each passing hour. But they'd hovered in the distance, far away from the red clay streets of Jexville. Now they were on the move. They came toward us, thunder rumbling louder with each tick of the clock. Lightning shot out from the low-lying clouds in nasty forks.

I knelt down and put my hand on JoHanna's shoulder. "Let's take her inside," I said.

She ignored me, murmuring softly to her dead baby in that strange, lilting pattern. I didn't know then, but it's the same noises a mother cat makes when she's trying to lick life into a kitten. Cows and dogs and horses have their same version of the noise. All animals do, I suppose.

"Mrs. McVay, let's take her inside. It's going to storm." I lowered my grip to her arm, trying to move her gently away from the corpse. When I looked behind me, no one else had moved. They were watching us as if we were some strange creatures imported from an exotic land doing things they'd never seen before.

"Will someone help me get them inside?" I tried not to sound angry, but I hated their cow-like faces, the stupid way they stood, slack jawed.

"She's not dead." JoHanna whispered the words, but I knew they were meant for me. In that moment, I swear I thought I'd die from pity.

How could she look at that burned body that had been flung halfway across the yard and not realize that the life had gone?

Finally, Nell Anderson stepped forward. "The doctor is on his way, JoHanna. Let's take Duncan in the house, where he can examine her." She spoke with gentleness.

"She's not dead." JoHanna shrugged away from both of us. "Just leave us alone. Go away and leave us alone." She bent down lower, shielding Duncan from our sight.

Behind me, Rachel Carpenter started to cry softly. "Somebody get Reverend Bates," she said. I heard another of the children slam out of the house and run. I never turned around to look. All I could think of was Duncan, alive one minute and dancing her heart out. Now she was gone.

I knelt beside JoHanna just as the first big drops of rain began to fall. They struck the dust where Duncan had been dancing, causing little flares of orange to jump up, as if the ground were alive and pulsing. The stump of the pine tree sizzled.

"Mrs. McVay, let's take her inside. It's going to rain."

"She's isn't dead." JoHanna never stopped rocking. "She can't be."

I could hear the rain in the magnolia tree beside the gramophone. It hit the slick green leaves with snaps and pops. It hit me, too, but I didn't feel it. I could see it striking JoHanna's shoulders, fat drops soaking into her coppery dress.

Nell Anderson knelt beside JoHanna on her right. "We need to send for Will. Where is he this week?" She reached out to straighten one of Duncan's little socks. Her shoe was missing. It had been blown clean off her foot.

"He's in Natchez."

"We'll send a telegram."

"Try the Claremont House. He'll be in there sometime today."

Nell was crying, and I was crying. Only JoHanna didn't cry. Nell got up to send the telegram, but I stayed, watching the rain soak into JoHanna McVay as she keened softly to her dead girl.

When I looked up, the other children and mothers had left or gone inside. Agnes and Annabelle Lee were standing at the door, watching. They were both crying, too.

The ground had begun to puddle with water, but JoHanna refused to consider going inside. Dr. Westfall arrived, his white hair flying around his head and his black bag in his hand. He tried to lift JoHanna, but she hunkered down over the body and cried out to be left alone. I saw his hand move out to Duncan's neck and rest there for a moment, and then he reached up and closed her eyes. When he stood, he shook his head at Agnes and walked to the back door.

They spoke in low whispers for a moment, and then he went inside.

"JoHanna, we have to move out of the rain." I knew if she didn't get up and move they were going to come back outside and force her. I could imagine what they were doing. They'd send for the undertaker. They'd give JoHanna a shot. Then they'd tear them apart. I put my hand on her arm. "We have to go inside if you want to keep her a little longer."

"Make them leave me alone." She finally looked at me, and she was crying. "She isn't dead. I can feel her. Make them leave us alone for just a little while."

"Move under the magnolia tree." It didn't offer much protection, but it was better than nothing. The rain had leveled off to where it was a steady drum on the leaves. Together we picked up Duncan and carried her the few feet to the tree.

JoHanna sat with her back to the trunk, cradling her child. "Make them leave us alone." She didn't beg or plead. She asked.

"Just for a while." I didn't know how long I could hold them off. I didn't know why I felt like I needed to. All I knew was that once they took her baby, she'd never get her back. A little time wasn't much to ask.

I walked across the yard, my gray dress sopping. Inside the house I heard the murmur of low voices. They were already planning what to do, how to do it. The undertaker was on the way, and Dr. Westfall was filling a glass syringe with something. It certainly wasn't for Duncan.

"Leave her alone."

Everyone in the room turned to look at me. I could see from their faces that I gave them a fright.

"She's in shock. The girl is dead, and we can't leave her out there in the rain." Agnes wrung her hands as she spoke. She wasn't hardhearted, just unable to think beyond what appeared proper.

"Leave her alone. It's her child. There's nothing to be done for Duncan. Let Mrs. McVay have the time."

No one had ever paid the least attention to anything I'd ever said before. Maybe they didn't know what to do, so what I said was better than nothing. But we stood there for fifteen or twenty minutes, looking at one another and listening to the rain. Agnes made a pot of coffee and gave us all a cup, and we took seats around the kitchen table, where the unfinished bowls of ice cream had melted and begun to draw flies.

The undertaker came in the front door, along with the Methodist minister. We were a sorry group, but no one wanted to go to the back door and look out in the yard.

Sitting there in that hot kitchen, I knew that JoHanna was not liked, but no one could have possibly wished that tragedy off on her.

No woman is capable of wishing the death of a child on another. At least that's what I believed.

Finally the rain stopped. It had been thirty minutes or more. I knew there wasn't much longer to wait. I could see on their faces that they feared for JoHanna's sanity. They were repulsed by the idea that she could embrace a dead body. To their way of thinking, it was best to get it over with.

"Let me talk to her." I stood up and waited, but no one else volunteered. Walking across the kitchen and out the door, I saw things with a clarity that was painful. The leaves of the magnolia had been washed a deep hunter green. Part of the red dirt from the road had flooded into the yard, creating muddy red miniature rivers that cut around the magnolia, as if Duncan and JoHanna were stranded on an island. Up above, the sky was a perfect blue, deeper in color than it had been all summer.

JoHanna was as I'd left her, all energy and attention focused on her child. She was brushing Duncan's face with her fingertips, talking so softly I couldn't make out the words. Her hair had come down from the bun she wore and it was longer than I'd expected, and wet now, so that it was darker. It clung to her neck and shoulders and molded to her breasts beneath the wet dress.

I walked across the yard, slowly, dreading every step. I wanted to cry but I didn't. About ten feet away, I stopped. "It's time to go inside now, JoHanna."

She looked up but said nothing.

I heard the screen door close behind me and I turned to find nine-year-old Mary Lincoln and Annabelle Lee coming toward me. They stopped.

"Is she dead?" Mary asked. "I've never seen a dead person."

"I have." Annabelle Lee looked at the ground. "Lots of times."

"Go back inside." I tried not to snap at them but couldn't help myself. "Git! Right now."

Mary darted around me and ran up to the tree. At the sight of Duncan she froze.

I wanted to scalp her on the spot, and I was just reaching out to do that when Duncan's eyes opened. She stared directly at Mary.

"Don't sing with your mouth open, Mary, or you'll drown," she said.

This is a book I'm reissuing. TOUCHED was originally published in 1996 by Dutton, it is part of the Jexville Trilogy , which includes SUMMER OF THE REDEEMERS and JUDAS BURNING.

When I was growing up in the small town of Lucedale, Mississippi, I had big dreams. I wanted to be a cowgirl, a writer, and Nancy Drew. Life has surely thrown me more than a few twists, but dreams are hard to destroy. Today, I'm all three—sort of. Of course the only mysteries I solve are in Zinnia, Mississippi. And I have the help of Sarah Booth Delaney, Tinkie, Cece, Coleman, Millie and a host of other characters. They'll be quick to tell you they do all the hard work—I'm just the writer.

As to the horses, I have three. But no cows. I'm a little too tenderhearted. If I had a herd of cows, they'd live with me until they died of old age. But I do have the horses, Miss Scrapiron, a Thoroughbred, Mirage, a half-Arabian, and Cogar, a Thoroughbred-Connemara cross.

In the dog department, I have my very own Sweetie Pie, a red tic hound; Maybelline, a tall beagle; Zelda, a husky; and Rosie, a red dog. All of the dogs are strays, as are the cats, Miss Vesta, Gumbo, Poe, Chester, and Maggie.

A lot of people ask me how I started writing about the Mississippi Delta. My hometown, Lucedale, is way down in the Southeast corner of the state. That section is called the pine barrens, and it lives up to its name. Pine trees are a cash crop, and thousands of acres were once owned by the big paper companies. It's a world very different from the Mississippi Delta.

My first visit to the Delta was as a photojournalist. I went to Parchman State Prison to do a newspaper story. Parchman was notorious at that time, and I can still remember the terrible desolation I felt when I looked out and saw mile after mile of heat and cotton. But the Delta also has fabulous wealth. And it has the blues. I knew then, at the age of twenty-one, that I would one day write about that land of stark contrasts and strange beauty.

Sarah Booth and Jitty came to me in tandem, arguing just as they do in the books. When such fully developed characters visit a writer, it's truly a gift. I didn't know Sarah Booth was a private investigator–in fact she didn't either–until I'd started writing the book (Them Bones. Now, it's become my challenge to give her interesting cases to solve.

Before I wrote fiction I worked for nearly a decade as a journalist. That experience has been invaluable as a writer. It was a fabulous life for a young woman, and I had some terrific adventures. I once covered an armed robbery on horseback and on another occasion had to climb a tree to cover a hostage situation in a graveyard. It's a good thing I was a tomboy growing up.

Along with riding my bicycle, building forts in the woods with my brothers, playing baseball and touch football, and getting into mischief, I also spent a lot of time with my grandmother. She lived with us when I was a child, and she was a wonderful storyteller. She'd emigrated from Sweden when she was six, and she had a host of stories that kept me riveted for hours.

Many of the stories my grandmother told were ghost stories. When she really wanted us kids to be good, she'd recite that James Whitcomb Riley poem, "Little Orphan Annie." We'd be terrified to even let a hand dangle off the bed, so we were very, very good! During spend-the-night parties, I often repeated Grandma's stories to my friends, usually ending in a squealing, writhing heap of girls trying to find an adult to protect us. But my true love was mysteries. I devoured them as a reader. As early as high school I started trying to write short mysteries.

Prior to the Bones series, I wrote *Summer of the Redeemers* (1994) and *Touched* (1996). Though they were published as general fiction, they both contain strong mystery elements. But it wasn't until Sarah Booth stole that dog that I realized I had hold of a real mystery. I've spent the last five years in the company of the Zinnia crowd, and I have to say I've had a great time.

TOUCHED tells the story of a great love shared by a mother and daughter, and the power of such a bond. In 1993 I had a two-book contract with Dutton. *Summer of the Redeemers*, a coming of age story set in rural Mississippi in 1964, was the first book. *Touched*, set in the same town of Jexville in 1926, was the second. Johanna McVay is a woman ahead of her time in a religious, repressive town. She is a "free thinker" which can only bring tragedy in a world where that is never allowed for a woman. The story opens at a birthday party for a contemporary of Johanna's daughter, Duncan, a nine-year-old girl who has been raised to be her own person. Shocking the town residents, Duncan has brought a gramophone to the party and is outside dancing, an activity frowned upon. Out of a blue sky, she is struck by lightning. Against all odds, Duncan survives. Johanna begins to realize her daughter, while nearly killed, has also been given a gift. She is prophetic, but she can only predict drownings. The town believes she is "touched" by Satan. The story is narrated by a 16-year-old mail-order bride, Mattie. The third book in the Jexville trilogy is *Judas Burning.* All three books will be reissued this winter.

Carolyn Haines is the USA Today bestselling author of over 80 books in a number of genres. Her latest book is *Independent Bones,* the 23rd Sarah Booth Delaney mystery. She has been honored with the Harper Lee Award for Distinguished Writing and the Richard Wright Award for Literary Excellence as well as being inducted into the Alabama Writers Hall of Fame. Her website is www.carolynhaines.com

From Pangaea, a Novel

Debra Thomas

Chapter Two

Pangaea

Binghamton, NY: 1971

The light hit her bedroom wall and fell seemingly through the floor. Josie tried to focus on the light and not the image of a car descending the hill beyond their house. It could be like counting sheep, she thought, kicking off the sheet and turning her face toward the small fan beside her bed. Warm air tickled her cheeks and blew about the few strands of hair that weren't soaked with sweat. Another dash of light. "One," she began, closing her eyes, but she couldn't stop her ears from hearing the motor as it descended and approached the house. If it started to slow, as cars often did to take the dip in the road, she'd be tempted to jump out of bed and run to the window. It was a habit she couldn't shake, not since her father left eight years before, and she and her brother, Vic, then five and eleven, would lie side by side on her bed, watching the wall for that flash of light and then listening hard. The cars never stopped; they only left a silence that was filled, some nights, by their mother's muffled sobs beyond the wall that caught the light.

This car was noisy, pulling Josie up and out of bed. The linoleum felt cool to her feet as she hurried to the window in time to see a pickup roar by. She watched the taillights bounce in the distance. "Damn," she said out loud. "Now I'm wide awake." She'd known it was too early to be Vic. When he finished working on cars at the service station, he often met up with friends at Thirsty's Tavern. Plus, that motor wasn't anything like the coughing of his old Mustang, despite all the work he'd put into it. She knew the sound of his car, just like she knew the sounds of her mother coming home from the hospital at night—her heavy sighs, the hiss of a match as she lit up another cigarette and settled into the darkened living room. Josie had learned long ago not to interrupt that moment; it was her mother's special time to be alone. When she woke at the sound of her mother's keys, she never came down, but lay back and listened, wondering what her mother was thinking.

Josie pressed her forehead against the well-worn bulge in the screen. She didn't have to wonder tonight. Though they chose not to talk about it much, the air was thick with one fact: Vic would be leaving for basic training, the army, and—most likely— Vietnam.

Two weeks before, on August 5th, they had listened together to the draft lottery on the radio. Since Vic had turned eighteen the previous year, his August 10th birthday was randomly assigned the draft number twenty-five, which meant he was certain to be drafted. After much thought, Vic had made the decision to enlist in the army, a four-year stint instead of two as a draftee, but it meant he'd have a better chance of applying for and getting a specialty training assignment as a helicopter mechanic. This way he could avoid direct combat and add to his skills as an auto mechanic.

"Kinda like goin' off to college," he had joked. "Just four years." So, on his unlucky birthday, he had officially enlisted and was set to leave in a couple of months.

Josie couldn't imagine this house without his presence. Even when he wasn't home, there was always the anticipation of when he'd sweep in. What he'd done. Where he'd been. He could make an aimless three-hour drive down to New York City sound exciting, even though he had simply driven around Yankee Stadium, stopped for gas, and come back. She swallowed hard at the thought of his leaving and pushed herself away from the window toward the door and the dull rays of light beyond the stairway.

She switched on the eleven o'clock news and sprawled onto the faded, floral sofa in front of the large fan. That's where she'd spent most of the day, devouring a stack of old National Geographic magazines that Vic had picked up for her at a garage sale the week before. He had come home early that day and stopped at the kitchen doorway, beaming like a boy with a secret, then stepped aside to reveal the two large boxes filled with magazines, and said, "Ought to keep you out of trouble this summer." He'd looked younger than his nineteen years, his bushy dark curls tousled and his cheeks flushed. She'd wanted to fly at him and wrap her arms around him tight. Instead, she'd said, "Cool!" and bent down to look through the boxes as he walked away, whistling.

Her mother wanted Josie to be a nurse. The local hospital, where her mother worked evenings as a nurse's aide, had a reputable school of nursing, and that's where she saw Josie's future. But Vic had always scoffed at that. "Josie's no nurse. She's a doctor," he'd say. "Hell, she's too smart to be just one of the crew; she's gonna be the captain." He'd make his usual comments and little jokes. But one night, just last winter, when he'd teasingly asked what book she was buried in this time, instead of answering with a wrinkled nose and continuing to read, Josie had taken a deep breath and said, "I'm reading about Pangaea, the super-continent." Vic had stopped and looked at her for what seemed like a long time, until she started to talk and he sat down beside her.

She told him how the mountains were formed by constantly moving plates of earth. How scientists were uncovering facts every day that supported this theory called continental drift. She pulled out a map and showed him how the continents had once fit together like a puzzle. "Pangaea," she said again. "That's what they call it. But it all broke apart, over millions of years. And it's still moving, still changing."

Vic had bent over the books and maps with the same concentration he used under the hood of a car, so she'd kept talking. She showed him the articles that her science teacher had given her, and the ones she'd found on her own.

"What kills me," she said, "what just kills me is that it's always been there. All these rocks, and mountains, and these ocean trenches, all the secrets of our earth's past just waiting to be uncovered and made sense of."

When she finally paused to catch her breath, she saw that Vic was slowly flipping through pages until he stopped and asked, "Who's this? With the hammer?"

He pointed to a picture of a thin, young woman standing by a cliff. Her smile was slight, and forced at that, but Josie noticed how sure her footing was on the rocks, and how firm her grasp of the tool.

"You mean her name?" she asked.

"No. No," Vic said impatiently. "What is she?"

"I don't know. A geologist? Maybe a paleontologist?" She leaned forward to read the caption beneath, but her eyes blurred when she heard Vic say firmly in her ear, "Then that's what you're gonna be."

Now stretched out on the sofa, too tired to read, but too hot to sleep, Josie stared at the bright TV screen. The drone of the fan blocked out the words of the newscaster, but his face was hypnotizing just the same. His eyes seemed to smile, though his brow was creased and his lips settled into a slight frown. Then scenes of war filled the screen. Soldiers in sweat- soaked fatigues, an old man peering up from under a large brimmed hat, the somber dirty face of a child. Josie shuddered. She just couldn't see Vic there. Not at all.

Startled at the sound of the door and her mother's raspy cough, Josie sat up. She watched as her mother walked wearily to the front of the fan, where she stopped, let the air blow on her face and neck, then leaned forward and let it billow down the front of her white uniform. Her short dark hair was tucked behind her ears. Her uniform, damp under the armpits, hung loosely on her ever-thinning frame. Her mother ate so little, Josie worried she'd waste away. Coffee and cigarettes were her main staple. When she did have time to make Josie and Vic a meal, she'd take one or two bites, scoot back her chair, and then light up another cigarette.

Turning slightly, her mother glanced at the TV and said in one long sigh, "Turn that off, Josie, for chrissakes. I don't want to hear about that place."

Josie jumped up and turned the knob on their beige console TV. Her mother looked at her expectantly, then with a slight, sad smile, she ran her fingers through Josie's long dark hair.

"You too, huh?" she said. "All the patients were restless again tonight. Too hot to sleep, too hot to breathe. You should tie this up in a ponytail." She gathered Josie's hair up off of her neck, then let it fall gently over her shoulders.

Josie shrugged. "I did. Took it out 'cause it was giving me a headache."

Her mother turned toward the kitchen. "Vic not home yet?" she asked.

"No," Josie answered. Then she heard herself say, "Maybe he won't go."

"Go where? Where'd he go?" Her mother stopped.

"To Vietnam, I mean. Maybe he won't go."

Her mother's face filled with color as she turned back and said in a hushed tone,

"What'd he tell you?"

That was one way to get her attention, Josie thought.

Where'd he go? What'd he say? Who's he seeing? Sometimes she told and sometimes she didn't.

"Is he planning to run? Go to Canada or something?" Her mother was holding Josie by the arms now, looking hard into her face.

"No," Josie said. "That's not what I mean. He didn't say anything.

125

I just keep thinking that maybe he won't have to go."

Her mother grunted and let go, then heading toward the kitchen, she said, "Oh Josie … I thought . . . oh, Christ."

Josie considered following her and telling her what little she did know, but the most Vic had actually said on the subject was, "What the hell else am I gonna do?" and there wasn't any comfort in that. So she settled back on the sofa and tried to make out the blades of the fan as they whirled.

~~~

She was dreaming of children running down a long tunnel that began to turn, first slowly, then faster and faster until the children's laughter became shrieks of terror. When she opened her eyes, she couldn't be sure if she'd been one of the kids or just a spectator watching.

A high-pitched squeal filled her ears again, followed by her mother's uncharacteristically cheerful voice saying, "Now Vic, cut that out. You're embarrassing me."

"Well, you are, you know," Vic was saying. "The foxy lady of my life. She is, Jay, and a great dancer, too. Come on Mom, dance with me. Come on."

"That's enough, Vittorio." Her voice was firm now. "You've had a bit too much to drink tonight, and you know my feelings on that. Now if you boys will excuse me, I'm going on up to bed."

Josie sat up. Boys? Who was here? she wondered, then lay back down when her mother's shadow filled the doorway. "Jay, in case my son doesn't follow through on his hospitality, there are towels in the closet at the top of the stairs . . . Vic, stop it, for chrissakes, I swear."

Josie smiled at the giggle of her brother's otherwise deep voice, then closed her eyes and feigned sleep as her mother passed by, stopping to linger for a moment beside the sofa. Thinking what? Josie wondered. Then she felt something laid over her legs, heard her mother's slow panting as she climbed the stairs, then the water running in the bathroom.

Kicking off the afghan, Josie stood up and smoothed out the

oversized T-shirt that she slept in. It covered the gym shorts she wore underneath and was longer than most of her miniskirts, but when she edged to the doorway, the stranger's dark eyes that met hers swept down to her legs and stayed there. He was sitting on the opposite end of the Formica kitchen table, holding a can of Genesee beer and looking like an ad in a magazine—his handsome face, neatly trimmed mustache, and slight smile, as he held up the red and white can that matched their red and white dinette set.

Then Vic was beside her, his voice booming. "Josie! Sleeping beauty. This here's a new friend of mine, Jay."

Vic was always making new friends. He drew people to him like some movie star, she thought, yet he'd never been a star at anything. He just seemed to pull people in. Being near him made you feel good. That was it, she decided, as he hooked an arm around her neck and led her into the brightly lit kitchen: He made you feel as if you were the star.

"Now Josie's goin' to college, too, someday," he was saying. "I'm seeing to that. Hell, she's so smart she's gonna get her picture in the National Geographic magazine one day." Then he pulled her down onto the red and white chair beside him and said, "Jay here goes to Penn State. He's from Wilkes-Barre but is on his way to Syracuse to visit his girl. Car broke down on 81, got towed to our service station. I've been showing him the town a little."

Briefly glancing at the dark eyes, Josie laughed and said, "I'll bet you've seen the real high parts of Binghamton tonight." She was glad she had left her long, wavy hair loose, covering her breasts on both sides. Without a bra, she felt exposed.

"Yeah," he said with a slight laugh. "It's a nice town though, kind of like my own." Then he shrugged and looked down at his hands. When he looked up again, he tried to smile, but his lips seemed to settle in a frown.

~~~

The next day felt like the longest day of her life. Josie was certain that something had happened the night before. She felt it, though she couldn't put her finger on what it might be. She'd slept till ten and woke to find that "The boys're already down- at-the-station," as her mother put it, "working on Jay's car." Josie had left them at the table the night before talking baseball, although there'd been tension, some awkward pauses, that Vic seemed to be easing with small talk. But later, she'd heard their voices rising and falling, a continuous ebb and flow that seemed to vibrate up the walls to her room long into the night. She wondered if they'd slept at all.

Her mother left for work early to run a couple of errands, then called at four to say she'd be working a double. That meant she'd be gone until the morning.

"I called Vic at the station," she said. "Told him not to stay out too late."

Her mother paused and Josie said, "Mom, you didn't have to do that. I'm okay alone, and anyway . . ." But she couldn't finish. They both knew calling Vic would not be an option soon.

When his Mustang pulled up shortly after nine, Josie met him at the door. "Vic, you don't have to stay. God, it's only nine! Mom is nuts. You can go out. I'm fine." But he just walked past her to the sofa, where he sank down, head back, eyes closed.

"You okay?" she asked, sitting across from him on the edge of the coffee table.

He opened his eyes and looked at her a long time. "You're growing up," he said in a soft, strange voice. "Most times I look at you and don't really see you. I just see my little sister. But you are."

Josie hit him on the leg. "Cut it out," she said. But he kept on staring at her with a seriousness that made her uncomfortable.

"That guy, last night, Jay, he didn't look at you like you were some kid," he said with a slight smile. "I could tell."

"Why? What did he say?" Her voice sounded childlike, yet a part of her felt older inside, like she was two people in the same body.

"He didn't say anything. I could just tell . . . just like I knew he wasn't on his way to visit some girlfriend." He studied his hands for a minute. When he looked up, she saw his eyes were wet. He leaned forward.

"He was on his way north," he said slowly. "Goin' to Canada. When we finally got it all out in the open last night, he almost had me talked into goin' with him. He's got a place to stay, a job waiting. It's all been arranged. He flunked outta Penn State. I guess he was on one of those college deferments. And now his lottery number is pretty low, like mine, and . . ." He paused and shook his head. "His dad doesn't believe in the war, so he worked it all out for him."

She heard the words, tried to sort it all out in her mind.

"Why?" she finally asked. "Why didn't you go?"

He shook his head and lowered it into his hands. "I can't. I just can't. It's not right . . . for me. It's not my life."

"What do you mean?" she cried. "My god, it's a way out of that war. That's not your life, Vic. Why didn't you go with him?"

"I almost did," he said, pushing up from the sofa and pacing around. "Right up until he drove away. But all I could think about was . . . him. Two kids and a wife and just running off with some bitch!"

The mention of their father, so unexpectedly, hit Josie like a blast of heat. Her face felt hot, but her hands felt prickly and cold. She struggled to catch her breath.

"But it's not the same, Vic," she said. "It's not. You've been given a chance, a choice. And . . . and you said he has a place and a job. That's not running away."

"He, Josie. Jay has the place and the job. That's his life, not mine, that I'd be chasing."

Josie shook her head. She knew he was wrong, irrationally wrong. She wished there was someone or someway to convince him.

"All right then," she said standing to face him. "What you're saying is I'm crazy to dream of being anything but a nurse. Staying in this town, at that hospital, as a nurse. That's what you're saying then."

He looked at her a moment with a tenderness that made her want even more to send him north. "Oh Josie, that's just it. You have a gift that has to come first. You have to see that through to the end. Not doing it would be your desertion. But me, this is where life's put me.

And Jay's been put in a car heading north. That's his life. And he's not so crazy about what he's got ahead either. He's leaving a girl behind, a family, a town. Man, he's scared of all that too. But that's his life. He's gotta face it, and I gotta face mine. That's all there is to it."

What silenced her more than the words was the set of his chin and the hard look in his eyes. He seemed to age years right before her.

~~~

What she regretted most was agreeing not to tell their mother. Several months later, after Vic had shipped out to Vietnam, she ached to talk about it, wondered if perhaps together she and her mom could have persuaded him to ride it out in Canada. Then, at least, she wouldn't feel so responsible, especially on those long, empty nights when her imagination, fueled with graphic news-footage from Vietnam, created endless visions and versions of his possible death.

One such night, she fell asleep on the sofa and awoke in complete darkness just as her mother came in the door.

Expecting her to turn on a light, Josie quickly closed her eyes, but instead, her mother carefully made her way in the dark and eased down on the sofa by Josie's feet. She heard the click of a lighter, a deep intake of breath.

Through squinted eyes, Josie watched the angry glow in the darkness. One cigarette . . . two. Then Josie shifted, resting her feet on her mother's lap. Her mother began to stroke them.

"You okay, baby?" she asked.

As Josie tried to answer a simple, "Uh huh," a croaking sound leapt from her throat, split right through the air with an unexpected force. It startled her at first, pulling her forward, eyes wide open. For a moment, she felt suspended, until the shaking began, convulsive sobs that seemed to come from deep inside her chest. At first, there were no tears, but soon they came, cascading down between gulps and gasps.

Her mother was holding her, rocking her, crooning like she was a baby. "Jo-Jo," she kept saying, "Jo-Jo."

When the shaking eased a bit, her mother softly said, "Oh, I miss him, Josie. I miss him, too."

Josie heard her own voice whimper from somewhere far away, "But it's not fair. It's just not fair. Why did he have to go? Why?"

"I don't know, baby," her mother said while she smoothed Josie's hair back again and again and again.

Suddenly it struck Josie that, perhaps, if she started out small, a chip here, a chip there, it might somehow all make sense.

She looked up into her mother's weary face and asked gently, carefully, "Tell me, Mom. Tell me about Dad. What was he like . . . before things got bad? Tell me any little thing that comes to your mind."

Her mother was startled at first, a quick intake of breath, then slowly, haltingly, she began. Together they talked until dawn.

"Pangaea" was actually a short story that I wrote decades ago. The sister and brother, Josie and Vic, have always held a special place in my heart, as characters often do for writers.

But in this case, I knew they would end up in another story—or novel—one day. That's exactly what's happened. *"Pangaea"* is now a flashback chapter in a novel, currently titled *Pangaea*, which will be published by She Writes Press in Spring 223.

Most of the novel takes place thirty years after this short story. Josie and Vic are now in their forties. This flashback chapter captures the importance to Josie of the image of the supercontinent Pangaea, and it establishes the deep bond between brother and sister, which is the heart of this novel.

Novel Synopsis: When Josie's brother Vic experiences a devastating tragedy, Josie leaves her home in upstate New York to join him in Los Angeles. While hoping to help Vic pick up the pieces of his shattered life, Josie finds herself confronting her own broken relationships when their estranged father Tony suddenly appears, and Josie's rebellious daughter Ellie arrives as well. As this fragmented family is forced together on an unexpected journey, they are given a chance to reconnect.

Debra Thomas is a writer, teacher, and immigrant rights advocate.

Originally from Binghamton, New York, she has lived in Southern California most of her adult life. She taught literature and writing at James Monroe High School, a Los Angeles public school, as well as English as a Second Language (ESL) at adult schools in LA. Her debut novel, Luz, won the 2020 Sarton Award for Contemporary Fiction and the 2020 Next Generation Indie Book Award for Multicultural Fiction. Her second novel, Pangaea, will be published by She Writes Press in Spring 2023.

Buried Beneath

Debbie Baldwin

Thirty miles north of Stowe,
Vermont November 20

The small cabin sat nestled in a clearing in the snowy wood. Smoke puffed amiably into the starry sky.

The setting might have inspired Robert Frost but for the rotting roof and supporting wall threatening collapse. The crumbling chimney sat at a Seussian angle, and most of the windows were boarded up.

Then, of course, there were the men inside.

Dressed in winter camouflage, Camilo Canto moved silently through the wet snow, approaching the house from the side. He was the newest member of the team, but with each day that passed and every op they ran, Cam grew more certain that leaving the CIA to join Bishop Security was one of the best decisions he had ever made. In eight short months, he had found a home and had slammed the door on the demons of his past undercover work.

If only those demons would stop knocking.

Cam stepped on a twig, the small snap like an explosion in the quiet. He was distracted, and it didn't matter if he was a SEAL, an undercover officer, or a Bishop Security operator; distraction could get you killed.

Before they boarded the jet in South Carolina, Cam had received word from the CIA that someone had called the cell phone belonging to Cam's cover identity, Miguel Ramirez. The call had not connected and had come from an untraceable burner phone. It was a nonevent—no message, no caller to identify—and yet it needled him. It was the country code where the phone call originated that spurred his disquiet: Crimea.

There was one man who might have called him from that part of the world. Cam didn't have friends in the CIA, but Raymond Greene came close. He and Raymond shared a common interest in a very uncommon criminal. Greene knew Cam was out of the CIA, which only made the phone call more confounding. If it even was Greene who had attempted to contact him.

A voice in his ear forced Cam into the here and now. "Cam, what's your twenty?" Miller "Tox" Buchanan, their team leader, spoke in an even voice.

"About thirty yards to the north. I have a clear view of what looks like the kitchen. No activity." Cam refocused—if there was one thing he could do without hesitation after living for more than two years as his cover identity, Miguel Ramirez, it was compartmentalize.

"I thought Vermont was supposed to be quaint, like where they tap maple trees and churn butter and shit. This isn't one bit quaint." Hercules Reynolds, their sniper, spoke into the comm from his perch in a White Poplar. "Very un-fucking-quaint."

"Fuck off, Herc. At least you're in a tree. I'm stuck in an ice swamp," Jonah "Steady" Lockhart muttered from thirty feet below Herc's roost. Steady had earned his nickname on his SEAL squad for his ability to keep an even keel under the most trying of circumstances. Despite the griping, today was no exception.

The crunch of tires on gravel had the men snapping to attention.

"Incoming." Looking through binoculars, Leo "Ren" Jameson spoke from behind a tree to Cam's left. Ren was short for Renaissance Man. Leo Jameson was officially their medic; he also possessed an encyclopedic knowledge of topics ranging from astrophysics to zoology.

Bishop Security had been contracted to locate and rescue the daughter of a prominent insurance executive. Amy Rafferty had been driving from Bloomington, Indiana to Colorado to meet up with friends for a ski trip when she went missing. Her car was located at a truck stop outside of Lincoln, Nebraska.

The FBI was only too happy to hand over the case. Their list of investigations into killings and abductions potentially involving long-haul truckers was so long, the agency had an entire database dedicated to it.

The evidence—security footage and some blood droplets at the primary crime scene—had led the team to Alfred Winston Bell. Bell was a forty-three-year-old trucker with a string of offenses, including public indecency and peeking while loitering—a lawyerly way of saying he was a peeping tom. It appeared Mr. Bell had decided to take it up a notch.

Unfortunately for him, he chose the wrong girl. Amy Rafferty's father was an influential businessman with a network of connections that looked like an airline route map.

A rusted-out pickup rumbled up the drive, pulled onto the grass, and stopped with a sputter. A tall man with a beer gut jumped down, then turned back to the cab to grab four pizza boxes and a six-pack. He entered the cabin through a side door.

"Is that Bell?" Herc asked.

"Negative," Steady responded.

Cam crept through the wet snow to a closer tree, confident in his ingrained training. He had served as a SEAL with most of these guys before leaving the Navy to work for the CIA. He spoke softly into his comm. "I've got three men in the cabin. I don't have a visual on the girl, but Asshole Number One brought four pizzas when he came in, so it's a safe assumption there are more people in there."

"Unless Tox is in there," Steady ribbed. "Four pizzas would be about right."

Tox fired back, "I'm currently in a warm, dry van getting some very provocative texts from my wife, but by all means, you boys keep up the trash talk." Tox was a newlywed. He had fallen in love on an op last spring, and the six-foot, five-inch warrior was like putty in his new wife's hands.

Steady and Ren both groaned from their positions in the icy snow.

"Got a visual on the girl," Herc said, staring through the scope of his rifle. "She's in an upstairs bedroom. Looks like she's alone."

"Tox, Asshole Number Two just polished off the fifth of Wild

Turkey they've been passing around. I'm going to move to the window," Cam said.

"Good copy. Any of these assholes our guy?" Tox asked.

"Negative. Moving in now," Cam answered.

"We've got you covered. Chat's on your six," Ren added.

Andrew Dunlap moved into position, his dark skin and bald head masked by the night. The guys on his SEAL squad called him "Chat," a facetious nod to the fact that he was a man of few words. His instincts, however, were razor-sharp—when he did speak, they listened.

"Right behind you, Cam," Chat spoke into the comm. "Looks like Asshole Number Two is going outside to use the facilities, and by 'facilities,' I mean tree."

"Neutralize and move in. Nathan wants to avoid a body count on this one. The local sheriff is a friendly, but he hates paperwork," Tox instructed, referring to their boss, Nathan Bishop.

A minute passed, the silence cut by the drunken man's crunching footsteps in the snow, and then by Chat's neutral words, "Asshole Number Two is hogtied and napping."

Steady whispered, "Chat and Cam, take the back. Welcome Wagon is coming in through the front door." Cam watched Steady, with Ren at his back, make a low run to the entrance.

"Copy that," Cam acknowledged. Then, with practiced movements, he and Chat darted to the unlocked rear door.

If a mini-fridge, a hot plate, and a card table qualified as a kitchen, then the kitchen is where Cam spotted Asshole Number Three standing with a slice of pizza in each hand and a look of confusion on his face. Cam dropped him with one punch. Chat restrained the unconscious man with zip ties, and they continued into the cabin. By the time Chat and Cam got to the main room, Steady and Ren had taken down Asshole Number One.

A dingy back hall led to opposing bedrooms and either a very narrow staircase or a very wide ladder that went to a loft above the front room. Cam took point. The step-rungs groaned their protest as he climbed. When his head cleared the second floor, he immediately spotted the girl. Appearing unharmed, she was sitting on the side of the bed shivering in jeans and a T-shirt. When she looked up at him, he recognized Amy Rafferty from the photo her parents had provided. The picture... That's when he remembered. They also had a photo of the perp. None of the assholes downstairs matched the description of their suspect, Alfred Winston Bell.

When Cam looked at Amy again, she was indicating frantically with just her eyes that someone was behind her. He reached for his sidearm, but not before the man himself, Alfred Winston Bell, popped up from the far side of the bed on his knees, pump-action shotgun pointed directly at Cam's head.

Cam was torn between cursing himself for the rookie mistake and trying to recall some sort of Catholic invocation from his childhood when he heard the tinkling shatter of glass. Alfred Winston Bell fell forward onto the bed. The back of his head did not follow. Amy released a pent-up scream and raced to her rescuer. Cam moved her against the wall, cleared the room, and crossed to the window where he spotted Herc in the tree, sighting Cam through the scope of his Remington. Herc lifted his head and gave a thumbs up. Cam nodded his thanks and turned his attention to Amy just as Chat, with Steady on his heels, leapt up into the loft.

"Amy Rafferty?" Cam held her upper arms gently as she nodded confirmation.

"You're safe now," he reassured her.

She took in their tactical gear and face paint. "What are you guys? Commandos or something?"

Cam explained, "We're security specialists hired to get you out."

Amy started to shake. Chat threw an emergency blanket around her shoulders and spoke softly. "Your parents are nearby waiting to bring you home. Ready to go home?"

She gripped the edges of the silver blanket and nodded again through her shivers.

Ren called up from the bottom of the stairs. "Local law enforcement is en route with an ambulance. Tox is going to sort it out. Her parents are meeting us at the hospital in Stowe."

Twenty minutes later, Cam stood in front of the cabin and watched the commotion. Tox was shooting the shit with the sheriff while two deputies loaded the three assholes into the back of a police cruiser and a body bag into the coroner's van. Chat climbed into the ambulance with Amy. Steady and Ren flanked Cam and clocked Herc as he swung down from the tree, long gun in its soft case over his back. He joined the group with fist bumps for the team.

Steady pointed to Cam. "You may not be the new guy anymore, but you're still buying the beers."

Cam smacked Herc on the shoulder, and they turned as a group to head to the van. "Yeah, sure. I guess you clowns have earned a free beer."

Cam joked and trash-talked with the guys as they left, but in the back of his mind, that phone call to his old CIA cell phone continued to plague his thoughts.

Camilo Canto has unfinished business.

As the newest member of the Bishop Security team, Cam has left the dark world of undercover work with the CIA and is starting a new life in South Carolina. Unfortunately, there is a haunting figure from his past with an agenda. The Conductor is a criminal mastermind who wants Cam eliminated along with the evidence Cam compiled while working undercover. A devious plot is in place to do just that. Cam is abducted and awakes on the island paradise of Mallorca, where crime, danger, and obsession are buried beneath the picture-perfect surface. In order to stop The Conductor, Cam must sift through layers of diversion, including an infatuated supermodel, a corrupt mine owner, and an obsessed treasure hunter. As he fits the puzzle together, Cam crosses paths with a beautiful archaeologist searching for answers to another mystery hidden in the caves beneath the island.

Evangeline Cole is a Ph.D. candidate in Mallorca with an archaeological team. When Evan stumbles upon a strange marker, she is compelled to follow the clues to solve a centuries-old mystery buried in the caves. When Evan's treasure hunt crosses paths with Cam's investigation, passion and danger ignite. Cam is forced to confront both the real and psychological demons from his years undercover to find the true treasure buried beneath.

Fans of Lori Foster, Sandra Brown, and Toni Anderson will love Illicit Intent.

Be advised: this story contains scenes of violence equivalent to an R-rated movie and explicit sexual situations.

Debbie Baldwin is a successful print media and television writer. She is a graduate of Princeton University and the University of Virginia School of Law. Debbie and her husband live in Saint Louis, Missouri with their puggle, Pebbles. They have three children in college.

The Black Sheep

Johnnie Bernhard

He started early in life - challenging the teacher's authority, sneaking out at night, questioning city ordinances, ignoring speed signs. At sixteen, he adopted the moniker "Live Free or Die." Some say he marched to his own drum. In time, the family realized, he was the bandleader.

The family shared many theories as to how the black sheep came to be. Mom blamed it on genes inherited from Dad's side of the family; Grandma called it growing pains, and Dad's one comment was, "he's a tough row to hoe." His sister marked his transgressions in life by the same, tired conversation she had always had with him. At seven years of age she would warn him, "MMMM, I'm telling Mom!" At thirty-four, she pleaded, "Please don't make me tell Mom."

There's that person in every family who refuses to live by everyone else's standards of behavior, while most succumb to following the rules of a civilized society without question.

Church attendance, the litmus test of a solid citizenry, is without debate in a small town in Mississippi. There are those who do and those who don't. He never wasted a breath on making excuses for not going to church-stomachache, backache, headache, everything aches. He simply said he wasn't going. At first there were patient lectures on why he should go. No deal.

In desperation for the saving of his soul and the family's

reputation, there were fierce arguments in hope he would be shamed into going. It didn't raise an eyebrow. The final solution came: go to church or stay home and work. He chose to edge the front sidewalk with a pair of blunt scissors.

Once or twice during his adult years, and on religious holidays, he would attend church. He would greet the family at the front steps of the church supporting a black eye, hickey or shirt in poor taste, or sometimes all three. This caused his mother to cry during the service. His sister, patting mother's hand for comfort, questioned what kind of woman still gives hickeys in the 21st Century.

He spent much of his early adulthood saying the Man would never get him. The rest of us spent years trying to figure out what man he was talking about. There was some courage to how he lived his life – he did not react to anyone's dares or expectations, but acted on his own impulses.

He cruised through town for twenty years flickin' filterless Camels out of the truck window whenever he passed the "Do Not Litter" sign. For 20 years, select members of the garden club mentioned his littering habit and refusal to support the city's beautification campaign to his mother. For twenty years, his mother remained speechless on the issue.

He wasn't a liar or a gossip, and because of that, people could count on him in a pinch, especially when the line was crossed between civilities into hedonism. He knew the underbelly and he navigated through it as if it were an amusement park.   He took calls made in the hours between a bar closing and the time people got up to go to work - true witches' hours. Those hours before dawn when nothing fruitful or of merit can happen if you're still awake and not getting ready for work. He could be counted on for pick up and delivery, never mentioning the lapse of judgment on your part. He had a talent of keeping secrets from the rest of the family – he knew what shame could do, and he silently grieved that you had to know it too.

There were attempts over the years by do-good girlfriends. The end of the relationship was marked by her buying him clothes. As if by putting on the right shirt, recognizable to others that this is the shirt a successful man would wear, he would somehow become exactly what she wanted. He truly was a rebel without a cause, living in a time when the most passion that could be aroused was what people were wearing and where they were going to eat supper.

Some say the black sheep is the most sensitive in the family. The family continues to pray for their black sheep; hoping for the day that prince of a guy will jump through the hoop and deliver, becoming the man they thought he should be. And he, he forgave them years ago for not loving him for who he is.

In this creative essay, Johnnie Bernhard explores the meaning of unconditional love within family.

A former teacher and journalist, Johnnie Bernhard is passionate about reading and writing. Her works have appeared in the following publications: University of Michigan Graduate Studies Publications, Heart of Ann Arbor Magazine, Houston Style Magazine, World Oil Magazine, The Suburban Reporter of Houston, The Mississippi Press, the international Word Among Us, Southern Writers Magazine, The Texas Review, Southern Literary Review, and the Cowbird-NPR production on small town America essays.

A Good Girl (2017) was shortlisted in the 2015 William Faulkner-William Wisdom Writing Competition, as well as featured novel for panel discussion at the 2017 Mississippi and Louisiana Book Festivals. The novel was shortlisted in the 2017 Kindle Book Award for Literary Fiction, a nominee for the 2018 PEN/Robert W. Bingham Prize, shortlisted by the Mississippi Institute of Arts and Letters Fiction of the Year Award, and placed in the permanent collection of the Texas State Library and Archive Commission, Texas Center for the Book.

Johnnie's second novel, *How We Came to Be* (2018) was a finalist in the 2017 Faulkner-Wisdom Competition. Named a "Must Read" by Southern Writers Magazine, the novel was featured for panel discussion for the 2018 Louisiana Book Festival and Mississippi Book Festival. It was selected for the 2019 Deep South Magazine recommended reading list and shortlisted by the Mississippi Institute of Arts and Letters for 2019 Fiction of the Year. It is the recipient of the Summerlee Book Prize, HM by the Center for History and Culture at Lamar University.

Her third novel, *Sisters of the Undertow* (2020 was chosen for discussion at the 2020 national AWP Conference, the Pat Conroy Literary Center of South Carolina, the Southern Book Festival/ Humanities Tennessee, and Words and Music Literary Feast of New Orleans. It was an official selection for the 2020 International Pulpwood Queens Book Club and Deep South Magazine's recommended reading list for 2020. Named "Best of the University Presses, 100 Books" by the Association of University Presses, *Sisters of the Undertow* was shortlisted in the Kindle Book Awards for literary fiction. It was placed in the Texas Center for the Book, State

Library Collection and received First Place in the Press Women of Texas Communications Contest.

Johnnie was chosen as a selected speaker in the 2020 TEDx Fearless Women Series. She also supports young writers in public schools through the Letters About Literature program with the Texas Center for the Book and with the Write for Mississippi program. In 2021, she was named a teaching artist with Gemini Ink Writing Arts Center and the national TAP Summer Institute 2021.

CONTACT

Johnnie Bernhard, author: johnniebernhardauthor@gmail.com www.johnniebernhardauthor.com

For orders, Texas A&M University Press: 800-826-8911

Guesthouse for Ganesha

Judith Teitelman

Chapter One

Esther Grünspan arrived in Köln with a hardened heart as her sole luggage.

An uncommonly sweltering September day was her welcome, as well as a language that sounded like her native Yiddish, yet foreign in structure and comprehension. A formidable determination guided her actions.

"*Stantsye, ikh darf a stantsye.* Lodging, I need lodging," Esther demanded of the first person in uniform that crossed her path. "*Vu ken ikh opzukhn stantsye?* Where can I find lodging?" Her articulation was clear and direct, emphatic.

Quizzical, the man's eyes skimmed this plain-faced young woman from her faded, long-sleeved cotton frock with white rounded collar to her scuffed, lace up shoes. Small in stature with thick blond hair pulled away from her face in a tight bun, she was unadorned and clearly out of place.

"*Was? Ich verstehe Sie nicht*! I don't understand you," he said, waving her away and pointing toward the train terminal.

Without a note of thanks, Esther headed in the direction he indicated. Once inside the terminal, she strode through the cavernous building to consider every booth, kiosk and stand until she found a corner counter with a large sign overhead announcing *Information.* This was close enough to the Yiddish *informatsye* for Esther to push her way to the front of the line, disregarding the glares and loud protests of those in her way.

She paid them no heed. Patience was no longer a part of her framework. It had been displaced by entitlement and self-preservation. The recent, devastating turn of events—Tadeusz's action, his rejection—and such a public spurn—of her, of them, of all their plans—had shaped an impossibly conceived scenario. Esther's one priority now was Esther.

She repeated her request to the man behind the counter three times. Each time she enunciated every syllable more precisely, then more slowly but colored by rising frustration.

The official, while clearly annoyed, noticed her youth and asked, *"Wie alt sind Sie?"*

Alt? Esther thought quickly, alt—old. Just like in my language. Although the other words made no sense, she correctly assumed he was asking her age.

"Zibitsn," she said.

The man shrugged his shoulders, rolled his eyes and turned to help the person next in line. Esther leaned over and grabbed the pen on his desk. In clear, thick lettering she wrote the numbers one and seven on her palm. Standing on the tips of her shoes, she stretched her left arm high and held it up close to his face.

With a snort, he reached into a pile under his desk and thrust a piece of paper in Esther's expectant hands. She looked intently at the page's Gothic script and line drawing of a building.

This must be a place for young people to stay, she deduced, for next to a name and address the numbers 16 - 22 were printed. A map of the area with a large X seemed to mark its location. Expressing no appreciation, Esther turned quickly, jostled the three people beside her, and ventured out into her first metropolis—a location as far away from all she had ever known as her meager resources enabled. A place with an assurance of anonymity and seclusion.

If she could still muster gratitude for anything, it would be for this.

And in the only way anguish can be subdued, if not entirely

vanquished, Esther never stopped moving during those first self-exiled months. She couldn't. She could not allow herself to sit idle, not even for a few minutes, for if she did memories of him, of them, of what was, would deluge her mind. Emotions that she now strained to destroy or deny ever existed would take over and she would be rendered helpless, powerless, as she had been and as she promised herself she would never be again.

She devoted her time to establish a formula for sustenance. Sewing was her foundation. While she strived to grasp the rudiments of German speech, her willpower propelled her to walk up and down the streets of Köln seeking work. She entered every dress boutique and tailor shop she could find with samples of her handiwork as calling cards.

"*Schauen Sie*—Look!" She ordered those she met, holding up one of her tasteful blouses for inspection. The caliber of her skill and artistry supplanted language barriers.

She was rewarded with small assignments from four tailors after just two weeks. Basic tasks—shortening a dress and repairing a pants cuff—were soon replaced by more complex responsibilities for her mastery was revealed in the simplest exercise. Her stitches were precise, her hems and seams were even, and the presentation of each project was flawless.

Stitching, basting, pleating, hemming, altering, darning, tucking, grading, embellishing, blocking, mending—these activities were second in nature only to breathing for Esther.

Daily she sewed from the first hint of light to its last shadow to ensure her new clients received the quality work of which she alone was capable. No matter if her eyes burned, her neck strained or her fingers ached without respite.

Here, in the windowless room cramped by a single bed, rickety table, rough wood chair and hot plate at the noisy, dilapidated youth hostel, Esther's stoic nature took root— growing deeper and thicker by each day's passing. She barely spoke, except as needed to secure a sewing assignment, purchase necessary supplies, or tell one of the other residents to quiet down. It was a raucous building, filled with too many young people, constant comings and goings, stair stompings, door slammings and shouting. For much of the day, with her focused concentration on work, she was able to ignore any distractions. But when she couldn't, Esther found her nerves rattled, her posture tested. Such sounds were common to someone who had grown up in a home with twelve siblings. At these instances, she forbade the pent-up tears behind each eye to fall, and she quashed all but the most basic thoughts if one dared enter her head.

After darkness fell, she spent the better part of the night trudging along the riverfront. In 1923, Köln was a chiaroscuro palette of grays and blacks with a few patches of deep brown or the darkest blue breaking through the visual monotony. Most structures housed three stories; a few had four or even five.

Although some were stout like marshmallows and a handful of others were lean as poles, each was indistinguishable in design, color and pattern from its neighbor. Esther faded easily into this cityscape, apart from the occasional streetlamp illuminating her face's stony glaze.

On these walks Esther contemplated how long it would take the cold, fast-moving Rhein to swallow the torment that she, as yet, could not fully ignore. The memory refused to dissipate: every feather, overcast and edging stitch in her simple white dress, the posies in her hands, family and friends gathered in the town center, their excited chatter overlaid by *klezmer* music as the musicians frolicked, and her, standing unaccompanied under their tenderly crafted *chuppah.* Waiting. Until too much time passed. Until she could no longer remain there—alone. Surely the weight of Tadeusz's abandonment would supersede her ability to swim.

Over successive evenings, Esther marked a route that covered six kilometers in total. Once established, her steps never varied, every evening the same. She always headed toward the river via Trankgasse near the Kölner Dom, the city's glorious cathedral, and then crossed over Hohenzollern Bridge. When she reached its crown, water on either side, only sky above, Esther paused to relish the cool breeze of the river blowing on her face. One of the few joys she permitted herself.

From there she went north where she plodded the full length of the cobblestone path that followed the Rhein's left bank. Her movements were precise, not unlike her stitches. Each step she took landed in the exact center of the unvarying stones. A low, wrought iron fence ran the river's expanse, providing a demarcation of choice. Her choice. To stay on one side or cross over to the other.

At the furthermost edge of Rheinpark, the area defined by its thick row of uniform trees, Esther would stop, squeeze her eyes tight, inhale deeply—and consider. A few minutes might pass or just a handful of seconds. Inevitably the mantra "he cannot prevail, he will not prevail," would resound in her thoughts. With a toss of her head, she would then turn around to retrace the course. Some nights she traversed this route twice, sometimes more. She moved steadily. Eyes most often directed downward with fixed attention on the patterned cobblestone. Esther never cared to look around to explore, for there was nothing of significance to see.

At the close of the day after darkness reigned, her evenings unfolded exactly like the one before and the one that would follow.

Until—

— fourth of December, a bitter Friday twilight with the promise of snow nearly four months after Esther's arrival in this city. It began like the others: Esther treading, once again, the familiar course that bordered the Rhein. However tonight her pace was limp. As she walked, she stretched, one arm extended long and high above her and then the other. She rounded her shoulders up and down and back and forth and rolled her head from side-to-side until her neck cracked. She pulled on each finger to extend the ligaments and when she reached the last digit she returned to the first. The weariness of her heart had been compounded by what had been a tedious day creating 10 flawless buttonholes on each of two dozen long-sleeved white shirts for the members of a youth band. She was lost in thought, eyes focused on her feet and the cobblestones, as she reviewed the deft movements she had taken to ensure every stitch's identical length, when—

Esther stopped abruptly.

— she glanced up to take care she didn't overstep the sharp curve in the path and saw, juxtaposed against Köln's muddy landscape, streaks of luminous color burst through the trees barely 50 meters away. Like a beacon.

"*U va! Vos iz dos?* What in the world is this?" Esther said out loud, startled. Quickly she looked around to see if anyone had heard her or saw what she saw. She was alone. Focused again on the phenomenon before her, she thought: I've not seen this before here, or anything like it—anywhere!

Just ahead, in the grassy area near the north edge of Rheinpark, stood a small, poorly constructed wood stand. Its only defense against the open sky was a square canopy of fabric—a cacophony of vibrant, garish colors—supported by four thick poles at each corner. Tiny mirrors and tinted glass were stitched throughout this material, along with fringe, sequins, ribbons, tassels and beads.

Utterly incongruous to the surrounding dim setting, this was a vision from a dream gone awry—a sight she could never have possibly conceived. Intoxicating smells—pungent, sweet, musty, sharp, woody, comforting—wafted from within the stand. Esther inhaled deeply. This bouquet impelled further exploration.

She moved closer to peer inside and saw that the interior of the stand's makeshift plywood walls was covered in a motley array of printed pictures of people—or were they people? Such strange characters! Perhaps these are images from a theatrical production taking place somewhere in the city, Esther mused. Or maybe a circus? Certainly nothing like this ever came through Przeworsk.

Most of the images were of scantily dressed figures in bright colored sheer fabrics. Some had far too many hands and arms, one had too many heads, and one face possessed three eyes. There was a picture of a woman who was completely blue and an image that seemed more monkey than man. Larger than the others was a rotund man with the head of an elephant.

Both women and men were heavily made up, with most covered in strange elaborate jewelry. Many wore outrageous headdresses. Whether seated on one large, stuffed cushion or on an ornamented throne or standing in front of a glowing orange background, all were encircled by a variety of objects, some recognizable, others not— books, shells, musical instruments, candles, bowls, crescent moon, pillows, swords, snakes, fruit, flowers—too extensive and too confusing to register on first look.

Esther's eyes widened and she began to feel lightheaded. The lone man in the back of the booth smiled at her, exposing a stained cracked front tooth. Thin, dark-skinned with thick black hair and a deeply angular face, he also looked like no one she had seen before. In imprecise German with a peculiar accent, he asked:

"Würde Sie, einen Samosa mögen? Would you, a samosa, like?"

Intrigued, though not knowing what he offered, she nodded, and he began to fry a small, doughy turnover. The strong smells that had originally lured her inside now overpowered the modest space.

As Esther waited, she once again scanned the gallery of images that filled these crude walls. Truly an archive of the bizarre, they were at once compelling and absurd. Her eyes came to rest on the elephant-headed man. He, above the others, captivated her. Esther felt, in the oddest of ways, he was calling out, seeking her notice—demanding attention.

This man's—

Is it even a man, Esther wondered?

— large animal head and ears, wide mouth, four arms, broken left tusk and huge protruding belly bordered on the comical. His body, seated with one leg folded inward and the second resting on the ground, was loosely draped in sheer yellow and red fabrics. He held a highly wrought axe in his upper right hand and some type of flower in his upper left.

Another hand held a thick rope, while the fourth was outstretched, its palm facing toward her.

Esther inched closer and squinted. She observed that a mark, similar to a single cross stitch, but turned upright with short lines like flags on each end, was carved on his palm. A mouse staring at a tray that overflowed with what she thought were cookies, sat near his left foot. The scene was outlandish, but alluring nonetheless.

Esther took a step backward to grasp this image full on and stared steadily into the elephant-headed man's eyes. It was only a picture, this she understood; nevertheless she was struck by a gentleness and profound compassion. She descended into his eyes full on. Consciousness of time and space evanesced. A forgotten sense of warm, soothing calm wholly embraced her. All feelings of suffering and loss dissipated.

And... I... looked deeply back into her eyes...

In that penetrating gaze... I learned what had passed... and saw what was to come. Her life's path could not be evaded... but I knew from this point onward we would travel together.

The man handed her the warm pastry, transporting Esther back to the stand. She began to nibble the savory treat filled with new tastes and impressions—she recognized potato and perhaps a pea—when an abrupt shudder coursed through her body as though a hidden switch had been flipped on at the core of her being. Her eyes began to water and she let out a quick breath.

No doubt, she thought, from the heat of these unusual spices.

It was too soon.

She would not... no... could not understand...

I watched her walk away... and toward her future.

———————

Back in her room at the youth hostel Esther could not oust the image of the elephant-headed man from her mind, nor could she escape the feeling he invoked within her.

She paced back and forth between the bed and the chair.

Three equal steps in either direction. She twisted her hair around her index finger and chewed on the inside of her right cheek. Normally after these evening walks to the riverfront, she would simply go to bed, exhausted from the day's work. But this night sleep would not come. When she attempted to lie down or just sit, her legs would tremble as though they had somewhere to be.

Oy, gevalt—Good grief, Esther thought. This is crazy— *Meshuge*! If I can't sleep, I'll work. That's what I'll do. There is much to get done, and I'm certain sewing will set me right. It always does.

So though the light in the room was poor, she began the next day's assignments and gathered needles, threads and fabrics. Esther first lined up the necessary materials as she did each morning: measuring tape, shears, pins, seam ripper and thimble. She matched the cloth with the proper thread, in thickness and color. Threading a blue strand in her milliner's needle, Esther began to baste a pleated skirt. But the gathers kept bunching, so she put that project aside and turned to another. Then another. And then one more.

Surprisingly, needle and thread were not able to bring composure. This had never occurred before. But all was not the same, something

154

had shifted—of this Esther was sure. Yet, she was not capable of putting into words what that difference implied or what exactly had changed.

For the first time since Esther had moved to Koln, she felt the need for someone—most especially one of her sisters— to talk to, to share what happened. To help her understand.

"Am I going mad?" she said out loud. Questions overflowed—

Why do I feel so strange? It's like my head and body are no longer connected! What was that place? Those pictures? Did the stand even exist? Was my imagination playing tricks on me? I was overstrained from the day's work after all.

Perhaps it was some type of dreaming while being awake?

All the while knowing she had had no dreams since leaving Przeworsk.

It's so very late now, really the middle of the night.

Perhaps that's why I can't concentrate on any of my assignments, she ruminated. For even the most straightforward task, re-seaming a pair of men's trousers and adding cuffs seemed beyond her abilities. She kept making mistakes.

Repeatedly she pulled the stitches out and began the process anew. Her slender, normally dexterous hands would not stop shaking, her fingers refused to cooperate.

"*Nit vider*—Not again!" Esther cried out, after the fifth time she pricked herself. "A chorbn—Disaster!"

What is wrong with me, she wondered. This is crazy.

Silly, silly me!

After two and a half hours passed without progress, Esther put down her needles and thread. "Enough!"

I must go back. I don't know why, this makes no sense at all. I must revisit that place. Perhaps I need to return for no other reason than to assure myself that the stand and the experience were, without a doubt, real.

For a second time that evening, she put on coat, hat, gloves, shoes and scarf and, at a swift pace, retraced the nearly three kilometers to the site of the stand. In the middle of the night, the riverfront was devoid of people, serene. Until Esther was close to one hundred meters from the location she sought. From this distance she heard cries— screams—that became increasingly pronounced with each step forward.

Moving as stealthily as possible, Esther ran to the edge of the nearby park and hid behind a tree.

"*Helfen Sie mir*! Help me! Help me!" A male voice shouted, "Bitte! Please, please help me!"

Esther's body stiffened. Like stone. She could only watch as two Polizisten ferociously beat and kicked and pounded the same man who had so kindly offered her the doughy treat a few hours earlier. These supposed officers of the law shouted epithets at him,

"*Dreckiger Ausländer! Mistkerl! Arschloch*!

"*Geh' zurück in deinen Dschungel*! Go back to your jungle!"

And they laughed and joked. Each goaded the other on. Esther had never witnessed such violence. While able to acknowledge the horror of what was taking place, she willed herself not to physically react. Honing stoicism served her well here, allowing her to smother compassion and the desire to shout out, to let the man know he was not alone. For to reveal herself would only bring peril to her and, likely, even worse to him. So Esther shut her eyes tightly and tuned out all sounds. Her mind traveled back to the evening's earlier encounter and the sensations it invoked. This is the place she would like to remain.

As the man lay on the ground, writhing and bleeding, one of the officers poured gasoline, lit a torch and set the stand ablaze—intensifying its color and vibrancy for a few moments until it, too, became black and gray and ash like the environment. Like all of Köln. Like Esther herself.

Charred bits of fabric and pictures flew in the wind.

All too soon, not a remnant remained—only a vision, a taste, and an enduring longing.

Left at the altar, spurned—what does that do to a young woman's heart? And why would a Hindu God care?

In 1923, seventeen-year-old Esther Grünspan arrives in Köln "with a hardened heart as her sole luggage." Thus begins a twenty-two-year journey, woven against the backdrops of the European Holocaust and the Hindu Kali Yuga (the *"Age of Darkness"* when human civilization degenerates spiritually), in search of a place of sanctuary. Throughout her travails, using cunning and shrewdness, Esther relies on her masterful tailoring skills to help mask her Jewish heritage, navigate war-torn Europe, and emigrate to India.

Esther's traveling companion and the novel's narrator is Ganesha, the elephant-headed Hindu God worshipped by millions for his abilities to destroy obstacles, bestow wishes, and avenge evils. Impressed by Esther's fortitude and relentless determination, born of her deep—though unconscious—understanding of the meaning and purpose of love, Ganesha, with compassion, insight, and poetry, chooses to highlight her story because he recognizes it is all of our stories—for truth resides at the essence of its telling.

Weaving Eastern beliefs and perspectives with Western realities and pragmatism, *Guesthouse for Ganesha* is a tale of love, loss, and spirit reclaimed.

Judith Teitelman has straddled the worlds of arts, literature, and business since she was a teenager and worked her first job as a salesperson at a B. Dalton/Pickwick Bookstore. Life's journeys took her from bookstores to commercial fine art galleries to the nonprofit arts and cultural sector, in which she has worked as staff, consultant, and educator for more than three decades. Throughout this time, Teitelman continued her pursuit of all things literary, and over the years her writing has been published in a variety of formats and publications. *Guesthouse for Ganesha* is her award-winning debut novel. She lives in Los Angeles with her husband and three beloved cats.

Of Locusts and Wild Honey

Joe Palmer

Prologue

South Vietnam Mekong River
Delta Summer, 1970

A dying green dragonfly, my mortally wounded helicopter corkscrews toward the muddy waters of the Mekong River below. The deafening clamor of my door-mounted, 50-caliber machine gun moments earlier has been abruptly superseded by an otherworldly silence, punctuated only by the rush of humid air whistling through the ragged holes in the fuselage. The chopper must be auto-rotating down, I imagine; otherwise, we'd simply fall from the sky like a dead bird. The pilot must still be at least alive, I reason, with what wits remain. My lips are numb and my mouth doesn't want to move but I somehow manage to call out in a slurry voice that doesn't seem to belong to me.

"Jimmy? There? Okay?" But there's no reply. Only the eerie quietness.

"They're all dead," I think, and I comprehend in that moment that soon I'll also be nothing more than pulverized flesh, my own life erased from the roll call of the living. And then my mind starts to wander, nonsensical fashion. A berserk merry-go-round I can't seem to exit. Every time I try, it changes directions.

"*Cicadas,*" I randomly muse about the loud buzzing sound in my ears. "*No. Locusts,*" I remind myself as warm blood pours from my wound and pools around me. But there are no locusts here, no trees here, only the expansive and seemingly endless delta and rice paddies, reeking of manure and stagnant water beneath a pitiless sun. I wonder why I'm thinking about locusts but my mind ventures away again. Then tranquility fills me like a mother's warm milk. Accepting the death that awaits me, my mind drifts back to a small Southern town and my final farewells to my three best friends and the girl I love.

Locusts. One of the enduring devotions of my life is the lowly and cacophonous cicada, which we mistakenly called locusts. I still think of them as such, clinging to the old and soothing familiar. The lofty green pines oozing sticky, pungent sap and lifting their arms as if in Pentecostal rhapsody, full of them, singing their songs of doomed love. When they molted, they left their diaphanous, translucent husks clinging to the tree bark for us to find and play with. Their discordant trilling was the soundtrack of our summers together. I cannot hear their relentless, inharmonious strain without my heart brimming with the memory of faces and places that seem so long ago. It was the place where profound love had its dawn in the summer I went to live with my grandparents and aunt after my mother's death.

I reach for the cache of photographs I keep stowed in my heart and go home. I see all of us again the way I remember us the day before, and the day of, my departure from a bus station parking lot in that small town. Some of the photos are fading somewhat but still tell their story. Counting me, there were five of us. By the end of our first languid summer together when we were twelve, we were, as my grandmother said of us, tighter than green corn in the husk. By the time we were thirteen, we were as inseparable as iron filings on a magnet. There was Bart, short and muscular as a young bull, with gray eyes and a mop of dishwater blonde hair that always needed combing; Rusty, who got his nickname because he was always the first to tan in the summer, tall and rangy with hazel eyes and mousy brown hair; Jeannie, with her carrot-colored hair, bright blue eyes, a constellation of freckles and sturdy Celtic milkmaid stature. And then there was Vivian, my Vivian, with hair as black and shiny as the starlings that filled the woodlands and fields, flashing dark eyes and sultry, gypsy features. Alongside of them, I felt ungainly – pale skin that seemed permanently burned and peeling, cotton white hair and faded blue eyes, a newborn colt's awkwardness, with ears too big and teeth too crooked.

I shuffle the photographs and study them one by one. Then I spread them out side by side and look at them together, the way I remember us in those final days with each other. The faces and smiles shining back at me are fresher than the peaches we stole from a neighbor's tree one summer day, gorging ourselves on the dripping flesh until our bellies griped. We're shoulder to shoulder on that late autumn afternoon, striking our favorite pose on my grandmother's wide porch.

We're leaning into one another laughing and making silly faces as we mug for the camera, trying to outdo one another's outlandishness. My Aunt Susie snaps the photos with one of those old cameras with the flashbulbs that always left you momentarily blinded, with white spots drifting apparition-like in front of your eyes. Vivian's wearing the Beatles' *Abbey Road* Album T-shirt I bought for her eighteenth birthday. She's braless, and I remember the swell of her breasts and her nipples pressing against the thin cotton. That evening, as we lounge drinking wine and smoking pot in our favorite hangout, a cave at the bottom of a limestone sinkhole in the woods outside of town, Bart passes the sweet smelling joint to me and points at Vivian and begins singing *She Came In Through The Bathroom Window*: She scoops up a handful of dirt and flings it at him.

Then we're laughing so hard I think it will go one forever. But it doesn't. That night full of stoned giggles and foolishness almost eludes me now.

No one's there with a camera to snap our pictures the next day. No one need be, for the photos I have in my stash of that afternoon are from the camera lens of my eyes and seem preordained to outlive the others. They're seared into my mind like the afterimage of a flashbulb. The five of us linger inside a dinghy Greyhound Bus Station that stinks of cheap aftershave, stale cigarettes, sweat and sadness. Bart and Rusty conceal burdened hearts behind tough guy sneers. They feign coolness and make crude comments about a tawdry prostitute arranging her next assignation at a nearby payphone. Jeannie sniffles and tries to be brave, fussing with the black silk neckerchief on my dress-white cotton Navy uniform blouse so many times that I finally push her hand away in embarrassment.

Vivian cries while we wait for the big silver and blue bus to come and deliver me to a far distant runway where other scared and dejected young men like me clutch their own melancholy photographs. She's pressed to my side, eyes pinched shut. Her eyes, veiled by her long black hair, dribble an unbroken stream of tears on the unforgiving brown linoleum floor. She's still wearing the Beatles T-shirt. When I bend and press my face against hers, the musk of our lovemaking in the cave late into the night before still lingers. She squeezes my hand so tightly that my fingertips grow numb. Her breaths come in hitches, eruptions of crippling pain catching in her slender throat, and cruel sobs that threaten to cleave her. In the numbness of my own grief, I'm unable to comfort the person for whom I'd gladly give my life. The pledge we all sealed with our blood long ago to never leave each other's sides is cold ashes in my mouth. I choke on them when I try to tell her I'm sorry. From time to time, she manages to give voice to her agony in a keening, whimper that cracks my heart and fills my own eyes with unshed tears.

"Denny. Please. Denny, please don't go."

And then the anguish rushes her away in its flood until she can find her voice again: "Denny, please. Please don't leave me."

When my bus arrives, they follow me outside into the reek of oily, black exhaust, the grumbling of bus engines and the parking lot littered with crushed paper cups and broken dreams. I try to pull away but Vivian has my hand locked in hers.

Tenderly, Jeannie reaches down and releases her fingers one by one until I'm free. I take her into my arms and hold her. I feel her scalding tears spill down my collar and onto my neck. Then I step across the grimy asphalt lot and onto the bus. I make my way toward the back and take a seat behind a hoar frost-haired old black man who's already snoring. As the driver closes the door and begins to pull away from the shabby concrete building, I press my face to the tinted glass window. I cup my hands around my eyes and commit them to memory: Bart, with a psychedelic head band binding his long hair, flashing me the peace sign. Rusty, shoulder length hair, wearing John Lennon sunglasses and a T-shirt with an upside down American flag that drew glares from old men in the bus station, playfully giving me

162

the finger. Jeannie, in a tie-dyed peasant dress and yellow wildflowers woven into her hair, blowing me kisses. Vivian, presses her face against Jeannie's shoulder, sobbing. Jeannie begins to cry and wraps Vivian in her arms and holds her, the two of them swaying slowly back and forth.

A matronly looking woman wearing a navy blue dress and boxy, black shoes pauses and glances out the window, then turns and fixes me with a disapproving stare before harrumphing away to take her seat. The bus begins to edge forward. I crane my neck to look back one more time. Vivian's face is still on Jeannie's broad shoulder, her mouth opened in a scream. Then she tears free of Jeannie and runs to the bus, and, seeing my face pressed against the smoky glass, lifts her hands toward mine, reaching for me. Jeannie rushes to her and wraps her in her arms, pulling her away. As the bus begins to nose into the traffic, I watch as Vivian finally collapses, falling to her knees on the filthy pavement, bent forward at the waist, hands over her eyes and wailing. I put my own hands over my own face and weep. When I hear her final scream, it's one so piercing that I sometimes hear it in the murky delta at night and mistake it for that of a wild animal. Then I hear another voice, a familiar one that lingers on the cusp of recognition but does not cross the border. It leaves my body prickled with cold gooseflesh. It's far away and hollow sounding as if from some pitch-dark abyss.

"Out of the depths I cry to you!" it wails. *"Out of the depths I cry to you!"*

And then silence as the Mekong River rushes in and fills me.

Of Locusts And Wild Honey is Joe Palmer's second novel. In a small, South Georgia town, five misfit 12-year-olds - three boys and two girls - swear a blood oath in the summer of 1962 never to part company with each other. But fate has other plans, and when Denny Kershaw, the story's narrator, returns from Vietnam physically and emotionally wounded, he sets out on a quest to find out not only what happened to his friends, one of whom was the love of his life, but to unravel a family mystery.

Joe Palmer is a former newspaper reporter and columnist and author. A sailor, terrible surfer, unapologetic beach bum, he was raised in Waycross, Georgia, he's lived in Florida most of his life. He and his wife, Pam live in Fernandina Beach with a huge Great Dane named Harley, who is the owner of their home. His debut novel, *A Mariner's Tale,* was published by Koehler Books on October 25, 2020

Samuel's Wife

Brenda Sutton Rose

Here she comes. Samuel's wife. That must be her boy Isaac with the reins. I watch their arrival from the window, my grandmother's dough bowl in my hands, the ingredients for baking spread on the table behind me. The boy drives the horse and buggy to an open area near the barn and halts.

As dust settles around the rig, Isaac unfolds his long body from the seat and springs to the ground with the litheness of his father, in one smooth movement. He stretches beside the buggy, the sun's rays glistening on his curls, tarnishing the copper locks with a rich patina.

Isaac takes his mother's hand and helps her descend. After she's planted her feet on my soil, Samuel's wife tucks loosened hair inside her bonnet while turning left and right, appearing to take stock of my place, my land, my garden, my fruit trees, my corn crib, my smokehouse, my cabin. All mine and not a thing she can do about it.

Champ, my most striking rooster, swaggers back and forth near the buggy, the bulk of his feathers taking on a blue hue in the sunlight.

My fingers caress the marred wooden bowl, its scars and indentations honest, the result of two generations of women baking bread: My mother who died when I was a child, and my grandmother, Mala, who raised me. Today, observing Samuel's wife, I clutch Mala's bowl to my chest like a bible, a holy armor in an unspoken battle. I knew she would come, but I didn't expect her so soon.

Isaac combs long fingers through his curls. If his hair smells like his father's, it carries the unmistakable spice of his activities. After a morning of fishing, Samuel's hair reeked of pond water; after plowing in the fields, his hair retained the odors of sweat and earth; and when he slipped under my blankets at night, I read the geography of his day in silence, my nose buried in auburn hair threaded with gray, my body pressed against his.

Samuel's wife turns to Isaac and speaks. He frowns and places his hands on her shoulders, anchoring her where she stands. A flock of blackbirds fly overhead, a traveling convoy of darkness in the sky, and a shadow passes over mother and son. Isaac's lips convulse in a rush, words tumbling from his mouth. I wish I could hear what he's saying.

His mother shakes her head in response, a stern negative motion, then halts and stares at him. Faced with the wall of her resistance, Isaac drops his hands and steps back. Her mouth terse, Samuel's wife pulls a black shawl tight around her shoulders and wheels around to face my cabin head on.

Under sprawling oak trees, squirrels collect acorns too soon, the sign of an unusually cold winter to come. Champ scratches at the ground, pecking for food. Isaac leans against a wheel and rolls a smoke, pausing now and then to watch his mother's determined march toward the porch. He frowns. Shakes his head. I suspect he is defeated in this contest of wills between mother and son.

As she nears the porch, Samuel's wife halts and closes her eyes. Her pale lips move. She must be praying. If she believes her prayer will rise from her lips and ride on the wind to the heavens, she'll be mighty disappointed. Not a puff whispers over this place today. Last night, death swallowed all circulating air from Arabi, Georgia. It's as dead as a cemetery here. Without a breeze, her prayer will fall flat on my land, and the red dirt will bury it beneath her feet.

I hold the dough bowl with one hand, open the door with the other, and study Samuel's wife as she approaches. He never spoke of her to me, and I never asked. This is the first time I've seen her up close.

Faded beauty clings like dust to the shadows of her chiseled face. A straight-spined woman, she holds her head stiff and elevated, her chin jutting out, her lips tight and cobwebbed, as though she's never spoken poetry, never prayed with a smile on her mouth, never licked syrup from her lips. A black crinoline dress reaches with starch and lace up to her neck, concealing her sharp angles and flat bosom. Our eyes meet. Lock. She lifts the hem of her dress and takes the steps without looking down, a risky undertaking.

On the porch, an arm's length from me, Samuel's wife stops. Her greenish-blue eyes pause at the black braid hanging across my shoulder and over my bosom. She lifts her chin and looks me in the eyes. The name handed down to me by my mother and handed down to my mother from her mother rolls thick and layered with purpose from her mouth. "Mahala."

My tongue loosens a single syllable, curled, ready to strike, and I toss it between us like a rattlesnake. "Bess."

She nods, a slight movement of her head, and I motion for her to come inside. Champ crows. He's feisty today, perhaps warning of bad weather, perhaps disturbed by the arrival of strangers.

Samuel's wife idles inside the door and surveys the interior of my home. Her body carries no scent of her husband, not a trace of his lye soap or his horse or his hair or his pipe or his lovemaking. With darting eyes, she plunders my belongings. I turn from her and fix my attention on Isaac. He exhales a puff of smoke, his gaze trained on me until I close the door.

Samuel's wife pivots and watches me take the bowl to the table. She sighs, expels the sound with impatience. *If this high falutin' woman thinks I'm going to ask her to take a seat, she's wrong. She has come to me. Let her make the first move.*

Stone silent and attentive, her body too thin to hold laughter, Samuel's wife inches closer to the table and watches me sift flour. I used to cook biscuits for Samuel after we made love, his juices sliding slick between my legs. He would eat the biscuits straight from the oven, sliced, stuffed with butter and cane syrup.

Turning from me, she loosens her bonnet and rambles into the room that serves as living area, an open extension of the kitchen that leads to the back door of the cabin. The hem of her dress drops red dust from my land onto the floors, leaving a ghostly trail behind her.

At the hearth, she warms her hands near the flames and studies the items on the mantel. She takes an arrowhead and the piece of flint used to cut the birth cord between my mother and my mother's mother, between my mother and me, and between me and my two babies. She rocks the arrowhead and flint between her palms. Back and forth. Back and forth. Back and forth. The click of flint against flint taps out a rhythm, the steady pulsing of a heartbeat. Tap. Tap. Tap.

My fist hollows out a crater in the flour, stirring up white dust.

Still fiddling with the arrowhead and flint, Samuel's wife turns and gazes at me, as though searching for secrets in my face. I feel the intensity of her eyes uncovering my youth, the color of my skin, my full lips, the fervor of her concentration taking in my simple dress and unadorned fingers.

I scoop lard about the size of an egg from a container and drop it into the depression I've made in the flour. I am hungry. Ravenous.

Logs settle and crackle. Sparks shoot up the chimney. Samuel and I used to sit for hours mesmerized before the fire, and today, his wife stands between me and the flames.

She replaces the tools, arranging them with care on the fireplace shelf, and fingers the spine of two books stacked together, one on top of the other. Without the tapping, the room is silent, as if holding its breath.

I survey my furnishings through Samuel's wife's eyes, my past and present laid out before me. Pottery. Vessels of all kinds. The kitchen table Samuel built. A handmade blanket. Two books. Two handwoven baskets. A pie safe. Four cane-back chairs. The arrowhead and flint on the mantel. A rifle in the corner. A sewing box. The dough bowl carved from walnut.

When I look again, Samuel's wife is flipping through the pages of *Aesop's Fables,* her face a frown, her head shaking, as if she doubts I can read. Let her think what she will. I've read the slave's book numerous times, yet it doesn't hold a single tale as rich as my grandmother's story.

Mala could read and write the white man's language when Jackson and his men rounded up her and her people and forced them down the trail of death. By the time Mala was abandoned along a back road in Kentucky, her belly heavy with child, the dead and rotting bodies of her family were spread for hundreds of miles behind her, their shallow graves a rich supply of food for buzzards and wild animals. And when Mala crawled into the forest, overtaken by cramps, crying for her dead mother, not one soldier stepped out of line to help her. Jackson and his men rode on, driving their dwindling herd of human cattle, and left Mala and her unborn baby to die.

Hours after the soldiers had moved on, Mala gave birth to a healthy baby girl. She cut the birth cord with a piece of flint, nursed the infant from her breasts, and mapped out a path of survival. She kept the flint, as sacred as the dough bowl in our family of women.

Samuel's wife whispers the inscription Mala wrote to my mother: *Read, my daughter, and you will never crawl.* She clutches the opened book and stares at me. Her expression makes me wonder if she came here expecting an illiterate savage with scalps hanging from the mantel. *Let her stare.*

I squish lard and flour between my fingers until the texture breaks into small lumps and turns grainy. This is what I do best: make bread. I spent many hours during my childhood standing on a three-legged stool, watching Mala's fingers dance in this dough bowl, hand-carved by her white lover. I spent glorious mornings and evenings captivated by the magic of bread-making, hearing the stories of my people, listening to Mala describe how she had learned to bake buttermilk biscuits for the white man who found her and her newborn baby, the man who took them into his home, who made love to her with gentle hands and raised the baby, my mother, as his own, the man I called grandpa. Storytelling tastes best in the kitchen, told deep inside the aroma of cooking, told with stomachs growling and mouths salivating. In Mala's kitchen, partnerships formed, bargains began, forgiveness came with the sharing of food.

I pour buttermilk into the crater and work the mixture until it is pasty. Using my fingers, I pull dry flour into the wet ingredients, building on the dough, kneading it, drawing meal from the sides. My fingers make small circles while my hand makes a larger circular motion, working around the bowl.

Samuel's wife pivots and the hem of her dress twirls around her. For several moments, she stands motionless, her skirt settling around her ankles. When she walks, it is with hesitation, the awkward timing of her feet without rhythm or cadence, her shoes striking the plank floors. She stops at the table where I work, *Aesop's Fables* tight in her hands, her eyes brimming with questions.

Folding dough from the top, from one side, from the bottom, from the other side, I work, the twirl of my hands grounding my emotions.

Using the fingers of my left hand, I rake the sticky mixture from my right hand into the bowl, wasting nothing. I know the rhythm of this poem by heart.

Without looking at me, Samuel's wife places the book on the table, her hands lingering on the cover. A moment later, she shatters the silence. "My husband died last night."

I wipe my forehead with the back of a floured hand. "I know."

She recoils, her head jerking back. Surprise colors her face and alters her voice. Her words come at me stretched with enough tension to snap apart and slap me in the face. "How do you know, Mahala? Samuel went to bed with a healthy constitution and died in his sleep. I found him this morning."

I take no pleasure in what I must say. I simply speak the truth. "Samuel's spirit woke me during the night. If you stand near my bedroom, you will find his scent still hanging in the air."

Anguish and fear distort her face. She narrows her eyes and studies the bedroom door, closed to her.

Whether she smells these things, I do not know, but the odors of soil and pipe tobacco hover nearby, as if my man still walks these floors, as if my man still lives, as if he is waiting for me to serve him the biscuits I'm making. And she has come to tell me he's gone. I knew Samuel Story had passed from this world before she stirred from sleep this morning. Perhaps she rolled over and found him cold beside her. All I know is Samuel's spirit found me in my bedroom, hovered above me, and breathed over my belly, over my breasts, my neck, my face. He placed his warm lips on mine and exhaled his life into my lungs. She can't take that from me.

The fire hisses and spits in the hearth, and blazing arms dance high, swaying this way and that. "For thirteen years you didn't care that he was a married man?"

I fold and knead the dough. The flurry of my fingers and hands comes without forethought, comes from deep inside me, comes instinctively.

She slaps the table with an open hand. "Mahala, talk to me."

I shoot my eyes at hers, dark brown against blue-green, miles of mistrust rising between us. She turns her back to me.

The finished mixture is soft and smooth, warm and alive. I lift the dough in my palms, lower my face, and breathe deeply, inhaling memories of loving Samuel in the night, of cupping his most private parts in my hands while a bobcat cries in the woods outside my bedroom window. If Samuel smelled of rich earth, I must smell of fresh bread.

She spins around. "Samuel kept you here all these years. He deeded this cabin and forty acres of land to you. But my husband was never yours. Never! I am his wife. I intend to bury my husband in the family plot."

With floured hands, I pinch off enough dough to fill my cupped palm and roll the mixture into a perfect ball. After patting the ball of dough onto a greased and floured iron skillet, I pull off another bit and repeat the process.

Samuel's wife crosses the room, her shoes punching the floor. She snatches a lap blanket thrown across a chair, holds it against her face, and inhales.

The cast iron oven is fired up. When I've filled the skillet, I press my knuckles into each biscuit, leaving my mark on the dough.

"It's a private plot for family. We buried Samuel's parents and four of my babies there." Her voice quivers. "There's a place for Isaac and his wife, if he ever marries. There's a place for Samuel and me, side by side, husband and wife." She bunches the blanket to her barren bosom. "There is even a place for your girls. Samuel's girls. But not you," she whispers. "Not you. You are not family."

My knuckle prints branded on the uncooked dough, I slide the skillet into the oven, heat rushing over me.

On tired legs I cross the room, putting space between us, trying to untangle myself from Samuel's wife and the web she is spinning around me. Idling near the window, I wipe my hands on a dish rag and spot Isaac standing on the far side of the buggy. Smoke swirls gray and ghostly around him, a sign that he's rolled more tobacco. For a moment, I see his father. From this distance, it is hard to tell. The lines between life and death are blurred. The lines between right and wrong are blurred.

Bess carries the blanket back to the chair and folds it. With the unblemished hands of a lady, she adjusts her bonnet, as though preparing to leave, then stops when she spies Samuel's hat hanging on a peg by the bedroom door. Her cry splits the air. "How did you get this?" She lifts the wide-brimmed fedora and examines it, her lips quivering. "Samuel slept at home last night. How did you come to have his hat?" She holds the hat between us. "It doesn't matter. Keep it. Keep the cabin. The land. Keep it all. I ask for only one thing— leave Samuel's burial to me. Let me bury my husband with dignity, without interference."

The knot I've been carrying in my gut ignites like fatwood and sizzles me from the inside out. I have no stomach for this kind of talk. *You better leave before I expose your sorrow, before I crack open the shell of your sorrow, before I force you to hold your sorrow raw in your hands. You better get yourself home and wash your husband's dead body and lay it out for viewing before I sharpen your sorrow into a lethal weapon and turn it on you.*

I check to be sure the biscuits haven't cooked too long, taking note of my knuckle prints in the dough. After closing the oven, I put away the ingredients scattered across the table.

She lowers the hat, the brim gripped in her hand. "Isaac and I saw the girls hanging clothes on the line." She hesitates, fingering Samuel's hat. "I'd like to meet them and tell them their father has passed away. They are innocent in all this."

I make for her, crossing the room in a breath, and snatch Samuel's hat. How dare she stalk through my house, dropping red dust like a trail of bloody tears across my floors, plundering through my things, talking about my daughters as though she has a claim to them. I raise my right hand to hit her but stop in mid-air and hold it there. Frozen. She steps back once, twice, three times. Cornered against the log wall with nowhere to retreat, she rakes my face with sharp eyes, as if daring me to assault her. My hand drops, and, in my rage, I ram Samuel's hat onto the peg.

Heart racing, my mouth stuffed with words, I chew on every consonant and vowel, tasting the bitterness before spitting them at Samuel's wife, knowing my honesty will sicken her. "My daughters knew their father was dead before you ever crawled out of the bed this morning. You might be his wife, but you were the last to know of Samuel's death."

She sinks against the wall, legs bent, barely standing, and sobs. I wait for her to regain her composure before attacking again. "Samuel was their father, and I am their mother." I sharpen the words she had flung at me earlier and attack her with her own ammunition. "But not you. Not you. You are not family." I cannot stop myself. "Your stillborn daughters are buried in your cemetery, the one with plots for Isaac and his wife, the one with plots for you and Samuel. You inherited a cemetery, and it is filling up fast."

White as chalk, she twists her head from me and groans. Tired, depleted, I take a step back.

She pushes away from the wall and stands to full height. Her chin extended, she runs her hands across her bonnet, over her shawl, down her waist, and over her dress, smoothing out the wrinkles, tidying herself. I recognize her struggle to show no weakness, but she can't fool me; I smell her open wound.

In the silence that follows, a change comes out of nowhere. An unfamiliar air seeps vaporous, up from the floors and around the windowsills, as if something dead has arisen. Goose bumps sprout from my body, creeping upwards from my toes, over my curves, crawling over my flesh, tingling across my scalp. The cabin breathes.

Samuel's wife shudders and inhales sharply, fear splayed across her face. She whispers, "My God."

Warm and cold air swirls around me. I close my eyes and wait, knowing something more will come. I hold my breath, and the innocent spirits of four stillborn babies pass through me. *Whoosh. Whoosh. Whoosh. Whoosh.*

I stand alone, lost, unsure of myself in many ways, strange sensations seeping into my bones, yet I know with certainty that her babies passed through my soul like a prayer. I taste the sweetness of a blessing.

Shivering, I notice the flames in the fireplace have faded, giving way to a soft crackling sound. Turning my back to Samuel's wife, I move to the hearth and place a split log over the embers.

The wind howls, a long miserable sound, drawing me from the fireplace to the window. The sky is shifting colors, melting into shades of green, casting an eerie glow over my piece of land. During twister weather, anything can happen.

Searching to see if my daughters have taken cover from the approaching storm, I press my face against the window and gaze toward the clothesline. Under clouds as bloated as the breasts of a nursing mother, my girls, holding hands, race this way, dark hair flying around their faces. As I watch, Isaac sprints to them and leads them to safety inside the barn, where he has moved the horse and buggy.

The path Samuel's wife walked to my door, the path where she appeared to pray, has begun to stir, dirt swaying, lifting, dancing in the air. The wind screams, bending trees, and breaking branches. I tell her, "Isaac and the girls are in the barn. It is sturdy."

An anemic smile lifts Samuel's wife's lips and relief spreads across her face. I watch her, and suddenly I understand. This woman with no dough bowl, no stories of strong women in her family, this woman with buried babies, babies whose deaths left her breasts aching, swollen, and leaking with milk, this woman with a dead husband who never loved her—this woman stands damaged before me. We are bound together in our grief.

The wind moans and whips up leaves and red dust, whips up wisps of cotton from surrounding fields. When the twisting stops, a drumroll of rain attacks the tin roof, faster and faster it falls.

While the pummeling overhead continues, the aroma of bread fills the cabin. Bess follows me to the kitchen, her dress swishing with each step, and watches me pull the skillet from the oven and toss fat golden biscuits with crispy bottoms upside down on the table.

I pull a biscuit apart, stuff it with butter and syrup, and offer it to her straight from my callused hand. Butter melts and slides down my outstretched hand.

Bess takes the biscuit and sinks her teeth into it. She licks syrup and butter from her lips and takes another bite.

"Samuel's Wife," a short story published by *The Broadkill Review,* was nominated for a Pushcart Prize for Fiction. It was my first nomination.

A work of fiction, scarred with truth and wrinkled with secrets, the story about Samuel's life grew from my own family history. My 4th great grandfather, Samuel Story, who lived in Arabi, Georgia in the early 1800s, was married to the daughter of a prominent reverend. While married and fathering children with his wife, Samuel kept a woman in a cabin down the road from his house. She was the daughter of a man called "Indian Jim." The "kept woman" gave him numerous children, many more than he had with his wife. Those illegitimate children took his last name: Story. Most would be buried in the family Story-Odom Cemetery.

After uncovering this startling story of love and betrayal, and after plundering through the gray areas of Samuel's life, I knew I had to write about it in some way. Through writing, I often make sense of life. Among the spaces of the written word, I come to know my characters and their numerous flaws and strengths.

A DNA test revealed that Samuel's lover was my 4th great grandmother.

I plan to write a novel based on Samuel Story.

Brenda Sutton Rose, *Author of Dogwood Blues*

www.authorbrendasuttonrose.com

Those Colorful Streets

Nancy J. Martin

Shopping at Britex on Post Street in San Francisco was my idea of heaven on earth in 1968. Fabulous combinations of cotton candy pink and bright, bright tangerine, or purple, teal, and lime green prints on fresh bolts of multi-fibered fabrics filled the entire store, roof to basement. Getting down on my knees, digging through oversized cardboard cartons of cool remnants for the best deals was a big part of the fun. I was always on the lookout for fabric remnants covered with huge geometric shapes in bright colors and sleek Asian prints to create huge, fluffy, floor pillows. Those comfy creations sold the minute I left them in the crafts stores or consignment shops, providing me with additional dollars to help make ends meet.

After thoroughly scouring all the remnant boxes, the next step was moving on to the sewing patterns stored in their huge, heavy, grey metal filing cabinets. Everything was Carnaby Street style then-colors, fashion, and music. Humming along to "Georgy Girl" playing on the store sound system, I'd slide open one of the drawers and leaf through the selection of sewing patterns. Discovering a pattern for a perfect little minidress inspired me to find an ideal fabric to complement the design. Even the smell of the tissue paper patterns did a number on me, exactly like the smell of books in the library or bookstore.

Gleefully toting a stuffed Britex bag, my next stop would always be the dance store nearby where they sold leotards and tights in every bright, primary color. Taking my new fabrics out of the bag, I'd come away with two or three pair of tights in colors to match. This was my look: Psychedelic patterned mini-dress, jewel-toned tights, knee-high boots, dangling earrings from Cost Plus and handmade strands of love beads. My colorful bead necklaces were strung on string, while I sat on the edge of my bed, quaffing cheap Red Mountain wine out of a sticky water glass and listening to the very hip sounds of Thelonious Monk.

Prior to the London Mod look, my wardrobe was simply basic black: Black headband, black turtleneck, black bell-bottoms or a black mini-skirt, black tights, and black boots. As protection from the fog and cold I had a heavy, waterproof navy blue pea jacket purchased cheaply from the local Army/Navy surplus store. This look plus the fact that I wore no makeup at all, simplified getting dressed in the morning.

At the time I was living in a nine-dollar-a-week bare-bones room with a funky bathroom in the hall (shared with junkies, winos, and lots of Ajax) in a run-down, multi-storied hotel above a bar on Grant Avenue. My lumpy single bed was under a window overlooking the street where I could see, smell, and hear all the action. A distinctive bar odor of booze and cigarettes rising from the raucous establishment below permeated our building.

Because upper Grant Avenue and North Beach were predominantly Italian neighborhoods, that lovely garlicky scent of simmering sauce would come wafting down the street from the Old Spaghetti Factory as soon as they started sautéing the sugo in the morning, enhanced by yeasty mouth-watering aromas from the ovens of various bakeries in the neighborhood. Always there was Italian opera leaking through the walls and windows out onto the street, in competition with Jimmy Hendricks coming from the kid's rooms.

The neighborhood was a wonder. On my days and nights off I walked the colorful neighborhood streets soaking it all up. Because I was under twenty-one and not yet allowed to purchase alcohol, I'd usually end up nursing a cappuccino at Caffe Trieste on the corner of Grant and Vallejo Streets. On any given evening, one of the local beat poets like Philip Whalen, Diane de Prima or Lew Welch (who honest-to-god invited me to "come up and see my etchings?") would read and chant their poems. Sometimes someone would bring bongos offering a beat to the verse-our 1960's rap. Later, filled with inspiration I'd always end up at City Lights Books to spend money I should have saved for food.

Records were my other obsession. There was a great record store on the corner where I also spent money I didn't have on music. There wasn't much in my room, but I had everything I needed. My portable sewing machine and a record player, both propped up on boxes and a pile of books in the corner filled it up. Classical chamber music would start me off to work in the morning and always jazz at night. I was learning to appreciate rock music, but disdained hippies. Although I was too young, in my own opinion I was a member of the beat generation.

Working at Pacific Bell as a long-distance telephone operator, I got my exercise walking from North Beach to work in a huge, grey building near the financial district. It was a gig and provided me with the money to support my fabric, book, and record habits. Sometimes there might be five dollars left over to buy a lid of pot.

Grant Avenue is split down the middle with Italians on one end and Chinatown at the other. My favorite place for cheap eats was a very funky Chinese diner called Fuey Guey Louie's. Perching on a red swivel stool at the counter I could fill up for practically nothing. Since I didn't speak Chinese, I'd just point to a plate that looked good. Best to finish it up as I had no kitchen or even a tiny fridge to store leftovers. Unlike today, there were no homeless people sitting on the curb who would want leftover food.

On sunny days, I would wander down to Washington Square Park in the heart of Little Italy, across the street from Saints Peter and Paul church, first stopping at Liguria Bakery for a café latte and some cannoli so fresh they would melt on my tongue. Lazily lying back on the grass, I loved listening to mothers cooing to their beautiful dark-eyed babies in mellifluous Italian. Or maybe a hike up Telegraph Hill for a visit to Coit Tower to take in the incredible 360-degree view and brilliantly colored historic wall murals would be just the ticket.

At the intersection of Broadway and Columbus near Grant stood the Condor Club in the "seedy" part of the hood. From far and wide one could see the infamous blinking breasts of Carol Doda in neon lights on the flashing marquee. Barkers stood in the doorways of clubs and peepshows, loudly beckoning roving gentlemen to enter and harassing girls on the street. I knew to always watch my back at night. Best to avoid being noticed, unless you were in the business of selling sex.

My friend Sally, worked at Joseph Magnin on Stockton and O'Farrell, an upscale fashion emporium selling hip styles, which appealed to us young working girls. If I was lucky, I might have a few extra bucks to buy a new hairclip there, and also got great ideas for fashion knock-offs. With her silky, lustrous hair shimmering almost down to her hips and even longer legs, Sally always looked like she had just stepped out of the store window. Guys were always trying to pick us up-"*wanna smoke a joint?*"-which we politely declined-not wanting to get busted. Sally was always a hoot and full of good ideas. "How about if we catch a bus on Saturday and ride down to Sausalito to hang out for the day?"

Having grown up in Marin, after leaving behind the foggy Avenues in the city when I was in third grade, I was more than familiar with Sausalito. If there were any place I'd ever been that would qualify as the most awesome place on earth, it would be Sausalito. So, when the weekend rolled around, we hopped onto the bus, eagerly anticipating whatever the day might offer.

The bus dropped us off on Bridgeway-Sausalito's picturesque main drag, the entirety of which curved around Richardson Bay. A bright sun sparkled out on the water, wrapping all the sailboats in diamond necklaces and the breeze so fresh it literally smacked me in the face with a big kiss. This was an entirely different world only fifteen minutes out of the city. We made a beeline for The Tides Bookstore. Inside, the old board and batten building was warm and fragrant with its comforting redolence of books, coffee, and donuts. The Tides always had great music playing and the people-watching was the best. We wandered around taking our time, checking out titles and reading poetry. When each of us had selected something, we met up for a cup of strong, hot coffee, settling in some cozy, well-worn chairs in a corner and blissfully whiled away the morning.

Fortified with caffeine, we made our way down the main drag and through the side-streets, meandering in and out of chic shops and jewelry stores. The Village Shops-a multistoried mélange of delightful little specialty shops filled with assorted treasures had long been a favorite haunt of mine. In a Scandinavian shop on the upper level I had a forest green hand knit cardigan with sterling silver buttons on a lay-away plan for what seemed like forever. The owner was so patient with me as I doled out my pitiful payments. I adored that green sweater, so beautifully constructed that someone is probably still wearing it to this day. Further down Richardson Street on the bayside was a tiny shop in a beat-up little shack. If you didn't sew or knit you'd probably pass it by, but I always had to go in and check out the handcrafted buttons and other lovely artistic notions which included exquisite ribbon trims which everyone, back in the day, sewed to the hems of their bell-bottoms. These unique little items made a huge fashion statement in the 60's.

Crossing the street Sally and I agreed that we were starving. Soupcon was my favorite place in Sausalito for cheap eats. You could smell the enticing fragrance of the soups long before stepping through the door. Every day the chefs would cook up huge kettles of a few mouthwatering varieties and serve huge, steaming bowls with a hunk of freshly baked sourdough French bread for mopping up the savory goodness. Soup-the ultimate comfort food. It just didn't get any better than that.

Not wanting to miss the sun setting over the city, we typically made it a point to get back on the bus just before sundown. No matter how many years I had lived in San Francisco, it always blew my mind to cross the Golden Gate Bridge, coming home to a panoramic sunset settling over downtown. From our seats on the bus as it approached the bridge we watched the lights across the bay, illuminating the skyline of downtown high-rises and around the coastline to the Sea Cliff neighborhood, always an unforgettable moment. Hanging out in marvelous Marin was fun, but we loved returning to The City.

Those Colorful Streets is a prequel to *From the Summer of Love to the Valley of the Moon.* It is a story about my early years living in North Beach, San Francisco.

Nancy J. Martin was born in San Francisco, raised in Marin County and migrated north to the Valley of the Moon, where she has resided since 1976. She is the author of a memoir-*From the Summer of Love to the Valley of the Moon.* www.nancyjmartinauthor.com

Ferry to Freedom

Eileen Harrison Sanchez

Chapter 1 ~ Ninety Miles to Key West

The day I began the journey to leave Cuba with my father and my brothers more than fifty years ago, I saw my grandfather cry. He wiped tears as they dripped from his mustache. My mother and sisters waved as my father backed the car out of the driveway. We left our home in Cuabitas, a suburban area outside of Santiago, to attend a camp in Canada for reasons I would soon understand. But not yet. I was disappointed. My team needed me to catch for the final games of the season. Summer was for baseball not camp in another country.

***

Cuabitas is about 600 miles from Havana, and it would take eleven or twelve hours before we would arrive. We left at sunrise and drove and drove and drove, stopping only for gas and bathroom breaks. My mother packed a cooler with sandwiches, galleticas, hunks of cheese, fresh baked bread, bananas and orange juice. I worried that my father would fall asleep behind the wheel. He wasn't a good driver and he kept yawning as he shrugged his shoulders. I was thirteen years old and knew how to drive if it was necessary. My grandfather's chauffeur had secretly taught me and my brother Fernando how to shift the gears. The first problem was that he always sat next to us as he engaged the clutch. The second problem was that I wasn't sure if either of us were tall enough to reach the pedals for the accelerator. Although Fernando was thirteen months older than me, we were the same height and sometimes mistaken as twins. I knew I had grown a few inches since I needed new pants for the trip, and I was confident I could drive if I had to.

"Miguelito, I need you to sit with me to read the maps.

Fernando can sit in the back with Pedro. I could see that Fernando wasn't happy with that assignment, but he would get carsick if he read the maps. At eleven years old, Pedro was a more seasoned traveler than the two of us. He had been to the US numerous times for polio treatments when he was younger. He was excited to return but didn't understand why our mother wasn't coming with us. Our father expected obedience and not a lot of questions.

We arrived at my Uncle Javier's house before dark. At dinner, our travel plans were questioned by my aunt and uncle. My brothers and I were sent away as the adults left to another room and spoke in hushed voices. That had happened at home too. I knew that there was more to our trip than we were being told. We were told that my father needed to take care of some business in the US. He is an attorney and has an important role with the Catholic Archdiocese in Oriente. Being obedient and not asking a lot of questions gave us a chance to have a game of catch. After the long car ride, I was happy to grab my catcher's mitt and run to the yard. The branches of several mango trees restricted my tosses while I waited for my brothers to follow me. No one did.

The back door led to a hallway and I found my brothers in the pantry with the base of drinking glasses held to their ears. Fernando handed me a glass from the shelf as he raised fingers to his mouth to keep me quiet. I copied him and placed the open end against the wall.

My father's voice was as clear as if we were in the room. He said, "They closed my office and my children's school so we could attend rallies! Waving Cuban flags and singing the Revolution's song! All for Castro to be on TV! Que lastima!"

My father's brother had been active in our family's support of "La Revolucion," told my father, "Jorge, tu estas loco!!!..." "Jorge, you are crazy!!! How can you leave your wife and daughters behind?"

Pedro choked back his surprise at hearing about Mama's absence in this way. She had always accompanied him to the United States for his polio checkups. And one was scheduled at the end of the summer.

Fernando looked at me with worried eyes and then to Ramon as he ran his fingers across his lips.

My father's voice was strong and determined, "I will send for them soon, it's too risky if we all leave together."

"Jorge, Jorge, think about this! Things will get better, you will see," my uncle pleaded.

I strained to hear my father's words, now he sounded desperate.

"If I am wrong, we can always come back. My fear is that if we do not leave now," "… we may not be able to leave later."

We all heard his voice break with emotion. Pedro leaned into Fernando with tears in his eyes. I stood straighter and taller.

"Papa says *Dios Provera* and I say God helps those who help themselves. God can only provide the Grace. We will help Papa."

The next morning, my uncle tried once more to delay our leaving. But our tickets were purchased for that day and it would be difficult to exchange them. He reluctantly drove us to the "Havana-Florida" Ferry Terminal. My father was deathly afraid of airplanes. The ferry was the only way for us to travel out of the country, and less expensive with three kids and luggage.

Our arrival was uneventful, and we had time to find the way without rushing. We followed the signs for departures and got on the end of a long line of passengers with all sizes of luggage. We each had one large suitcase. My father also carried his briefcase, and a zippered canvas bag with leather handles filled with linens and towels.

Since we were early, we stood on this line for at least an hour before the passengers were asked to show their Exit Visas, ferry tickets and paperwork which included permission to leave Cuba and proof of return to Cuba. It was finally our turn and my father had to get out paperwork for the four of us. The woman behind us started to complain as he slowly made his way toward the agent. I took his suitcase from him as I saw him struggle with the canvas bag and his briefcase.

"Señor, cual es el problema?" muttered as the line stopped moving. Reviewing the papers of the four of us traveling together was going to take too much time.

Another agent approached us and said, "Senor, por favor, step away from the line and wait here for the agent to collect you."

We were escorted to a nearby table where a government official reviewed our papers. We had passports, visas and a return ticket for the ferry. The packet with baptismal certificates and our report cards began a careful inspection.

"Senor, why do your sons need these for summer camp," asked the official?

"We are Catholic. They do well in school. I want the camp to know," answered my father.

I was surprised to see my report card. It wasn't my best, as my father had recently reminded me. I hoped that the camp didn't have tutors. Swimming and baseball had been the promise.

The questions continued as the official searched each piece of luggage. Mine was last. He held up my catcher's mitt and asked, "Whose is this?"

I raised my hand.

"What is your name?" asked the official.

"Miguel de Jesus Rodriquez, señor."

"How old are you Miguel?"

He sorted through the passports to find mine. "Thirteen, fourteen in October, señor."

I watched him look from my documents and then at me, holding my gaze as if we were friends in a staring contest. He returned my mitt to my suitcase and clicked the latches to close it. I didn't look away. Neither did he until he turned to pick up my father's briefcase which was locked.

When my father opened his briefcase, his watch was on top of the paperwork. I wondered why? I was sure that he had it on when he was driving. The contents of the briefcase received a lot of attention from the official and the discussion continued.

"What are these files for, señor?" asked the official.

"I am a law professor at the university, and I have some work to finish."

"When do you return to Havana?" asked the official.

Impatiently, my father replied, "My documents have my return date. We have permission to travel until September."

"Si, señor, but you are an important man with all this work. Cuba needs you back."

At last, the official closed the briefcase and said we could board the ferry. I had kept my gaze low after the staring contest, low enough that I saw the watch slip into his pocket as he snapped the latches on the briefcase with the other hand.

He handed the case back as he said, "Viva La Revolucion!"

We were finally able to board the ferry.

Standing on the deck, high above the dock took my breath away. I don't mind heights, but I didn't realize how big the ferry was until I looked down at the crew pulling up the gangplank we had just walked up. My father didn't say anything about his watch, and I didn't ask. He would only say, "Dios Provera, God Will Provide, and I can get another watch."

As the ferry left the port, we all relaxed. My father's pacing lessened as the ship started heaving in rougher waters. He took a seat next to Fernando and put his arm around Pedro who tended to get seasick and looked like he might throw up. I felt good knowing we were on the way to Key West. I was proud that I was able to win the staring game but the interrogation by the ferry official worried me more than the whisperings back at my grandfather's house and again at my uncle's. I kept thinking about the watch I saw the agent take. I was sure that my father had it on his wrist in the car. The watch was a bribe. He wanted the agent to take it. His watch was a small price to pay to insure our passage.

A refugee story that asks what does freedom mean to you?

Patria o Muerte, County or Death? What would cause you to flee from your homeland? Skirmishes between rebels and soldiers in the hills near your home? Checkpoints when you travel? Death threats for family members?

This is the first chapter of my work in progress. *Ferry to Freedom* is the working title. It might change but for now it connects this story with my first novel. *Ferry to Freedom* is based on facts and personal experience assisted by research and personal interviews. And like my first novel I have fictionalized the facts and the research to create historical fiction.

Readers met Miguel as secondary character in *Freedom Lessons*. He had been in the US for nine years in 1969. It was at the height of civil rights protests, war protests and mandated school integration. In *Ferry to Freedom* the reader backs up in time to meet Miguel in 1960, as a thirteen year old boy when he leaves his mother and extended family in Cuba for the US. He left with his father and his brothers under the pretense of attending camp in Canada for the summer. He was unaware that his father had no intention of returning to Santiago de Cuba or that the rest of the family would soon follow. He never saw his beloved grandfather again. His youthful dreams of a baseball career were left behind.

Follow his journey which starts on a ferry to Key West with nothing but family and a suitcase. Teenage years were challenged with the American culture clashes of generations. The Vietnam War was raging, and he was drafted into the Army before he was a citizen. The freedom promised by his adopted country's laws was important to him, so important that he became an attorney. But what did he lose and at what cost?

Eileen Harrison Sanchez is now retired after a forty-year career in education. She started as a teacher and ended as a district administrator. A reader, a writer and a perennial – a person with a no-age mindset – Sanchez considers family and friends to be the most important parts of her life, followed by traveling and bird watching from her gazebo. *Freedom Lessons* is her first published novel. Eileen is an administrator of Prose and the Pandemic and blogs as Gram's Book Club – Recommending books to inform young people of the small stories that make up our history. Before retirement she presented numerous workshops to educators at district, state and national levels. She continues to present in person and virtually, to readers and educators at conferences, book clubs and in libraries on using historical fiction to teach social justice.

Website: https://www.eileensanchez.com

Facebook: https://www.facebook.com/eileensanchezwriter/
Twitter: https://twitter.com/EileenHSanchez

Instagram: https://www.instagram.com/ eileensanchezwriter/
https://bookshop.org/shop/Jersey_Girl

"Debut novelist Sanchez has crafted a moving and timely story, based on her own experiences, about school integration in the South in 1969 and the issues that still linger today. This powerful tale offers a beacon of hope that individuals can inspire change."

–Library Journal http://bit.ly/googleplayFreedomLessons
http://bit.ly/KoboFreedomLessons
 https://bit.ly/BNFreedomLessons
https://bit.ly/FreedomLessons-ANovel
http://bit.ly/NookFreedomLessons

Lacewood

Jessica James

Katie felt the rough edge of the old key in her hand as she walked toward the padlocked gate of her new home. It sent electric currents of excitement through her—along with a ripple of pure terror. This was hers. All of it. Thirty days ago she hadn't known this place existed. Now it was home.

She paused before opening the old gate and took a deep, slow breath. The air was clean. The sky was vast. The birds singing from the branches of the sycamore trees sounded jubilant—as if they were serenading her into this new world. She glanced up at the sunlight streaking through the tree limbs but couldn't see the source of the joyful chorus through the thick new leaves.

Katie couldn't explain the mystical pull of this house, the strange magic it created. Her friends in New York thought she'd gone off the deep end—and maybe she had. Why else would she be wearing this ridiculous smile as she pushed open the rusty gate of a decrepit, abandoned house? Why else would she feel downright giddy at the thought of owning all these weeds and shrubs and rocks?

The sycamores on either side of the house loomed before her, even more stunning and towering than when Katie first saw them. Back then, of course, the limbs were cloaked only in buds and a promise of what was to come. Now they were in full leaf, their immense white trunks standing in deep contrast to the green overhead, their boughs nodding and whispering mysteriously to one another as she passed. She tried to imagine what her view from the house would be like in the fall, when the trees around Lacewood erupted into a carnival of color, creating a tapestry of hues in every direction, as far as the eye could see.

Katie took her time making her way to the house. *Mine. All mine*, kept running through her head. Followed by, *what in the heck am I doing?* As she swept her eyes over the expansive vista of deterioration before her, she couldn't help but think of the extravagant penthouse she left behind.

One moment she was excited, the next shaking with fear. She was completely alone here. No neighbors above and below her. No housekeeper to make her bed, or restaurant to deliver her dinner. So simple, yet so complicated. So exciting and terrifying…so daunting and thrilling.

Pure, stark fear, bordering on hysteria, bubbled up—and was swallowed. Bright sunlight and singing birds had a way of making panic over unknown things seem trivial. By the time Katie reached the front steps, she'd conquered her misgivings. *I need this*, she told herself. *And heaven knows, it needs me.*

After sticking the key into the lock with a trembling hand, Katie gave a firm turn. The resulting click sent an emotional charge straight through her. This was it. She'd just unlocked the door to her new home…her new life.

Closing the door behind her, Katie stood perfectly still in the foyer, her heart pounding in her ears. Dried leaves made a scuffling sound as they whisked across the floor in a hurried dance, settling into the shadows as if hiding from a stranger.

"A little fresh air will do wonders." Katie said the words out loud and was startled when her voice echoed and reverberated back to her in the nearly-empty room. She hurried to a window on the south side of the house and wrestled with the monstrous pane until at last it moved. Warm air full of birdsong and the alluring fragrances of spring rushed in, creating a completely different atmosphere.

The intense satisfaction from that simple act made Katie sigh with happiness. Yes, this was a far cry from a condo at the beach—or even a rustic cabin in the mountains. But her jet-setting days of glamor and glitz were behind her. Lacewood was home, providing a haven she needed and longed for.

Katie walked through the imposing foyer, trying to avoid the shards of glass glittering in the sunlight. Her mother would never approve of this, that's for sure. She often scolded Katie for wrapping herself in a cloak of isolation rather than enjoying the spotlight. Katie always responded by pulling the cloak even tighter.

The mere thought of what her mother's reaction would be made Katie cringe, and then smile. For the first time, *she* was in charge of her life. No more trying to be what someone else wanted—or the world expected.

Katie's sandals made a scuffing sound as she walked down the corridor to the room in the back. This was where she planned to put her air mattress and belongings until other parts of the house were made livable. Sizeable yet homey, the room had a masculine feel to it, and an aura of protection and warmth.

Walking over to a built-in seat on the far wall, Katie rested her knee on the wooden ledge, and unlatched the French-style window behind it. Leaning forward as far as she could, Katie was disheartened at the confusion of vines and vegetation that had taken over the garden. But even without flowers, this house was abundant with exactly what her soul needed.

Peace and quiet.

No more disruptions or distractions. No more interruptions or intrusions. On any given day, she could do as much—or as little—as she wanted. The debilitating headaches that had plagued her since childhood had all but vanished in the last month. She hadn't even bothered to refill her prescription medications, or pack anything stronger than aspirin.

In that regard, the healing powers of the house were already evident. "I'll fix you and you'll fix me." Katie felt silly making the promise out loud, but it was true. The house's issues were countless and vast—but they were mostly superficial, paling in comparison to her deep-seated ones.

Pulling out her phone, Katie prepared to make the call she'd been dreading. *Better to get it over with before the news begins to spread.*

As she dialed the number, she steeled herself for the conversation to come. Her mother would be frantic with disbelief and dismay when she learned Katie made this decision without her. She would ask the inevitable question and demand an immediate answer. *"What in the world are you DOING?"*

Katie smiled with a deep sense of contentment at what her response would be.

Living.

***

"You're not actually *staying* here, right?" Elliott C. Fairfax III pulled a handkerchief out of his hand-tailored suit and batted at some cobwebs near his head before entering the room.

Katie placed the groceries he brought for her on the bare floor before answering. "Why wouldn't I?"

"It's disgusting."

"It's a little dusty."

"It's filthy."

"But it has possibilities."

Elliott cast one eye toward the crack in the plaster overhead. "Yes, like the possibility of a piece of the ceiling falling down on your head at any moment."

"All it needs is a little cleaning—"

"And a lot of *fixing*."

"Okay. I'll grant you it needs some fixing." Katie put her hands on her hips. "But nothing a little TLC can't take care of."

"I think you mean *TNT*," he replied, still looking around. "A stick of dynamite and a bulldozer would do wonders."

Katie frowned and shook her head. "You're my agent, a friend. I thought you'd be happy for me. Maybe offer some encouragement..."

"Okay. I *encourage* you to come back to New York with me and will be *happy* when you're out of here." He scanned the room again with a shudder of revulsion. "I brought you enough food to last a week because I wanted to give you time to settle into your new home. I didn't realize you were living in something only slightly more sophisticated than a cave."

"Did my mother send you?"

Elliott glanced away from Katie's accusing eyes, suspiciously eager to change the subject. "Honey, I know you're burned out. You need some time off. I get it. But this..." He took a deep breath and rolled his eyes. "This is going a bit too far."

"Too late. It's mine, and I'm staying."

"This is ridiculous. How will I even get in touch with you about contract offers? Do they have phone service around here?"

"Send a note by Pony Express." Katie bent down to move a box of cleaning supplies out of the way. She was trying to lighten her agent's mood, but he didn't crack a smile. In fact, he seemed to be trying to decide if she was serious. When his nine-hundred-dollar Italian shoes crunched on some broken glass, he froze in place, and winced as if afraid to look down and see what he stepped on.

"This is crazy," he complained under his breath as he carefully repositioned his foot.

Katie picked up a broom and began sweeping the glass into a pile, which only served to increase the particles of dust hanging in the air. "I appreciate your concern, but I'll be fine. I wanted some peace and quiet and I know I'll find it here."

"You can find peace and quiet in Central Park. It's not nearly as dirty." He put the handkerchief back to his nose as he noticed the new cloud of dust.

"Depends on your definition of *dirty*," Kate shot back. "Just like it depends what your definition of *civilized* is."

He fixed his unsmiling gaze on hers. "This is like another planet. Where's the nearest store?"

"I think it's only about three miles."

"Excuse me? Did you say three *miles*?"

Katie smiled. Naturally he was upset, since he would cringe at the idea of having to travel three blocks to find a good restaurant or gourmet food store.

"Where do you get a cup of coffee around here?" Elliott flapped the handkerchief over his head as if clear away more cobwebs while he walked into the next room.

"From my coffeepot, as soon as I get it set up." He stopped abruptly in the doorway of the parlor.

"Where's your TV? Do you have internet service? What in the world are you going to do all day?"

"Take long walks, sit on the porch, write, drink beer…" Katie sighed. She'd found peace. A reconnection to her roots…far away from the materialistic, covetous world she'd escaped.

"Wait a minute. Stop." Elliott put his hands up, palms out, and then forced a laugh. "For a minute there, I thought you said you were going to drink *beer*."

"That *is* what I said. Champagne doesn't taste nearly as good after a hard day's work as an ice-cold beer."

"This is getting out of hand," Elliott said in a serious, low tone. "You can't possibly want to live like a hermit and be completely antisocial. Remember how you used to enjoy getting all dolled up and going to cocktails parties in the city?"

"To which I reply, *No-o-o*."

"But you went," he countered. "You *acted* like you enjoyed it— and the society pages loved you."

"I *pretended* to enjoy it." Katie crossed her arms. "To please my mother. Big difference."

"You had me fooled. You must be a helluva good actress."

"Thank you." Katie bowed. "My therapist would be glad to know you believe I actually enjoy being around people."

Elliott's brow creased in confusion. "Speaking of which, how in the world are you going to get a therapist down *here*?"

"Why would I need one? I'm going to relax. Keep to myself. I won't be attending events solely to please Mom…Speaking of which, *did* she send you?"

"No, she didn't *send* me…exactly." Elliott wiped his forehead with the handkerchief. "I mean, she did want me to see if you would go to the next—"

"No."

"You don't even know what I'm going to ask."

"That's because I don't even care. I'm not going."

"But she has this wonderful new gown she wants to show off, and your figure is perfect—"

"N. O."

Elliott took a deep breath, as if to respond, but Katie cut him off. "I told her, and I will now tell you, I'm done with it. No more public appearances."

He glanced around distractedly, making it obvious he was seeking a subtle way to change the subject. "So, what are your neighbors like? Have you met any yet?"

"No one but the sheriff." Katie shrugged. "He seems like a nice guy."

"Sheriff?" Elliott stood motionless in the middle of the room. "Does he carry a gun?"

Katie had to close one eye to remember whether or not the kind, blond-haired man with the broad shoulders carried a gun. "Yes. He carries a gun. It's what sheriffs do in the country."

"Country? You mean the Wild West."

Katie couldn't help laughing at the incredulous scowl on her agent's face. "Seriously, Elliott. Not having a Starbucks or an Italian restaurant every few hundred feet does not make this the Wild West."

"Men walking around with guns on their hips do."

"I know this takes a little getting used to…"

"Getting used to? You're a city girl, born and bred."

"Yes, born and bred, but I lived with Grammy every summer." Katie sighed. "The best days of my life."

"Really? Running around barefoot in the dirt and going fishing were better than having a view of the Manhattan skyline from your penthouse living room?"

"Absolutely. And I like the view *here* even better."

Both of their gazes spontaneously turned to an oversized window where a jumble of trees and shrubs had taken over what was once the garden. A vine had even found its way through a crack and was climbing up the inside of the pane.

Elliott reached over and put his hand to her forehead. "I think you have a fever."

Reading his thoughts easily, Katie glared at him. "Are you really worried about me? Or are you worried you'll have trouble handling my mother without my help?"

Elliott shot her one of the priceless smiles she knew cost him a small fortune. "You know I'm only worried about you, baby."

Katie felt a little sorry for Elliott. She knew he was here to check up on her because of the rumors floating around New York. Heck, some of them had even made their way into the tabloids. One claimed the house purchase was a ruse—that Katie was actually at a beach resort in South America recovering from some unknown addiction. Another insisted she'd had a breakdown and bought a run-down, dilapidated old house during a period of decreased mental capacity.

It was Elliott's job to dispel the rumors, set the record straight, and protect his client's reputation. Katie knew she was pushing him way beyond his comfort zone.

"You can live anywhere in the world, and you chose this rinky-dink, hillbilly town and this run-down, abandoned property?"

"I can't explain it." Katie studied the room, noting its potential, not its pitfalls. "This place called to me."

"It *called* to you." He repeated the words, not as a question, but as if he had to hear them from his own lips in order to understand what she meant. "Let me guess. It said, *help me, I'm falling down.*"

"Elliott, give me a break."

"I'm trying to, honey, but this just isn't *you.*"

"Actually it *is* me. What you saw before wasn't." Katie spoke in a low, serious tone. "You of all people should understand. Remember how liberating it was when you came out?"

"Oh heavens, don't go there." Elliott waved his hand. "Coming out of the closet in downtown Manhattan is a little different from coming out to be a recluse in the middle of nowhere."

"It's not the middle of nowhere." She shook her head and inhaled deeply. "It's *home.*"

Elliott blinked repeatedly, as if by doing so he could change the view. The once-elegant wallpaper in front of him drooped in long strips, exposing the plaster wall beneath. As he lifted his gaze, Katie hoped he would focus on the priceless quality of the chandelier—not the brown spot around its base.

Katie chalked up their difference of opinion to values and upbringing. Elliott thought of her house as the individual elements of wood, stone, columns and beams, that to him were old, tattered, inadequate, and useless.

She, on the other hand, thought of Lacewood as a collection of features that somehow managed to remain steadfast and persevere despite decades of neglect and hardship. That alone made the house worth saving.

Bending down to pick up a paint scraper, Katie gestured toward the ladder on the other side of the room. "Someone left me a ladder. If you want to stick around, you can give me a hand..."

He took a step back. "Who, *me?*" He sounded appalled, as if she'd asked him to pick something up for her at the local Dollar General. At the same time he brushed some imagined dust off his Armani suit, making it clear the mere act of standing in the room was beneath his normal standards. "I think I'll pass. I've got to get back..." he glanced out the window at his car "...to civilization."

"Okay. Well then, thanks for stopping by. And thanks for the groceries...and the roses." Katie nodded toward the bunch of yellow roses, now wilted and droopy from Elliott's long drive.

She knew he brought them to brighten up her new home, but right now they were anything but vibrant and cheerful. "I'm going to grow my own flowers—all kinds—and pick fresh bouquets every day." When Elliott didn't respond, she came out of her daydream. He appeared to be frozen in the middle of the room.

"Who. In. The. Heck. Is. That?" He pointed a shaking finger at the portrait over the fireplace.

"I'm not sure yet. A previous owner, maybe." Katie studied the woman's image again. A lustrous coil of hair crowned her head, and her melancholy brown eyes gazed out imploringly.

"Oh, my gawd, she's watching us." Elliott walked to the far side of the room, and indeed, it seemed like her eyes followed his movements. "Take that hideous thing down, for the love of Pete," he said dramatically, moving to another part of the room. "It's possessed, I'm sure of it."

Katie studied the beautiful woman with the sad face. "It's not scary. I feel like she's protecting me."

"From what? Is this place *haunted*?" Elliott was no longer stationary. He strode toward the door at a clip she had never seen him move before.

"Safe travels, Elliott. Tell my mother I'm fine."

"I'll tell her you've bitten off more than you can chew," he said, his shoes echoing through the empty room as he made a hasty retreat. "How do you think you're going to do all of this by yourself?"

"I'm not. The sheriff said he knows someone in town who might be interested in helping."

"Probably your everyday, small-town, run-of-the-mill chainsaw murderer," Elliott said under his breath as he unlatched the door. He gave a tug, but the door didn't open.

"The door sticks a little." Katie nudged him aside and put both hands on the handle. After a few tugs with all of her weight behind it, the door creaked open. "See? I'm a big girl. I can handle it."

"You're a *city* girl. You've never had to do anything for yourself in your life."

"Then I guess it's high time for me to start." She walked onto the front porch with him. "Anyway, that's what the Internet is for. These days I can watch a five-minute video and learn how to install a toilet."

"Excuse me?" Elliott stopped with his foot hovering over the first step. "Do you *need* to install a toilet? Don't you have indoor plumbing?"

Katie noticed his sprayed-on tan had turned two shades paler, and beads of sweat dotted his forehead.

"It was simply an *example.* Yes, I have indoor plumbing." Elliott let out his breath. "It was a bad example to use.

"Don't scare me like that." He put one hand on his chest and pulled his phone out of his pocket with the other. "That does it. I'm giving Jules a call right now and telling her to make arrangements for you to go to Paris. Or would you prefer somewhere in the South Pacific? Your choice. You need some time to think. And don't worry about a thing. It's on me."

"Put your phone away."

He glared at the device in his hand and shook his head. "Might as well. I don't have any reception here anyway."

"Makes me love it here even more," Katie said dreamily. "No contact from the outside world."

"When you come to your senses, give me a call." Elliott gave her a hug and a peck on the cheek. "Or send smoke signals, or however it is you communicate with each other out here."

"Maybe the next time you visit I'll have some chickens," Katie said cheerfully.

Elliott stopped walking, but he didn't turn around this time. "I beg your pardon?"

"Chickens. Those feathered things that produce the food you eat every morning. Believe it or not, eggs don't grow on trees."

"I know where eggs come from." He turned around now. "But you're not going to pick up eggs fresh out of their butts, and then *eat* them."

Katie tilted her head. "They don't get delivered on a plate with Hollandaise sauce and a side of bacon."

"They do where I come from."

"Bye, Elliott," Katie said as he made his way toward a dusty Mercedes parked in a patch of tall weeds.

"Call me when you're ready to leave." He made the sign of a phone with his hand.

Katie laughed and waved. "Sure thing!"

Elliott quickly put his window up before throwing the car into reverse and turning around.

"Watch out for bears," Katie yelled as he drove away. Elliott didn't hear. He had his foot on the gas pedal and was leaving Lacewood as fast as the condition of the road and the density of the dust would allow.

I often get asked how a story comes about, so I thought I'd share a little bit about this sometimes painful, always unpredictable, adventure with you.

The inspiration for the novel *Lacewood* began very innocently. I started noticing sycamore trees while driving to work. Suddenly they were everywhere…along the road, dotting the creeks, stretching their ivory white limbs up to the sky in the distant fields. Most people would ignore this sudden fascination, but being an author, I knew it was the prodding of my writing angel (that's what I call her)—and I don't ignore the writing angel.

I did some research and found an article that referred to sycamore trees as lacewood.

Lacewood sounded beautiful…like the title of a novel. This was wonderful news, because I usually struggle with a book's title long after it is completed. The bad news was…that's all I had.

After much thought and deliberation, I decided my novel would be part love story, part ghost story and focus on a disillusioned socialite and a wounded veteran who find a shared purpose through the restoration of an abandoned mansion. Secrets are divulged, riddles are unraveled, and mysteries are solved, as the house reveals a love story in danger of being lost forever.

Jessica James is an award-winning author of historical fiction and suspense/thrillers who loves old houses and big trees. She lives in Gettysburg, Pa. Find out more at jessicajamesbooks.com or her travel and history blog: pastlanetravels.com.

Champagne Widows

Rebecca Rosenberg

"Champagne. In victory one deserves it, in defeat one needs it."
Napoleon Bonaparte

Le Nez The Nose
Reims, Champagne, France 1797

Grand-mère sways over the edge of the stone stairs into the cavern, and I step between her and eternity, dizzy from the bloody tang of her head bandage.

"Let's go back. We'll come another time." I try to turn her around, so we don't tumble into the dark crayère, but she holds firm.

"There won't be another time if I know your maman and her heretic doctor."

They drilled into Grand-mère's skull again for a disease they call hysteria. The hole was supposed to let out evil spirits, but the gruesome treatment hasn't stopped her sniffing every book, pillow, and candle, trying to capture its essence, agitated that her sense of smell has disappeared.

"This is how you know you are alive, Barbe-Nicole." She taps her nose frantically. "The aromas of brioche fresh from the oven, lavender water ironed into your clothes, your father's pipe smoke. You must understand. Time is running out." Her fingernails claw my arm, the whale oil lamp sputtering and smoking in her other hand.

"Let me lead." Taking the stinking lantern, I let her grip my shoulders from behind. Grand-mère shrunk so much, she's my height of five feet, though she's a step above. For as long as I remember, she has tried to justify my worst fault. My cursed proboscis, as Maman calls my over-sensitive nose, has been a battle between us since I was little. I remember walking with her through town, avoiding chamber pots dumped from windows, horse excrement paving the roads, and factories belching black gases. Excruciating pain surged to my nose, making my eyes water and sending me into sneezing fits.

Maman left me standing alone on the street.

From then on, my sense of smell swelled beyond reason.

Mostly ordinary odors, but sometimes I imagine I can smell the stink of a lie. Or the perfume of a pure heart. Or the heartbreaking smell of what could have been.

Maman complains my cursed sense of smell makes me too particular, too demanding, and frankly, too peculiar. Decidedly troublesome traits for a daughter she's tried to marry off since I was sixteen. But why must the suitors she picks have to smell so bad?

Grand-mère squeezes my shoulder. "It is not your fault you are the way you are, Barbe-Nicole; it's a gift." She chirped this over and over this afternoon until Maman threatened to have the doctor drill her skull again.

The lantern casts ghoulish shadows on the chalk walls as my bare toes reach for the next stair and the next. I'll have hell to pay if we're caught down here. Part of me came tonight to humor Grand-mère, but part of me craves more time with her. I've witnessed her tremors, her shuffling feet, her crazy obsessions, which now seem to focus on my nose.

As we descend, the dank air chills my legs; feathery chalk dust makes my feet slip on the steps. The Romans excavated these chalk quarries a thousand years ago, creating a sprawling web of crayères under our ancient town of Reims. What exactly does Grand-mère have in mind bringing me down here? The lantern throws a halo on grape clusters laying on the rough-hewn table.

Ah, she wants to play her sniffing game.

"How did you set this up?" My toes recoil from cold puddles of spring water.

"I'm not dead yet," she croaks. Taking off her fringed bed shawl, she ties it like a blindfold over my eyes. "Don't peek."

"Wouldn't dare." I lift a corner of the shawl, and she raps my fingers like the nuns at St.-Pierre-Les-Dames where Maman sent me to school before the Revolution shut down convents.

"Quit lollygagging and breathe deep." Grand-mère's knobby fingertips knead below my cheekbones, opening my nasal passages to the mineral smell of chalk, pristine groundwater, oak barrels, the purple aroma of fermenting wine.

But these profound smells can't stop me fretting about Maman's determination to marry me off before the year is out. I told her I'd only marry a suitor that smells like springtime.

"Men do not smell like that," she scolded.

But men do. Or one did, anyway. He was conscriped to war several years ago, so he probably doesn't smell like springtime anymore. His green-sprout smell ruined me for anyone else.

Grand-mère places a bunch of grapes in my hands and brings it to my nose. "What comes to you?"

"The grapes smell like ripening pears and a hint of Hawthorne berry."

She chortles and replaces the grapes with another bunch. "What about these?"

Drawing the aroma into the top of my palate, I picture gypsies around a campfire, smoky, deep, and complex. "Grilled toast and coffee."

Her next handful of grapes are sticky and soft, the aroma so robust and delicious, my tongue longs for a taste. "Smells like chocolate-covered cherries."

Grand-mère wheezes with a rasp and rattle that scares me. I yank off the blindfold. "Grand-mère?"

"You're ready." She slides me a wooden box carved with vineyards and women carrying baskets of grapes on their heads. "Open it."

Inside lays a gold tastevin, a wine-tasting cup on a long, heavy neck chain.

"Your great Grand-père, Nicolas Ruinart, used this cup to taste wine with the monks at Hautvillers Abbey. Just by smelling the grapes, he could tell you the slope of the hill on which they grew, the exposure to the sun, the minerals in the soil." She closes her papery eyelids and inhales. "He'd lift his nose to the west and smell the ocean." She turns. "He'd smell German bratwurst to the northeast." Her head swivels. "To the south, the perfume of lavender fields in Provence." Her snaggletooth protrudes when she smiles. "Your great Grand-père was Le Nez." The Nose. "He passed down his precious gift to you."

Here she goes again with her crazy notions. "Maman says Le Nez is a curse."

Grand-mère clucks her tongue. "Your maman didn't inherit Le Nez, so she doesn't understand it. It's a rare and precious gift, smelling the hidden essence of things. I took it for granted, and now it's gone." Her wrinkled hand picks up the gold tastevin and christens my nose.

A prickling clusters in my sinuses like a powerful sneeze that won't release. I wish there were truth to Grand-mère's ramblings; it would explain so much about my finicky nature.

"You are Le Nez, Barbe-Nicole." She lifts the chain over my head, and the cup nestles above my breasts. "You must carry on Grand-père Ruinart's gift."

"Why haven't you told me about this until now?"

"Your maman forbid it." She wags her finger. "But I'm taking matters into my own hands before I die."

I feel an etching on the bottom of the cup. "Is this an anchor?"

"Ah, yes, the anchor. The anchor symbolizes clarity and courage during chaos and confusion."

"Chaos and confusion?" Now I know the story is a delusion. "Aren't those your cat's names?"

"I have cats?" She stares vacantly into the beyond, and her eerie, foreboding voice echoes through the chamber. "To whom much is given, much is expected."

Holding her bandaged head, Grand-mère keens incoherently. The lantern casts her monstrous shadow on the crayère wall; her tasting game has become a nightmare.

"Let's get you back to your room." I try to walk her to the stairs, but her legs give out. Lifting her bird-like body in my arms, I carry her as she carried me as a child, trying not to topple over into the crayère.

"Promise you'll carry on Le Nez," she says, exhaling sentir le sapin, the smell of fir coffins.

My dear Grand-mère is dying in my arms. Now I know Le Nez is a curse.

"Promise me." Her eyelids flutter and close.

"I won't let you down, Grand-mère," I whisper. She feels suddenly light in my arms, but the gold tastevin feels heavy, so very heavy, around my neck.

CHAMPAGNE WIDOWS by Rebecca Rosenberg is about Veuve Clicquot (Widow Clicquot). Barbe-Nicole Clicquot used Le Nez (extraordinary sense of smell) to found the first champagne house owned by a woman in the early nineteenth century, a time when married women were not allowed to own a business and Napoleon Bonaparte ravaged Europe with fifteen years of war.

Rebecca Rosenberg is a triple-gold award-winning author of CHAMPAGNE WIDOWS, champagne historian, tour guide, and champagne cocktail creator for Breathless Wines, Moderator of Breathless Bubbles & Books, and American Historical Novels facebook groups. Rebecca writes novels about history's real-life women of substance who made an indelible mark on the world. Her latest novel begins a series about the true champagne widows, the first of whom was Veuve Clicquot. A University of Colorado alumni, she holds a Stanford University novel-writing certificate. Her novels have garnered many awards including IBPA, IPPY, and starred Publisher Weekly reviews for her novels, THE SECRET LIFE OF MRS. LONDON (Lake Union 2018) and GOLD DIGGER, *The Remarkable Baby Doe Tabor* (Lion Heart 2019). As lavender farmer and founder of the largest lavender gift manufacturer in America, Rebecca's debut book was LAVENDER FIELDS OF AMERICA. https://www.Rebecca- rosenberg.com Facebook page: https://facebook.com/rebeccarosenbergnovels

The Art of Traveling Strangers
Zoe Disigny

The odor—a peculiar blend of disinfectant, ozone, and jet fuel—tainted the air but enticed me. I liked the smell of escape.

Taking a deep breath, I pressed my head against the cold window and watched Los Angeles shrink below me into a Cubist painting. Those once massive buildings of concrete, glass, and steel were now the abstract geometric shapes of Picasso. I smiled. Life imitating art. That idea had always intrigued me—the belief that art could change our perception of reality. But this time, my attraction to the concept was even stronger. It offered hope. If chaotic LA could transform into a well-designed composition, why couldn't I?

Leaning back in my seat, I embraced the escapist fantasy and pondered the art form I'd want to mimic. Certainly not Cubism. It was too cerebral, and I already spent way too much time in my head. Expressionism was also out—too emotional. But the work of Niki de Saint Phalle struck a chord. She was part of a twentieth-century art movement committed to "new ways of perceiving the real." I liked that, and I adored her work. She was known for her whimsical sculptures of triumphant women—an art form I'd be happy to emulate.

I envisioned myself as one of her creations: an imposing female figure wearing bold primary colors, lustrous metallic wings, and twirling confidently on tiptoe. But just as that vision began to take hold, a cabin light above me blinked off.

"Ladies and gentlemen, the captain has turned off the No Smoking sign, and you are free to smoke at this time. Please refrain from smoking in the aisles, lavatories, and non-smoking sections of this aircraft. Thank you for your attention and enjoy your flight."

Enjoy my flight. Now that posed a challenge. Although I was grateful to be traveling to Europe, far from the emotional turmoil of home, my getaway plan had a serious flaw: the thirty-something woman seated next to me.

She chewed her gum with mindless enthusiasm while reading the July issue of *Fashion First* magazine, apparently to discover the health benefits of crotchless pantyhose. Her name was Viv Chancey, and I, Claire Markham, a thirty-something myself, would be her art guide in Europe for the next three weeks.

"Ya know, I never thought of it before," Viv said, "but I think they're on to somethin' here. I'm gonna get some. Don't get me wrong. I hate pantyhose. They're just so damned uncomfortable. But sometimes a girl's got no choice, and they're a hell of a lot better than garter belts or girdles. Know what I mean? Remember girdles? So stupid. What teenage girl needed a girdle? But we all bought into it back then, hook, line, and sinker. Ya know, you should get some too. Pantyhose, I mean. The crotchless kind." She turned back to her magazine, looking so pleased to have enlightened me, a response to her call to action seemed unnecessary.

I breathed a silent sigh of relief and returned my attention to the window. My Cubist painting had now morphed into the San Bernardino Mountains, home of Big Bear Lake and my daughter's summer camp. I'd taken Amber to camp only two days earlier. We'd sung her favorite camp songs as we snaked up the mountain: "Make New Friends," "This Land is Your Land," and "My Bonnie Lies over the Ocean." My voice faltered on the last song, an unwelcome reminder that I would be "over the ocean" soon and far from Amber.

After I'd helped her settle into her cabin, we'd hugged goodbye, and I watched her join her friends in spontaneous jubilation. Her long red hair spiraled in the wind while her blue eyes sparkled mischievously, and her freckled cheeks dimpled as she smiled. With each passing year, we looked more alike, and that thrilled me. I wanted everyone to know I was her mom.

I could see the lake below us now and tried to pinpoint the exact location of her camp, wishing I could parachute down and steal her away. But that was a purely selfish thought.

Amber loved being at camp. And I'd already exceeded my lifetime limit for selfishness.

Catching one last glimpse of the lake, I pictured her standing on the shore and squealing as the mountain-cold water splashed her toes. It made me smile. As much as I wished I could reinvent my life, it didn't mean without her. She was the best thing in it.

"Hey," Viv said, "I got lots of stuff to read here. Help yourself." She plopped a stack of magazines on my lap, all fashion rags with people like Brooke Shields and Cindy Crawford on the covers.

"Oh, thank you." I offered a disinterested smile and scanned the glossy covers for a featured article to read. *Clown Makeup Be Gone!* My, what a serious topic. *Ten Things to Do with Your Old Falsies.* Ah, guaranteed titillation with that one. *Is He the Great Pretender?* Oh no, way too close for comfort.

I handed the magazines back to Viv. "Thanks anyway. I think I'll just rest my eyes for a minute." Reclining against the headrest, I took another deep breath, hoping to recapture that earlier whiff of escape.

"Okay, suit yourself. Are ya gonna sleep? It's kinda soon for that, don't you think? The stuff I read about flying says it's best to wait 'til after they serve a meal before ya try to sleep. That way, you won't wake up because you're hungry. I don't sleep good on planes anyway. It's too bumpy. Some people love that, though. I have a friend who flies all the time and thinks the best thing about flying's all the bumps. Can you imagine? Ya wanna chill-pill? It'll help you sleep. I got a bunch if you need one."

"No. What I need is peace and quiet. Do you think you could help me out here?" I immediately regretted my comment. I usually filtered my thoughts better than that.

"Well, aren't you Miss Cranky Pants. I was just trying to help." Viv popped her gum as if adding an exclamation point.

"I'm sorry. I guess I'm a little uptight at the moment. Thank you for your offer, though."

Viv chewed in silence, but not for long. "Ya know, the pills I got are good for lots a things, not just sleeping. They help bad moods too. They can really take the edge off. Here's one for you just in case."

Viv pressed a small, round tablet into my hand. It reminded me of the pill bottle in my purse. The one Viv's husband gave me right before we left for the airport. The one he said was only a precaution and not to worry. But I hadn't stopped worrying since I got it.

I looked down at the pill in my palm, and a lump rose in my throat. The thought of spending three weeks with Viv in Italy and Paris overwhelmed me. Yes, I was qualified to be her art guide, but not her caretaker. Taking care of myself was hard enough.

For one irrational moment, I wanted to tell Viv everything— everything about my marriage, my mother, and my shattered heart. I wanted her to understand how emotionally vulnerable I felt. But I barely knew her. She was my employer, and I couldn't risk coming off like a basket case. I needed to lock those negative feelings away and stay positive. I excelled at that.

Slipping the pill into my pocket, I noticed that my cuticles were raw from my nervous picking. How did I get here?

Things were different before. I wasn't a basket case. I'd led a normal life. A few ups and downs and danger zones to avoid, but I'd learned to navigate them well. At least until my fourteenth wedding anniversary, a year and a half ago. That marked the start of a maelstrom I'd been caught in ever since. Every time I thought I could escape, it scooped me up again.

"Isn't this place cute? *The Beachfront Bugle* calls Café Piccolo the

best up-and-coming restaurant in town. And it's so close to our house."
I surveyed the garden terrace with its trickling fountain and candlelit
tables, hoping Kurt would approve.

"Sure, it's fine," he said, eyeing the menu. His smooth, angular
face looked like carved marble in the shadowy light.

"You don't think it's going to be too cold, do you? I could have
made reservations inside, but I thought outside would be more
romantic."

"It's fine, Claire."

I handed him an envelope. "Happy anniversary."

He looked up, surprised. "Should I open it now?"

"Of course, open it," I said, bouncing in my chair with excitement.

Kurt opened the envelope slowly as if to tease me. I couldn't wait.
"It's tickets—one for the PGA Championship Tournament and one for
your flight." I beamed at him. I never knew what to get for Kurt. He
had such specific tastes. But this time I knew I'd bought the ideal gift.

"Wow, thanks, Button. This is so thoughtful." He slid the tickets
back in the envelope and reached across the table to pat my hand. "But
you know, if everything goes the way I'm hoping, we won't be living
here in August."

"What?"

"Not to worry, though. We'll just need to change the plane ticket,
that's all."

"What do you mean we won't be living here?"

"Well"—he looked pleased with himself—"I hesitated to say
anything before, but things are going so well with my sporting goods
store right now, I think it's safe to say we could be living in Dubois by
August. Happy anniversary!"

My heart sank. I knew this could happen, but I never thought it
would. I should have objected to a business in Wyoming the minute he
brought it up. But he was so excited. And I didn't want to burst his
bubble. Didn't want to make waves, either. It was easier to hope this
pipe dream would dissolve on its own than to contradict Kurt.

"Wow. That's . . . quite a surprise." I could feel my hands begin to fidget. "I don't know what to say."

"Well, you could start with 'congratulations.'"

"Yes, of course, congratulations, but"—I swallowed—"I don't want to move to Wyoming. We're established here."

For the first years of our marriage, I had followed Kurt wherever his employment took him and never objected. I liked the excitement of moving and enjoyed my new role as a supportive wife—something I knew he needed. Kurt's work was hard on him, or perhaps I should say Kurt was hard on himself. My mission was to bolster his spirits and show him his worth—something his parents never did. I felt sure with enough love, he would blossom.

I wanted only two things in life besides Kurt—my own career and a family. Given our gypsy lifestyle, I put my vocation on hold and focused on a baby. But now that we'd settled down—or so I thought—it was time to pursue my profession.

Kurt stared at the envelope on the table, creasing its flap with origami precision. His lips pressed tightly together like the folds in the paper. His grimace alone should have warned me— now was not the time to plead my case. But he'd caught me off guard, and I couldn't stop myself.

"What about my job? You know how hard it was for me to get that tenure track position at the college. If we leave, I'll have to start all over again. And there's no guarantee I'd even find a job in Wyoming. Art history professors are not exactly in demand." My voice cracked as it rose to a higher pitch. "This is a problem for me. We need to talk about this. Please."

"There's nothing to talk about, Claire. You've pulled this stunt way too many times—acting like everything's fine until all of a sudden, it's not. I can't read your mind. You know full well how much this means to me, and you never said a thing about wanting to stay here until now. And now is too late. But you are right about one thing. This *is* your problem." He stood up, aligning the carefully crimped envelope with the table edge. "So you're going to have to figure this one out on your own."

I watched him walk out of the restaurant with the slow, deliberate steps he took when trying to control his anger. My stomach tightened into a familiar knot. But maybe he had a right to be mad. I'd never objected to moving before, so how was he supposed to know what I felt about Wyoming if I never told him? Did I always do that—pretend things were fine when they weren't? Did I really expect him to read my mind, or did I simply want him to be sensitive to my needs? And was that the same thing?

As I lingered in the restaurant, my thoughts kept going in circles. And even though sitting alone at our table for two made me feel self-conscious, I didn't want to leave—not then for home and never to live in Wyoming. There had to be another option.

But the only alternative I could come up with was to live apart and travel back and forth to see each other. I'd heard that kind of arrangement could be exciting and even rekindle the romance in a marriage. But I knew Kurt would never go for it. Keeping two households would be too expensive, traveling back and forth would take too much effort, and he'd never let me out of his sight for that long. So I tried to be more open to the idea of moving. But the more I thought about it, the more resolute I became about staying put. I had waited so long and worked so hard to get where I was in my job, I could not—would not—throw it all away now.

When I told my colleague and best friend, Mara Bellamy, about my dilemma, she suggested I go to therapy. She'd gone to see a psychologist when her marriage fell apart, and she said he was a tremendous help. I balked at the idea. My marriage wasn't falling apart, and I certainly didn't need a therapist. I needed options. But after days of getting the silent treatment from Kurt, nights with no sleep, and no solution in sight, I asked Mara for her therapist's name. She was thrilled to be able to help and said I would love Dr. Alexander McPherson.

I told Kurt my plan and he seemed relieved that I was dealing with the situation by going to see a shrink. I guess he thought that took the pressure off of him to talk about it. I, though, felt wary. I had no idea what to expect from therapy, but since I'd hit a wall with Kurt, I decided I had nothing to lose.

※

Waiting to be called into the doctor's inner office, I flipped through his magazines and began to doubt the wisdom of being there. What could a shrink possibly do to solve my problem? I threw the magazines back on the table and got up to stretch.

Moving always helped me think. Maybe the doctor could give me strategies to get Kurt to talk. That alone would make the visit worthwhile. I smirked, recalling Mara's comment about Kurt's communication skills. Talking to Kurt, she said, made her feel like a courtroom lawyer cross-examining an unwilling witness.

"Come in," Dr. McPherson said. "May I call you by your first name?"

I nodded.

"Okay, great. Please sit down, Claire." He gestured toward the couch before sitting in the armchair facing it. I knew he intended for the arrangement to appear conversational, but it felt confrontational to me. It only lacked an interrogation lamp.

The cold leather couch sent a chill through my body on contact, and I crossed my arms over my chest. Scanning the room to avoid the doctor's eyes, I noticed a tall mahogany cabinet crammed with books, and a large window, its light softened by cream-colored sheers. A small ink drawing beside the window depicted a man and woman reclining together in a loving embrace while being transported over a village by a winged horse. I recognized the artist as Chagall.

"Tell me why you're here, Claire."

Although I'd agreed that Dr. McPherson could use my first name, it annoyed me when he did. It seemed phony, like now we were pals and I should have felt comfortable divulging all. But I didn't. I felt manipulated.

"Is that a Chagall?" I asked.

"Yes, it is. Do you like it?"

"Yes, a lot." I got up for a closer look, an unusually bold move on my part, but it was meant to signal that I was calling the shots, not him.

Unlike the images in most doctors' offices, this drawing was an original. A nice personal and revealing touch. The good doctor appeared to be a romantic. But looking at it longer, I came up with a different perspective. Maybe the work's true purpose was to send subliminal vibes to the couples he counseled.

I returned to the couch and considered the doctor. He looked nothing like Kurt. He seemed more like the sensitive type—slight of build; sweet, almost effeminate face; and disheveled blond hair, as if he ran his hands through it too often. He was nice-looking in an understated kind of way.

Soulful looking.

"I'm glad that piece pleases you," he said, undisturbed by my bid for control. "I take it as a good sign when my clients notice it. To me, the work is all about trust. The man and woman embrace, trusting themselves in each other's arms, but they make an even bigger leap of faith. They trust the horse to fly them safely where they want to go." He stopped for a moment to look at the drawing. "For counseling to work, there must be that kind of trust. My clients need to feel safe in my care. They have to believe that I can help them achieve their goals."

I knew it. The artwork functioned purely as a manipulative ploy.

"Do you feel safe enough with me, Claire, to tell me what you'd like to accomplish with therapy?"

I didn't, but I felt . . . something. Not safety or trust— something else—something I couldn't identify, but it compelled me to admit what I wanted to deny.

"My marriage is a mess, Dr. McPherson."

"I'm sorry to hear that," he said, his eyes filled with concern. "It sounds like you need couples counseling. And please, call me Alec."

"There's no way my husband will do counseling. Can't you work with just me?" I stopped short of using the doctor's first name—much too chummy.

"I can, but it won't be as effective if your goal is to improve your marriage. Have you asked your husband if he'll do counseling with you?"

"No, I already know he won't."

"Oh, that's too bad."

What did that mean? I thought. *Too bad Kurt wouldn't do counseling, or too bad I answered for him without asking first?* I pulled my skirt self-consciously over my knees.

"So, without your husband here, what are you hoping to gain from individual counseling?"

"I don't know . . . sanity, I guess." I gave a nervous laugh and picked at my fingers.

Dr. McPherson didn't smile. "Why do you say that?"

"I'm just kidding." Couldn't the man tell when someone was joking?

He still didn't smile. Instead, he slid his fingers across his lips, in a way that was both thoughtful and sensual, appearing in no hurry to say anything.

"I think I'm frustrated," I finally blurted out.

"Okay, then, let's talk about that. What's making you frustrated?"

I wanted to say *he* made me frustrated, but I held back. I was paying for this and decided I should at least try to get something out of it. "I'm frustrated with my husband. He won't talk to me."

"He won't talk to you at all, or just about certain topics?"

"No, he talks, some, but not about the elephant in the room. He wants to move to Wyoming, and I don't."

"Okay. What happens when you share your feelings with him about this move?"

"He told me it's a done deal, and I have to face it."

"How does that make you feel?"

"Frustrated, like I said."

"And what do you do with those frustrated feelings? How do you express them?"

"What do I do? Nothing. What can I do? He already said what he thinks, so there's nothing more for him to say, I guess. It's frustrating to me, sure, but I can see his point."

"What about your point, Claire? You have a point too."

"Yes, well, he doesn't think so."

"And how does that make you feel?"

"Like I said, frustrated. Are we going in circles here?" During the silence that followed, I twisted in my seat, suddenly unable to find a comfortable position, until his voice interrupted my squirming.

"Do you ever yell at him? Stomp your feet? Storm out?"

"No," I said with indignation, wondering what kind of unhinged neurotic he took me for.

"Do you pout or withhold affection?"

"Well, I guess I pout, but so does he." No way would I admit to withholding affection. "I'm not sure where you're going with this, Dr. McPherson."

He looked at me with the softest eyes I'd ever seen on a man. "You say you feel frustrated, but from your responses, it sounds like you're intellectualizing your feelings rather than allowing yourself to feel them." He rubbed his lips again. "How often do you get angry, Claire?"

I bristled at the question. "Anger is a waste of energy, a totally nonproductive emotion. It just makes people do crazy things."

I cast my eyes to the floor, far from his gaze. What was I doing there?

"I'm not going back to that guy," I told Kurt when he came home from work that evening.

"What guy?" "The shrink."

"Not a good fit, huh? Well, there are lots of therapists out there. I'm sure you'll find one that works."

"Yes, I suppose." I dragged my feet into the kitchen to start dinner. Cooking had never been my strong suit, even on a good day.

I scanned the contents of the pantry, refrigerator, and freezer. Nothing inspired me. I could have fixed macaroni and cheese—our favorite family comfort food—but even that left me feeling cold.

As a last resort, I pulled out the only cookbook I owned, *The Joy of Cooking,* and flipped through the pages for a recipe. But instead of seeing words, I saw Dr. McPherson's soft blue eyes and his fingers gliding lightly across his lips.

~For lovers of art and travelers at heart~

It's the 1980s, and art historian Claire Markham reels from a series of heartbreaking losses. Desperate to escape her shattered reality, she becomes an art guide in Europe for quirky stranger Viv Chancey and embarks on a life-changing journey through the art-filled cities of Milan, Venice, Ravenna, Florence, Siena, Rome, and Paris.

But when Claire's woes follow her abroad, she must learn from the spirit of her eccentric companion and the lessons from the artworks they encounter to take charge of her life or lose the most precious thing in it.

The Art of Traveling Strangers is a journey of self- discovery and personal empowerment inspired by the great art masterpieces of Italy and Paris. It's a tale of female bonding and the amazing powers of perception. After all, reality, like art, is just an illusion.

Zoe Disigny holds a master's degree in art history and taught college courses for thirty years. She also worked as an art gallery director, a lecturer for The Norton Simon Museum of Art, and most recently, as a lecturer for Road Scholar, an educational travel organization for adults.

Zoe has led numerous art tours in Europe and, at one point, established a business in Paris offering art history adventures for American tourists.

You may contact Zoe by emailing zoe@zoedisigny.com or going to her website: zoedisigny.com.

Five Will Die

Trace Conger

Chapter 1

"Get over here right now and see what those Richardson boys done to my barn!"

Sheriff Tim Burke jerked the receiver away from his ear to save his hearing. He waited for Walt Tanner to stop talking before he pressed it back against the side of his face.

"Why don't you just tell me over the phone, Walt? It's too damn hot to be trekking out there."

"No. You have to come out here and see what they done. Those kids spray-painted the whole side of the barn. There's curse words and a Nazi swastika and everything. Vulgar stuff. I think that's a hate crime."

"How do you know it was the Richardson boys? Did you see them?"

Walt paused. "No. I guess I didn't see them. They done it in the middle of the night, Sheriff. Saw it today when I went out to fix that busted beam. I want you to round 'em up. I want to press charges."

"I think we're getting ahead of ourselves, Walt. Give me a bit and I'll head out and have a look."

"You better be quick, Sheriff. I'm steaming mad. Steaming mad!"

"I get that impression. I'll be out as soon as I can." Burke hung up the phone and tugged on his earlobe, hoping Walt hadn't done any permanent damage to his eardrum. He sighed, willed himself out of his chair, and headed for the coatrack next to the front door. The last thing Burke wanted to do was leave his air-conditioned office for Walt Tanner's farm. It was late June, and Lincoln, Ohio, was damn hot. The kind of hot that dominated the local newscast and gave the weathermen more screen time than they needed.

Collecting his tan hat, he placed it neatly upon his head, ran his thumb and index finger across the crisp brim, and walked into the office kitchen, where Deputy Corey Poteet was pouring a cup of coffee.

"What does Walt Tanner want now?" asked Corey.

"You heard him all the way in here?"

Corey nodded. "Likely could hear him from out back too. In the squad car with the radio cranked up."

"He said someone vandalized his barn last night. Thinks it's the Richardson boys."

"Probably was," said Corey between sips. "Those kids are all trouble. People call them the Dirty Dozen. Course, that's not so accurate on account there's only six of them, but they got the dirty part right."

Burke refilled his coffee mug and slipped the glass pot back onto the warmer.

"You going to knock some sense into those boys?" asked Corey.

"Might want to make sure it's them first."

"It's them, Sheriff."

"Yeah, I reckon you're right."

Burke left the Sheriff's Office. He walked down Broadway past Dalt's Ice Cream Parlor and the city building to the small parking lot on the corner of Broadway and Main. His aging white Ford Explorer rested in front of the sign Mayor Brewster erected last year. Reserved for Sheriff Tim Burke.

Burke always left the Explorer unlocked. It was a habit he'd developed while working with the Cleveland PD years earlier. Unlocked cars were easier to get into quickly, and if you were responding to a violent situation, which in Cleveland was an everyday occurrence, fumbling to get your key into the car door could mean the difference between life and death.

Such stakes weren't so common in Lincoln. Aside from the occasional barn vandalism, it was a quiet town. Quiet enough for a sheriff and two deputies to have a lot of free time. Still, old habits die hard.

He grabbed the door handle but quickly pulled his stinging hand back, shaking off the burn. Lincoln was in the middle of a heatwave, had been for weeks, and metal door handles didn't play nice with the high-noon sun. He tried again, this time using a single finger to open the door.

Burke knocked the Explorer into reverse and backed out of his parking spot, careful not to ding the mayor's red convertible, which was parked a little too close to his passenger side. A moment later, he was encouraging the AC to do its job while he drove west on St. Rt. 63.

Walt Tanner's farm was perched atop a hill two miles west of downtown Lincoln. Burke turned off 63 and crawled up the winding road to the white farmhouse. After stepping out of the Explorer, Burke took a moment to take in the horizon. A hazy mist hung over the town like a visiting relative who wouldn't leave. It wasn't the first time he'd been to Walt's place, but it was the first time he'd taken the time to savor the view. He looked down, noticing the shops on Broadway, the Sheriff's Office, the primary and elementary school campuses, and the new high school they had just completed north of town. The Presbyterian church's steeple stood tall in the distance, dwarfed only by the water tower on the east side of town.

Burke retrieved his hat from the passenger seat and closed the driver's door to seal in what little cool air the AC had delivered. When he turned, he saw Walt running at him faster than any eighty-year-old should. The old man waved wildly the entire way, as if shooing away a bothersome horsefly.

"Sheriff, I've been wait'n for you."

Burke slipped his hat on, took a deep breath, and walked toward the charging farmer.

"Why don't you show me the barn, Walt?"

"You gonna go arrest those boys? I want to press charges."

"Let me take a look at what happened first."

Walt looked unsettled. "Alright. It's this way."

Burke followed him to a white barn on the back of the property. Six twelve-foot two-by-fours propped under the eaves supported the leaning structure, keeping it upright. The barn was on the losing end of a decades-long war with the weather, and Burke thought the next strong wind could deliver its death knell.

"It's on this side here," said Walt, pointing.

Burke followed him around the side, careful not to trip over the wooden supports.

"See?" He jabbed his finger in the air. "That's what those lil bastards did."

Burke crossed his arms and examined the barn. The side was maybe twenty-feet long, but the graffiti only covered an area six-feet long by five-feet high. There was what looked like a crude cow spray-painted in yellow and various obscenities scrawled in black. Less than half of them were spelled correctly. In the center of it all was a large red swastika. To the right of that, in large misshapen letters, was a name. Bucky.

"You Jewish, Walt?"

"No. What does that matter?"

"Just wondering. On account of the graffiti."

"Do I have to be Jewish for it to be a hate crime? It's hateful either way."

Burke shrugged, wiped the sweat from his forehead with his arm, then snapped a few photos with his cell phone.

"I don't think anyone hates you, Walt. I just think your farm is conveniently located, that's all."

"You know there's twelve of them boys. The Dirty Dozen, they call 'em. Like the Lee Marvin movie."

"There's only six of them."

"That's still too many if you ask me. Nuth'n but trouble."

"That's enough."

"You gonna go over there to talk to them?" Burke nodded.

"I'm come'n with you."

"You'll do no such thing, Walt." He wiped his forehead again. "No, you're going to go down to Hader Hardware." Burke pulled his wallet from his back pocket, slipped out a twenty, and handed it to Walt. "Pick up a gallon of white paint."

"I want them to pay for it," said Walt, staring at the bill. "I doubt those kids are eating three squares a day. You know their father can't afford any paint."

"Still, no reason you should pay for it."

"You want the barn repainted or not?"

Walt nodded and took the bill. "Yes, but I don't want you out any money."

"Don't worry about that." Burke eyeballed the wall again and then plucked another twenty from his wallet and handed it to Walt. "Pick up a few rollers and paint trays too. If that's not enough, tell Jack to put in on my tab and I'll settle up with him later."

"It ain't right that this is come'n out of your pocket, Sheriff."

"It'll all even out in the end. Gather up the supplies and leave them inside the barn. I'll have those boys come up tomorrow or the next day and repaint it." Burke pressed his palm against the side of the barn. "How stable is this thing?"

"It's fine."

"Those two-by-fours say otherwise."

"It's fine. Why?"

"Because I don't need this thing collapsing on top of those kids when they're painting over this crap."

"It'll hold."

"All right. I'll go talk to them. Pick up those supplies and leave them in the barn. And don't come out and cause a ruckus when you see them painting. I'm not saying what they did wasn't wrong, but just let them make it right. I don't want anything to escalate."

"Fine. But how do you know they'll show up?"

"They'll show up, Walt."

Burke left Walt at the decaying barn and went back to his Explorer. He drove toward town, turning off St. Rt. 63 and onto 99. A quarter mile later, he was parked in front of the Richardson home.

The Richardson homestead sat alone in what remained of the Haven Mobile Home Park. The park closed a decade ago and all of the other residents up and left. Any house trailers that couldn't be moved on account of not being roadworthy were demolished. The Richardsons were the only family that didn't have a house trailer. They lived in a manufactured home, which was the size of a house trailer but had no way to be relocated outside of hoisting it onto the back of a flatbed and driving it out of town. After Haven closed, the city brokered a deal with Dan Richardson, the family patriarch, allowing him to purchase the parcel of land below the sixty-foot by thirty-foot home. The mortgage terms were loose, allowing Dan to pay when he could, and Burke wondered if anyone was really keeping track of the payments.

The home itself was falling apart, but Dan kept up repairs as best as he could. It was a losing battle. Most of the home's vinyl siding was missing, exposing long strips of housewrap. Two of the four front windows were broken, but only one was taped up with silver duct tape. Several shingles had been blown off the roof and there was a toppled television antenna in the side yard. Dan's red pickup truck wasn't there.

Burke had been to the home once before. Six months ago, he responded to a call when Brenda, Dan's wife, went after him with a baseball bat. By the time Burke got there, Brenda had up and left town, and as far as anyone knew, she'd never been back. Burke had helped patch up Dan's forearm, which had taken the brunt of his wife's fury. It could have been much worse.

Burke parked on the side of the street and walked toward the home. There was no grass, and it was hard to determine where the dirt road ended and the front yard began. He walked up the rotting wooden front steps and noted the pile of tangled bicycles on the right and the four spray paint cans on the left. He knocked on the door.

One of the Richardson boys cracked open the door, and a rush of cold air hit Burke. One by one, more children gathered around each other and stared at Burke. They looked him up and down but seemed most interested in his sidearm, which was eye level to them.

Burke looked at the boy who had opened the door and asked his name.

"Raymond," he said quietly.

A shirtless boy pulled Raymond out of the way and pressed his face against the screen door. He looked to be around fifteen.

"Whatchu want?" said the shirtless boy. "Pop ain't here."

"I see that," said Burke. "What's your name, son?"

"Buck."

"Well, Buck, I'm Sheriff Burke." He reached out his hand. "Nice to meet you."

Buck hesitated, but after a moment, he opened the screen door and reached out his hand.

As Burke shook the young boy's hand, he turned his wrist, revealing yellow paint on three of his fingers.

"You the oldest one home?"

"Yep."

Burke released his grip. "Can you step outside for a moment? I'd like to talk to you."

"I don't think my dad would want me talking to you."

"He still working at the bus garage?"

"Yep."

"Well, I can drive over there and get him and then we can all have a chat about Walt Tanner's barn, or you can step out here, and we can talk about it man-to-man, just the two of us."

The boy thought for a moment, stepped through the door, and sat on the wooden steps. The rest of the boys watched from inside until Buck grunted, then they closed the door.

"I suspect you know why I'm here," said Burke, looking at the boy's legs, which were caked in dried dirt.

The boy hung his head. "I think so."

"Why did you tag the barn?"

He shrugged. "We found the paint in the shed out back and Scott dared me to do it."

"How many of you went up there?"

"Just me, Scott and Danny Jr."

"You know, Walt's pretty upset about the barn. Wants me to toss all you boys in jail and throw away the key." Burke knelt down in front of the boy. "But, I'd rather not do that. I'd prefer to keep that space available for people who really deserve it."

"Are you going to tell Pop?"

"Your pop work tomorrow?"

"Yes. Goes to the garage from lunch to dinner."

"Okay. I'll make you a deal. Tomorrow, after your pop goes to work, you go back up there to Walt's farm and repaint that barn. You'll find the paint and supplies inside. You know how to use a paint roller?"

"Yes."

"Good. Paint the whole side of the barn that you tagged. Two coats. With three of you, it won't take but an hour. Get more of your brothers to help and you'll make even quicker work of it."

"And you won't say anything to Pop?"

"You do a good job on that barn and I'll keep this between us. Deal?"

"Deal, Sheriff."

"After tomorrow, I don't want to hear about you ever going back up there. Let's just chalk this up to a stupid mistake that you're not

232

going to make again."

Buck nodded but didn't say anything. Satisfied, Burke returned to the Explorer aching for the AC. He felt Buck's eyes on him the entire way.

Corey was pouring water into the coffeemaker, preparing to brew another pot, when Burke returned to the office. Burke looked at his massive hands wrapped around the handle of the glass decanter. Corey Poteet's hands seemed too big for his body, but Burke couldn't decide if they were too large or his forearms were too thin. The proportion just seemed off. Corey had no other peculiar features, except for a grin that often invited a punch.

"You get to the bottom of Walt Tanner's fiasco?" asked Corey, placing the pot under the drip basket.

"I think all is right in the world. For now, anyway."

Corey raised his meat hooks in the air like a Baptist preacher. "And peace is restored once more in Lincoln." He returned to his desk, where a Post-it note stuck to the telephone's receiver jogged his memory. Corey snatched the note and leaned back in his chair. "Boss, your wife called. Said not to forget the wine for tonight."

"Got it."

"You throwing a big party or something?"

Burke thought about how to answer. "No, just the two us."

At four o'clock, Burke stepped out of the office and crossed Broadway. He passed the Ram's Head Inn, the city's historic hotel and restaurant, and Lincoln's biggest claim to fame. Most people in southern Ohio had heard of the Ram's Head, even if they hadn't heard of Lincoln. A hulking brass plaque listing all the famous people who had stayed there over the years hung next to the inn's front door. At last count, it was twelve US presidents, as many dignitaries and statesmen, and a half dozen famous authors, including Mark Twain and Charles Dickens.

The idea of so many famous people calling Lincoln home for a night always made Burke laugh given the small town lacked everything except charm. But back in the day, when people traveled by horse or coach, Lincoln's central location between Cincinnati and Dayton made it the perfect stopover.

Next to the Ram's Head was Lot 7, the town coffee shop.

Lot 7 got its name from its physical location. The land it occupied was the city's seventh plot, laid out back in 1802. As far as Burke knew, no presidents, authors, or other people worth namedropping ever set foot inside the place. They did have the best coffee in town, though. They also had a policy for arming the local sheriff and his two deputies with free coffee whenever they wanted. Of course, it didn't hurt that Burke and his wife, Gwen, owned the place.

Gwen, a former nurse, had always dreamed of opening a shop of some kind when she retired. She realized coffee would be a hot commodity when the Burkes moved to Lincoln two years ago from Cleveland and couldn't find a decent cup of coffee outside their kitchen. Having fond memories of spending time in their neighborhood coffee shop up north, they looked into what it would take to hang out their own percolated shingle. They only needed to look at one vacant property, an abandoned building that used to be a book store, to find the one they wanted. The place was in good shape for being as old as it was. It needed some work here and there, but the bones were good. "Character" was the term Gwen used.

They signed the lease and hired a contractor, and four months later, they poured their first cup of coffee for Mayor Anne Brewster at the ribbon cutting.

Gwen would usually be working the counter on Friday afternoon, but she only worked a half-day today. She'd left early for the same reason Burke did.

Burke glanced through Lot 7's large front window, as was his habit, and waved. Amanda Marie, the shop's only other employee, waved back. He walked another two blocks before arriving at the King

Kwik convenience store.

Opening the door, he ducked to avoid the low-hanging bell that danced over his head. Joyce Riggins was restocking a rack of donuts.

"Hello, Sheriff." She held up a glazed donut. "Cop vitamin?"

Burke laughed. "Not today, thanks. Just here for alcohol."

"Been one of those days, has it?"

"No, celebrating a birthday at home. Nothing too fancy."

"Ah-ha. Your birthday?"

"No." Burke didn't elaborate.

Joyce climbed down from the wooden stool. "We've got a few different types." She pointed to the back of the store. "I don't claim to be a wine expert, but if you have any questions, I can try my best to answer them."

"We're not picky." Burke walked toward the back. "I usually just buy it based on the label."

"Me too." Joyce smacked the top of the stool. "I usually buy the one with the most clever name."

Burke picked up two bottles, one red and one white. "Looks like a party to me," said Joyce, ringing up the sale.

He smiled. "I stopped partying when I turned fifty." Burke winked, paid the tab, took the brown paper bag, and walked back to the town parking lot to retrieve his Explorer.

When Burke arrived home, he found Gwen hanging a HAPPY BIRTHDAY banner. She brushed a handful of silver hair out of her face as she struggled to tape the end of the banner above the fireplace. Burke set the paper bag on the dining room table and double-timed it over to lend a helpful finger. Gwen taped off the final corner of the banner and stepped back to admire her handiwork.

"I think we do less every year," she said. "A few years ago, and this place would have been filled with balloons and streamers."

"The thought is still there," said Burke.

"I know, I just feel like we're letting her down."

"Nonsense." He wrapped his arms around her and squeezed. "She'd love it."

When he broke the embrace, Gwen stepped into the kitchen and Burke unpacked the two bottles of wine.

An hour later, Gwen emerged from the kitchen with a steaming pepperoni and pineapple pizza on a round, wooden cutting board. The end of her long, maroon skirt, which was dusted with flour, swept the hardwood floor as she walked.

Gwen was almost as tall as Burke, but much thinner. Her shoulder-length gray hair just touched the shoulders of her white, short-sleeved T-shirt. She looked tired, but not the kind of tired from working a half-day or making a pizza from scratch. She looked as though she hadn't slept, even though Burke knew she had. It was the kind of look that came with a tragedy you didn't want to forget but wish you didn't have to remember. Burke imagined he looked the same way. They both drew in a deep breath and forced a smile.

Burke poured a glass of red wine for Gwen and a glass of white for himself and they sat across from each other staring at the pizza in front of them.

"How in the hell did Kristen ever come up with this combination?" said Burke. "Pepperoni and pineapple? It should be illegal."

Gwen shrugged. "As far as favorite meals go, I can't see too many people picking this, but then again, she was one of a kind."

"I'll drink to that," said Burke holding up his glass. "One of a kind."

They clinked glasses.

"Happy birthday, kiddo," said Burke to the room. Gwen smiled and began the cut the pizza.

After dinner, Burke and Gwen made their way to the living room, where they shared stories and memories of their daughter, Kristen. There were laughs, tears, and the occasional regret, but they both went to bed with a smile, just as they had done for the past twelve years.

These are the first two chapters of my forthcoming thriller, FIVE WILL DIE. The novel is about a serial killer stalking a sleepy Ohio town.

I've always been fascinated by serial killers, especially those who taunt the police throughout an investigation. FIVE WILL DIE explores what I thought was an exciting idea. What if a serial killer contacted the police BEFORE he began his spree? How would a small-town police force respond?

Especially when the most pressing crime they've faced was finding who vandalized Walt Tanner's barn.

Toss in a local sheriff who is dealing with a panic disorder, a result of the violence he witnessed as part of Cleveland's Homicide Division, and I think you've got a recipe for a good story.

Trace Conger is a Shamus award-winning author in the crime, thriller, and suspense genres. He writes the Connor Harding (Thriller) series and the Mr. Finn (PI) series.

His Connor Harding series follows freelance "Mirage Man" Connor Harding as he solves problems for the world's most dangerous criminals. The Mr. Finn series follows private investigator Finn Harding as he straddles the fine line between right and wrong.

He is known for his tight writing style, dark themes, and subtle humor. Trace lives in Cincinnati with his wonderfully supportive family. Visit him online at www.traceconger.com.

Hepburn's Necklace

Jan Moran

Rome, 1952

Niccolò held out his hand to her. Tentatively, Ruby rested her fingers in the fold of his palm, setting off the sizzle that coursed through her every time she touched him. Instead of giving their *lire* to street vendors for hot paninis made from the finest thin-sliced prosciutto, the freshest tomatoes and basil, and the creamiest mozzarella and then nursing small, strong espressos at a café where they could sit for hours and watch people, he'd suggested a surprise.

"Do you trust me?" Niccolò's vivid blue eyes sparkled with mischief, and his subtle, melodic accent mesmerized her.

For some reason she couldn't fathom, Ruby nodded. "Where are you taking me?"

Shifting the cloth bag he had thrown over his shoulder, Niccolò grinned. "I want to show you the very best performance in all of Rome. Maybe the best you'll ever see."

Ruby glanced down at her clothes. She wore a simple cotton seersucker dress she'd made before she left Texas. "I hope it's nothing fancy."

"It's very fancy," he said, guiding her in the direction of trailers that were being used for various filming needs. "But I have a plan. Come on."

They'd finished the first week of filming, which had commenced with the opening reception scene shot at the baroque Palazzo Brancaccio filled with Italian nobles in their gowns and jewels who'd answered a casting call for *Roman Holiday*. They were just as intrigued by the Hollywood film as the ordinary people who lined the streets during filming.

Now, much of the cast had dispersed to explore the city on their day off. She'd heard Audrey Hepburn mention that her mother, Baroness Ella, had made reservations for high tea at Babington's, an English tea house near the exclusive Hassler hotel where Miss Hepburn was staying. Others, including the director, might be watching dailies or sipping a Bellini or Negroni on Via Veneto, a fashionable street filled with cafés.

Ruby had heard about the Italian cocktails and wondered what they tasted like, but she'd promised her parents not to drink alcohol and to watch herself around boys. Once this week, she'd settled for a chilled latte macchiato and had felt very grown-up, indeed.

Wine didn't count, she'd decided after a few days in Rome. Even kids her age sipped red wine as they ate lasagna or ravioli or other pasta she could hardly pronounce. And she was supposed to be eighteen, so she had to act the part. *A part within a part*, she mused, making herself laugh.

Holding his fingers to his lips, Niccolò led her into the costume trailer. He tapped on the door. "David, it's me. Niccolò."

The door swung open, and the sound of jazz music wafted out. Niccolò handed his bag to a young male assistant to the wardrobe supervisor.

"Amaretto and limoncello," Niccolò said. "Very fine."

"Excellent. You surprise me," David said in a Midwestern drawl. He looked inside the bag and then motioned them in. "You can borrow

240

most anything but items reserved for Miss Hepburn, Mr. Peck, or Mr. Arnold. And don't spill anything on the clothes. Niccolò, I have your suit ready over there."

"I don't know where to start," Ruby said, gazing at the racks of costumes.

David swung his attention toward Ruby and stroked his chin. " You're about the same size as Miss Hepburn. I know just what will suit you."

Niccolò laughed. "David wants to be a fashion designer like Coco Chanel."

"More like Elsa Schiaparelli," David said, smirking with glee as he flipped a silver high heel and balanced it on his head like a hat. "Elsa created a shoe *chapeau* in collaboration with Salvador Dali in 1937. Darling, it was all the rage in the pages of *Vogue*."

Ruby giggled. She'd never met anyone quite like David, but he was fun. Another assistant had fitted her costume when she'd reported to work, but David had retied her scarf just so.

He pointed Niccolò toward the rear of the trailer. "Now, off with you while I work with your girlfriend."

"Oh, no," Ruby said, feeling herself blush. "I'm not his girlfriend." Although, as she said the word, she felt flutters in her chest. Ruby had never had a proper boyfriend, but if Niccolò asked her, she would consider being his girlfriend.

David smiled. "The night's still young, my dear. I'll be right back."

Ruby stopped in front of the costumes reserved for Miss Hepburn, whose cotton shirts and full skirts were similar to Ruby's. But the regal outfits for the Princess Ann character were extraordinary. Hanging before Ruby was a lace dress with full sleeves that looked as sweet and delicate as the spun sugar she'd once had at a fair.

Ruby caught her breath at the ballgown displayed on a dressmaker's form. The dress was spectacular, which wasn't a word she'd used much on the farm. The off-the-shoulder gown of silver brocade had a narrow bodice and an impossibly full skirt. Even without accessories, it was regal and awe-inspiring.

"Magical," she whispered, daring to touch the fabric. Ruby could sew, but she'd never seen such beautiful material. The craftsmanship was exquisite. She inspected tiny stitches rendered as her mother had shown her, though her work would never be that fine. As long as she could sew, she wouldn't starve in Los Angeles, but neither would she ever have what she craved.

David returned, carrying a sleeveless aquamarine dress with a boatneck neckline and a full skirt. "How about this?"

"Oh, I couldn't," she replied, although it was a stunning dress. She ran her fingers down the fabric, which was so fine it was almost iridescent. A petticoat filled out the skirt, emphasizing the tiny waist.

"Pure Italian silk, made in Como," David said. "Try it on. For me."

Ruby twirled her finger. "Turn around, please." She unbuttoned her shirt and slid the dress over her head before taking off her skirt. She eased the dress over her slip. "Okay, you can look."

When David turned around, his mouth opened in surprise. "Oh, mercy me. You're an absolute star!" He finished zipping the dress. "We'll add pearls, *faux*, of course, and flat silver sandals. Mind if I style your hair, my pet? I've never seen that exquisite shade before." He lowered his voice to a whisper. "Is it natural?"

"Since I was a little girl." Ruby giggled. "Where are you from?"

"Omaha," David replied with a drawl.

"You're funny," she said. She'd never met anyone like David, who was so fashionable and fun. "Is everyone from Omaha like you?" She had no idea where that was, but it sounded exotic.

"Darling, no one from Omaha is like me. That's why I high-tailed it to California. Even so, I was nervous about showing my costume portfolio to Miss Head, but she hired me right away after seeing it."

"Aren't you nervous that you could be fired for this?" Ruby whispered. Edith Head had designed costumes for all the stars, and she'd won more awards than any other costume designer. She wouldn't stand for a transgression like this.

"She's far away in Hollywood. If you ain't telling, neither am I." David winked at her. "What drove you to Tinseltown?"

"I love the movies," Ruby said, smiling at the glittering term for the film industry. "You get to pretend you're someone else. And get paid for it." She dropped her voice to a whisper. "A lot, if you're good. My family could sure use the money, so I'm going to learn everything there is to know about acting."

She caught a glimpse of her transformation in the mirror. The icy blue color contrasted beautifully with her dark red hair.

"Stay right there," David said. After turning up the dial on a record player in the corner that was spinning a black-and-gold 78-rpm record, he scooped up a hairbrush and a makeup bag. "Mmm, that's my desire," he sang along. "Can you believe I found a Louis Armstrong record in a shop here?"

"I've heard him on the radio," Ruby said, excited.

Although her father seldom let her tune the dial to anything but country and western stations.

David snapped his fingers to the music. "That's jazz, baby. Satchmo—that's his nickname—tours often in Italy, so folks here know his music." David's eyes brightened. "He made a film right here in Rome, *Botta e Risposta*, which means, 'I'm in the revue.' It's a screwball comedy, and this song is from that. It's called *You're My Desire*. And you should hear the Italian jazz. Wow." He fanned his face.

Ruby laughed, but soon she was tapping her toe to the music. As she stood still, David brushed her hair from her face and secured it with a pair of rhinestone combs. Using a fine cosmetic brush, he dabbed red lipstick on her lips, and then he stepped back, admiring his work.

"I need to record this for my portfolio," he said. "Hold still."

David angled a bright light toward her, which threw a long shadow. He adjusted the lens on a complicated looking camera. "Don't smile," he said. "Look just over my shoulder."

As she did, Niccolò sauntered out, snapping his fingers to the music. He wore a dark, slim-cut suit that made him look much older. Her heart quickened, and her lips parted in awe.

"That's it," David exclaimed.

A flash popped in her eyes, momentarily blinding her.

Niccolò knelt beside her and clasped her hand. "Do you know how beautiful you are?" His voice was thick with emotion.

"And you, too," Ruby managed to say.

"Dress-up time is over," David said, clapping his hands. "Bring these clothes back by tomorrow afternoon. Four o'clock sharp. No earlier. I have a date with a hangover."

Ruby and Niccolò raced out the door, laughing and hugging each other.

On the way, Niccolò bought a snack from a street vendor of *arancini*, delicious little fried balls of rice, cheese, and peas that Ruby ate with care so as not to smudge her lipstick. As they sat in a square with napkins draped over their finery, the setting sun cast its gossamer glow over them. So far, the evening had been magical. One that Ruby knew she would hold tight and remember.

Afterward, they took a taxi past the Pantheon, the Roman Forum, and the Colosseum. Niccolò pointed out his favorite places. He'd lived here in Rome with his family, but he also spoke of Lago di Como in the north where his mother's family lived.

"How did your parents meet?" Ruby asked as they sat with their legs touching in the back of the cab. The warmth of his body next to hers was enthralling.

"My mother's father has vineyards in the north, and my other grandfather had an art gallery in Rome. One day my mother traveled with her father to deliver wine to a gallery, where my father was working. Wine and art—a good match, they always say."

She lifted her face to the warm breeze through the open window. "And is it, do you think?"

Niccolò laughed. "What a funny thing to ask. We have so much love in our family." He kissed her on the cheek.

Niccolò's simple kiss sent tingles clear down to Ruby's toes. Giggling, she returned the kiss on his cheek. The driver smiled at them in the rearview mirror as he slowed in front of their destination.

"This is Terme di Caracalla," Niccolò said, gesturing toward towering ruins. "That means Caracalla's bathhouse," he added, chuckling. "My mother loves opera."

Ruby stared out the window. "Opera?" "You've seen opera, yes?"

"No, but I can't wait." Beautifully dressed people milled about, laughing and kissing each other on the cheeks. *Ciao! Come stai?* She frowned. "Is it expensive to get in?"

Niccolò laughed. "I have a cousin." He paid the driver and took her hand, helping her slide across the bench seat in her dress.

As she slid from the car, she noticed a few people looking at her. Frowning, she pressed a hand to her chest and asked Niccolò, "Do I look okay? People are staring."

"That's because you are mesmerizing," he said, sliding his arm protectively around her.

Relieved, she raised her face to his. Niccolò pressed his cheek against hers, kissing her cheek and neck. Her heart was bursting with such emotion she'd never felt. *This is passion.* A warm feeling flooded her. The passion she'd seen portrayed on the screen was actually real.

Niccolò pulled away and cradled her face in his hands. "*Anima mia,*" he said in a husky voice. "My soul."

"*Anima mia,*" she repeated.

He laughed. "Not bad. I'll teach you Italian if you want to learn."

"Oh yes," she cried, completely lost in his embrace. And yet, she was found—by another soul so much like hers. She'd never dared hope he might exist, but here he was in her arms. She felt like the luckiest girl in the world and a million miles away from Texas.

He motioned toward the front of the crowd. "*Andiamo.*"

Clasping her hand, he led her through the crowd. "*Teatro dell'Opera* performs here in the summer. This year, they are performing *Aida*. You know *Aida,* yes?"

Ruby shook her head. She was hardly paying attention to anything but him and the passion she saw in his eyes, too.

"Wait until you see it and hear it." Niccolò touched his fingers to his lips. *"L'opera è magnifica.* Sensational. Maria Pedrini is performing, and she has the voice of an angel. If I ever have a daughter, I would name her Mariangela. It even sounds musical." He grinned. "Say it for me."

"Mariangela." Ruby laughed with him, but she loved what he was saying. And the name did flow off the tongue.

When they reached Niccolò's cousin, the man, who was a little older than Niccolò, nodded and waved them in with a smile.

"Now, we have to look for empty seats, but don't be too obvious about it," Niccolò said in a low, conspiratorial voice. "Act like we're looking for friends."

"I can do that," Ruby said, grinning.

They waited with nonchalance near a row that had open seats until the lights went down. Quickly, they scurried into the empty seats, stifling their laughter. But as soon as lights illuminated the stage, which was positioned between massive stone pillars, Ruby and Niccolò watched in rapturous awe.

Ruby loved everything about the opera—the music, the story, the performers, the costumes. The soaring passion of the performance reflected what she felt in her heart. Niccolò whispered a little about the story, but even without understanding a word, she comprehended the meaning deep within her being.

If given a chance, she vowed silently, she would bring these emotions to the stage and to film—in her way, of course, but she would be just as strong and memorable.

After the opera ended, the crowd erupted in applause and cheers. Ruby and Niccolò stood with everyone else, and Ruby was amazed at the outpouring of love.

As they made their way out, Niccolò snatched a program from a chair for her. *Aida, Giuseppe Verdi, 1870.* Taking a pen from his jacket, he drew hearts on a page before giving it to her. "For you to remember tonight."

"How could I ever forget it?"

They splurged again and took a taxi.

"Scalinata di Trinità dei Monti," Niccolò told the driver.

The Spanish Steps were near where Ruby was staying with the rest of the cast. Her pensione wasn't as fancy as the Hotel Hassler where the stars were staying, but she loved simply being in Rome and having a chance to be a part of the production.

At the base of the broad steps, they lingered in the Piazza di Spagna, perching on a low wall near a large sculpted fountain. The sound of rippling water muted nearby conversations and the breeze off the water cooled Ruby's bare arms.

Gazing at the fountain, Ruby recalled something she'd heard from a fellow cast member. "Baroque style, right?"

"You know art?" Niccolò smiled. "This is the Fontana della Barcaccia. Fountain of the boat."

Ruby regarded it with a finger to her chin. "Aptly named, seeing as how someone left their boat in the middle of the fountain."

Niccolò chuckled and drew close to her, lifting his arm around her shoulder. "You make me smile so much inside." He'd removed his jacket in the balmy night air.

Ruby shivered in his embrace with anticipation.

Sliding his fingers under her chin, he tilted her face and grazed her lips with his in question.

Responding, she kissed him back, softly but surely. This was her first kiss, here in Rome with a boy whose heart beat in rhythm with hers and whose eyes saw into her very soul. She would never forget this night. *"Anima mia,"* she whispered.

Hepburn's Necklace – From a USA Today Bestselling Author, A Dual Timeline Saga from the Film Set of Roman Holiday to Lake Como, Italy

A vintage necklace. A long-hidden secret. A second chance for love.

When costume designer Ariana Ricci leaves her groom at the altar, she seeks solace with her great-aunt, a Texas-born Hollywood legend who worked on the film Roman Holiday as an extra. There, Ariana discovers Audrey Hepburn gave Ruby Raines an intriguing necklace during filming, and a cache of 1950s letters, postmarked Italy, raises more questions about Ruby's hidden past.

Aching for a fresh start and the chance to resolve an unfinished story, the two embark on a journey to the sun- dappled shores of Lake Como, Italy that will illuminate secrets of a bygone era and offer second chances to each of them—if they are bold enough to seize them.

Jan Moran is a USA Today bestselling author of heartfelt women's fiction series, family sagas, and 20th-century historical novels. She dreams up her popular, contemporary beach books on sunny shores in Southern California, not far from where she lives.

Jan has been an avid traveler throughout her life, so you'll find her books infused with authentic locales and things she loves to research—from chocolate, wine, and food to history, fashion, and more. Readers often say that along with a heartwarming story, they also learn many fascinating details. As a native of Texas who lived on the east coast and worked in Paris, Hong Kong, and Canada, Jan brings a wealth of experience to every book she writes. Pour a cup of tea or a glass of wine, open one of her books, and find yourself transported with characters you'll soon be rooting for as friends.

A Coffee Stain

Anju Gattani

"Hello, Sheetal." The 'l' from Arvind 's lips rolled long and deep as snow fell like a laced curtain between them. "How are you?"

Sheetal's heart welled up in her throat. The memory of his mocha kiss from ten years ago rained down with the flakes.

Was it really him after all these years or some mirage the snow had sculpted? She swallowed, but bubbles of air refused to sink. "I'm fine. *Tum bhi.*" She paused to weigh her comment in Hindi, *"Acche lag rahe ho." He looked good. He always did.*

At five-foot eleven, Arvind's warm, brown skin bronzed by the Indian sun curved around his gentle features and melted along the slant of his French beard. Strands of salt-and-pepper hair combed back in gentle waves. A thick layer of flesh now padded Arvind's frame and a slight paunch pressed against the fabric of his blue shirt and camel-colored blazer peeking from behind his thick, brown coat. He raised his eyebrows and wrinkles crusted his forehead. To think ten years ago on her wedding day, he had climbed up her bedroom balcony and begged her to elope.

If only… Sheetal bit her lower lip and looked past him and the footprints he'd left behind. He smiled, and her heart skipped a beat.

"You look beautiful." Hadn't he said that when they last met?

"I…" She curled her fingers into fists.

"I thought it was you but wasn't sure." He slid a gloved hand in the jacket pocket. "I'm Yash's science teacher and House Master," he quickly added by way of explanation.

Yash. Sheetal turned right and Yash's gloved fingers were locked around her wrist. When did Yash come to her side, and how did she not realize? From the corner of her left eye she noticed Arvind staring, and warmth spiraled up her chest.

"You two know each other?" Yash asked.

"I…yes." The unsaid words lay trapped on her tongue, and she pursed her lips.

"We were good friends a long time ago. You could say we were in the same school."

"Like me and my friends?" Yash asked. "We're in the same room, the same dorm and we're together all the time."

"Not quite," Arvind laughed. "I knew your mother from classes we had together. We were just friends back then, that's all." He shrugged like it didn't matter.

Anger riled up her veins. Had Arvind forgotten the after-lecture coffees they drank at the cafeteria? And what about plans they'd made of a future together? Is that all she was to him ten years later—a friend? Sheetal tightened her grip round Yash's fingers and tugged. "Let's go."

"Arrey! So soon?" Arvind asked. "We meet after such a long time, and you want to walk away?"

"Just friends, right? Isn't that what you said? Come on Yash." Sheetal walked past Arvind toward the boarders' lodging and Arvind's footprints filling with snow. "It's too cold out here, anyway."

"Sheetal." Arvind called out.

She looked over her shoulder.

"It's been a while. Surely we can chat and catch up a little."

"Our meeting here, isn't it like a coincidence? I mean, you left

Raigun, I never heard from you since, and we suddenly meet out here in the middle of Mansali."

"I didn't have a choice at the time. Better late than never. Anyway, I have some work in Dr. Chaturvedi's office and was on my way there when I saw Yash in a snow fight. I couldn't resist and thought I'd check what he was up to. Last thing I expected was to find Yash throwing snowballs at his mother. Anyway, if you don't have time, I understand. I should get going." He gestured to the brick building ahead. "I'm late for my appointment. Maybe I'll see you around sometime." He trudged ahead.

Her heart sank with disappointment. Ten years later and he was more concerned about being late for an appointment than being with her. Sheetal walked on, holding Yash's hand as Yash talked about his busy morning.

"How is Daddy?"

Rakesh. Regret stirred in her chest. "He's fine."

"He didn't come?"

Sheetal pivoted for a view of the two-story brick building and saw the double-doors close behind Arvind. His footprints had filled to the brim, and soon the snow between them would soon level. "He has work, *Beta.* He's busy." She led Yash to a bench and they sat down.

"He's always busy. It's not fair." Yash pouted.

"He works hard." Recently, Rakesh had been working harder to make sure they spent no time together.

Yash swung his feet that didn't meet the ground and his shoelaces, twisted at the ends and bound with thin plastic caps, tapped against his leather shoes, making a tic-tic-tic sound. "Does Daddy miss me?"

Miss me? Miss me not. Miss me? Sheetal synched the questions with the swinging motion of Yash's legs. As a girl she would pluck petals off a rose and chant one sentence with a petal, in the hope of one day meeting her true love. Tic-tic-tic- tic. Sheetal firmed her heels in the ground and crushed the thought. What was the point of holding on to long forgotten dreams when their juices had been squeezed and drained from life? She turned to the brick building on the far left. Was

Arvind still there or had he exited through a rear door?

"Mum?" Yash tugged at her coat. "Does Dad miss me?"

"Of course. He's your father. Don't you think he would?"

"I don't know," he shrugged.

The ground, the sky and the falling snowflakes misted a fog of confusion. How was she supposed to convince Yash of Rakesh's love when she wasn't sure of it herself? "He loves you a lot. Just because he couldn't come doesn't mean he loves you any less."

Yash pointed to the dorms on the other side of the black, iron-gated wall. "Let's go there."

"How about we wait here a little longer?" Sheetal willed the door to open and for Arvind to emerge. She reached over and pulled Yash onto her lap.

"But it's cold out here. You said so just now."

"Isn't it fun to watch the snow fall? We never get to do this in Raigun." She would never get to wait for Arvind in Raigun either. She needed to stay put for just a little longer. Sheetal pulled Yash on her lap and wrapped him in a tight embrace.

"You won't believe what happened at break today…" Yash chatted about his friends, classes and life at boarding school while Sheetal glanced back at the brick building. "…and then the House Captain said lights out and we had to…"

A frigid wind blew, and Sheetal tightened her embrace around Yash. A hot cup of coffee would soothe her chilled nerves. Or maybe, hot chocolate for a change? They'd been here for fifteen minutes and no sign of Arvind. "How about—"

"Coffee? Hot chocolate, anyone?"

Sheetal's heart skipped a beat, and she looked over her shoulder. Arvind. And he'd stolen the words right out of her mouth.

# # #

Sheetal entered the campus cafeteria, known as the mess. The enormous hall brimmed with five-hundred-and-fifty uniformed students who were seating themselves around long, rectangular tables for their afternoon snack. The boys sat in groups of sixteen, eight on each side, and waited to be served. Yash let go of Sheetal's hand and wove between the bustling crowd of navy-blue blazers and gray trousers until he blurred with them.

"Come."

She followed Arvind to a serving counter on the other side of the cafeteria. A slab of granite spanning the hall's width divided the mess from the kitchen. A wooden swinging gate slicing down the counter's middle allowed servers to rush back and forth without having to push open the door with their hands. A wall behind the counter sealed off the kitchen, and on the other side of glass-paneled wooden doors servers in gray jumpsuits whizzed back and forth armed with trays of food and drink. A minute later, the servers emerged carrying steaming mugs, baskets of French fries and puff pastry as the hall buzzed with chatter.

"Coffee?" Arvind asked. Sheetal nodded. "Something to eat?"

Sheetal shook her head. "I had a late lunch."

Arvind signaled a server. "*Do coffee, dena. Doodh aur shakkar alag se.*" He asked to set aside some milk and sugar separately.

Sheetal's attention meandered to Arvind's profile, and a dry heat swelled in her chest.

The server placed a tray on the counter with two Styrofoam cups of black liquid, two plastic lids, spoons, a small steel pot of milk and a matching lidded sugar container.

Arvind poured some milk in both cups, added a cube of sugar in each and stirred both with a spoon.

In ten years, Rakesh had never bothered to pour her coffee.

The servants did everything. "Two more cubes, please."

"Two?" He shook his head and grinned. "It's not good for you."

"You still give free advice?"

"Only if you want to hear." Arvind added two more sugar cubes to her coffee, stirred the liquid, snapped the lid on her Styrofoam cup and gave her the cup.

Ten years and Rakesh still didn't know that she took milk and sugar with her coffee. How would he when he was hardly ever around. And the times that he was, he didn't care to know.

"Something wrong?"

"Oh no, I…" Heat welled up her neck and Sheetal turned away. She didn't realize she'd been staring at him.

"Your coffee." He gestured to her cup. "Take a sip and let me know if it tastes alright."

Her opinion mattered?

"I guess we should sit somewhere and maybe catch up on…" His lips fluttered at the speed of a butterfly's wings and he led her to the door. "Sheetal? Are you listening?"

She was, to everything he said.

"I said the staff room is less than five minutes' walk. We can chat there if you want."

Too many people. "How about somewhere outside in the open?"

Arvind shrugged, and she followed him down the center aisle as a few students paused between sips of hot chocolate to watch them pass and then resumed their drink. Sheetal spotted Yash at a table with his friends and lip-synched "I'll meet you outside later." Lip synching was one of many secret connections she shared with Yash.

"Okay," Yash lip-synched back.

Arvind opened the door. "Ladies first."

Sheetal paused. Always ranked last on the family rung, it was hard to believe someone waited for her to go first.

"Sheetal?"

"You still believe in the ladies' first policy?" He grinned.

"You haven't changed."

"Neither have you."

"Silly." She bit her lower lip suppressing the urge to laugh and followed him to a green metal bench looking out to a running track. The snow had stopped falling and her feet crunched the white ground as he walked beside her. She sat on the bench's right, leaned against the armrest and balanced the cup on the metal arm as metal creaked under Arvind's weight. A two-inch gap separated them, and her thumb nervously flicked the plastic lid's edge. Heat from the cup seeped into her skin and she peeled back a tiny opening in the lid, cracking the silence between them.

"Careful. It's hot," he cautioned. "Let it cool a little."

Sheetal gently clawed back the entire lid, and a mist of steam rose. "Still at the free advice thing?"

"It's for your own good."

Her heart melted. Wasn't this how they used to argue?

Over sweet nothings? Such a contrast to arguments with Rakesh where she simply obeyed. "I know my own good."

"What if you burnt your lips?"

"I'd heal."

"I'm trying to help."

She blew away the mist, snapped the lid back on and sipped the coffee through the tiny hole. Too strong. She lowered the cup on the bench's armrest and balanced it with the tips of her fingers.

"I still think of you every day, Sheetal."

Her fingers numbed, the cup toppled, and coffee spilled. Fool! Rakesh would have said, and she shuddered at the thought. "I'm so sorry. I…somehow…keep making mistakes." Not having married Arvind—her biggest mistake? She bent over to pick up the cup as the brown puddle melted into the snow.

"Don't worry. Now we know what happens."

"What's that supposed to mean?"

"When the truth spills." He grinned, cracking open a tiny hole in his cup's lid. "You take my coffee. I'll get another."

She tensed. "I'm not that thirsty anyway."

"Calm down, Sheetal. It'll only take a minute." "It's okay. Really."

He took a deep breath then. "*Acchha.* We'll share."

Share Arvind's coffee? She was a married woman now.

Sitting and talking alone with Arvind wasn't appropriate. But sharing from the same cup? She stiffened.

"You look lost." He laughed. "Here, have a sip, it'll warm you up." Arvind handed her the drink.

She imagined his invisible lip-prints stamped over the edge. Would he still taste of mocha?

"I haven't sipped it yet," he added, as if reading her mind. "Ladies first."

He was going to taste her first, not let her taste him. "But be careful," he warned. "It's hot."

He was hot. She parted her lips when laughter rolled off her tongue. The coffee sloshed from side to side, spilled over the edge and she almost lost her grip.

"What's so funny?" Arvind reached for the cup, and a fire ignited her soul. Her gaze fell to his brown fingers wrapping her milky whites, and her heart pounded as they both held on to the cup in silence, the past and present sloshing between them. She had to let go. But if she moved, the coffee would spill and another moment would disappear into the snow. Sheetal slid her left hand beneath the cup and withdrew the right. "It's yours." She returned the cup and the moment; both his to keep.

"No, you have it."

Her attention meandered to the brown puddle near her feet. "It's yours, I insist."

"You agreed to share."

"I agreed to a sip."

Arvind took the coffee and shrugged. "So, let's talk about you. Your husband. Is he still the same?"

"What do you mean?"

"All these high-flying marriages make headlines, you know. Sometimes ordinary people like us happen to read them. And I've been reading a lot about him lately."

She didn't like the assumption in his voice. "We're happily married."

"*Acchha hai.*" He nodded. "You're both still together."

"What do you mean still?" She pulled her gloves out the coat pocket.

"Nothing much. Just that your marriage is successful and you're happy. That's what matters."

Her heart ached, and she turned away.

He pointed to the princess-cut diamond on her third finger. "Looks expensive."

"Ten carats." Dhanraj blood rushed to Sheetal's head and she straightened her posture with pride.

"I'm not surprised. A woman like you deserves beautiful things."

She sucked in her lips wishing she could take back the words and the patronizing tone she hadn't intended.

He inched away, but damage like the brown stain in the snow couldn't be erased.

"What about your family and wife?"

"They live here with me. My parents on the other hand, they died about five years ago." He paused. "They were riding the bus uphill to visit me from Lower Mansali. The driver swerved to avoid colliding with an oncoming lorry, over-turned and the bus fell down a cliff. No one survived."

The air thickened. "I'm so sorry."

"So am I. I've been so for a long time."

"It must have been hard. I can't imagine how you—"

"Harder than you can imagine. But that's life." He fanned the fingers of one hand in the air and shook his head. "All in God's hands."

"I...Mama told me you'd gone to our place in Raigun...sometime after my marriage."

"I was naïve and foolish. For so long I didn't understand why your parents wouldn't let you marry me. Then I saw where you lived. How you lived. They were right. I could have never kept you happy."

She lived a wealthier life with Rakesh than she ever had at Mama's. But Rakesh wasn't able to keep her happy. Her heart grated with guilt. Was she one of those demanding types who couldn't find happiness with what she had?

"I don't know what I was thinking when I came to save you that day. What made me think I could rescue you? From what? I was such a fool."

"You're not."

He turned to look at her. "So you're saying you would have come with me?"

Sheetal blinked and firmed her tone of voice so Arvind wouldn't think she was weak. "You know I—"

"Of course you couldn't. I understand now why you couldn't, but not back then."

Sheetal shifted, uncomfortable with the conversation. Why couldn't he just leave the past alone? "So...how many children do you have?"

"Five."

"Oh." Did that mean he loved his wife five times more than he had loved her? Sheetal reached for the *mangalsutra* around her neck and rolled the black and gold beads strung on a religious thread to signify her married status as jealousy roiled in her heart. "Boys and girls?"

"Boys." He took a sip. "All five hundred-and-fifty." Her heart skipped a beat.

He laughed. "Oh, come on, Sheetal, lighten up. Every single boy here at St. Paul's is like my own. It's a joke."

Sheetal raised her eyebrows and turned away. His sense of humor hadn't changed. "What about your wife?"

"What about her?"

"Where does she live?"

"She doesn't."

Her forehead throbbed. "So where is she?"

"Who?"

"Your wife?"

"Why?"

"Why, what?"

"Why do you want to know about my wife? What difference does it make where she lives, how she lives and what she does?"

Anger clawed at Sheetal's heart. What difference did it make how big or expensive her diamond ring was? Arvind had asked. She had answered, and now she wanted to know something about him in turn. So what if they were two people from two different worlds and snow was the only common ground between them? Her heart sank and she leaned against the bench's back rails, her attention fixed on the purity of the white landscape. All this snow would melt and disappear once the season passed.

"Did you ever bother, once, in the last ten years to worry about me and find out where I live? How I live?" His voice hardened. "Well? Did you think of me?"

"I'm married, Arvind."

"I was supposed to pick up my parents from Lower Mansali and ride the bus with them. But they said not to bother and they'd manage on their own because it was just a two-and-half-hour ride uphill. They died. And here I am, still alive."

A ten-carat lump pummeled her throat and the breath tightened.

"But how does it matter to you, Sheetal? Honestly?" Just then a beeping disturbed the silence and Arvind flicked open his mobile. "Hello? Aryan speaking. Yes. I know I'm late. I'll be there in five minutes."

Why did he call himself Aryan?

"Umm…I have to go." He glanced at the watch on his wrist. "There's a staff meeting at four."

"I didn't have a choice, Arvind. I was forced to—"

"We all have choices." He dusted snow off his coat. "It all depends on the ones you make and choose to live with. I chose you above everything. Foolish, wasn't I? Naïve? Yes. But that's how much I love you. I gave up everything for you. And you gave me up for everything."

Didn't he understand? There had been nothing for him to give up because he had nothing to lose.

"Come, I think you should go back indoors too or you'll fall sick."

Bile raced up her throat as a gust of icy wind blew. "I didn't leave you. I was never meant to go with you in the first place. You just turned up on my balcony on my wedding day expecting me to elope with you while my family, friends and the world waited for me to marry Rakesh."

"And now you're happily married."

The remark bit. "Yes, I am happily married."

"Good. At least one of us is." He rose, abandoned the cup on the bench's rails and turned to leave as snowflakes cascaded again. "Coming?"

"What do you mean, one of us?"

He pivoted to face her and walked backwards. "I never had the heart to marry anyone after you." Then he turned his back and left, his figure diminishing in the growing distance as more flakes curtained his exit, filling his footprints, their past and padding his Styrofoam cup with snow. Soon the ground would level and there would be nothing left except for one abandoned cup of coffee.

Sheetal turned and searched for the brown spill, but the puddle with the moment had gone.

In book 1, *Winds of Fire* series, set in Raigun, India, Sheetal was forced to surrender her true love, Arvind Chopra, to marry playboy millionaire, Rakesh Dhanraj, in accordance with her parents' wishes. Sheetal endured an emotionally abusive marriage and regrets the ugly turn her life has taken. However, the birth of Sheetal's baby boy, Yash, gives her inner strength and courage to fight for her rights.

In book 2, Yash is now eight. To protect Yash from the dysfunctional Dhanrajs and Rakesh, Sheetal enrolled Yash three years ago at the prestigious St. Paul's Boarding School (an all-boys' school) in Mansali, the foothills of the Himalayas. Sheetal and Rakesh take their annual vacation to Mansali around mid-October and then bring Yash home for a three week-long Diwali break (from mid-October to November).

However, this year, Rakesh can't join Sheetal on the trip, so Sheetal travels alone to Mansali.

Sheetal meets Yash on the school campus and the two just shared some fun and laughter in a mother-son snow fight. Then Sheetal meets Arvind for the first time after ten years.

The excerpt is a deleted scene from Book 2.

Fiction author, freelance journalist, fiction writing instructor, blogger and former newspaper reporter, Anju was born in India but grew up in Hong Kong. She has also lived and been published in Singapore, India, Australia, and USA in cover stories, fiction, feature, news, interviews, travel, perspective pieces and more. She finally dug her roots in Atlanta, Georgia, USA, with her husband, 2 dashing boys and a rebel lion-head rabbit.

Her *Winds of Fire* series, was optioned for film / TV to Double Strings, Inc, ranked on the Amazon Bestsellers List and is honored to be a book of the month pick by International Pulpwood Queen and Timber Guy Book Cub Reading Nation. Reviewed as *Crazy Rich Asians* in India "Downton Abbey-style saga, but set in India!" by BooksByWomen.org. The series advocates for awareness of abuse, domestic violence, mental health and more...

Anju also interviews writers and publishing industry professionals on her Youtube channel, Story Mantra. Anju hopes her books will Bridge Cultures and Break Barriers.

Social Media:
Website: www.anjugattani.com
Facebook: Anju Gattani Author
Twitter: @Anju_Gattani
Instagram: Anju_Gattani27
Bookbub: @Anju_Gattani
Youtube: Anju Gattani, Story Mantra
https://www.youtube.com/channel/ChijH5uk4DoWU9AlBq0rzFw

They Killed Papa!

J. Lawrence Matthews

It was Friday, April 14th. Good Friday.

A mood of unrestrained jubilation gripped the crowds of Washington City as I pushed my way from the Stanton home to the White House to fulfill my new assignment from the War Secretary.

That assignment involved young Tad Lincoln.

The President and Mrs. Lincoln—as the entire city of Washington knew—were to attend *My American Cousin* at Ford's Theatre that evening in the company of General and Mrs. Grant. And as General Grant and President Lincoln were the most popular figures of the day, and as they had never appeared together in public, it was expected to be the most sensational event of the year.

Mr. Stanton wanted nothing to go awry.

"I want you to keep that boy out of the President's hair," he had said, handing me two tickets to a performance of *Aladdin* at Grover's Theatre, a few streets from Ford's. "You'll take him to this show, and until the President and Mrs. Lincoln have returned General and Mrs. Grant to the Willard Hotel for the night, you will not bring that boy back to the White House. Under *any* circumstances"

The crowds at the White House gate were thicker than usual—

everyone in Washington, it seemed, wanted to shake the President's hand, or beg a favour of him, or steal a souvenir—but soon enough I was admitted upstairs to the family quarters, where I came upon the President engaged in a wrestling match of sorts with Tad, who was delirious with joy at having his father to himself.

"Your charge is here, Tad," said the President, raising himself slowly to his feet, a great unfolding of limbs that brought him a full two heads taller than myself. He dismissed the guard and frowned at his disheveled son. "Best tuck in that shirt and tell Mother your companion is here."

The boy dutifully scampered away into Mrs. Lincoln's parlour just as the door from the President's office opened and John Nicolay entered, fuming.

"What is it, Nicolay? Bobby Lee hasn't changed his mind, has he?"

"No, but General Grant has. Sends his regrets. Says he and Mrs. Grant must take the evening train to visit family in New Jersey if he is to return in time for his conference with Sherman on Sunday. He begs your pardon and thanks you for your kind invitation, etc. etc."

Lincoln appeared not in the least surprised at this news, but a cloud had descended upon his features, and lines of fatigue and care returned. "This will not go over well with Mother," he said in a somber voice.

At that moment, Mrs. Lincoln appeared at the doorway with Tad, now dressed for the evening. "What news, Mr. Nicolay?"

"General Grant sends his regrets—"

Nicolay's words were cut short by a hideous screech and the sight of the President's wife tearing off her gloves, flinging them to the carpet and stomping on them like a child. The imprecations that woman heaped upon poor Julia Grant were such that I would blush to repeat them, Watson—and no publisher would print them. The President said nothing, but slumped ever more deeply into his chair. Nicolay grabbed Tad decisively by the hand and motioned me to follow him into the President's office, shutting the door behind us.

I found myself in a large room with tall windows, its walls lined with shelves of books and displays of regimental flags.

Several bell-pulls hung from the ceiling, and in the center of the room was a long, oval table covered in maps and surrounded by a half-dozen chairs, all beneath a bright, many-globed gas chandelier. The President's desk in the far corner was piled with books, letters and documents.

Mrs. L's screams were still somewhat audible through the library door, and Tad exhibited a manic nervousness that I had witnessed during similar episodes, so I occupied the boy by drilling him on the regimental flags while Nicolay sent messengers to find a suitable couple to take the Grants' place.

Eventually he secured the services of one Henry Rathbone, an Army major who, with his fiancée, had accompanied the Lincolns on similar occasions. By that time, the fires of Mrs. L's tirade had burned themselves out, so I escaped to Grover's Theatre with Tad while father and mother prepared to see *My American Cousin.*

Without General Grant and his poor, abused wife.

It should have taken us only a few minutes to reach Grover's, it being a mere two streets away from the White House, but so crowded was Pennsylvania Avenue and so jubilant were the celebrants that we would have missed the curtain rising but for the foresight of Nicolay. Seeing the crowds from the window of the President's office and fearing for Tad's safety, he had insisted we be accompanied by the White House doorkeeper—a tall, burly policeman named Donn.

And it was well that Donn came with us, Watson, for Tad very nearly lost himself more than once on that short walk, so full of energy and excitement was he.

"There's Pa!" he would shout as the serenaders marched by, waving portraits of the President and General Grant, whence he would disappear into the crowd until Donn pulled him back.

We reached Grover's just before the curtain rose, and Donn excused himself to take dinner at the tavern across the street. Tad was soon engrossed in the fairy-tale story upon the stage whilst I, as was my habit, employed the time to make an intensive study of the actors—and of the tools and techniques they employed.

Needless to say, *Aladdin* was by no means a work of distinction, but the adventure was portrayed with some little competence, and the evening passed swiftly enough. It was what occurred between the second and third acts, however, and not the play or those who performed it, that is forever etched in my mind.

It was, as I have said, common for theatre performances in America in those days to be interrupted with patriotic songs and poetry readings. During one such interval at Grover's an actor stepped up to the gaslights to recite a rousing poem he called "The Flag of Sumter."

I remember being impressed with the fiery delivery, which brought the men in the crowd to their feet, stamping and whistling in approval—but my recollection of the poem's contents has been erased in the aftermath of what was to come, when the cheers and whistles were interrupted by a new sound, discordant and out of place, emanating from somewhere in the darkness of the theater behind me.

It was the voice of a man in distress.

His cries were hoarse and indistinct at first—and masked somewhat by the actor's recitation from the stage—but they persisted until the actor became flustered and paused, allowing the words being cried from the back to ring throughout the theatre, blasting the ears of everyone in their seats:

"President Lincoln is assassinated in his private box at Ford's!"

I write the words precisely as they were shouted, Watson—although I cannot adequately portray the manner in which the man's voice fairly choked on the passive verb, nor can I convey the profound hush that fell upon the audience as the full import of that horrible word reverberated in the very air.

Next—well, the history books tell us that pandemonium erupted, but that is not what happened next. No, what happened next, Watson, was this: nothing. And for the very simple reason that almost nobody in the theatre believed what they heard.

Confused silence lingered until another voice, a reassuring voice of authority, cried out:

"*Pay no heed! It is a ruse of the pickpockets!*"

A murmur of approbation arose from the crowd—in those days, Watson, pickpockets were never far from any gathering in Washington City—and all around me the men and women settled their children in their seats for the resumption of the entertainment.

And who might blame them?

The words seemed impossible, unbelievable, absurd. After four years of insurrection and war, subterfuge domestic and foreign, could anyone believe America's Great Man had been taken away only days after the very moment his vision, so strongly held and so firmly pursued, had finally triumphed? In something so prosaic as a theatre box? Watching an entertainment so lightly thought of that no one would remember the point of the play—only what happened during it?

Who could believe it?

But I believed it, Watson. And not because of the skills of observation and deduction I had been practicing since my days in the gunpowder laboratory at DuPont.

It was the instincts of a street urchin that told me it was so.

No pickpocket would have thought to raise such a cry in such a place at such a time. Merely shouting "fire" would have cleared the theatre and provided ready prey for the cutpurses. Nor would he have spoken with such precision—*in his private box at Ford's* was a detail only an eyewitness would have known.

Without a second thought I grabbed my charge by the wrist, pulled him out of his seat and raced him to the lobby, where a knot of anxious men had gathered around the stranger who had brought the news.

The men included, to my relief, Donn, the White House doorkeeper. He had finished his meal and was smoking on the steps of Grover's when the man had begun shouting, and he was interrogating the man now—rather roughly, I thought, holding the poor fellow by the throat and shouting, "It's *not* so!" But the man—hatless and disheveled, with a face whose spectral pallor was streaked with real tears—insisted that it was so.

And forcefully enough that Donn finally let go the man and listened as he told the entire, horrible story.

He was an usher at Grover's, he said, sent by Mr. Grover as a spy to count the house at Ford's. He had been watching the President's box when the explosion occurred; had seen the puff of smoke billow from the box; had heard the commotion and watched an actor—J. Wilkes Booth—leap from the box to the stage; had seen him come down hard on one leg before rising awkwardly to his feet, brandishing a knife and shouting wildly as he limped off through the wings.

Donn listened carefully to each detail, repeating them to himself to make certain that even in such a trying circumstance he had ascertained precisely what this fellow had seen. Then he set about to question the man, whose answers sent a chill to my heart.

No, the man said, he didn't know if Booth was holding a gun—he only remembered the knife; yes, Booth had been followed—by a major named Stewart; no, the major had not been able to stop Booth from his flight; yes, President Lincoln was being attended to by a doctor, an Army doctor. No, he didn't know the doctor's name. Yes, he knew the President was dead.

"*How?*" pressed Donn.

"Mary Lincoln screamed it."

At this last, Donn nodded gravely and turned away, taking Tad's hand and hissing an emphatic command to me: "*Get to Franklin Square and tell Mr. Stanton what you have heard, at once!*" Then he picked up Tad and trotted away down the steps.

As they disappeared into the surging crowds, I could hear Tad screaming, "They killed Papa! They killed Papa!"

I pushed and ran my way to Franklin Square as quickly as I could manage, though my progress was slowed by the crowds, for I was intent on helping in whatever way was necessary.

I could never have imagined, my dear Watson, what form that help would take…

Excerpt from *One Must Tell the Bees: Abraham Lincoln and The Final Education of Sherlock Holmes*

Published in 2021 by East Dean Press, *One Must Tell the Bees: Abraham Lincoln and the Final Education of Sherlock Holmes* tells the story of a young English chemist named Holmes whose work at the DuPont gunpowder mills in Delaware brings him to the White House of Abraham Lincoln and, after Lincoln's assignation, secures him a role in the breathtaking pursuit of John Wilkes Booth—the most infamous manhunt in history.

It is the very first case of the man who would become the great detective known to the world as Sherlock Holmes.

The following excerpt from the typewritten memoirs of Sherlock Holmes (which he addresses to his old friend, Dr. John Watson) takes place on the evening of Lincoln's assassination in 1865, one week after Confederate General Robert E. Lee's surrender to General Ulysses S. Grant at Appomattox.

Holmes's keen abilities caught the eye of President Lincoln's powerful Secretary of War, Edwin Stanton, early on during Holmes's time in America, and on this historic and tragic evening, the youthful Holmes has been given a modest but important task to perform.

He is to keep the rambunctious young Tad Lincoln occupied while Mr. and Mrs. Lincoln attend a performance at Ford's Theatre.

Before the night is through, Holmes will do just that. And much, much more…

J. Lawrence Matthews has contributed fiction to the New York Times and NPR and is the author of three non-fiction books as Jeff Matthews. *"One Must Tell the Bees"* is his first novel. Written at a time when American history is being scrutinized and recast in the light of 21st Century mores, this fast-paced account of Sherlock Holmes's visit to America during the final year of the Civil War illuminates the profound impact of Abraham Lincoln and his Emancipation Proclamation on slavery, the war and America itself. Matthews is now researching the sequel, which takes place a bit further afield - in Florence, Mecca and Tibet - but readers may contact him at jlawrencematthews@gmail.com. Those interested in the history behind *"One Must Tell the Bees"* will find it at jlawrencematthews.com.

The Poisoning
James Garrison

Through a printed window, I saw my forebears encapsulated in amber and pinned on a page, a pause in time captured and frozen in a news clipping of a death by poisoning deemed suspicious and meriting a formal inquest in rural North Carolina in 1888 and memorialized in statements written by educated others and signed with an "X" as his or her mark: the four children still at home (Ben, Em, Mary, and their half- brother, Sam), there with the old man, Smith Bell, when he died—and "the colored boy," Will, who they said stayed at the house during the day and ate the leftover food in the kitchen pots when the white family was done. He was the only one who didn't get sick and vomit his guts out two weeks before or again after breakfast the day the old man died, both times when they all were sick, except the "negro boy who lives here was not sick either time," according to the youngest son Sam's statement in the inquest.

This was August 1888, and Grover Cleveland was president. Reconstruction in the South was long past, ended ten years before, and all the blue-clad Federal troops withdrawn, leaving the Ku Klux Klan, white robes flying, rising from the ashes of defeat to restore the old balances of race and class and fear and maintain the established order for a desperate white society.

So how did it end, and equally curious, how did it start there on old Smith Bell's farm? All of them living together, farmers, not sharecroppers, the old man a blacksmith and landowner, twice widowed, his grown sons going off to catch the horses before breakfast and then to plow the fields afterwards and getting sick, and the old man dying like that, the father of Ben, Em, Mary, and Sam, and also the father of Thomas Smith Bell, my great-grandfather, whom I know only from a black-and-white photograph taken in his old age—long white beard and bib overalls, standing with two succeeding generations, all relatives of mine, in front of a makeshift sawmill, and who died in 1922, falling off the porch, stone dead, while my mother, age ten, watched and then told me about it fifty years later: my great-grandfather dropping dead before her eyes; how was it that his father came to die by poisoning in August 1888?

In his statement at the inquest: Benjamin Bell, age twenty-seven, after being duly sworn, says: "Our family consists of (or did) my father, one brother, two sisters & my self [sic.] & a black boy about 16 years old. We all stay here at night except the boy & he goes to a black mans [sic.] to sleep (Cal Allison)."

How did the six of them arrive here at this moment in time, together in old Smith Bell's house on an August morning in 1888? The seventy-year-old father and four of his children by two dead wives and Will, "a black boy about 16 years old." Two older children— Lieuhanna and Thomas Smith Bell, my great- grandfather, who dropped dead and fell off the porch of a farmhouse in 1922 while my mother watched (and later held funerals and made a graveyard, she said, for all the birds and chickens who died in the yard)—had both gone off to start their own lives, still close by, working the same red-dirt farmland where the family had lived for a hundred years and more and where my mother grew up in a four-room farmhouse and chopped cotton instead of going to school when she was ten years old—and after until she went to work at the cotton mill when she was fourteen.

Before the War (the only one that counted here in 1888), Smith Bell and his family did not have a plantation, only a farm, where one supposes they grew cotton for cash, corn for animal feed (and liquor), garden vegetables for the table, and peaches for the pie that Ben ate that morning for breakfast.

Before the War, one may ask with some misgivings, did old Smith Bell own slaves, perhaps the parents of Will. From a few surviving documents in an estate settlement, we know that *circa* 1850 Smith Bell inherited "one-half the value of Hannah, about 20 years of age—$700," the other half divided among the other heirs of Nancy Bell, his mother, also the first cousin of his father, not so unusual in those days, in small close-knit communities.

How do you divide a person, or the value of a person? Was Hannah sold and the proceeds allocated among the owners?

Owners of another human person, with her own hopes and fears, and no freedom or say in what happens to her that day or the next.

According to county records, before the War old Smith Bell was sometimes a "patroller" in his "militia district," in other words, part of a "slave patrol" to keep the subject race in check and prevent insurrection. How is it that neither he nor anyone else in his immediate family served in the War? Where were they and what were they doing while the armies of blue and gray surged across the land and thousands were dying of violence and disease? Were they older, younger, lamer, or just wiser than the others?

And why did Will, "a black boy," full name Will Allison, come to stay with the Bell family during the day in 1888? He ate alone, in the kitchen, the food the white folks left on the stove that last day old man Bell was alive, my great-great- grandfather, who, his daughter Em says, had only a cup of coffee for breakfast.

Foul play was suspected, and the coroner cut out the old man's stomach and sent it to the State Chemist in Raleigh for analysis of its contents. There was a headline in the local newspaper, *Statesville Landmark*, **August 16, 1888: A Probable Poisoning.** "There is every reason to suspect that poison was given the family," the article said.

And who was suspected but Will. "With [the family] … lived a colored boy about 15 years old, who spent the night at the house of his grandfather, … [and he] was not taken sick either time when the white members of the family were. He always ate in the kitchen, his meals being left in the vessels in which the cooking was done." What capped off Will as the prime suspect was that "Neither he [Mr. Bell] nor his family had any enemies, so far as they or any of their neighbors know."

So there it is, in rural North Carolina in 1888, in the trusted local newspaper, the finger of suspicion pointed at Will, "a colored boy about 15 years old." Was Will interrogated, threatened, whipped? Held in the county jail? What kind of life did he have after that? Did the local chapter of the Ku Klux Klan or some random lynching party show up at his grandfather's house? Did he flee?

The day after old man Bell died, Will appeared at the inquest. I wonder where it was held, perhaps at the family home, the old man's decaying body in a wooden coffin in the next room, the coroner and jury sitting in straight-back chairs around the dining room table, the children and Will talking as the scribe wrote out their statements and they signed with an "X" in the middle of their written name.

Will says in his written testimony: "I live here, have been here a year & a half. Eat here but sleep down at grand paps." He admits he did not get sick the day the old man died or two weeks before when all the others were sick. Will says "[I] was not here yesterday morning until the boys were catching the horses and then ate my breakfast, ate three biscuits and some butter, did not have any coffee, don't drink it in the summer."

Em says that the only thing the old man had for breakfast was a cup of coffee.

It was August 9, 1888.

Benjamin, Emily, Mary, and Sam lived long lives, remained close to their old homestead and the land their family had held onto and farmed for generations. Thomas Smith Bell, Smith Bell's oldest son, was not a blacksmith. He continued to farm nearby and in his later years had an unfortunate encounter with a train that severed a heel, my mother said, so that he walked on the ball of his foot. HE WAS NOT DRUNK is reported in the family history. What happened to the mule and wagon is not reported.

As to old Smith Bell, my great-grandfather's father, the coroner's jury of "six good and lawful men" concluded that "the deceased came to his death under very suspicious circumstances & by some unknown causes to us." The two doctors who conducted a postmortem examination found that it "did not clearly reveal to us that he was poisoned since we have not examined the contents of his stomach." They reserved their final opinion "until such examination should be made as prescribed by law."

Sam Bell, the youngest son at age twenty-four, being sworn, says at the end of his statement in the inquest: "I do not suspect any person of poisoning us."

Many months later there was an answer to one of the questions, or so it seems: "NOT a case of poisoning – a satisfactory explanation" is the heading of an article in the *Statesville Landmark*, **May 23, 1889.** "It will be remembered that about the first of August last year," so the article begins; it then recapitulates old man Bell's death "under circumstances which suggested poisoning. A small colored boy who lived with the family was suspected." But the long-awaited report by the State Chemist in Raleigh concluded that: "[A]fter an extended examination for all classes of poisons I have not found any substance of a poisonous nature … It is possible that the symptoms observed may have been due to the peculiar class of ptomaine compounds which are not thoroughly understood—possibly to some substance resembling tyrotoxicon, which owes its origin to putrefactive matter in meats, milk or vegetables. The symptoms for tyrotoxicon poisoning seem to resemble those observed in the case of T. Smith Bell."

So in 1889, in post-Reconstruction North Carolina, on the cusp of Edison's lights and another Bell's telephone, there was a victory for science and justice even if the odor of foul murder had lingered in the air for a long nine months. The State Chemist's letter to the Board of

County Commissioners goes on to justify his delay doing the analysis and sending the report by the press of other business, including the responsibility of the State Chemist for analyzing fertilizers, an issue "in which the farmers of the State are interested to the amount of millions of dollars."

Who knew that fertilizer was so important to the farm economy in North Carolina in 1888? Certainly not I. But it was. After the War, by 1888 production of cash crops like cotton and tobacco, along with farm animals, had returned to pre-War levels, but the farmers' incomes had not.[1] There was over production, nationally and locally, and commodity prices were severely depressed in the years since 1865, cotton dropping "from 25 cents a pound in 1868 to ... 9 cents in the 1880's" while the farmers' expenses for machinery, fertilizer, and freight rates had declined little or not at all. Farm tenancy and crop liens were on the rise. Farm income was depressed not only by costs but also by a monetary policy that deflated the wages of labor along with the prices of cotton and other fruits of the land, to the ultimate benefit of the lenders, railroads, and robber barons—and led to William Jennings Bryans' call to arms: "you shall not crucify mankind on a cross of gold."

Around them the farmers could see the manufacturers, bankers, and urban professionals prospering while they did not. "In 1890 the wealthiest three percent of the American population owned sixty-five percent of the national wealth while the poorest eighty-seven percent owned only ten percent."[2]

So the farmers went deeper in debt and struggled to make crops grow on tired land that, in the absence of Twentieth-century farm technology and knowledge, required ever more fertilizer every year. They were squeezed and bled by bankers, manufacturers, and politicians who raised taxes on their land and crops. And they organized granges and alliances to make their voices heard and their votes count. So in North Carolina, a farm state, fertilizer was extremely important to the farmers, and the farmers to the politicians and the State Chemist.

But what about Will, whose fate hung in the balance because fertilizer was more important to the State Chemist?

What happened to Will, the "small colored boy who lived with the family"? What became of him during all of this, during the nine months it took for the report to be concluded and sent to the Iredell County Commissioners: "NOT a case of poisoning"?

Could this be the same Will Allison who appears in the county census records of 1900, the Will Allison who has his own story and family history? And his descendants, progeny of slaves, still compelled to struggle against the grasping tendrils of American slavery and Jim Crow, where are they now?

Chicago, Los Angeles? Or still tied to the land, the red-dirt soil and rolling hills of Piedmont North Carolina, like many of Thomas Smith Bell's descendants.

Perhaps none of this matters, only the present moment, while the past remains forever fixed in time, frozen in amber, and rarely remembered.

---

[1] North Carolina, Lefler and Newsome (The University of North Carolina Press 1963) pp. 490-493. This is the text we used in a North Carolina history course at the state university in 1964. In another first-year class, Western Civilization I believe it was called, the professor announced on the very first day: "The WAR is over! And you lost." That made sense to me, based on what I knew then, but I'm not sure it did to everyone there, fifty or so students, most from North Carolina, assembled in a large auditorium for the mandatory course.

[2] Lefler and Newsome, p. 493.

Acknowledgments: With special thanks to R.C. and Irene Black for sharing their research into the Bell family history along with copies of the news clippings from the Statesville Landmark and documents from the coroner's inquest into the death of Thomas Smith Bell, who died on August 9, 1888.

"The Poisoning" is based on my family's history in Piedmont North Carolina, where most of my forbears have lived since the early 1700s. The poisoning incident and coroner's inquest at the center of the story occurred in 1888, a decade after the end of Reconstruction in the South, near the small farming community of Turnersburg, NC. The narrative closely follows the official documents, witness statements, and newspaper accounts of an inquest into the death of Smith Bell, age 70, at the family farmhouse where he lived with four of his six children and Will, "a black boy about 16 years old." My cousin R.C. Black and his wife Irene dug up the Bell family history and shared it with me to use in my writing. My mother, who grew up chopping cotton near Turnersburg, NC—and confessed to only a first-grade education—also contributed by sharing her memories over the years in vivid detail.

A graduate of the University of North Carolina and Duke Law School, James Garrison practiced law until returning to his first loves: writing and reading good literature. His first novel, *QL 4* (TouchPoint Press 2017), based on his experiences as a military cop the Mekong Delta during the Vietnam War, has won awards for literary and military fiction, and it was a finalist for the 2018 Montaigne Medal. His novel, *The Safecracker* (TouchPoint Press 2019), has won legal thriller awards, and it was a category finalist in the 2020 Eric Hoffer Book Awards. His creative nonfiction and fiction works and poems have appeared in literary magazines and anthologies.

Sheila-Na-Gig online nominated his poem *"Lost: On the Staten Island Ferry'"* for a 2018 Pushcart prize. His most recent novel, *What Seems True,* set for release by TouchPoint Press on September 20, 2021, was inspired by the 1979 murder of the first Black supervisor at a Texas Gulf Coast refinery, a crime for which the shooter was never convicted.

Webpage: https://jamesgarrison-author.com/

Twitter: @JimGarrison10

FaceBook: https://www.facebook.com/JamesGarrisonauthor/

The Old Lady

T. K. Thorne

It may be a mistake I'll regret, but I pull over onto the side of Highway 11, a backroad somewhere between the city of Trussville and Argo, Alabama. Not much traffic this time of night. This is a crazy move. I'm not a cop anymore. I'm an old lady with osteopenia, for God's sake; I could break something.

I hear this voice every time I step onto the mat for training or swing a leg over my horse. For thirty-odd years, I listened to that voice. Playing with martial arts and horses was an over-and-done part of my life. But here I am. In fact, I'm on the way home from jujitsu class, and I'm dead tired. All I want to do is eat dinner and crash.

But I saw something. Correction: I thought I saw something, but I'm not sure what to do about it. I don't even know where I am except I'm pretty sure I haven't passed Argo yet.

I look around for something familiar. Two nights a week I drive this stretch of road. I should know where I am. But I am not particularly observant when I'm driving. Especially when I'm tired. And to be totally honest, that part of being a police officer was never my strong suit. I looked out the window a lot and daydreamed. Dealing with people was a better skill, and it got me through most situations.

But if something is wrong. If I saw what I thought I saw, I need to be able to give a location. Wait. That old barn up ahead. I do know approximately where I am, and all I need to do is call 911 *and report it. They can check on the radio and make sure he is okay.*

This is actually a decent idea. I pick up my phone. "Damn it!" It's stone dead. I plug it in every night, but the charger end must have been loose again.

I should go home and forget about it.

Stubbornly, I twist in the seat and back my pickup carefully along the dirt edge of the road. I can only see a few feet behind me at a time. Thankfully, my truck has four-wheel drive, so if it's muddy, I won't get stuck, but I hate backing and doing it with mirrors just makes it worse.

"Steady, don't oversteer."

I can't remember when I started talking to myself. Somehow, as I grew older, it got easier and easier to get distracted. I often can't remember why I walk from one room to the next. My thoughts skip like a skimmed stone over still water. It helps focus if I talk out loud:

"I'm going to the kitchen to get my water bottle. Don't forget the water bottle. Pay no attention to the cat litter box that needs cleaning . . . or that jacket on the chair. Aim. Kitchen. Water bottle."

It seems forever until the front of the white car I had passed is a dim pink in my backup lights. Behind it is the marked car, lights flashing. I grab a flashlight and purse, my chest ticking like a grandfather clock on steroids and do the body slide that brings my feet closer to the ground with less jar before dropping. Trucks are made for men, not short old women. But I do love the feeling of all that steel around me.

The white car's headlights and the flashing blue lights behind it hit my eyes. The trooper is probably sitting in his car writing a ticket and approaching him at night is going to make him go for his gun. I can see the headlines, "Crazy Woman Shot by State Trooper."

I flatten against my truck as the vehicle parked just behind me switches the headlights to bright, blinding me, and takes off in a spray of mud, missing me by inches. Out of reflex or maybe out of pique, I aim the flashlight into the driver's face. Only a brief glimpse—white male, scruffy beard—as he gives me a quick hard stare and then he's gone.

"B-three nine six." It's all I could see of the tag. I repeat them to myself to keep from forgetting.

"Three nine six. Three nine six." Smallest first (three) then triple (nine), then double (six). I have never been good with identifying vehicles, which all look alike, but it is a four-door white sedan, and I recognized the Chevrolet "bowtie" emblem. I turn back to the trooper car and the flashing blue lights.

Something about that intense color has such allure for me. It's the same blue as airport runway lights and the "on" of a Bluetooth device, a siren-song blue you could get lost in, float away in. Maybe when it's time to go, I could get one to stare into to escort me to the Darkness. That and the hypnotic sound of ocean surf. Then I'm set to meet my maker. . . or whatever.

I pocket the flashlight, which could look like a weapon in the dark, step to the side of the truck and keep my hands up, palms forward, waiting politely for the trooper to open his door and ask what I'm doing.

Nothing happens. I wait a few more seconds. Nothing. I can't really see inside because his headlights are on in addition to the blue lights. Careful to keep my hands up, I step around to the passenger side, not too close. If he's concentrating on writing that ticket or whatever, I don't want to appear suddenly in his space.

Maybe I should just back up, get into the truck and go home.

"Yeah, maybe," I mutter. "But I'm here, so I might as well make sure—"

I see the body now, crumpled beside the front tire. *Oh my God . . . the blood.*

#

"Coffee?" The plain clothes detective asks.

I shake my head. "Can't drink caffeine after 3 pm, and I'm wired plenty." What I don't say is my body is harboring all this stress, and I'll probably be constipated for a month. That would be TMI—too much information. I have become my grandmother.

He grins and nods, putting his mug on the table between us and taking a seat in the tiny interview room. To be honest, I'm a little surprised Argo has a Black detective. It's a tiny town in St. Clair County, which is mostly rural.

I eye the steaming cup, probably left over from the day shift and reheated in a microwave. I heard it ding. The miracle of hearing aids.

Focusing on details helps keep emotions stuffed into the box created so many years ago when I needed not to feel things no matter what was happening. That's the only way you can do your job when someone is screaming at you or shooting at you or you have to deal with a dead body. The box is located in my gut, just out of reach. Probably why I have to eat prunes.

"Thanks for coming to the office," the detective says. His eyes are dark with crinkles at the edges. Maybe in his twenties or early thirties. Who knows? To me, he looks like he just graduated from high school. Did I ever look that young? How does a criminal take him seriously?

We've been over what happened several times, but now he hits me with what he's been wanting to ask. "I listened to the tape of the call. You sounded very calm on the radio, considering—"

Oh crap. He thinks I'm a suspect!

I take a breath, wishing I had agreed to the coffee, if only to have something to do with my hands. It never occurred to me that I would be a suspect. When I found the trooper's body, I automatically shoved down the panic into the box, checked for a pulse, and crawled across the front seat of the patrol car to the radio.

"Most people would have called 911 on their cell phone," the detective says casually.

"My phone was dead."

"Really?"

I dig into my purse and hand it over to him. "Radio is quicker, anyway. Anyone close by could have started that way."

"Good thinking, just . . . unusual."

You are a suspect! Ask for an attorney. Now.

"Am I a suspect?"

"I never said that."

Then it hit me. He has no idea who I am. I'm a short, somewhat dumpy gray-haired old grandma, but I could be a little shorty, dumpy gray-haired grandma that killed a trooper or I could be connected to the killer. It's just my word that I'm a witness.

"I guess I went for the radio out of old habit. I'm a retired police officer."

His eyebrows raise. "Really?"

He's not believing me. I'm used to that. I never looked like a police officer, whatever that means, even when I was one.

The first time I appeared at my sister's house in my uniform, she laughed. I don't blame her. My hat was too big and fell over my eyes. Every inch of my several-inches-smaller waist was occupied by a piece of equipment. My gun was twice as big as my hand. And God knows, the silver hair and turkey skin under my neck don't help make it more believable.

"How long were you an officer?" he asks.

I know this actually means he is trying to wrap his head around the absurdity and hopes for a mental escape hatch from the idea—that maybe I tried it for a little while and it didn't work out.

"Twenty-nine years."

His mind is spinning again, trying to decide whether to believe me or call me out. After a long pause, he leans back and nods. "That would explain why you went for the radio instead of calling it in."

I let out a breath. Maybe I don't need the lawyer.

"Tell me one more time why you stopped."

I am tired. I want to go home and drink a glass of wine, but I know the drill—ask the same question different ways and see if there is a hole or something the witness forgot to say. At least I'm a possible witness now and not a probable suspect.

Maybe.

"I slowed down when I saw the blue lights," I repeat. "A flash of movement between the trooper car and the sedan caught my eye."

I don't tell him that I always do that—slow down and check when I see a patrol car on the side of the road. It's something buried into who I am. If a fellow law enforcement officer is in trouble, you do not pass by without giving aid. If the situation just looked hinky, I would hang back and call 911 for backup. That would be the safe and sane thing to do. If my phone wasn't dead.

But if something were going down, I know myself well enough to know I could not just sit, even if I get so old, it amounts to bopping somebody with a cane or throwing my false teeth at them.

"It was so fast," I say, "just a blur of movement, but it worried me, and I pulled over. I should have just called, but my phone was dead, so I backed up to check on him."

"It was a stupid thing to do." I say out loud and bite my lip. "And it didn't make a difference." I don't want to think about that trooper who gave his all, whether he had a wife, children. I can't think about that or the walls of the box might dissolve. I sure as hell don't want to start crying.

"It might have made a difference. You didn't know. And it might still make a difference in finding the bastard who slit his throat." He hesitated. "We have a name."

His attitude has shifted. I feel it. And he wouldn't have said "bastard" otherwise. I'm not a suspect anymore.

"The trooper," he says, "the victim . . . called in a driver's check before things got nasty."

"Good." That is a relief. "It's just a matter of finding him then."

"Unfortunately, the tag on the car was stolen and it looks like it might be a fake ID."

Back to not being good.

He sighs and sips at the coffee crud. "So, all we really have at the moment is you."

"And hopefully something from forensics."

He nods. "Hopefully."

#

Mucking out a barn is not something I thought I would still be doing in my seventies. But it's not unpleasant. Horse apples don't stink like meat eaters' poop. In fact, it's a comforting smell, earthy. And there's an art to working the rake under the apples and lifting them in a smooth movement that keeps them on the tines until you dump them in the muck bucket.

I like being outside and working with my hands, though there are some mornings when I need a hot shower and some aspirin to be able to move without pain. But today wasn't one of those.

At least a couple of hours of daylight remain before I need to head to class, though the sky has grayed over, and the wind is suddenly speaking of rain and a summer storm. I worked in the city for decades, but up here on my mountain is where I truly feel alive, with cows and tall pines for neighbors. If I can't have blue lights and the sound of an ocean in my ears when I die, the tease of wind and pungent smell of horse will do. I've thought about simplifying my life since Five died.

That's what I called my last husband. It would make sense to move into a condo in town where I wouldn't have to keep up a yard, much less forty acres. But I keep putting it off. And where would I put my horses? Some fancy-ass barn I'd have to drive fifty miles to get to?

Through the open stall door, I can see my three horses grazing, keeping me in visual range in case I decide twice a day is not enough to feed them. Hope burns eternal. I take a moment to admire my latest treasure, Nickie Jones, a rescue off the track, an old lady like me. She ran until she wasn't winning and then was sold to the Amish, who worked her until she was too old for that and then sold her at auction. She was in a kill pen in Louisiana, headed for dog food in Mexico when I bought her sight unseen right in the middle of the Covid pandemic. All she needed was good food and attention, and now her black coat gleams, and although she's a little stiff in the right hip, she no longer favors her back leg. She's the bottom rung in the horse social ladder, but she is happy, and I'm happy to have her.

I'm about to go for the last pile in the corner when Nickie Jones jerks her head up, ears pricked toward the road. A horse has a wide range of vision, but to focus on something in the distance, she raises her head. That movement also signals as a warning that a predator might be in tall grass beyond the herd, and the other horses go on alert. I smile. It's likely a stray dog or a fox or a coyote, even though it's early in the day for them. No one ever comes down my dusty road.

I go back to the horse apples. My back is turned to the stall door, so the first time I'm aware that I'm not alone is when a man's gravelly voice speaks.

"Well, there you are."

My head jerks around, as startled as Nickie Jones had been. A burly man stands in the doorway, an open knife in his hand. It's not a pocketknife.

My heart goes into accelerated percussion, the demand of blood from my extremities making me momentarily light-headed. I am back in the night on the side of the road, pressed against my truck door, a face illuminated in my flashlight— scruffy beard, hard eyes, the same face and hard eyes considering me now. I got a partial tag number from his car as he sped away, but he had plenty of time to see mine when I backed toward him and, if he had connections, to trace my address.

It's hard to breathe.

He takes a step into the stall.

Lights flash. I am kneeling beside the trooper, *his skin chills under my fingers*. My knees weaken. They will bend to the ground when the steel slices.

Why didn't I bring my gun to the barn?

But I didn't. If I am not going to go down to the Dark, I better get with it. The study of martial arts is the study of violence, but the key is intent. We learn principles of the human body, where the weak points

286

are to disable, how to take someone off balance, how to use a wrist lock or an arm bar.

The aim is to defend. But there are two kinds of attack. One, the more likely, is at heart a social message—the establishing of who's the tough guy, the top dog, usually mano-to-mano or gang-to-mano. The intent is to brawl or prove bravado or maybe even to rob or maim in anger.

This is different. The intent here is to kill. Me. I must meet that intent with a total commitment to violence. Anything else and I lose. I die.

He takes another step forward, the knife lifting waist high, the grip easy, confident. He sees a short, slightly dumpy old lady trapped in a box far from witnesses or help. He sees prey.

I see death.

My old sensei was shorter than I and was still teaching at eighty-plus-years. He understood he would always be the prey unless . . . He wasn't.

A loose grin on his face, the man comes for me. As I step forward to meet him, I flip the grip of my right hand on the handle of the muck rake, jabbing the end of the stick hard into his throat.

\#

For the second time in a matter of weeks, blue lights play on my face. This time in my pasture. I know the officer walking toward me is going to have a hard time believing who killed the man that lies sprawled in my barn. Certainly not me. I'm just a little old lady.

When the world fell apart in 2020, the muse deserted me. I could not put pen to paper except to edit and to write blog posts. Fortunately, I had a lot of material to edit, but the more days that turned into weeks and month, the drier the well of creativity seemed. Then I was asked to submit a short story to an editor in Australia who was putting together a crime anthology featuring law enforcement authors and wanted some submissions from women. I am both of those things—an author and a cop, a retired one anyway, a short, gray-haired old lady. I agreed to submit a story. The catch is I had to write it. I had to create it. I promised, so I had to do it. One word at a time.

I was delighted and surprised that the character emerged as a short, gray-haired old lady who is an ex-cop, a martial artist, and a horse woman who witnesses a murder. It was accepted, and I'm exploring whether this (awfully familiar) character and story can support a novel.

T. K. Thorne has been passionate about storytelling and writing since she was a young girl, and that passion only deepened when she became a police officer. She served for more than two decades in the Birmingham police force, retiring as a precinct captain and then as the executive director of a downtown business improvement district focused on safety, retiring to write full time. Her books and essays include two award-winning historical novels (*Noah's Wife* and *Angels at the Gate*); two nonfiction civil rights era works (*Last Chance for Justice* and *Behind the Magic Curtain: Secrets, Spies, and Unsung White Allies of Birmingham's Civil Rights Days*); and a dally with murder, mystery, and magic in *House of Rose* and *House of Stone*, the first two novels in the *Magic City Stories trilogy*. She writes from her mountaintop home northeast of Birmingham, often with a dog and cat vying for her lap and horses hanging out in the yard.

www.TKThorne.com

Murder at the Thunderbird Inn

Rebecca Barret

Chapter One

The Neon Phoenix stood out starkly against the night as it rose above the horizon with wings spread wide. Hugo ran his palm down his face and felt the stubble of a five o'clock shadow. He angled his watch toward the dim light of the instrument panel on the dashboard of the Thunderbird. A quarter past four in the morning. "Christ."

The two-way radio on the seat next to him crackled with the dispatcher's voice. "ETA to scene?"

He picked it up and adjusted the volume knob with his thumb, "Arriving now."

"The forensic team is enroute."

"Copy."

The flashing lights atop a patrol car formed a landmark in the mist rising off the water that edged both sides of the seven mile long narrow strip of land that bridged Mobile Bay and linked the city of Mobile with the Eastern Shore. Hugo pulled onto the oyster shell parking lot and surveyed the scene as he put the Thunderbird into park and killed the engine.

Chief Goode was easily identifiable, the beginning of a paunch at his midsection well defined by the back lighting of the motel entrance. He stood with another man in civilian clothing. Behind and just to the right of them, under the peaked portico over the glass double doors leading into the building, two people stood in intimate conversation. Smoke from the cigarette in the woman's hand drifted upward.

Hugo folded a stick of Juicy Fruit gum into his mouth and got out of the car.

The Chief let his gaze travel over Hugo's tall frame. "You look like shit."

"It's four in the morning."

"You sober?"

"As a judge."

The Chief studied Hugo a moment longer. "This is Chief Stanton. Spanish Fort Police."

Hugo shook the man's hand, waiting for an explanation as to why the Mobile Police Chief, and more particularly, he, was standing outside a motel in the wee hours of the morning in what was clearly not their jurisdiction.

After another brief hesitation, the Chief cleared his throat, "We have a murder in one of the rooms. The victim is Stanton's niece. Ruby."

Hugo looked from the Chief to Stanton. "How?"

Stanton looked off across the highway into the mist dancing in the swamp grass along the far shore. "Single gunshot to the heart."

"What was she doing here?"

Neither Goode nor Stanton replied.

The female smoker caught Hugo's eye as she ground out her cigarette. One corner of her mouth lifted in a knowing half smile as she touched her companion on the arm and the two of them went through the double doors into the motel lobby.

"Okay," Hugo said. "The forensics team should be here any minute. Anything I need to know before they get here? Like why we're there and not the state police? Or the county?"

"Ruby was engaged to Arnie Hollingsworth. He's one of the highway patrol officers for Baldwin County. She broke it off about a year and a half ago." Stanton rubbed the back of his neck and exhaled a weary sigh, "And I don't want the new sheriff all up in my business, if you want to know the truth of it."

Chief Goode gave Stanton a slap of consolation on his upper arm. "Buzz and I go way back, don't we?"

Stanton nodded, studied the ground at his feet, and blinked rapidly. "God Almighty," he said in a soft voice. "How am I going to tell Nora?"

Goode cleared his throat. "Look, Buzz, you pull your guy and hi-tail it out of here before anyone shows up. We'll do what we can to keep everything as low key as possible. Won't mention the family connection but you know it'll get out. Be sure Nora's prepared. And Ruby's mama."

Hugo and the Chief watched as Stanton walked toward the motel entrance. Just before he reached the door, he swayed a couple of steps, a small drunken dance of grief, or perhaps it was simply a trick of the flashing light of the neon sign. The weight of the door almost defeated him as he went inside to collect the patrolman guarding the room. As soon as it closed behind him, Goode turned to Hugo, his voice a fierce, low growl.

"Keep a lid on this, August. Not one word to the press about it. Not one, you hear me? Make sure everyone else gets the message." He opened the door of his car and as he slid onto the seat he looked up at Hugo. "I want a detailed report of the initial findings and progress reports on every little detail. I don't want to be blindsided. This is going to be one hot mess."

The Chief sped away as Stanton and a uniformed patrolman came out of the entrance of the motel. Both of them looked shell shocked. Neither of them spoke to Hugo as they got into the patrol car. As they pulled away, the driver killed the flashing lights and turned east toward Spanish Fort.

The smoker was behind the registration counter when Hugo entered the motel. She was already lighting another cigarette. With a flick of her head she sent blond curls cascading behind her shoulder. She appraised him from head to toe as he crossed the small lobby.

"What's your name?" Hugo asked.

"Dixie."

"You the night manager?"

She nodded.

"Who found the body?"

"Me."

"What time?"

"Two forty-five or there about."

"You randomly check the rooms at two forty-five every morning?"

That garnered him a hint of a smile.

"Not usually. She wanted a wake-up call for two. No one answered so after a couple more calls, I decided she had left already and I went around to check the room."

"Was anyone else in the room?"

"Not when I got there."

"How'd you get in?"

"Pass key."

"Anyone else have a key?"

"There are generally two keys for each room. The guest gets one. Sometimes two if the circumstances call for it."

"And what might those circumstances be?"

"Oh, shuga, you know what circumstances. This ain't the Ritz."

"By that you mean The Thunderbird Inn is a rendezvous establishment."

"You didn't hear it from me."

"Were you here when she checked in?"

Dixie nodded.

"When was that?"

"About ten, I think. Something like that."

"Was anyone with her?"

292

"No."

"Anyone show up looking for her?"

"Not that I know of."

Hugo looked past Dixie into the open office where a pegboard mounted to the wall held keys under their allotted numbers. "Which room is it?"

"Lucky number seven."

"You think it's lucky?"

"She did."

"Yeah?"

"Always the same room. Lucky number seven."

"She asked for it specifically. On a number of occasions."

"You are a bright boy."

Hugo let his gaze travel around the lobby. Off to his right a glass door led into a darkened room that appeared to be the restaurant. To his left a long hallway was the conduit to the rooms. There were only two dimly lit fixtures spaced far apart along the whole length. At the far end he could barely make out what appeared to be a door to the outside.

"Is the door at the end of the hallway locked at night?"

"It's supposed to be."

"Was it tonight?"

"I haven't checked."

"Did the police officer who was here earlier check it?"

"I don't know."

Hugo walked around the counter and into the office. Hanging under number seven was a single key. "Is this the key you used?"

"No." Dixie opened a drawer of the registration counter and pulled out a ring of keys. "People are always walking off with the keys so we keep a back-up on a master ring." She handed them to Hugo then leaned against the doorframe of the office, the smoke from her cigarette spiraling upward. "They're all marked with the room numbers."

"Is the desk always manned?"

"Mostly."

Hugo looked around the office at the recliner with a blanket over the arm rest, the empty coffee cup with Dixie's hot pink lipstick smudging the rim, and a plate with the remains of a sandwich on it.

"Did you use the master key to let the police into the room?"

"Yes."

He nodded at the single key still on the pegboard. "Has anyone touched this one?"

She shrugged. "Not since it was placed there after the last occupant, I guess."

Hugo opened drawers on the office desk until he found a stack of envelopes. He took a tissue from the box of Kleenex on the desk and used it to remove the key from the pegboard and drop it into the envelope. Dixie watched without comment.

"Did anyone go into the room after you found the body?" He saw the flicker of indecision before she could control her reaction.

"Who?"

"I didn't know what to do. So, I told Harry."

"Did he go in alone?"

"No, I was with him."

"Did either of you touch anything?"

She thought a second and shook her head. "No. Except the light switch. When I opened the door, I flipped the switch. That's when I saw her."

"How did you know she was dead?"

"The bullet hole in her chest and the blood."

"You didn't touch her? Check for a pulse?"

Dixie shook her head and looked away from his steady regard as she rubbed her hands up and down her upper arms.

Hugo jangled the master keys in his hand then walked the length of the hallway to the emergency escape door. There was a deadbolt lock mounted above the door handle which had a thumb lock. When Hugo turned it, the door opened onto the pre-dawn light and the smell of damp and decay.

He retraced his steps to room number seven. It was locked.

He used the master key and stepped inside, closing the door behind him. The room lay in darkness, broken only by pulsing flashes of neon light slanting intermittently through the partially open venetian blinds.

Ruby lay on her back on the floor at the foot of the bed.

Her face was turned slightly toward the window, her lips parted as if on a sigh, her eyes open as if watching the strobing light of the motel sign. One hand lay on the floor in the tangle of long red curls that framed her face, the other lay across her abdomen. Her legs were pulled up slightly as one does in sleep. A short, sheer robe was tied at the waist. A single dark ribbon of red trailed from an entry wound on the inside rise of her left breast. Her face and limbs were the white of a delicately sculpted marble statue. She was beautiful, and she was dead.

As writers, we all come to a story from a unique perspective. Each story is different and the spark for each is different. For the Hugo August series it was the music. A friend gave me a CD of Leonard Cohen's greatest hits. It took me back to that era of the best music ever written. It was all about love, drugs, protest, and social injustice.

Every region of the nation has its own unique form of social stratification but, in my experience, the South lends itself to a rich tapestry of old families, old money, and a whisper of royalty. This is particularly true of one of the oldest port cities, Mobile, Alabama.

Then you ask yourself, what would one such character do to preserve the mantle of such position and prestige. And so, the story begins.

Rebecca Barrett writes historical fiction, cozy mysteries, and short stories of life in the South. An avid reader all her life and a product of "front porch" socializing, she became a story-teller at an early age. Her current project is a detective series, *Hugo August*, set in the deep South amid the upheaval of the Vietnam War and the social unrest of the hippie movement.

To learn more about Rebecca Barrett or to read some of her short fiction, go to: www.rebeccabarrett.com

Rebecca can be reached by email at: barrett.author@gmail.com

You may follow this author on the following sites: BookBub, Goodreads, Amazon Author Page, Life Intervened Blog

Lulu
Jodie Cain Smith

To ignore the swamp is a fool's game. It takes on many forms—ponds, creeks, rivers, even a trickle of a stream over smooth rocks. It may swell to a lake in places, with roped cedars rising in shadows, sometimes five, six feet wide. A pirogue can snake through the tall reeds then float onto the deafening quiet of a lagoon. There, the cedars disappear. The expanse of water suggests safe passage, but consider what lies beneath the murky surface. Cedar stumps, those mighty trees Mother Nature with her impulsive temperament deemed cut down for whatever reason, hold their ground. Wait to be known. Only a fool forgets the stumps or underestimates their treacherous value.

"If I was born with a last name, no one bothered to tell me," Lulu grabbed the whiskey bottle and poured two fingers into a cut crystal glass. She slid the bottle back across the table. "Help yourself, Father."

"Thank you," the priest glanced at the empty glass before pouring. "This is lovely. New Orleans?"

"New York. A present to myself. Surely you have a set over in the rectory."

"Not this nice."

"Well, temptations of the flesh," Lulu tipped her glass toward the priest.

He eyed her, but not with contempt. His slate blue eyes suggested an understanding. "You should come to the church. I imagine confession is a necessity in your line of work."

"Needing and doing are two very different things. And, to confess, shouldn't I be truly sorry, or at least attempt repentance?"

"Ideally, yes," Father Healy flinched against a clash of thunder, one so invasive the oil lamps flickered. A drop of scotch splashed against the table.

"Little jumpy tonight, Father? Not quite used to the rumblings of Huet Pointe? Well, then, why don't you just sit in that comfy chair, drink my good scotch from my lovely glass, and enjoy the view," Lulu waved her right hand toward the open parlor, draped in purple velvet with settees, sofas, and chairs draped in women too old to be brides and too young to be wives. That scrumptious age when half-dressed is accomplished without guilt or regret or shame. Shame had no place in the House of Dann. "That is why you come to see me, correct? Even on those nights you must fight the wet and cold? Or, are you one of those types who believe God will prevent you from succumbing to the demon flu?" Lulu still carried herself with the ego of that lesser, haphazard age, but by the time Father Healy began his weekly visits, she had earned petticoats, overskirts, full corset, and sleeves, the privileges of a madam.

"God's protection is nothing to scoff at," Father Healy dabbed his finger against the errant drop then licked his fingertip clean. "I like to care for all my flock, not just those who fulfill their weekly obligation." He looked about the room, unrevealing of whether he admired the décor or the product.

"Because my name is written in your Book of Lambs? I think you'll find a hundred Lulabells and Lurlines and even a few Lulus, but none of them me. I wasn't born into your registry."

"But one may be you."

"Of course not, Padre. God has no idea what my name is. I made

298

it up, the last part. Some things can only be accomplished with a full name. As you can see, I had goals. Things to accomplish with that free will you harp about. See, Rev, back then, when I's lying beneath some sweaty mass of a man, I'd imagine myself with his last name. Lulu Jones. Lulu Thompson. Lulu Little. Not Little. A lifetime with that turd would've been a slow death by constant, boring twaddle and barely noticeable twaddling," Lulu laughed, something she did when she thought of her beginnings and was sober enough to laugh. "Lulu Boudreaux? Hell, with all the Boudreauxs in these parts that coulda been my real last name."

Father Healy downed his scotch, licked his lips for any stray drops, and reached for the bottle as if waiting to have his hand slapped away. He was a naughty child who wanted too many cookies.

"So, on one particular night," Lulu continued, "the man pumping and thrusting on top of me like he's trying to turn sweat into butter was a Love. No, not my love. I wanted a last name, but not his. Every time he came to see me, I'd crack up at the irony. Mister Love and his whore."

"Is that how you think of yourself ? The whore?" Healy lifted his full glass to his nose and inhaled.

"You know, that stuff works a whole lot better if you drink it. Anyway, that's what I am, well, was. I've no shame in how I started," Lulu pounded her own glass empty, her jade eyes barely closing against the singe on the back of her throat.

"Mister Love was sweet, but that man played my nerves better than he coulda ever played my ... well you know," a grin flashed across Lulu's face at the sight of the blush heating up Healy's. "Or maybe you don't? Surely you had yourself a taste before tuckin' it away for good."

Healy met Lulu's eyes and held her stare for a moment as if allowing her to enjoy teasing him. "I believe you were in the middle of a story," he said, then took another sip while the storm outside threatened to burst through the doors.

"Sure. Sure. So, Mister Love insisted I talk to him all the while. Not dirty, filthy words like you men like. Well, maybe not you," she curled one corner of her mouth and waited for a reaction that didn't come. "Anyway, he wanted me to talk to him like I actually, truthfully loved him. Poor thing. He had no idea I'm incapable of such a feeling."

"Everyone is born with the capacity to love."

"I don't doubt that. But I believe that capacity can be drained. Like the swamp at low tide. Or that muddy street out there. Eventually all that water will just disappear."

"So, you believe that your capacity to love—that great gift of God—has been drained from you? Just disappeared?"

"Father, I told you already. This isn't confession. I've just no need for love. Love's got no place in my life. I mean who in this world has shown me love? My momma? I assume she's the one who brought me to Ruth in the first place. My daddy? I'm guessing if he knew about me and gave a damn, I'd have had a last name and wouldn't have spent eight years as 'Second story, two doors down the hall Lulu.' Eight damn years under that woman's thumb and any man she sent to my room."

Father Healy reached for a third pass on the bottle, but Lulu grabbed it instead.

"How 'bout something of substance in that belly of yours? Chip," she called to the barkeep, "Get Father here a big steak. You like it a little bloody?"

"I like it any way you wanna fix it."

"Well, Chip'll fry it up for you. I don't cook for anybody but myself," Lulu poured scotch in her own glass, watching as the brown liquid raised three fingers high. "Now, Mister Love. Lord, he was a strange breed of sinner. That night Mister Love went on and on with his usual 'Lulu, my pet, my sweet,' and then waiting for me to respond. 'Oh, yes, my love, yes,' I'd tell him. I may not know love, but I'm a damn fine actress. I shoulda been on a stage in front of thousands for the talent it took to utter those words to Mister Huey Love. Mister Huey Love of Huet Pointe. Silly name for a silly man."

The priest allowed a short chortle to escape his lips.

"Careful, Father, the scotch is showing," Lulu smiled, almost. It was the kind of smile that betrayed the thick armor she had crafted link by link so that seeing beneath it was as difficult as through muddy water. "That dullard Love kept it going like that the whole time. 'What else, my pet? How do I love you?' Then, he'd prop himself up on his elbows so his face was directly above mine. So close I smelled his dinner. He wanted me to express to him for the thousandth time that what he was doing to me was exactly what I needed. That his churning was the best I'd known. Well, I was all out of biscuits, so I didn't need no butter."

To that, Father Healy choked a bit, allowing a dribble of scotch to fall from his mouth to his chin.

"Chip needs to hurry with that steak. I don't need a sloppy man in here tonight," Lulu offered Father Healy a linen napkin.

"My apologies," said Father Healy, blotting his chin.

"Now, where was I before Mister Love and his silly pounding invaded my thoughts? Oh, yes, I remember. Incapable of love. Father, what purpose could love serve? Even if I'd tried. Cleaned myself up. Moved to New Orleans to start a new beginning and trapped myself a husband. To what end? Become his whore? Love didn't get the job done. Love didn't improve my station. Love didn't give me security or take care of old Ruth. Hell, Mister Love wouldn't even get off my hair that night with those damn elbows a' his before several strands ripped out of my head! 'Sweetheart, my hair. It's pulling,' I told him. 'Oh, goodness. Have I hurt you? I never wish to hurt you, my love. May I kiss the pain away?' he asked. I wanted to tell him, 'Just move your fat elbow,' but I didn't." Lulu drained her glass and poured another three fingers. "Insulting a man never gets ya a good tip."

"Perhaps Chip should fry a steak for you as well."

Lulu ignored the priest, as if he hadn't spoken at all.

"Instead, I'd say, 'Certainly. I can think of nothing better' or some kind of nonsense like that. Then he'd press his lips against my forehead allowing beads a' sweat to drip onto my face. If Ruth had allowed me more than one bath per week, she might still—" Lulu pressed her lips closed and breathed deeply through her nose. "Low tide. I bet the stumps are showing. The rain's churning up all that bottom stink. You know under the sandy layer; the bottom is just black clay. Full of sulfur. Stinks so bad you can taste it."

"Yes, the air here can be a bit foul."

"One of God's jokes, huh? Huet Pointe? Not that I'll ever leave this place, but I can't imagine a place more green, water more beautiful with all its colors. But underneath is all rotten eggs and gator shit," Lulu tugged the front right side of her corset, feeling her body swell from the scotch.

In Huet Pointe, ambition is as dangerous as the brackish water that surrounds the sliver of land. But, the women of this antebellum hamlet yearn for more than society insists they be-devout, feminine, and content with living according to cultural norms. So, what's a girl to do? She could employ poison, perhaps a bit of adultery, and drowning in alligator-infested waters is always a choice-whatever it takes to achieve her goal. A novel-in-stories, *Bayou Cresting: The Wanting Women of Huet Pointe*, tells the stories of ten women brought together by proximity, forever entangled by the actions they take.

Jodie Cain Smith is a graduate of the University of South Alabama and Northern Michigan University because earning a degree on both the southern and northern border happened by pure chance and a bit of study. She is the author of *The Woods at Barlow Bend*, her debut novel based on the true story of her grandmother's tumultuous adolescence in rural Alabama and *Bayou Cresting: The Wanting Women of Huet Pointe*. Her short works have appeared in *The Petigru Review, Pieces Anthology,* and *Chicken Soup for the Military Spouse's Soul*. When not creating fictional worlds on her laptop, Jodie hangs out with her long-suffering husband and the most precious little boy ever created. Seriously, the kid is amazing, and the husband puts up with a lot.

Simone and the Sweetness of Sound

Patricia Sands

In 1928, the north coast of Normandy is poor but peaceful ten years after the end of World War I. On a small farm, near the seaside village of Isigny-Ste-Mère, a typical family labors from before dawn until after dusk just to survive, as do most people. What to them is simply a natural product of their labor, is desired throughout the world.

The proud history of Isigny-Ste-Mère butter goes back to the 1600's.

To the west of Lower Normandy, the Isigny-Grandcamp pays is in a prime location, between the sea and the Bessin and Contentin marshlands. The terroir for the production of the sought after butter is almost perfect, with a mild, damp climate and fields near salt marshes. The grass on which the cattle graze is enriched with iodine and other minerals. It is flavored with the sweetness of apple blossoms, buttercups and other indigenous wildflowers amidst the grasses.

Simone is a precocious eight-year-old. Given to flights of fantasy, since infancy she has possessed special qualities.

"Churning butter is hard work, petit mouton," Lisette's words wrap warmly around her daughter, like the woolen shawls over their shoulders that keep away the evening's chill.

She places her hands over Simone's to help guide the pounding action of the wooden dasher in the baratte.

"Oui, Maman, but I love the feeling as the cream thickens and turns. I hear heartbeats as I work."

Lisette smiles at Simone's words. She knows those heartbeats are the air bubbles popping as the fat turns to cream. Her little lamb has a sense of hearing rooted deep within her. It became obvious in infancy that she felt all she heard and she heard what most did not.

In fact, her parents wondered as they became aware of her unique ability, did anyone else? It was an acuity that she demonstrated before words were ever available to her.

As a toddler, Simone would suddenly stop her play, cock her head, crowned with a mass of wild flaxen curls, and listen intently. At times she would close her eyes, a dreamy smile playing on her lips, as her mother wondered what amused her so.

"Simone is a child of light and calm, a gift to us in the midst of the hardship that is life," Lisette often relates to others as they tend their market stalls twice weekly in Isigny-Sainte- Mère.

Her three older brothers, Marcel, Luc, and Georges, cherish her in the same way, even as they gently tease, as brothers do. Simone is growing up feeling secure and loved. It never occurs to her that they are poor or lacking in any way.

Churning butter is one of many tasks mother and daughter share weekly, starting before sunrise in the warm months and at nightfall after the autumn solstice has begun. Cool temperatures are essential to the process. This has become a special time of a mother listening to her young daughter's dreams.

The fresh cream is left to sour before being ready to churn. This sour cream is part of what makes the Normandy butter so deliciously unique and separating the butter from the buttermilk is not a fast process.

To help pass the time, they make up rhymes and sing the tuneful ditty, handed down through generations:

Come butter, come
Come butter, come
Peter's standing at the gate
Waiting for a butter cake
Come butter, come

Simone's pet and constant companion, her donkey, Victor Hugo, bobs his head in time … or so Simone insists … from his position on the other side of the fence by the open stable.

As the butter thickens, Lisette takes charge. She adds a portion of the buttermilk to the earthenware crock from the kitchen and the remainder to a copper pot to slop into the pigpen.

"Maman, I can already hear the happiness of the pigs in their pen. They are calling me to hurry with the buttermilk you are draining off."

"We must keep some for my baking needs, ma petite. They will have to do with less this week. Bring the water now too, chérie."

As she skips to the well, Simone's thoughts float to images and aromas that will fill the simple cottage in the next few weeks. Noël is coming. The special seasonal breads, biscuits and the melt-in-your-mouth feuilleté, bring exclamations of joy from the whole family through the festive season.

Lisette's specialty is feuilleté avec pommes et chèvre. Her melt-in-your-mouth puff pastry is wrapped around slices of apples from their orchard. Goat cheese made from the milk of their small herd of goats, is molded into small crottins. These tasty morsels are crumbled and slipped between the apple slices.

Fresh and hot when served, no special acuity is required to hear the murmurs of appreciation.

For as long as she can remember, Simone has been in charge of crumbling the chèvre. She takes her task seriously, but enjoys it as it seems like play.

Lost as she is in her patisserie contemplation, Simone is abruptly interrupted.

"Simone, don't dawdle with the water bucket! You know we must do this part quickly."

The little girl suddenly has a flashback to the time she had tripped, spilling the water, and hitting her head on a rock. There had been blood everywhere. They were alone as her father and brothers were still working in the fields. Her mother had rushed to scoop up Simone and tend the bloody wound, which required her to apply a few stitches.

Left sitting, the butter turned bad. It didn't take long!

Simone's little heart filled with sorrow that day. She knew part of her family's livelihood depended on the creamy, rich butter they sold at the markets in Isigny. She felt responsible for the hardship, in spite of her mother's assurances.

"We can live a week without butter, petit mouton. We can't live without you!"

At the well, Simone stands on tiptoe to grasp the thick rope with her small fingers and pulls with all of her strength. Three times she returns, quickly but carefully, with the wooden bucket half-full of cold crystal clear water. She already feels the chill in it that comes with winter.

Simone knows she is not yet strong enough to pull a full bucket from the well. She hears the water send it's melodic message to her when the bucket is filled enough for her.

She watches her mother's worn, experienced fingers work the butter to ensure no water remains.

"May I add the salt, Maman?"

Once she finishes sprinkling the crystals of sea salt, Simone helps press the distinct yellow butter into a wooden box, to be stored in a cool place. For now, the task is complete. They will cut it into small blocks later and lightly press their mark on the surface with the wooden stamp Papa carved.

"Listen, Maman ... the stars are coming out." Dusk had fallen quickly as they worked under the thatch roof of the stable. The night sky is coming alive.

"And what aria are they twinkling this evening?" Maman asks.

Her warm smile settles on Simone like a gentle breeze.

Humming and la-la-ing in her soft dulcet tones, Simone goes to the fence to tenderly massage Victor Hugo's soft nose and scratch his tall ears. The donkey bends to lean his head gently into her shoulder and snuffles.

"Victor likes to sing along with me, doesn't he?"

Lisette nods, as she always does when this rhetorical question is expressed. She knows her daughter is hearing that which she cannot. She also knows it is part of the gift that Simone brings into their life and somehow that silly donkey is a gift brought into Simone's life.

It had been born in a fragile state just after Simone turned three. The mother had given birth to twins and immediately rejected the sickly newborn, tending only to the healthy sibling. Survival was not a cause for concern. There was no place on a poor farm for livestock that could not contribute.

Before they could stop her, Simone had lain down in the stinking damp hay, beside the pathetic-looking foal, stroking it as she softly sang her favorite lullaby. She begged her father to bring something for her to feed it and he could not resist her pleas. Her brothers were instructed to collect milk from the mother and Simone had bottle-fed and whispered nourishment and life into its soul until it grew to become her constant companion.

She called the little jack "Bébé" for one year. On the anniversary of its birth, the days of which she had ritually notched on a post in the stable, she gifted him with the name Victor Hugo.

"Because, Papa," she explained, "the night he was born you were reading us *Notre-Dame de Paris* and Quasimodo had just swooped down on bell ropes to rescue Esmeralda. I wanted to rescue Bébé."

Now Simone murmurs her goodnights to Victor before laying her ear at the side of his head. Lisette knows, as she does every day, her daughter is listening to his responses. Then Simone skips back to help her mother tidy up from their labors.

She slips her hand into that of her stout, strong mother as they cross the yard to the stone cottage. Her mother's hands still feel cool from the well water. The skin on those hands is rough by the end of the day, but in a good way.

Simone knows this is the sign of hard work. Dedicated work. To make her family's life the best it can be.

Once evening falls and gentler pursuits prevail, Maman has taught Simone to care for those hands with a small dab of the cream they make together. How? ......Stored in small clay pots in the cold cellar, it feels refreshing as it is absorbed.

"No matter how hard we work, petit mouton," Lisette would say in her most soothing voice, "we must never stop taking care of us."

Mother and daughter grin now. Long yodeling calls and whistles float through the air from the fields, as the men signal each other home in the quickening darkness.

Her father and her brothers work hard. There is no other way to survive. To work is to live and they make the most of it.

The most special time of their day approaches. Lingering younger pullets still peck the dirt, *out of habit* Papa says, *because they will find nothing in the almost-frozen ground*. With no night vision, the older hens are already settled on their roosts. Their soft, feathery breaths are calming to Simone and bring forth visions of fairies that stay with her later as she snuggles into her straw mattress.

Winter is nigh. Days are shorter and the stacks of firewood near the cottage are slowly showing signs of use.

Every evening, after the dishes have been washed and dried, Simone and her three brothers gather by their father's chair next to the fireplace. He waits patiently, book in hand, the bright embers of the fire still warming the room. Providing his family's food and livelihood from his hard labor on their farm is his daily work. Reading to them is his passion.

Simone loves to make up stories after listening to those read to the family.

Now it is father's time. When he is filled with exhaustion, their mother reads. But there is something about listening to Papa's rich strong baritone that brings the stories even more to life. Simone finds a deep pleasure in the fact that both of her parents share this time.

When Maman takes her turn reading, their father whittles quietly creating special gifts for his family.

The hourglass on the mantle is set. Bedtime comes early, as does the hour of rising to begin chores, heralded by the punctual cockerel that rules the barnyard.

Papa opens the clothbound book to where they left off. The man in the iron mask is listening to Aramis concoct a plan to free him and Papa builds the suspense with his voice. This is not the first time he has read this story to them but the excitement is no less thrilling.

Their library is small and treasured. The stories are read many times over.

The novels of Victor Hugo, along with some exciting tales by Jules Verne, incredible as they seemed to this simple family, allow them to dream of worlds beyond theirs. As their parents brought them into the adventures spun by Alexandre Dumas in *The Count of Monte Cristo* and *The Three Musketeers*, the room filled with excitement, suspense and fantasy.

Growing up, the children often recited their favorite passages. The boys play act the adventures. Simone dreams her dreams. She knows her brothers would laugh at them and her father would discourage her from being disappointed. She shares them with Maman ... and Victor Hugo.

Passed down through generations, the little library is stored in a leather trunk for protection from the smoke, dust or dampness that fills their small abode with the changing seasons.

Having two literate parents is most unusual. Maman, schooled by her own mother, in turn tutored Papa from soon after they met. Their love of language brought them together, along with her sweet nature and porcelain complexion, and he had been an enthusiastic student.

Farming is the necessity of Papa's life but in his fantasies he is a professor. He becomes that each evening with his children. His hope is to offer them a better life and his wife watches in admiration.

Lisette sits nearby carding wool sheared that spring from their small herd of sheep. She is pleased that the task is almost completed. Any day now, her sister and family will visit for a day and the wool must be ready to go. Her sister, Joceline, spins the wool into yarn for both families. The sisters have shared these tasks since childhood.

What is left of her current yarn supply is rolled neatly in cedar baskets to discourage moths. Set near her straight-backed chair, her wooden knitting needles are tucked into the skeins.

Months ago, Lisette chose this year's colors.

First, the brownish yellow butternut made by boiling the inner bark of the white walnut tree. Rusty red made from the roots of the madder plant and blue from blueberries. For Simone she gathered goldenrod blossoms to match the soft yellow of her daughter's curls.

Every Noël sees warm sweaters resting on the hearth for the four children and their father. Even though they watch their mother lovingly knit each sweater throughout the autumn months, their delight is genuine when they take turns unfolding their own sweater on that special night.

The massive stone fireplace is the heart of their home. Simone loves how the flames crackle and dance. The sound soothes her as the stones draw the heat into them and radiate warmth into the room. She hears soft murmurings that often lull her to sleep.

Preparing for la fête de Nöel, the mantle and hearth transform into a magical scene. After the boughs are arranged, the crèche is lovingly unwrapped from its storage box.

Everyone in the family takes a turn placing the beloved pieces in their place. These are their special santons. Not the clay pieces from the marché, but carved wooden pieces. The collection was begun by Papa's great-grandfather and carried on through the generations.

They know too, that their father's nightly carving will result in special gifts for each child. The rhythmic strokes of his knife on the wood signal bedtime is nigh. Maman tucks the treasures cleverly into the evergreen branches Simone has helped her artfully arrange across the large mantle of the fireplace.

The story hour passes quickly now. Before kissing each other's cheeks goodnight, they join hands and share a prayer of gratitude for the blessings of the day and safety through the night.

Simone climbs under the comforter on her straw mattress in the sleeping room she shares with her brothers. She lays with her cheek pillowed on her arm, gazing at the starlit sky through the small window on the wall across from her bed, and waits for the snoring serenade to begin.

Humming the melodies of the stars and filled with contentment, the little girl with the yellow curls and golden ears drifts into a dream-filled sleep.

Often when I am creating a character in a story, I become so involved with his or her specific personality that I find myself creating backstories. Such is the case with Simone Garnier, who enters the trilogy in Book 2, *Promises to Keep*. At the time she is 92 years old and a neighbour of the protagonist, Kat. Through one further novel in the trilogy and then the three Villa des Violettes novellas, Simone has emerged as a vital and beloved force in the series. Readers learn that she has always had a particularly heightened sense of sound and this trait allowed her to be indispensible in the Résistance during WWII and in later years helping the police track drug dealers through listening devices ... seriously. Here's a message a reader sent to me just a week ago ~ "I discovered your series through a Facebook event. Read first one in record time and ordered the next two as well as Christmas novella. Simone speaks to me. I can relate to her story. She's settled within herself now but her past still stirs her memory. I'm 73 and she's my new role model..along with Judi Dench! Old Crones don't mess around." It's comments like these from readers that keep authors writing!

Patricia Sands lives two hours north of Toronto, but her heart's other home is the South of France. She spends part of each year on the Cote d'Azur and once a year leads a women-only tour of the Riviera and Provence based on her novels. Her award-winning 2010 debut novel, *The Bridge Club,* is a book club favorite. *The Promise of Provence,* which launched her three-part *Love in Provence* series was a finalist for a 2013 USA Best Book Award and a 2014 National Indie Excellence Award, an Amazon Hot New Release in April 2013, and a 2015 nominee for a #RBRT Golden Rose award in the category of romance. Book Two, *Promises to Keep*, and Book Three, *I Promise You This*. This trilogy was published by Lake Union Publishing.

Drawing Lessons, Sands' fifth novel, also set in the south of France, was released by Lake Union Publishing on October 1, 2017 and a finalist in the Chanticleer Somerset Literary Fiction Awards. Her new 3-volume mini-series, *The Villa des Violettes*, is now available on

Amazon and Kobo, including in a new kindle boxset and paperback Complete Collection.

In December 2020, Sands published *The Bridge Club Tenth Anniversary Edition*, with revised content and a new Epilogue.

Patricia also contributes to such Francophile websites as The Good Life France and Perfectly Provence. Visit her online at www.patriciasandsauthor.com and find all of her links there. To enjoy her photography, follow her on Instagram @patricialsands.

This Time Around

Kimberly Packard

Chapter 1

There was a special place in Heaven for women who juggled it all. Successful career. Loving, harmonious marriage. Well-adjusted children who didn't require an armada of pills to make it through the day. Never forgetting a PTA meeting or snack duty.

It was Josie Gardner's goal in life to make it to this heavenly retreat. She imagined it was as quiet and serene as a spa. Hushed music. Always-flowing champagne. The softest bathrobe. Bookshelves filled with an eternity's worth of romance novels.

But she wouldn't be lounging on a chair, having her feet rubbed by a handsome, muscled masseuse who was also an incredible listener. Nope. She'd be standing outside looking in. Someone left off the guest list of an exclusive club, standing there waiting while her friends partied, holding all their coats.

"Mom, are you even listening to me?" The sardonic tone of her fifteen-year-old daughter, Aubrey, told her she'd zoned out at a crucial moment. Speaking teenager was like visiting a foreign country. One where she was once fluent in the language, but somehow she'd lost her ear for it. Not that different from her marriage. It was like she and her almost-ex woke up one more with that brain injury that makes one speak a completely different language. Suddenly she and Peter were no longer communicating.

"Yeah, you were saying…" Josie didn't even finish, Aubrey's dark blue eyes were focused on her phone. There it was again, a brief moment where they could speak in the same tongue and her daughter was back to the world of communicating in modern hieroglyphics.

Were her kids' lives better or worse with that device permanently attached? In some ways, they were smarter. Anything they wanted to know was a quick Google search away. In other ways, she worried they were giving up valuable life skills.

Josie hid her worry in a long sip of coffee. Then again, her mother constantly worried about drugs, devil worshippers and hidden messages in the music she listened to. And, aside from a few tries of pot in college and that Pagan wedding she attended, Josie made it into adulthood fairly sane and with her soul intact.

While Aubrey's thumbs flew across her phone in unnatural speed, Josie scrolled through her tablet. Meetings, meetings and more meetings. How was it that the more her company grew, the busier she got? New employees meant new product offerings, which lead to new distribution channels and then back again to more employees. It was a never-ending cycle.

And, while she should be thankful for the success, each win took her farther from the beginnings of her company, tinkering with oils and fragrances for an all-natural home in her kitchen with a newborn Aubrey sleeping nearby.

"Don't forget that your dad is picking you and Ben up from school," she scrolled past appointments on the shared calendar she and Peter kept for the kids. There it was, in a magenta meeting notice: *Peter getting kids, Spring Break ski trip.*

Aubrey dropped her phone on the kitchen counter with an exasperated sigh. "That's exactly what I thought. You weren't listening. I said that neither Ben nor I want to go."

Josie sat down the piece of toast she'd just picked up. "What do you mean? You guys love Vail."

The phone didn't stay out of her hands for long. "It's not where we're going, it's who's coming," her eyes stayed glued to her screen while she spoke.

Ah, the new girlfriend.

If Josie couldn't win at her marriage, she could definitely win at her divorce. And, by winning she meant to make everyone's lives as seamless as possible. As if nothing changed, they were all one big happy family. Even if Peter's new girlfriend was young enough to be their daughter, or that he moved into a contemporary condo in a downtown Austin high-rise that barely had space for his own upstart health and wellness company, much less his children. That didn't matter one bit, because Josie was going to win so frickin' hard that Peter would feel like a giant loser for letting her go.

"Kirsten is…nice." The pause was pregnant enough to be nearly full-term with twins.

Aubrey lifted an eyebrow and one side of her pretty mouth lifted into a proves-her-point smile.

Josie's breath caught. It was these moments when she felt like she was looking at an amalgamation of herself at that age and her dad. Where her hair was more reddish-blond, Aubrey got the full force of the red hair gene, but with enough of Peter's dark brown to come out in the perfect auburn color.

Josie's dad's hair was full-on red, but his eyes were a deep playful blue, the same blue that stared at her from across the kitchen island. The same blue eyes that never met her grandfather.

Josie often daydreamed about her dad and her daughter. They'd be thick as thieves, that's for sure. At least, she hoped they would. Hoped that his only granddaughter would pull him back into her life after she so horribly shoved him out of it.

That was the thing about cutting people off. Sometimes the universe had the last laugh and would cut them out permanently.

"Anyway," Josie said, clearing the emotion clogging her throat. "It's non-negotiable. You guys have to go."

"Because some lawyer said so?"

Damn. Kids today were too good at divorce.

"No, because your parents said so," Josie lifted her coffee cup to her lips, smiling into it. "Plus, I was going to have a huge orgy this weekend and I can't do that with minors in the house."

Aubrey appropriately rolled her eyes. "If Dad can have a bendy twenty-three-year-old girlfriend why can't you have something similar?"

"Because he's a few years ahead of me in the mid-life crisis phase of life," Josie leaned on her elbows. The classic we're-gonna-have-a-talk pose. "Aubrey, trust me on this one. There will be a day when you wished you'd put up with Kirsten, and whoever comes after her. And, after her."

Her daughter reached out and tugged on a strand of Josie's reddish-blond hair. She did the same on Aubrey's beautiful locks. A secret gesture they'd started when Aubrey could still barely speak. A way to show her shy little girl who just wanted to hide behind her mom that everything would be okay.

What she wouldn't give to go back in time. To hold Aubrey in her arms one more time. A perfect baby who wanted nothing but her mom. Josie was so busy simply keeping her alive that she didn't spend enough time just reveling in this tiny human she and Peter made.

That was the thing they succeeded at. Making two perfect children, individuals yet pieces of each of them. A living history of their families. It was hard to call their marriage a failure when she looked at it that way.

Ben stumbled into the kitchen. His dark blonde hair was rumpled, eyes half-open behind his glasses. Without a word, her twelve-year-old pulled a coffee mug from the tree and filled it to the top with black coffee.

"Since when did you let Ben drink coffee?" Aubrey said.

"Since never," Josie turned in her barstool. "Ahem, rough night?"

He tumbled into the stool next to his sister, one hand holding his head up while the other brought the cup to his lips. "I got like two hours of sleep."

Was he having nightmares again? There was a spell when he would have these vivid dreams. So vivid that instead of consulting a child psychologist she'd thought about calling an exorcist.

Before she could ask, he continued. "I had to rewrite the algorithm for the app. I realized it had a fatal flaw on the dashboard that would have made the whole thing crash."

Where Aubrey came out as a baby and grew to her ornery teenage self, Ben came out as a little adult. The way her cervix felt after he was born, he came with a briefcase in hand.

"Alright you two, get dressed for school and bring your bags down. I'll drop them off at your dad's on my way to the office."

Ben leveled a serious stare at her. "Are you sure you're going to be okay without us? I mean, you'll be here all by yourself. What if someone tries to break in and strangle you?"

Aubrey snorted. "That could happen with us here. Do you think you're the man of the house now?"

Her kids continued their bickering up the stairs. Josie grabbed her coffee cup and stared out the back window at the sun rising over Austin. They bought this house in the hills of west Austin after Peter's tech company got bought out. Even after all these years, the scenery of the hills, the green of newborn leaves and the sun sparkling off Lake Travis in the distance never failed to steal her breath.

She wasn't going to lie. When Peter told her she could keep the house and he would move downtown she was happier about that than sad to see their marriage dissolve.

It was in these quiet moments when her mind would drift to the past. To the summer nights with a chorus of cicadas. To a handsome boy with sun-bleached hair and green eyes that sparkled like the sun off the lake. To first loves. A future as wide and open as the Texas sky.

It was in these quiet moments that she'd find herself wondering what her life would be like if she hadn't panicked and shunned

Daniel's advances. Afraid to lose their friendship, that she'd somehow screw up an actual relationship and then she'd be left with nothing.

Maybe that's what made teenage love so special. The unrequitedness of it. The newness of every touch, every kiss, every murmur. Like babies learning to walk, teenage love was full of falls and stumbles.

It was also full of regrets that turned into scar tissue that lingered long after the feel of a stolen kiss faded from her lips.

———

The traffic into downtown Austin the Friday before spring break was schizophrenic. The normal slowdowns moved at warp speed, but then Josie crawled through areas where she usually gunned it.

It didn't matter. She barely saw the brake lights in front of her. Instead, her thoughts swirled around the boy who lived behind her throughout high school.

It wasn't the first time she'd found herself wondering about him. There were plenty of nights when she'd poured another glass of wine and spend hours scouring social media, Google search results and, during a night of too much rum punch, obituaries for any mention of her Daniel Palmer. The results were always the same.

Nada.

The music cut off and her best friend's name flashed up on her screen.

"Hey Em."

Heavy breathing answered her.

"Oh God, please don't tell me you accidentally called me during sex. Again."

"Happens one time," Emily was breathless, but the voice of a coach boomed. "I was just finishing a spin class. Are you free of dependents for the week?"

Josie's best friend since childhood never married, and the most she'd managed to keep alive was Ben's beta while they were on a two-week vacation. At least, she always assumed it was the same fish. Somehow it wouldn't surprise her if Emily had bought a replacement fish.

"Almost, just about to drop off their bags at Peter's and head into the office."

"So, what's the plan? A week of partying like we're teenagers? Living at the spa and getting every treatment available? Lots of meaningless sex?"

A sea of red brake lights lit up in front of her and she slowed. Josie hitched her left elbow on the door, cupping her head. "Mmm…I was thinking of catching up on Netflix, maybe eating meals that don't have vegetables. Drinking a bottle of wine a night and waking up the next morning to see what I drunk-bought. You know, the way a mid-life divorcee likes to party."

Emily's blender growled through the car speakers. "Okay, but don't go too crazy on the carbs. T-minus two months until the reunion and our metabolisms called it quits a while back."

Josie sighed, "Another thing lost on the youth, a fast metabolism." She looked behind her, hoping to flirt her way into changing lanes. Several cars drove by, their drivers staring sullenly straight. "Speaking of the reunion—Oh come on! I have my blinker on."

Flirting for a lane change. Also lost on the youth.

"Nope, you're not going to back out again."

"I need an appendectomy."

"Sounds like a personal problem."

She laughed. Would Aubrey find her person, the one she'd know her entire life, that would both cheer her up and call her bullshit? The person who knew her better than she knew herself. These friendships were priceless and more vital than air.

"Anyway, as I was saying. You've seen the guest list, right?"

Her friend waited several beats before answering, "You want to know if Daniel will be there." It wasn't a question. Didn't need to be. There'd been more than a few nights when Josie had called her friend drunk and despondent because she couldn't find any trace of him.

"Last time I looked he wasn't on the list," her voice was softer. "This is a crazy idea, but why don't you hire a PI and see if someone can find him."

"And risk a restraining order?" A car finally let Josie over and she started to make her way to the exit. "Anyway, that's a terrible use of money."

"Any worse than your ex being a regular with a dominatrix?"

She winced. That hurtful truth. It wasn't so much that he'd gone to a dominatrix. At that point, he was sleeping on the couch. It was the fact that when they finally had the divorce talk, his reason was that she was too domineering.

"Point. Set. Match," Josie pulled into the valet at Peter's downtown high rise. "I'll call you later."

She heaved the kids' bags out of the car and up to the thirtieth floor. Flashes of the Texas State Capitol flickered between the steel beams of the glass elevator. The nascent leaves of the springtime bloom cushioned the dome in a sea of green. The blue sky stretched overhead, like a baby waking up. Clear and bright, refreshed and ready to take on the day.

Kirsten answered Josie's quick knock. Her almost ex- husband's new "female friend" (apparently Kirsten was very offended by the term girlfriend. Maybe it was because she'd only been old enough to drink for a couple of years) opened the door.

"Hi, Mrs. Gardner. Happy Friday!"

Josie hated it when she called her that. It was like she thought she was Peter's mother or something.

Did she?

"Hey Kirsten, is Peter here? Dropping off the kids' stuff and making sure he's all set."

"Sure, I'll go get him," the girl turned and sashayed out of the foyer. Insanely long legs, freakishly long, thin arms. Did the human race evolve somewhere between when Josie was born and when Kirsten was? Her own limbs felt stubby, clunky.

Josie let herself in and walked over to the picture windows. The

324

morning traffic below reminded her of Ben's toy cars, rolling through a make-believe town. Off to make-believe jobs, at make-believe companies. With perfect make-believe families waiting back home at the end of the day. All she'd wanted out of life was for her kids to have a normal family. To have parents who loved each other as much as they loved them. It was an inevitable destination for Peter and Josie, but sucked still the same.

"Hey, Josie," her estranged husband's voice was warm and kind. It was always warm and kind, even when he told her he loved her but wasn't *in love* with her.

She turned. It was really unfair that he was more handsome at the end of their marriage than he was at the beginning. When they met in their mid-twenties, he was a pudgy geek with some coding skills and a business degree. Now, he was trim and fit, having sold the company he started for enough money that they could live comfortably, invest in Josie's growing business and the kids could go to any college they wanted, and he could invest in his own burgeoning business. A health and wellness app for men over fifty. His target audience: the kind who wanted to stay fit enough to attract a girlfriend half his age.

Female friend.

She rolled their suitcases toward him, delivering everything her kids would need for the next week.

He leaned in for a hug. Even though she agreed the marriage was over, there was something about clinging to the man who'd made love to her, held her hair back during morning sickness, smothered her in kisses after their babies were born that made her feel like she'd walked into a house she'd sold, yet it still felt like home.

"You look good," she said. It wasn't a lie. His hair had settled into the gray, which somehow made his steel blue eyes even more captivating. The gingham blue shirt was untucked, sleeves haphazardly rolled and the medium wash jeans sat perfectly on hips. *Dammit, why was Kirsten getting the best of him?*

"So do you."

Did she? She glanced down at her own outfit. Dark skinny jeans with a loose top to hide her softening middle. Luckily the teal color drew more attention to her blue-green eyes than her muffin top.

"This should have everything. Ben's backup inhaler is in the inside pocket." She immediately went into mom-mode, "Try to limit his screen time. I know you guys will be on the slopes most days, but he's going to want to fight it. Same with Aubrey, you'll have to pry that phone out of her hands, but it'll be good for her. Plus we don't need her breaking a leg because she tried to take a selfie flying down the slopes."

He snorted. "Hashtag embarrassing."

Josie laughed. He always made her laugh. Even when they were breaking up they somehow kept it light.

"Why don't you stay for a cup of coffee?"

"Thanks, but I have to get into the office. Million things to do," she tried to make her voice light, but she intended this to be a bag drop. If she could have left it with the concierge, she would have, but she just wanted to look in his eyes and make sure he'd bring her children home in the same condition. Her chest tightened with the thought of all the to-do's gathering dust on her list.

Peter's face dropped its friendly facade, his forehead wrinkled. "Sit with me, Josie. Let's talk."

Concern tumbled in her stomach like sneakers in a dryer. This was the same face he'd made when he took their marriage away. What else was he going to take from her?

"Is everything okay?"

He crossed into the kitchen, sliding a manila envelope off the counter, offering it to her. "You can have your attorney read through it, but I wanted you to hear it from me."

Josie stared at the envelope as if it were rigged to explode. Something deep inside her knew she was in the *before*. Before she opened it, read the document. Before she knew whatever it was that Peter was going to do to her. Before she had her heart ripped to shreds. Again. "What is it?"

"Look, we said we'd tackle the divorce this summer, but I wanted to go ahead and get the papers drawn up. What, with Kirsten…" his gaze drifted down the hall where the twenty- something had disappeared. "Anyway, with the custody arrangement, just hear me out. I was thinking the kids could stay here with me during the week, and see you on the weekends."

Like the old Graviton ride of her youth, the floor dropped out from under her. Disbelief pinned her to the spot, her hand halfway opening the envelope, her stomach flying up into her throat.

"What? Are you nuts?" Her shriek echoed around the sparse apartment. There was no way in Hell he'd bring her kids here to live. "I'm a good mother. I'm a great mother. You have absolutely no grounds to do this."

"You *are* a great mother. That's not what this is about."

She was finally able to convince her limbs to move. Josie crossed her arms, crumpling the half-opened envelope. "Oh? Well, then, enlighten me."

He blew out a sigh and ran his hands through his hair.

She'd done the same so many times. Yearned to do that now. Not sexually, but to cause him as much pain as she felt. "You did so much while I built my career. You stayed home with them, fed them, changed God knows how many diapers. I'm doing this so you can do the same for your career, not because you did anything wrong. You had your time, let me have mine."

A laugh bubbled up from deep inside her, hot, acrid, like magma from deep inside the earth. "Oh, so I get to deal with sleepless nights and shitty diapers while you get to hang out and play video games. No, Peter, you don't get to do this. You don't get to swoop in and do all the fun stuff. Not this time. You're not taking my kids from me."

"They're my kids too, Josie."

"Well, you should have thought that through before you decided you weren't in love with me anymore," she shoved the crumpled envelope into her bag, scrambling to find her car keys before remembering the valet had them. "Anyway, my attorney *will* be reaching out to your attorney."

Peter grabbed her wrist as she pushed past him, his thumb stroking the inside lightly. It had always been his way to calm her down, and Josie hated that he still used this. Hated even more that it still worked.

"Josie, look, maybe I said it all wrong then, but," he swallowed hard, the pain etched across his face was deep, as if it'd been there so long that it became part of his features. "You were always the one. For me. I just never felt like I was the one for you. I think I woke up one day and just didn't have enough love to hold us together."

Josie Gardner's life centered around two things: her amazing children and her burgeoning business. But, when both are at risk of slipping through her fingers, a panic attack releases her grip on reality… and the present.

She wakes up in her teenage bedroom, nearly thirty years into the past where she must encounter mistakes she made, heal broken hearts, and try to hang on to "the one who got away."

Kimberly Packard is an award-winning author of edgy women's fiction.

When she isn't writing, she can be found running, asking her dog what's in his mouth or curled up with a book. She resides in Texas with her husband Colby, a clever cat named Oliver and a precocious puppy named Tully.

Her debut novel, *Phoenix,* was awarded as Best General Fiction of 2013 by the Texas Association of Authors. She is also the author of a *Christmas novella, The Crazy Yates,* and the sequels to *Phoenix, Pardon Falls* and *Prospera Pass,* and her stand-alone titles *Vortex* and *Dire's Club.* She was honored as one of the Top 10 Haute Young Authors by Southern Methodist University in 2019.

Follow Kimberly online at www.kimberlypackard.com, Twitter or Instagram @kimberlypackard, or Facebook, www.facebook.com/kimberlypackardauthor.

The Bridge
Debra Bowling

Marilyn, 1960

She crouched forward on the car seat and leaned sideways against the door as they turned a curve in the road. The metal of the door handle was cool to her touch, and she looked down at her pale, thin fingers with long, red nails. She carefully filed and polished them in the early morning hours while CB and the girls banged on the bathroom door begging for her to come out. CB threatened to take down the "goddamned door," but she waited until each nail was perfect before pushing back the latch.

They were all asleep when she slipped from bed and quietly locked herself in the bathroom. She counted thirty-four aspirin in the bottle and ran her finger against the blade in CB's razor, gummed with old soap and tiny hairs. That's when she noticed the chipped polish. Now, in the car, their shiny redness seemed to stand out more against her pale white skin. The white fingers looked bloodless; maybe they were already dead.

She quickly let go of the door handle and smoothed back the soft waves of her hair, trying unsuccessfully to twist the ends into a knot.

Moments later, she gave up and flipped the strands back. One foot tapped nervously as she remembered the plan she made this morning to get CB to take her to the lake when he got home from work—and cross the bridge that recently opened after major renovations. The bridge had always loomed in the distance when she came with family to the lake as a young woman, but she never crossed it before, never saw the other side.

"The other side is miles and miles of trees on a bunch of little mountain tops. If you keep going, you get to Scant City, then Arab if you go south. Ain't really nothing to see, especially by the time we get there. It will already be dark."

He was sniffling now, and Marilyn shifted her eyes to look at CB next to her, his left hand on the steering wheel. He was a tall man, still lanky at thirty-six with huge hands and feet. His eyes glanced at her and she weaved her fingers together and dropped them into her lap.

Resisting the urge to bite her lip, she studied her hands. Red nails and white skin. Red and white. Red like blood. She closed her eyes tightly, comforted for a moment by the darkness. Then all she saw was red—liquid red. She wanted to open her eyes, instead she watched red blood trickling down her long, white fingers, dripping off the tips of her nails and falling in fat splotches that covered her dress and began to fill the car. She cupped her shaking hands trying to catch her blood into her hands then pressed them together, then tighter together.

Stop!

Did she say it out loud? Her eyes opened to see CB light a cigarette and she shifted slightly to keep him visible from the corner of her eye. His head turned toward her as she moved, and she stiffened. The blare of a horn made him lean forward suddenly and swerve closer to the curb. Several thick black curls fell on his forehead, and it reminded her of how good he looked. Even now. Even half drunk.

He slumped his six-foot-four frame back down to fit into the seat. Still, she knew his head was touching the headliner where a dark wet spot continued to grow from the daily squirt of Vitalis he religiously combed through his hair. One hand touched her stomach, almost flat.

She wondered if this baby would be a boy and would he look like him.

"Still upset?" CB's voice was deep and loud in the car, and she turned her head slightly toward him but did not answer. She flinched and squinted to see him in the darkness when he moved forward suddenly, his hand searching under the seat. He pulled out a brown paper bag. "Why don't you take a sip with me?"

Again, she did not answer, but turned toward the window, annoyed by the sound of whiskey sloshing in the bottle when he raised it several times. The highway was lined heavily with trees, dense and overgrown, blocking out much of the fading light from the sky.

As they turned the curve, two eyes glowed in the distance, returning the headlight's glare. The eyes held hers, and she wondered what animal had stopped, blinded by CB's lights, its motionless body waiting, frightened by the sound of the motor racing toward it. Maybe it was waiting for fate to decide if the car would smash it to death or pass on by. Was it too scared to run?

The road twisted to the right, and the eyes disappeared.

Marilyn felt vaguely disappointed as if the car failed its mission. She must have let out a sound because CB's fingers suddenly touched her shoulder, stroking the only part of her he could reach. She imagined their imprint on her skin like the dark purple spots his hands left around her neck and shoulder last night. She pulled her body closer to the door, and his hand slid to the seat. After a few seconds, he sighed loudly and returned his hand to the steering wheel.

Marilyn rolled down the window halfway as they turned another curve, and then sped down the mountain. The wind blew back her hair and filled the car with the sharp scent of pine trees. A string of lights revealed a clearing with two block buildings with peeling paint and a large metal white sign with black letters, LITTLE TEXAS. A smaller, hand-lettered sign was near the door with GO TO THE BACK FOR BAIT. She wondered again why this dump on the side of the road in Guntersville, Alabama would name their place after Texas, but it was one of the few places in the surrounding dry counties where CB could go to the back and buy liquor. This liquor was packaged, safer than the moonshine that almost killed CB when he was a teenager, but nearly twice as expensive. Although he was a frequent visitor, CB rarely stopped when she was with him, telling her it was too rough a place for women.

"If you weren't going to talk to me Marilyn, why did you want to take a drive together to see the bridge?" CB's voice whined like a child and as if she had no right to be upset with him. Pressing her lips together, she turned to face the window and wondered if her lipstick had worn off. She forgot to check before leaving the house even though she stared at a mirror while waiting for CB to get a neighbor to watch the girls.

CB turned the radio on and then quickly snapped it off, slowing down as they circled the last curve to Guntersville Bridge. From the side, the lights created long shadows from the tall, metal beams that soared high above the bridge and then dropped to disappear into the dark waters below. Even the road disappeared into the wilderness on the other side, or maybe it was just too dark to see it ahead.

Her heart fluttered, and she turned in the seat and looked back from the direction they came and saw the darkness closing in behind them; not even the lights of Little Texas shined through the trees.

"I told you it would be too dark to see anything by the time we got here."

There were no other cars in either direction on the bridge. Satisfied, she sat back, listening for the sound of water while trying to smell it in the breeze that lifted her hair. Shutting both eyes, she imagined the cool water washing over her and closing everything out. Her heart began pounding in her ears; irritated, she leaned closer to the window and struggled to hear the water. She thought she heard a voice then, "Maybe the baby's heart is beating hard, too." One hand pressed on her belly to comfort him, and she opened her eyes to the bridge looming before them. They drove up and inside the huge, metal cage that wrapped around the concrete with big, strong metal arms.

She wondered if the arms made the bridge safer or if it was only to make people think it was. The holes in the cage were still big enough to fall through. Or jump through. A shiver began but stopped as she looked at her husband, quietly sneaking sips of whiskey, the bottle still covered with a brown paper bag. He turned to her then, his eyes pleading for her, full of sadness and regret. His sadness always filled her, and she trusted it, took it in even with the drunken outbursts. This used to be all it took to get her back. She used to think she could make the sadness go away.

Her head quickly turned back to the window, and she heard him screw the cap on the bottle as she craned her neck out the window to see the water below. The side of the bridge was too high. The smell of damp earth and fishy water filled the car.

She turned back to CB. "I need to see it. I need to see the water."

CB's face grew soft, then relieved. He quickly slowed the car and pulled in closer to the edge. "Can you see it now, baby?" Her back stiffened at his voice. She would only be able to see it when she got out. They were near the center of the bridge. It had to be now.

He continued, his voice kind, almost a whisper, "If I had known you wanted to see the water, we would have gone to the swimming area on the other side of the lake."

Her hand grasped the handle, and she drew in a slow, shaky breath. She jerked the handle up and pushed against the door and used one foot to help shove it open.

Feet first. This was as far as she planned. The pavement scraped her foot, and the wind pushed the door against her. She held to the door to move her body out, but the car lunged forward, going faster. For a moment, she was afraid the car would pin her against the railing, but it swerved away, then back again, the headlight scraping against the railing when it stopped, and her body jerked forward. The door stayed open, and she was almost out when a big hand grabbed at the back of her head, taking strands of hair when it dug deep into her bruised neck and shoulder, tearing her blouse and she felt herself falling back.

Screams tore from her throat when she realized that his hands held her tightly inside the car. "I'm gonna jump. I'm gonna jump," she couldn't stop saying the words while trying to tear herself away from him.

"You goddamned crazy woman!" He released his hold on one shoulder for a second and leaned forward, quickly grabbing under her arm and pulling her back in toward him.

Her arms and legs continued to lock on the door frame until he stopped pulling and slapped her over and over, then pulled her fully inside. He reached over her, locking the door even though it wasn't shut tight.

A car from behind slowed down, then went around them. CB's hand held to her hair, pulling her head back. He glanced back to look at another car stopping behind them, then turned back to her, his eyes red from the liquor and rage. She flattened her body against the seat.

"You were going to jump the damn bridge!" He accused her, his breath hard and labored. She remained quiet and limp, matching his breath. "You're trying to get me in trouble, trying to make people think I threw you!"

Her head moved slightly to try to ease the strain from her scalp. His eyes narrowed at her move. He raised his other hand as if to slap her.

It was only a warning. A rush of anger stiffened her body.

His face was so close to hers that she wildly thought about plucking out his blue eyes and flinging them into the water.

"Let go." Her loud voice seemed to startle him. Her fingers were only tiny claws pulling at his huge hands, but his hold weakened when they both heard slamming car doors and strangers from cars talking to one another.

"Keep your mouth shut, Marilyn, or I swear I'll kill you and you won't have to jump off no damn bridge." She thought he smiled at her then, a twisted curl of his lips before he turned in his seat and opened the door.

"My wife and I are fine. Lost control of the car, but we were going so slow that everything seems okay." He got out and unsteadily walked in front of the car, stopping to examine the fender and headlight while talking to the two men. He moved over to lean against the railing, continuing to talk while watching her.

It was a mistake. Why did she choose this? Her face was burning, and she could feel sweat trickling down the sides of her face. Blood circled around her red fingernails, and she wondered if it was hers or CB's. She pulled back her hair with one hand while pulling the rear-view mirror down. She flinched at her swollen face and left eye and slowly pushed the mirror back in place.

She should run now. Her eyes focused across the bridge where the forest continued for miles without houses or people. It would be daylight before he could see to search for her.

She took a cigarette from his pack and lit it with shaking hands while imagining herself lighting a campfire. Breathing in the smoke made her calmer. As a child, she played in the woods, ran barefoot through the creek behind the family farm and sunned herself on large rocks. Could she get through the night here? She looked down at her skirt and bare ankles, the patches of scraped bleeding skin and one foot swollen over the edge of her shoe. Where would she go at daybreak?

CB moved from the railing and back around the car, still talking to the men. With the cigarette pointed up, she watched the tip burn down, breathing in the smoke through her nose. The door opened and CB slid in, moving the rear-view mirror to watch the last man get into his car behind them. He waved as the car passed and sat silent until the glow of taillights disappeared before turning suddenly and grabbing her arm, taking away the cigarette and throwing it out the window.

"I know what you're doing. What kind of wife and mother are you anyway? Don't you even think about the girls or the baby?" He stared into her eyes briefly, his eyes no longer sad, but cold and unrecognizable. Fear gripped her stomach. It was this stranger she feared the most. His nostrils flared, and he jerked her arm as he released his hold and found the keys in his pocket.

The car started quickly, and CB slowly continued across the bridge, then pulled the car onto the left side of the graveled shoulder of the road and reached for a cigarette. A metal railing continued from the bridge into the edge of the forest, holding back the baby pine trees and thick vines with tentacles that held to the metal and reached out for something more. A breeze made them sway like waving arms. Marilyn watched, shaking her head slightly, wondering again if she could have made it in the forest. Her arm slowly slipped out the window, her hand wide open and palm up. It began to shake, and she quickly turned the palm down, glancing at CB as he backed up the car, smoke streaming from his mouth. It was too late. She waved slightly to the vines before bringing her arm back inside the window.

The car sped back over the bridge, and she fanned away the fishy, damp air that filled the car along with CB's cigarette smoke. The car zipped back into the winding road and the waiting darkness where there was nothing more to see.

They were both silent as CB drove up the mountain, slowly turning sharp curves. There was no moonlight, and the headlights lit only a few feet of the pavement before the next curve. She rubbed her arms and neck where they had begun to ache and patted her swollen face. Her throat was sore and dry when she tried to swallow.

As the twists and turns of the road straightened out and they came into the edge of town, CB slowed down and turned the car into the driveway of a service station. "Can I trust you to stay put while I get us a Coke?"

Turning away, she stared at the screen door with a picture of a rosy cheeked little girl eating bread, and then changed her view to study fading letters on a wooden bench in order to keep from watching CB walk inside the store. A breeze cooled her face, and she heard the distant sound of thunder.

Children ran out of the store, slamming the screen door and laughing as they all crawled into the back of a truck parked near her. A tall older man came out next, nodding in her direction. "Evening."

She didn't answer. She knew CB would be watching her while in the store. He walked out then, holding two Cokes. He swallowed from the first can and held the other one out to her.

The older man started his car and waved, then pulled out of the driveway.

"Who is he?" CB turned and watched the car drive away. There would be no right answer, so she gave none.

"Will you take the damned Coke?" He set his on the top of the car, then reached inside the window and pulled her limp arm from her lap. There were bloody scratches on his hand, and she wondered if he noticed. He put the can in her hand, grabbed his own, and then walked back to the other side of the car.

Her throat ached, and she slowly brought the can up to her lips. A small sip of Coke fizzed against her raw throat moments before CB screeched the car out of the drive and onto the road. His hands tightly gripped the steering wheel, and she wondered why he stopped her from jumping? Was it only because he feared that everyone would think he did it? Sinking back, she closed her eyes, too weary to think anymore.

Maybe she was too tired. Maybe he put something in her Coke. She sat up and carefully brought the can up to her face and pretended to take a sip while rubbing a finger across the top, then smelling it. Only one side had a triangle cut into it; as usual, he didn't bother to make the second hole.

Glancing at CB, she wondered how long he would punish her when they got home. She just wanted it all to end. She leaned her head back and closed her eyes. If only she could just go to sleep and not wake up. She felt comforted at the thought and rose up to take large sips of the sweet Coke.

The Bridge is an excerpt from *The Memory of Flight*

A bridge is a structure carrying a pathway or roadway over a depression or obstacle, according to the Merriam Webster's Dictionary. The symbolism of bridges, as structures enabling one to pass from one side of something to the other, is one of the most widespread, according to the Penguin Dictionary of Symbols (1996). "Two points stand out: the symbolism of passage, and the dangerous nature of this transition, which is that of any 'journey' of initiation…It might be said that bridges symbolize the transition between two inner states or between two conflicting sets of desires." Further, the bridge must also lead to the solution to a confrontational situation and the crossing must not be avoided because avoidance solves nothing, and the situation remains.

The Bridge was initially written as a short story, the idea coming from a few known facts of an incident told to me by my grandmother when I was a teen. It seems that in the spring of 1960, a young wife asked her husband if they could go for a drive, if he would take them to a lake in the next county and across the bridge. The young woman was a mother of two school-age girls and was pregnant with her third child. She was terribly depressed and had told her sisters that her husband was violent when he drank and that he was drinking more often.

The young woman, Marilyn, chose the bridge as the destination for her conflict, which was deeply symbolic. I used fiction to bring the story to life, and soon it became the first chapter of a novel, *The Memory of Flight*, which received the 2015 Author of the Year Award for First Novel. The novel was originally published in 2014 by Little Feather Press of New York and has been reissued through the Back In Print Program of the Authors Guild in 2021.

Debra Bowling's debut novel, *THE MEMORY OF FLIGHT* received the 2015 Georgia Author of the Year Award for First Novel. She has published essays, short stories, poetry, and photographs. Bowling has also produced numerous video documentaries, including a series on Southern authors, Tina McElroy Ansa, Terry Kay, and Sara Flannigan, funded by the Atlanta Bureau of Cultural Affairs. *Walking Without Music: Raymond Andrews and the Storyteller's Tradition*, was purchased to be included in Andrew's special collection by Emory University and Stories of Survival, Refugees in Atlanta was a finalist in the 1989 Hometown USA Video Festival.

Spandex and Leg Warmers
Susan Cushman

As I watched Baby and Johnny heat up the stage in the 1987 hit movie, "Dirty Dancing," Bill Medley and Jennifer Warnes belted out the lyrics to the title song, and I made them my own: "I've… had the time of my life… and I owe it all to you!" And of course I fantasized about being on that stage with Patrick Swayze as I choreographed and practiced the routines to "Time of My Life" and other heart-thumping songs of the eighties for the aerobic dance business I managed for six years during that strange decade of dizzying discos, bad hair and really ugly clothes. But this session in August of 1988 would be my "swan song"—my last class to teach at Bill Johnson's Phidippides Sports in Jackson, Mississippi. I wept as I danced around the studio, knowing that in a few weeks I would leave that place where I had, in many ways, had the time of my life. The place wasn't Jackson, my home town, but Phidippides Sports Aerobics, the business my parents had opened alongside their retail athletic store.

It was the 1980s, and "the times they were a changing." The fitness craze finally made its way to Mississippi, and Dad became a runner, and a leader in the emerging world of distance running, competing in marathons and inspiring others to healthy lifestyles. In 1982, he opened a retail sports business and brought in his younger sister, my aunt Barbara Jo, to help manage the store. I think he agreed to Mom's idea to rent the adjacent space for an aerobic dance studio just to give her something to do.

I couldn't have been more shocked when they came to me and asked if I wanted to train to be one of the instructors for their new aerobic dance business. I was only thirty-one, but I was about thirty pounds overweight and completely out of shape. I hadn't exercised in years, nor did I have any training in aerobic dance.

"But you were a cheerleader, and you can *dance*," Mom said, and Dad smiled and nodded. Mom had been on the dance team in college, and had pretty much taught Dad all the right moves from the beginning of their courtship. I loved to watch them dance when I was growing up, and thrilled at the chance to join Daddy on the dance floor from time to time.

"But, what if … what if I can't do it? I'm really out of shape. Aren't aerobic instructors supposed to be models of fitness for their students? And… what would I have to *wear*?" Suddenly the thought of me in spandex in a room full of mirrors was more than I could bear.

"Well, we've just hired a coordinator for the program, and so why don't you come to one of the training sessions and see how you feel about it. And we're going to carry lots of cute leotards and tights and leg warmers in the store, and you can have them at cost!" Mom's face revealed the same hopefulness she always held out for her little girl— the fifth grade play princess, the little league queen, the cheerleader, and now, the aerobic dance instructor. Sometimes I couldn't delineate between her goals for me and my own dreams—her happiness and mine. This gift she was holding out to me couldn't disguise the fact that she would never give up on trying to get me to lose weight. But I wanted what she was offering, so I chose not to look the gift horse in the mouth.

Off I went to the practice sessions with the coordinator my parents had hired. She had been certified by the Aerobics and Fitness

Association of America (AFFA) and was also a seasoned runner, and when she put us through the paces on my parents' patio that steamy summer afternoon it was like déjà vu from cheerleading two-a-days in junior high school all over again. I was out of breath, bright red in the face, and struggling to keep up with the others who were "trying out" for this new role in the fitness industry. My thighs rubbed together as my nylon running shorts crawled up my butt and streams of sweat escaped my jog bra and found their way down my lower back into my athletic panties which were designed to whisk away perspiration and keep my skin cool.

None of this went unnoticed by my mother, who was watching through the French doors to the den. "Don't worry about your shorts riding up, Susan," she offered in her helpful June Cleaver voice, as she came out onto the patio carrying cold bottles of Gatorade and diet sodas. "You'll be wearing tights under your shorts while you're teaching." And sure enough, the precursors to Spanx saved the day when I was finally ready for my first appearance in front of a studio full of women waiting to be whipped into shape by the newly trained instructors at Phidippides Sports Aerobics.

I think I threw up half of the meals I ate the week before the first class I taught—partly out of nervousness, and partly from old bulimic habits returning to haunt my efforts. The voices in my head were saying, *You can't do this, you're too fat*. And sure enough, I was the chubbiest of the first flock of instructors, but not for long. It was almost magical how the pounds began to melt, week after week, as I led my students in three to six 60-minute workouts each week and practiced the routines at home between classes. And yes, the compliments helped, as I heard, for the first time in my life, "You look great!" and "How much weight have you lost?" and "Are you on a special diet?"

It was true. I went from 148 pounds to 115 in a few short months, and without dieting! After years of pleading with God through many tearful nights to please help me quit eating and please help me lose weight, it was as if my craving for food was suddenly gone. And of course my body had become a fat-burning machine that stayed tuned with workouts seven days a week. Yes, even when I wasn't teaching, I was always practicing. I remember going out of town with my husband on trips, and the first thing I would do when we arrived at our hotel was ask where the closest aerobics studio was. If I couldn't find a place to work out, I wouldn't eat, or I would eat and throw up, in order not to gain back the weight. I hadn't healed my dysfunctional eating at all—I had simply replaced it with an exercise addiction. The high I got from aerobics was better than the temporary high from carbohydrates. And I finally had what I always wanted—a thin, fit body. But the surprise that came with success was this: I wasn't happy. And I still thought I was fat.

I had developed body-image distortion, a condition that is rampant among women (and some men) of all ages now. But even in the 1980s, it was a growing disorder that left many women like me incapable of seeing ourselves as we really were. And there was lots of time to *look*—all the classes and practices for classes took place in a room full of mirrors. And dressing the part for those performances—because that's what they felt like—consumed lots of time and money. Thankfully, I got all my aerobics clothes at cost, since my parents owned the store, but my pursuit of the perfectly shaped leotard or just the right leg warmers was endless. In the early months of the business, we all wore running shorts over our tights, which made it easier for me to disguise my less than skinny thighs. But once the high-cut leotards—and even thongs!—became popular, I found myself scrutinizing my wardrobe even more critically.

My quest for perfection was exacerbated by the 1985 movie, "Perfect," starring Jamie Lee Curtis as the top aerobics instructor at a fitness center in L.A. Curtis' character showed no mercy on her students or herself, as she thrust her size two ass in their faces and yelled out drill sergeant commands over the throbbing disco beat of the music. Her ribs stuck out through her skin-tight leotards, and not a centimeter of flesh on her arms would jiggle as she pumped and punched her way through the routines. I remember running out to try and find a pale blue leotard like hers, with high-cut legs, which she wore over flesh-tone tights, but then I discovered that I looked best in black or dark blue, anything but the ballet pinks that the skinnier girls were wearing.

Leg warmers were one of the best inventions for bodies like mine. They camouflaged my skinny calves and balanced the girth of my thighs. I think I owned a pair in every color of the rainbow. And when everyone started wearing sleeveless leotards, I panicked at the thought of displaying my naked arms. But somehow I would always find just the right cut—the best design to flatter my body, which was surprisingly toned, a fact I rarely allowed myself to acknowledge.

After a couple of years our coordinator quit, and my folks asked if I would take over the business. I was thrilled, because by then I had attained a level of fitness and expertise, and, well, I've always loved being in charge! Off I went to AFFA conventions and workshops, where I honed my craft and brought back the latest fitness trends to all those former beauty queens who were now young mothers and career women, taking my classes to stay in shape. There were even former classmates from high school who surprised me by signing up to take classes from the girl who didn't make cheerleader or drill team fifteen years earlier. A few didn't recognize me at first. "You… you look better than you did in high school!" The words should have felt good, but there was always a sting to them. I'm sure they meant well, but it was what they *weren't* saying that hurt—that I wasn't good enough to be a cheerleader or Murrah Miss (drill team dancer) fifteen years and thirty pounds ago. The message couldn't have been clearer: my worth, my value as a woman, was tied directly to my weight and my appearance. I still believe that it was my skill as an administrator that saved the day.

Running an aerobic dance business isn't just about being fit. It's also about hiring, training, and sometimes firing instructors—something I had no preparation for, since I had only worked as a secretary up until that point. But I loved it. The power. The control. Some of the instructors I trained were successful in other areas of their lives—one was an emergency room physician, one was a successful business woman who ended up taking our program to the workplace, teaching our first off site classes. Several of our instructors were also runners, and were in better shape than I was. But they seemed to respect the time and organization that I put into the program, freeing them to do what they did best—teach classes.

Aerobics in the eighties was still about dancing, and the routines I choreographed were similar to what was happening with Jazzercise, although that franchise, which started in Chicago in 1969, hadn't hit Mississippi yet. I would listen to the radio constantly—in fact, I kept a notepad in my car—and write down the names of songs that had the right beat for the different parts of a 60-minute routine: five minutes for warm- up, twenty minutes for aerobics, five minutes for cool-down, and thirty minutes for floor exercises. Then I would go to the record store and buy 45s (yes!) of each song and record them onto a cassette player at home, without the benefit of a professional mixer. I spent hours on each amateur dance mix, trying to overlap them so that there was no pause between songs.

After each tape was made, I would choreograph the routines, writing down the steps to each song, and make copies of the tapes and routines for all the instructors. Every six to eight weeks we'd change routines, so the instructors would come in for practices to learn the new ones, take the tapes and instructions home with them and begin memorizing the routines for the next session while still teaching the current classes. All I can say when I think about it now is *we were young!*

The instructors would sometimes go out after practice or get together for lunch. Some of us put on demonstrations at local luncheon clubs to drum up business or promote fitness in the community at large. And my folks gave some great parties for all the instructors and store employees. One I remember fondly was on a summer night when they rented a houseboat on the Ross Barnett Reservoir complete with music and catered food and drinks. We danced on top of that houseboat on the same waters where Bill and I had enjoyed our first date on a sailboat fifteen years earlier. But this evening was more about fun than romance—with a bunch of dancers and athletes showing off their latest moves on a hot summer night under the stars. I think that was the last time I ever danced with my father, so it's a bittersweet memory.

One of my favorite experiences during my aerobics career was going with my mother and my aunt to market in Atlanta. Barbara Jo was the buyer for my parents' store, and I joined them on one of their buying trips because it coincided with an AFFA conference—one at which I learned new low-impact techniques, including the latest, "bench" aerobics. Stepping inside the World Congress Convention Center during the fitness clothing expo and AFFA conference, I imagined a similar scene inside the Olympic Village—athletes from every sport packed the halls and convention floor, sporting the latest trends in fitness. Vendors manned their booths and took orders from retailers from all over the country and beyond.

The sounds of music pumped out of the ballrooms, which had been transformed into aerobics studios for the convention. I found the class I had registered for and joined with my peers from other places in our common goal of improving our craft and taking the latest moves and information home to our fitness staff and students. Discussions often grew into arguments about the best ways to lose weight, build muscles, strengthen bones, and protect joints. The craze from the previous year—like the use of ankle and wrist weights during aerobic routines—was often this year's taboo. Target heart rates for aerobic workouts changed from time to time, as did recommended standards for fitness levels according to age and gender. My parents' aerobics business catered exclusively to women, so my experience teaching fitness to men was still to come, and I had no idea how different it would be.

Returning to Jackson with new routines, wardrobes, and inspiration, I continued to pour myself into the classes, and my newfound body and metabolism. Diets were out, but healthy eating was in, and one of the gurus I latched onto during those years was

Covert Bailey, whose first book, *Fit or Fat*, was published in 1978. The concepts I gleaned from Bailey were simple: it's what you eat (and do) 80% of the time that matters. So, if you exercise and eat wisely during the week, you should be able to relax on the weekends. Now I'm sure this precludes binge eating, and assumes a moderate diet during the week. But his message found in me a diet-weary and eager follower. After years of emotional over-eating, binging and purging, eating in secret, and experiencing the ups and downs of fad diets, Bailey's 80/20 principle was just the ticket to augment my newfound love of aerobic dancing. It was almost too good to be true. And actually, it *was* too good to be true, or too good to last, in that it presupposed life-long compliance—an unlikely occurrence for someone with a history of eating disorders. But it lasted the duration of my aerobics "career," which took an interesting turn in the summer of 1988.

When Bill and I moved to Memphis with our three children, one of the first things I did was look for an aerobics studio where I could continue to teach. The thought of what might happen to me if I didn't find this venue was frightening—I might gain back the weight I had lost and be overcome again with my former food addiction. It didn't take long for me to discover that the country mouse was now in the big city, as each studio I visited seemed more sophisticated than the last.

One of the first places I looked into was run by a woman with all the charisma of Jamie Lee Curtis' Jesse in "Perfect." She was considered the guru of aerobics in Memphis, and she wasn't hiring new instructors, so I signed up to take a class. I quickly learned that I wasn't in Kansas any more. Most of her followers were in better shape than many of the instructors we had back at Phidippides. And lots of her classes were co-ed, which attributed to its edgy dress code and sexy atmosphere. Suddenly my modest leotards and tights seemed parochial compared with the low-rise Capri tights, unadorned workout bras and off-the-shoulder midriff tank tops the Memphis women wore. When it became obvious I couldn't make the cut at this swanky studio, I headed downtown to the newly renovated YMCA, which was hiring a full staff for its grand reopening.

It turned out that they weren't only hiring aerobics instructors, but administrative help as well. I started as a part time secretary and early morning aerobics teacher. I'm exhausted just thinking about those mornings when I left the house—husband and kids still asleep—and headed downtown to lead the 6 a.m. class. I would take my secretary attire with me, and by 8 a.m. I was showered, dressed, and at my desk.

Eventually I worked my way up to assistant to the executive director. With that position, I would arrive at work every morning in professional dress suit and heels, since part of my work involved public relations and membership sales. But at noon I would change into workout clothes for the best gig in town—lunch hour coed bench aerobics instructor. By the late 80s, spandex-type clothing had advanced to high levels of jiggle control, and brighter and shinier colors and designs appeared every season. The wardrobe change was like stepping into a set of armor, which prepared me to enter the arena.

The workout room was huge, and the instructor stood on a stage and used a microphone to carry her commands across the state-of-the-art (wood-over-air) floors to the class, which often swelled to over fifty students. Many of them were lawyers and bankers and marketing professionals—the movers and shakers of downtown Memphis—but on the aerobics floor the playing field was leveled. Even the women who took the noon class were mostly professionals, and they took full advantage of their male classmates as they positioned themselves on the front rows, where their perfectly sculpted shoulders, back muscles and tight asses were literally in the men's faces during the workout.

And yes, it was a power trip for me, as well. Some of the guys on the weight machines upstairs would stop and peer over the rail during my class at times, even venturing a laugh or a snide comment to their buddies on the dance floor below.

"Dancing is for wusses!" was among the typical jeer.

"Come on down and try it yourself!" would be the offended guy's retort.

As I took my students through fifty minutes of high-intensity, low-impact steps targeting heart, quads, calves, hams, abs, and arms, my self-esteem was bolstered, even when every muscle in my body was screaming with pain. At age thirty-eight, osteoarthritis was already beginning to take its toll on my joints, especially my knees and feet, which had been victims of six years of high-impact exercise on a tile-over-concrete floor back at Phidippides. (And years on the tennis courts before that.) As my fortieth birthday drew near, the pain increased, and was joined by two new friends—exhaustion and depression. How could someone working at such a high-profile job which involved physical exercise and lots of interaction with the public possibly be exhausted and depressed? Wasn't exercise supposed to improve sleep and pump up the body with endorphins, keeping the mood elevated socially, biologically and physically?

It's true that I felt better about my body during those years, although I was always making comparisons. I even worked out on the weight machines upstairs whenever I had time, seeking that elusive perfect body. But after a while, the rush wore off. It just wasn't enough any more. In fact, I began to dread the classes, looking at them as times that I had to put on yet another show, no matter how I was feeling emotionally. And unlike the intimacy of the smaller classes at Phidippides, where I actually got to know my students on a personal level—we would chat about their families after class and I even counseled some of them about their weight loss methods—the classes at the Y were too large and impersonal for those kinds of relationships to develop. Everyone hurried to the locker rooms to shower and get back to their high-powered jobs immediately after class, leaving little or no time for socializing. Oh, sure, once or twice one of the guys would come up after class and say, "great workout, Susan!" and then add, "a few of us are going to Sleep Out Louie's after work for a drink if you'd like to join us." It was tempting, but my life only intersected with these folks for that one hour, which seemed almost outside of real time, on Mondays, Wednesdays and Fridays at the Downtown YMCA.

I think the image—and I know the fantasy is often better than the real thing—of a group of those thirty-something folks discussing the latest marketing trends over martinis at a swanky downtown bar probably added to my growing depression. It was that life-long craving for community, for belonging, that I had chased from childhood through adolescent cliques and college sororities and on into adult social circles. But somehow I knew these weren't my people— I was just getting too old and too tired. So on March 8, 1991, my fortieth birthday, I took off my spandex and leg warmers. I knew I couldn't stand to hang around the Y without teaching, so I quit my job working for the executive director as well.

There were some office politics involved (aren't there always?), but the main thing was that I was tired of the show.

When I quit working at the YMCA, I immediately went to work for the director of a graduate program in a local university. It was somewhat of a backhanded compliment that I was hired mainly on my looks and personality—something my boss didn't tell me until six months into the job.

My job was only part time, so I asked my boss if I could come in an hour later in order to take an aerobics class several mornings a week. He agreed, and I found myself back downtown at the Y, this time as a *student* in the 9 a.m. bench class. And was I in for a surprise. I could barely make it through the routines! Had I gotten that badly out of shape in the few weeks since I quit teaching? I found myself working at a lower pace than when I was leading the class, but I was still much more out of breath, and I wasn't even calling out the cues! And I could find a million excuses not to go on any given morning— headaches, exhaustion, and a vague but growing lack of motivation. The words I had drilled into my students' heads came back to haunt me: "Why can't you get here at least three times a week? If you don't make that effort, you won't see any benefit!" How easy it had seemed *when that was my job*. So after a few weeks, I quit aerobics. Forever. But I knew I needed to find an exercise program that would work.

The next stop on the exercise circuit for me would be Curves.

The first time I signed up for Curves, I was a bit turned off by the staff's insistence on weight and body measurements.

They do regular checks, and fill the walls with success stories of clients who shed pounds and inches each month. I let them know that I preferred to weigh myself, and didn't want to participate in the group "competition," so they left me alone after the first week. If you've never been to Curves, let me say that it's a pretty smart setup. The room is filled with a dozen or so exercise machines, each calibrated so that the faster the reps, the more resistance the machine delivers. This enables a group of women (Curves is for women only) to move quickly from one machine to the next without the need for making adjustments to the weights. A small mini-trampoline-type square is placed between each machine, so that the machines and squares form a circuit lining the walls of the rectangular room. A music tape plays continually, with a voice that instructs the participants to "change stations now" every minute!

One thing I loved about Curves immediately was that no one seemed to care about how cute their workout clothes were. Most women simply wore knit pants or leggings or shorts with loose T-shirts. A few of the younger ones showed up in spandex, but they were the exception rather than the norm. And the staff would not only monitor the workout to be sure everyone was using each machine correctly, but also distract us with trivia games and friendly chatter. The thirty minutes seemed to fly by. And in my first three months, I shocked myself by losing fifteen pounds, without consciously changing my eating habits during that time. Maybe I had found the perfect workout to replace aerobics. But then I plateaued. Months went by and I struggled, gaining and then losing two-three pounds on and off for about a year. And then the magic faded altogether: I needed to have surgery on my left foot, which had a painful bunion and a big toe that was gradually turned under its neighbor, creating the beginning of a hammer toe that would plague me for the rest of my life if I didn't take action.

The surgery went fine, but five weeks in a full cast up to my knee, and another five weeks in a steel boot cast set me back a few pounds, and all muscle tone from my year at Curves was gone. When I tried to return, most of the machines were okay, but I couldn't do much on the square mini-tramps to keep my heart rate up. Anything with impact hurt, not only the foot that had been operated on, but the other foot, which also would need surgery at some point. Arthritic pain continued to increase in both feet (surgery wouldn't cure it), so I was back at square one, looking for another exercise program. And the pounds kept creeping back on until I eventually regained the fifteen I had lost at Curves.

A younger friend suggested I try her Pilates class, which didn't require any foot impact, I reluctantly agreed. First I did my homework: I went online and read up on the history and design of the program, and I was impressed. But I was afraid I couldn't do it. The moves looked so difficult, but Patti assured me that there were different levels, and lots of women my age loved it.

So I pulled out my best exercise clothes—and yes, I even bought some new ones for the new environment I was about to enter—and signed up for a series of private lessons first. I liked the instructor, once I got past my extreme jealousy over her amazing body. She was knowledgeable and careful to teach me the science behind the movements. I got in touch with my "core" (possibly for the first time in my life) and learned to pay attention to my posture, even while driving a car or sitting at my computer. But three months later I was disappointed on two counts: my back was making a "clicking" noise when I stretched my upper body, followed by a new pain in the same region, and I hadn't lost any weight, not one pound.

When I joined a small mat class, the other women, all older than I, seemed to have slimmer, more toned bodies. I asked how long they had been doing Pilates.

"Oh, at least ten years," one of them answered, a bit too perkily.

"And, do you do any other exercise, something cardiovascular?" I asked.

"Oh, yes, I walk three miles with my husband, several times a week," another woman answered.

"And what about dieting?" I was almost afraid to ask.

"After I learned that I was diabetic, about six months ago," a third woman began, "I went on the South Beach Diet, and I've lost about twenty five pounds so far."

Sigh. It seemed that Pilates wasn't going to be the answer either, so once again, I found myself in the ranks of the quitters.

Through all my exercise adventures, my husband just kept on jogging, outdoors in good weather, and on the indoor track at a nearby college's athletic facility where we had a membership when it was cold or rainy. Sometimes he would venture into the gym and work out on some of the machines, and that's when he discovered something he thought might work for me—the elliptical machine.

I finally agreed to give it a try, but I was sure it wouldn't work. It seemed so much like the stair master, which killed my knees. And again, what would I wear? In a college gym, with all those buff young bodies, I was afraid I would be embarrassed just to show up. But show up I did, in my JJill yoga pants and soft comfy Under Armour tee shirt, and my Croc sandals. Yes—at this point all athletic shoes hurt my feet, and since the elliptical machine didn't require that either foot be lifted once they were in place, I hoped that my Crocs would work, and they did. And I was pleasantly surprised to find faculty members my age and older, as well as other community members from the neighborhood, in all shapes and sizes and manner of dress. Maybe this would be my exercise home. As I approached the machine, I put my earphones on and tuned my iPod to my exercise playlist and began pedaling. Twenty minutes later I wasn't out of breath and there was little or no pain in my knees or feet. My playlist was about to start over when I decided to go for three more minutes, just so I could listen to the first song one more time:

"With my body and soul I want you more than you'll ever know... 'cause I've... had the time of my life....!"

This would have been chapter 10 in a memoir I wrote but never published, titled, *Dressing the Part: What I Wore For Love*.

Susan Cushman's seven published books include *John and Mary Margaret* (novel), *Friends of the Library* (short stories), *Cherry Bomb* (novel), *Tangles and Plaques: A Mother and Daughter Face Alzheimer's* (memoir), and three anthologies she edited, *A Second Blooming: Becoming the Women We are Meant to Be, Southern Writers on Writing,* and *The Pulpwood Queens Celebrate 20 Years!* Susan writes with deep insight into the South's storied past, bringing elements of hope and healing to her short stories, memoir, and novels, honoring the heart, soul, and history of the South.

Before He Heard Her

Carol Van Den Hende

Before he heard her, he scented her. Lemon. Honey. Wild lavender. Feck.

"Ronan? Is that you?"

The familiar timbre came from behind. He had time to tuck his folded cane beneath his raincoat. He hoped it wasn't visible.

Ronan gripped the subway handle, and stared unseeing through his shades. Luckily, he'd donned his cool pair. The train swayed. Zoe's clothes brushed his as she rounded the space before him.

"Ronan. Oh my god. It's been what – six months?"

He knew exactly how long it'd been since he'd left his girlfriend. Half a year since the accident, so five months since they'd broken up. A different lifetime. The quiet nights and their missed anniversary should've inoculated him. Yet, even after all these fortnights, her voice rang as sweet as before.

"Aren't you going to say anything? Are you going to pretend you don't see me?"

A chuckle escaped. "I'm not pretending," he said.

"Not funny. You can't ignore me when I'm standing right in front of you."

"Try me." He grinned despite the harrowing situation. It was one thing to keep a secret over the phone, another in person.

Her breath reached him, warming his neck where his shirt lay unbuttoned.

"I thought you'd moved to another country the way you disappeared. Are you still here in the city? Because that would make you an even bigger jerk than I thought you were," she said.

"I told you, you're better off without me."

The edge in her tone triggered memories like a high school song bringing back prom night. Snatches of their last call tumbled in. Zoe had started out full of disbelief. She'd been away on business for two months. "Have you met someone else?" she'd demanded. He couldn't tell her the truth and still protect her. "This makes no sense. We were in love, weren't we?" she'd asked. He'd wanted to erase her anguish then, as he did now.

He heard the air in her throat catch, bringing him back to the present.

"Hey... Ronan, are you okay?" Fabric swished as she raised her arm. Oh no, not the hand in front of the eyes thing. That was worse than anything. Uncalled for. Cliché. A test that he couldn't pass. Even if he couldn't witness himself being demeaned.

The train's automated conductor announced the next station.

"What the—" Zoe's tone ratcheted up towards drama. *The sound of her uncovering his secret.*

"This is my stop. Good seeing you," he said, his free hand forming air quotes. His own private joke. He broke away from her before she could discover more, and lunged towards the door. Air released from the brakes and the doors slid open. He stumbled onto the platform, aiming for the exit. In the swirl of emotions, he hadn't even absorbed which station they'd entered. The echoes of footsteps against the tiled walls didn't sound familiar, like a station he'd previously traversed. Not since the accident, anyway. His commute tended to be unvaried. Here, among frenzied crowds, he didn't want to misstep onto the tracks. Or maybe he did.

"Ronan! Ronan!" she called, breathless, some yards behind him. Her heels tapped sharp and fast. Stilettos. Damn he wanted to see her. He could imagine the flash of red hair, the intensity of her hazel eyes.

He followed the sounds of the throngs, swept along with their motion. And his emotion. By some miracle, he fumbled his way through the turnstile. He'd worked hard to avoid this. This was never supposed to happen. And now he felt as lost as the day he'd woken in the hospital.

"Careful!" Zoe shouted, so close that she must just be an arm's length away.

But it was too late. His stride was fast and headlong. Until he struck something solid. The stairs felled him as easily as an axe splinters kindling. His knee twisted as he caught himself with the railing. His folded cane clattered onto the concrete, no longer hidden under his coat. The harsh echo reverberated in the cavernous station.

The crowd parted around him, commuters hurrying along their routes. Warm fingers grasped his elbow, and helped him up.

"Are you hurt?" she asked, her worry sounding close to grief.

He tested some weight on his leg. "Nah. You know me, I'll do anything for attention."

She let go of his arm and chuckled. "You always made me laugh. Tell me you're not seeing anyone."

"I'm not really dating material."

"Shut it."

He heard a hard plastic edge scrape against the cement floor.

He put out his hand for his cane, his face warming out of embarrassment for her seeing it. No question about it. His secret was eviscerated.

But instead of a lightweight cylinder, she shoved something small into his palm. He wrapped his fingers around the smooth circle topped by a sharp gemstone. "Oh."

Why today of all days, would she be wearing the promise ring he'd gifted her after the marathon? That summer morning, her mood had been buoyant, and her lips soft. It was the last time he'd raced.

"Here." She pressed the cool surface of his folded cane into his other hand.

"Thanks," he said. He tried to return the jewel and met air.

"Keep it," she said.

"It was for you."

"Not anymore." Her voice broke.

He pocketed the jewelry. It'd been the most dazzling piece in the store. One that shone almost as bright as Zoe's excitement when she was immersed in the beauty industry, attending fashion shows, or designing creative. She prized aesthetics, from the red lacquered bottoms of her Louboutins, to her twenty-one step skin regimen. In the midst of all that perfection, there was no space for damaged goods.

"Do you have time for coffee?" she asked.

"Nope." There was no point. He clutched the handle and flung open the cane's whole length. What did appearances matter now?

"How about something stronger?"

"It's eight in the morning," he laughed, and limped up the steps.

The tap of her heels kept pace with his. "I know an account up for grabs," she said. Smart. Talking shop would appeal to the entrepreneur in him.

"I'm not in design anymore," he said, trying to meter his bitterness. "How about you? You good? How was Korea?"

"K-beauty is amazing. Let me tell you about it over a bite to eat. You look too thin."

He shook his head. His cane found the top of the stairs. At street level, a chill mist wet his face.

"Oh c'mon. You owe me at least this. Weren't we serious? And you didn't even tell me the biggest thing to happen to you," she said.

"The biggest thing? Alright, you got me. The truth is, I pickpocketed your ring from a circus act."

She blew out some air. "Be serious for once. It's just five flippin' minutes."

He paused in the open air ten paces from the mouth of the station. His heart pounded, and his leg throbbed. This was ridiculous. A young able-bodied woman was not going to have problems keeping up with him.

He lifted his left arm to his face as if he was looking at a wristwatch. Even though he no longer had a need for a watch. "Five. Starting now. And then we go our separate ways."

"Right here?! Can't we go somewhere? Sit for a bit?"

"Four minutes and forty seconds," he said.

"Um. Okay. Jesus."

He imagined Zoe staring at him, and wondered what his expression revealed about the wreckage inside.

"I mean, I don't know if this is why you left me. But if it is… Is it? Is this why you broke up with me? Because I still had feelings. I still… Christ. Do you? Is this why?"

"Three minutes, fifty seconds," he responded.

"Stop being an ass." She smacked his arm. Then sounded guilty. "Oh god I'm sorry. What happened?"

"Bad accident. Three minutes."

He sucked a breath and inhaled citrus. She'd always been a cornucopia of scents – one for her hair, another along her neck, a third …Stop.

She grew so quiet he wondered if she'd left. Then, she drew a finger along the stubble that lined his jaw. Instinct shuttered his eyes. She leaned against his chest, tiptoeing up, and brushed the hollow of one cheek with her lips. Lavender. Lemon.

"Two minutes, thirty seconds," she whispered, so close that he could feel her exhale.

He grasped for an antidote as rational thought slipped away. "Stiletto, your place is the other way," he said, trying to dissuade her with pragmatism.

"Ha. Stilettos, that's right. How'd you know?"

"Blind men can still hear."

The air grew silent.

"Is there any chance…that your vision will…?"

"Nope. This is it," he said.

"I'm sorry. But you know, it doesn't matter. Between us," she said.

He pulled back, the tightness in his throat making it hard to talk. "I was protecting you," he said.

"By breaking my heart?" her tone rose to incredulous.

"By not screwing up your perfect life."

"That's bull. You're no chicken shit, but think about it, who are you really protecting?"

After months of friends and family treating him with kid gloves, afraid to upset him, Zoe's straight talk was like a slap upside his head. All those stories he'd told himself about why it was better to lie rewound themselves, now seen with a new lens.

He'd pictured her shirking away in horror, yet here she was, unwilling to leave him.

"Some days, this sucks," he said.

"And the days apart? Those suck worse," she said.

"Don't lie," he said but part of him wanted to hear this.

Had needed hearing this since…

"Shh." She slipped her hands under his overcoat and melted into his warmth, encircling his waist until one cheek nestled against his chest.

He wrapped his free arm around her. His lips imprinted her lavender-scented hair.

There weren't even two minutes left to his self-imposed deadline.

"I've missed you so hard," he said, his voice unexpectedly gruff.

Ronan let his cane tumble to the sidewalk. Inside his pocket, he located Zoe's ring.

One minute?

There must be more.

Before He Heard Her is a short story I'd written while penning my novel *Goodbye, Orchid*. It was initially meant purely for myself, to deepen my point of view for my main character, Phoenix Walker.

Pretty quickly, I realized that Ronan's story was special in its own right. Writer's Digest agreed, bestowing it with an Honorable Mention in its annual writing competition.

The story is close to my heart, as it shines a light on disability awareness, much like *Goodbye, Orchid* has. I'm particularly proud that sensitivity readers, including blind author Laurie Alice Eakes, and accessibility expert Darryl Adams, loved the story for its authenticity and resonance.

Carol is an author who inspires readers with her stories of resilience and hope. Her novel *Goodbye, Orchid* has been awarded thirteen times, for audiobook narration, best first fiction, best cover design, disability awareness, best interior design, best multi-cultural fiction and more. Her work has been featured in *Glamour, Buzzfeed, Parade, Travel+Leisure, POPSUGAR, Chicago Tribune, LA Times*, WABC Radio among others.

Carol speaks as a Climate Reality Leader, provides strategic counsel as a Board member for a special needs school, and drives vision and purpose as part of Mars, Incorporated's Digital Technologies Leadership Team.

One secret to her good fortune? Her humorous husband and teenaged twins, who prove that love really does conquer all. Please sign up for Carol's newsletter at carolvandenhende.com/contact or linktr.ee/cvdh

The Trip

Laura Davis

A month before my twenty-fourth birthday, my father and I made plans to spend a weekend together at Omland, my cousin Miriam and James' place in the Santa Cruz Mountains, for their annual "Back to the Land" party. Dad drove down from San Francisco and picked me up in Santa Cruz, and the two of us headed deep into the mountains. We drove up a dusty, rutted dirt road, full of crazy turns and drop-offs, the gears whining as Dad downshifted to keep from skidding in the dirt.

When we reached the end of the road, Dad backed onto a dusty shoulder, and we hoisted our backpacks. It was a steep one-third-mile hike straight up the trail to "up top." As we crested the final hill, we were both panting. Miriam greeted us, long hair flowing, wearing a floor-length cotton skirt of many colors, waiting to "water the guests." She hugged us and handed us each a tall glass of water.

Miriam introduced us to the other guests and led us to bunch of rusty metal chairs perched at the edge of the cliff, overlooking the valley. I gazed at the vast green forest below. An owl hooted and another answered the call. Some guy I'd never seen before lit a joint with a magnifying glass, holding it up to catch the sun. His hand was steady, and it took a few minutes, but the doobie caught fire. He took a long toke and passed it to Dad. He took a drag and passed it to me. Dad picked up a guitar. Soon he was singing *The Titanic* and I tapped out the beat on the weathered arm of the chair. Stared out into the wild. The owl hooted again.

Dad was singing the third verse of *The Grey Goose* when some other guy I'd never met offered us some acid. I knew my father liked psychedelics. I'd dropped acid a dozen times— with friends—never with Dad. Dad said yes and opened his mouth to whatever the next twelve hours would bring. Then the guy held a tab out to me. I considered it, a tiny square of possibility in the palm of his hand. Why not? I slid the tab under my tongue.

I hiked around Omland for the first hour, waiting for the trip to begin. At first, I felt a gentle spinning sensation. The greens became more vibrant. Trees started pulsing, a soft song emanating from their branches, embracing me. Leaves tinkled like bells. I fell into their rhythm, but then they got louder.

Soon they were shouting. An inferno of fierce sensations ricocheted through my body, and I couldn't get them to stop. Everything was repeating and loud, and the pattern was ugly. The world was ugly. I was ugly. And alone.

I'd been alone in that Isolette and now, I always would be.

That loneliness grew inside me and filled my entire being. I couldn't stop it. Skin no longer contained me. I was unraveling. I reached for my sister, and for a brief moment, felt her comforting heartbeat across the veil—something I'd craved for so long—but then she was gone.

A crow cawed; death was near. I desperately wanted to come down, but I was still going up. I needed help but couldn't move. Just let me get through this. I promise, I'll never take acid again. I followed my breath for hours. In, out. In, out.

Finally, the trees quieted, until only the wind was singing.

The rhythm stilled. My skin held my molecules in place. By the time the ground felt solid beneath me, the sun had transited the sky. I stood. On the dirt path, I heard voices—real ones.

The thwack of a knife cutting watermelon. The crow cawed again but this time its call blended naturally into the rhythm of the living, breathing world all around me. I was part of that world. I was going to be okay.

I found Dad alone in the tepee, staring into the woods. The distant chords of a guitar and two voices singing harmony wafted through the trees. The music was sweet, pulsing with a yellow glow, but I fell into its warmth. I was still high around the edges, but my core had returned. Thoughts moved in a line again. Dad was humming, as usual, but his hum was soaring.

No canvas draped the tepee poles that day, just eight carved tree trunks converging toward heaven. Cool white ash filled the central fire pit. A few mats lay scattered around the outside rim. Dad was perched cross-legged on one, wearing his smooth-bottomed moccasins, a pair of faded jeans, and his original Woodstock tee shirt. Small animals scurried through the brush. I plunked down in front of him, crossing my legs in the dust. The pulsing in my chest quieted as I stared into his familiar face.

His pale blue eyes fixed on mine, his pupils huge. His sing-song voice rolled over me like a light patter of summer rain. "You are so beautiful. I'm so happy to have you as a daughter. Do you know how lucky I am?"

"Yeah, I love you, too." But then something jagged ripped inside me. A tear in the fabric that kept everything in place. The truth pressed up and threatened to spill out. I could no longer contain it. Yeah, Dad. You know, you are lucky. You have a daughter who has never held you accountable. I never stopped worshipping you, even after you walked out on me. I spent my teenage years bragging about having a hippie father to visit out in California. Jesus. Yes, I know how lucky you are.

The scolding call of a hawk echoed above us. The sound reverberated, pressing into my chest like a flame. Why had I never held Dad responsible?

He beamed at me, face wide open. "I love you so much, Laura."

I know you do, but I have to tell you some things. Why hadn't I ever said them? Why wasn't I saying them now? The answer rose in my chest. Because I couldn't risk alienating the one parent who had always believed in me.

I slipped off my flip-flops and scuffed my feet in the dusty soil. The truth ignited inside me. Words pressed up from a bottomless place I didn't know. This was their time. "Dad, I've been mad at you for a long time. Your leaving really hurt me. I was fourteen years old, at sleep-away camp, and you told me in a fucking letter." As I spoke, a chasm opened inside me. I tried to jam it shut, but the opening tore wider. I had never cried, not once after Dad left me. I soldered myself shut, but now my fortress was cracking. I was risking everything.

Dad's face flushed with concern. He moved closer; his callused palms wiped the tears from my cheeks. The trail of his touch lingered long after his hands left my face.

It had taken me years to admit that I was outraged at my father. I'd locked that anger up inside me, just like everything else. But now, we were tripping together, and Dad was listening. He wanted to hear what I had to say. I just had to find the courage to say it. "Dad, you disappeared. You left a huge mess behind. Paul was gone. You were gone. You left me alone with Mom. You know how she is. How could you?"

That was it. Bingo. It wasn't that he'd escaped to Big Sur to "find himself." It wasn't that he gallivanted around with his hippie friends. It wasn't the divorce. It was that he'd stopped being my buffer.

Dad listened. His pale blue eyes peered deep into mine. The scar on his nose where he'd been whacked with a board while stocking shelves at his father's hardware store pulsed. I breathed into my belly. Laughter from nearby guests dappled the waning sunlight. I was still coming down.

The distant sounds of a guitar drifted over us. Goosebumps stippled my skin. I scooted closer. Dad took my hands in his.

They were big and warm, just like I remembered. The hands that had carried me. Hands that had cut silkscreens and carved woodcuts.

Hands that loved to play the congas. He held my hands and listened. I said everything I needed to say, everything I'd never said before. "Your freedom cost me. And it's still costing me."

Dad's eyes filled like a mountain stream. Unshed tears pressed beneath the surface of his words. "I'm so sorry, Laura. I just couldn't come back to New Jersey. That life was over for me. And you were the one who paid the price. I never meant to hurt you."

No one had ever apologized to me before. In our family, there were only radiating fingers of blame. Our eyes caught for a long moment. The father I could trust looked back at me. I breathed his apology into that ripped up place inside me. My jagged edges began to soften, like petals floating to the ground. Dad wrapped his arm around my shoulder. I leaned into his chest and my ragged breaths eased. Leaves rattled above us, like cellophane coming off a gift.

Maybe it was the acid that gave me the courage to speak or maybe it was just time. Whatever it was, I took my father's apology all the way down to my bones. My anger drained into the earth until all that was left was love. And it stayed that way. It didn't change when I came down. It didn't change in the years to come. I swallowed my father's apology whole, and it took root inside of me. That was the day I forgave him.

I had quite a bit more about my father in earlier drafts of my memoir, *The Burning Light of Two Stars*, but in the final analysis, the book was too long, and I needed to create more momentum, so everything that wasn't absolutely essential to my core story—the 57-year-relationship between me and my mother—had to go. For many drafts, I held on to this particular scene because I've always loved it, but eventually I had to "kill my babies" and let go of all the scenes, sentences, and words the book could live without. This scene is one of the scenes that unfortunately had to go. I'm glad I get to share it here with you.

The events I describe in this first scene took place in June 1980, a pivotal time in my relationship with my father, who left our suburban New Jersey home to drop out, move to California to become a free artist and hippie, nine years before this scene took place.

This scene makes reference to a couple of things you would have already known if you were reading it in context: I was a premature baby who spent the first six weeks of my life in an incubator called an Isolette. My older brother Paul is also mentioned in this scene. He left for college the same summer my father split to his new life in California, leaving my mother and me alone.

Laura Davis is the author of *The Burning Light of Two Stars: A Mother-Daughter Story*, the story of her loving yet tumultuous relationship with her mother, and six other non- fiction books. Her first books, *The Courage to Heal* and *The Courage to Heal Workbook*, paved the way for hundreds of thousands of women and men to heal from the trauma of sexual abuse. *Becoming the Parent You Want to Be*, a rich resource guide co-authored with parenting expert Janis Keyser, helped parents develop a vision for the families they want to create. *I Thought We'd Never Speak Again: The Road from Estrangement to Reconciliation* taught the skills of reconciliation and peace building, one relationship at a time. Laura's groundbreaking books have been translated into 11 languages and sold two million copies.

In addition to writing books that inspire and change people's lives, the work of Laura's heart is to teach. For more than twenty years, she's helped people find their voices, tell their stories, and hone their craft. Laura loves creating supportive, intimate writing communities online, in person, and internationally.

Laura loves meeting with her readers and believes that a book is meant to be a collaborative conversation between author and reader. She loves the unpredictable and often intimate conversations that occur when readers bring their own family stories and life experience to the books she has written.

You can learn about Laura's books and workshops, read the first five chapters of her new memoir, and receive a free ebook: *Writing Through Courage: A 30-Day Practice* at www.lauradavis.net.

Meet Me in Mumbai

Lovelace Cook

Chapter 1

I suppose at this age and stage of my life, I should have known to expect the unexpected. I pulled out my passport as the line of foreigners snaked its way through immigration, and I felt something sharp stab me in the back. Startled, I dropped the passport, bent down to pick it up and rammed my head into the generous buttocks of the turbaned Sikh standing in front of me. He glared.

I mumbled an apology, "Didn't mean to get familiar."

What stabbed me? I turned and saw a little girl with beautiful brown eyes. She giggled and held up her doll for me to admire. An Indian Barbie's high heels! Was this my welcome to India?

The airport was a colorful madhouse, the noise was deafening, and the chaos was exotic. Swarms of people surged past immigration. I was delirious with excitement and fueled by adrenaline. I rushed with the crowd to the baggage claim where Indian families pile mountains of suitcases on the large luggage carts. I grabbed my suitcase, passed through customs, and headed to the main terminal. Where was Trevor?

I stepped outside and the heat and humidity enveloped me. The night reeked of stale urine. Families shouted, waved, and jostled one another for the best positions behind control barriers. It was thrilling and terrifying. I saw Trevor wedged in the crush between saris and turbans, and I breathed a sigh of relief.

"You don't look like you've been traveling thirty-seven hours, Jesse." Trevor kissed me.

"I had a layover in Paris," I said.

He lifted my small backpack off my shoulder. "Crikey, babe, you got rocks in here?"

We walked to the row of parked taxis and waited for a taxi to be assigned. I said a silent prayer for a new taxi. No luck. Ours was ancient, a beat-up black and yellow cab, its trunk filled with plastic containers of gasoline and tied down with a rope.

The young driver took my bags from Trevor, "Uncle, let me." He put my suitcase in the passenger seat. We climbed into the back. Nasty ragged towels punctuated by faded red flowers covered the seat.

"Happy Birthday, babe." Trevor nuzzled my neck. "You smell great."

"Duty-free Chanel." I thought about Rodin's sensuous sculpture The Kiss in the exhibit at the Charles De Gaulle airport in Paris. I kissed him.

The driver turned to us, "I'll take you on the scenic route."

Backseat odors assaulted me. I rolled my window down. The air conditioner didn't work. Streetlights cast a strange yellow glow like the sky before a storm and hundreds of people slept on the sidewalks. Dogs lay beside people who were covered head-to-toe with saris, scarves, and blankets, or not at all. I was mystified. What was scenic about bodies lined up on sidewalks, block after block for miles? It was an apocalyptic landscape.

Our driver couldn't find the hotel and Trevor didn't remember the address. We were lost. A barricade blocked the road ahead.

"Slight detour, madam," the driver said.

The cab turned into a shadowy alley. I saw a group of men

huddled under a light outside a brick building. The men exchanged money.

"Drug dealers!" I panicked.

"No, Auntie," our driver said. "They're playing the stock market."

The taxi turned down another dark alley. A few meters ahead, I saw a blue building surrounded by sandbags and uniformed guards with machine guns. Trevor, the driver, and I spoke simultaneously.

"I know where we are," Trevor said.

"Oh my God!" I freaked out.

"Our hotel is around the corner," Trevor continued.

". . . *machine guns*!" My muscles tensed.

"Security is tight after a bombing at the synagogue," Trevor interrupted.

"It's a Mumbai landmark," the driver announced.

"Here it is," Trevor said. "The Hotel Lawrence."

The taxi stopped but I didn't see a sign for a hotel. The headlights shone on wooden steps leading to an open, dark hallway off the alley.

"The lift isn't working," Trevor said.

The lights weren't working either. I didn't know whether to laugh or cry.

"Bloody hell," Trevor said. "My torch isn't working."

He shook the small flashlight. I heard the batteries rattle around and a faint beam of light shone on the steps. A large roach scuttled out of the way.

"At least the cockroaches here aren't as big as the ones on the Gulf Coast," I said.

Trevor cut me a glare. His lips pursed in disapproval. I didn't mean to be sarcastic.

The driver took my suitcase and backpack from Trevor, "Uncle, I'll carry the bags."

The building smelled musty like the inside of an old wooden warehouse. Trevor led the way. His flashlight was useless in the dark. We walked up three flights of steps worn down by the years. We stepped over people who slept on each of the landings. I was horrified.

I thought our hotel, if it could be called that, must be a flophouse. I heard a loud crunch. Trevor smashed someone's glasses.

When we reached the third floor, he said, "This is it, Jesse."

I didn't see a reception desk but at least the overhead fluorescent light worked. Two battered wooden chairs with faded cushions sat next to a crude bookcase filled with dog-eared paperbacks. A sleepy Indian man opened the door opposite and peered out of an office. His mat lay on the floor beside a desk. He mumbled something and shut the door.

"He's the night guard," Trevor said.

We walked down a long corridor with a cracked linoleum floor and grimy walls. Only a handful of the overhead fluorescent bulbs weren't burned out. Trevor unlocked the door to our room.

I looked around and saw a small rotary fan mounted on the wall over the bed. The screened windows were open. The furnishings included an old wardrobe, a wooden table, two white plastic chairs and a wooden bed. At least the sheets looked clean. Trevor's orange backpack leaned against the wall, his gray sleeping bag lay open on the bed and a copy of *Lonely Planet* was beside it. A harsh strip light threw the room into stark relief. It was awful.

"I can't wait for a shower," I waited for Trevor to tell me what I already knew. The sad little hotel room only had one door.

"The bathrooms are at the far end of the hall," he paused. "We won't have hot water until morning."

I wandered back down the hall to brush my teeth, carrying the bottle of water Trevor gave me after he warned me not to drink the water from the tap. Three communal wet rooms, each with different doors, served the no-star hotel. The showers rained down on moldy tile floors and splashed appalling toilets and sinks. Water drained out through a hole in the floor. I hoped nothing stopped the drain. The open windows didn't have screens, and bugs circled a naked light bulb suspended from the high ceiling. Where was the toilet paper? The Hotel Lawrence might be every backpacker's dream, but I hadn't traveled on five-dollars-a-day since the 70s.

Back in the room, Trevor lay on the bed wearing nothing but his wicked grin. God, I'd missed him.

"I brought you a surprise," I said and gave him Mark Twain's *The Innocents Abroad.*

"Brilliant." After he stopped laughing, he said, "I haven't bought your birthday present."

I saw the hint of a shadow cross his face, but I forgot as soon as he wrapped his arms around me. Chanel's *Allure Sensuelle* perfume delivered on the promise of its name. We reveled in holding each other and fell asleep to the sounds of crows, cats in the alley and dogs barking.

I awoke before dawn and saw a full moon over Mumbai. It was quiet and cool. Trevor slept soundly. I traced the line of his cheek with my fingertips and wondered how much it would cost to take a return flight home the next day.

Lovelace Cook is a storyteller, writer and podcaster who lives in Fairhope, Alabama. She worked in NYC for magazine publishing and television and then moved to LA where she worked on feature films while attending film production and screenwriting classes at UCLA and the American Film Institute.

She traveled through and lived in India, SE Asia, and the UK from 2013-2016. The books and authors she discovered influenced her podcast Bollywood & Books. And her misadventures on the road, traveling like a 20-year-old on a gap year at age 63, were the inspiration for *Meet Me in Mumbai*, the novel she's revising. The first chapter appears here.

Mamma Mia! Here We Come Again...
Stephanie Chance

Chapter 15
Mamma Mia, We're in Greece - Ride to Chapel

A faint, distant roar grows louder as though a remote-controlled plane is coming in for landing.

"What is that noise?" We practically speak in unison, straining our ears. Soon the sound amplifies, and we realize a wand has been waved. A genie has arrived on a four-wheeled magic carpet.

Not one, but two tiny cars approach from behind us. Without hesitation, we wave and jump up and down in the middle of the road.

"Stop, stop!" We shout. Some of us dance in the middle of the road with arms in the air and bags of blossoms on the ground, while a few others stand wide-eyed, holding their bundles of freshly picked flowers.

The first car, a four-door model, has no choice but to stop and join in the parade of Americans.

"*Ciao!* Hello!"

We realize it's our lucky break; we're catching a ride, one way or the other.

The approaching car holds only the man sitting in the driver's seat.

"We're going to the Agios Ioannis Kastri chapel. The *Mamma Mia!* chapel. Our bus was too big to go around the hole in the road. How did you squeeze by?"

We bombard the man with our questions before he has even stopped. I shuffle my feet and hold my arms out on the chorus of "Mamma Mia!" Yes, here we go again.

"Can we please have a ride?" We shout loudly enough to wake the island.

The car skids to a sudden halt as the driver waves his arm out the window and yells a short sentence in Greek. His happy face needs no translation; it's telling us to "hop inside." He flashes a huge smile and jumps out of his car, speaking in broken English. We understand the words *"Mamma Mia! chapel."*

That's all the encouragement needed, and six of the Americans race to the doors and pile inside. Before the last door shuts in my face, they yell, "See you at the chapel! Have fun walking."

The little car peels away, sending off dusty smoke from the pavement.

Less than a second later, the second vehicle approaches us. The driver's arm extends out the window and waves heroically. We start the same welcoming dance in the middle of the road as the tiny vehicle abruptly stops.

"Hello!" We giggle and jump up and down like giddy teenagers.

A tall, robust man in the driver's seat throws the door open, causing us to hop back. Launched from the passenger's side, a lady with long, straight, brown hair and a body like a slim Tootsie Roll flies around the front of the vehicle.

"Howdy, mates! The big hole got you walking? Jump in, mates! We have room for some of you."

He's a fast talker, never pausing as his sentences run together. I immediately think of Crocodile Dundee. This guy is Australian, but with his flock of dark curls, he also resembles a young Tom Jones.

He smiles, showing tobacco-stained teeth, and goes straight for a tight, welcoming hug of long-lost friends and English-speaking comrades.

"Wow! You are British. Are you from England?" Dr. Clark's Texas dialect comes out as he rams Jeana and Scott Rabe into the back seat. He squeezes behind them as if he's afraid the car might leave without him.

"No, mate, we're from Australia. We were here yesterday at the chapel and came back today to experience it all again. We're going to take more photos." They open the back doors wider and gesture for more to hop inside.

"We're going to the little chapel, too." Kathy Murphy stands outside the car and scans the interior. "We have three couples renewing their wedding vows. Two of them are already in your back seat. We're going to reenact the whole thing, just like Meryl Streep did as she danced up the mountain. You know, where Sophia rode the donkey in the movie. Are you going up with us?"

There is no room for us. The other Americans are crammed in and packed on top of each other like sardines in a can but with arms and heads hanging out of the windows.

"Hop aboard," Scott's voice echoes from the back seat, and he laughs. His wife is on his lap, smiling radiantly. I suddenly wonder where her bridal bouquet is—smashed with the Americans in the tiny car, perhaps?

Only Kathy and I are left outside the Jeep-like vehicle with our arms full. Some of the others jogged ahead of us minutes ago. We are beasts of burden readying ourselves for the mountainous journey and trudging on foot to the chapel.

"Sorry, mates. It looks like you two will have to walk. No worries, though, it's only a few miles around the next five curves." Tom Jones, or rather Richard, the Australian heartthrob, jumps in the driver's seat. His fingers brush through his black curly hair that sprouts mere inches from his brow like a lawn of grass. As he drums his thumb against the steering wheel and waves his other arm through the window, we panic with the realization of what he said.

Only a "few miles"? Kathy and I simultaneously rush to the back of the vehicle, which holds a giant pile of stuff. No time to think. We pull and tug and manage to hoist ourselves up to perch on top of a tire. We grab the sidebars. My camera and large bag dangle, but I don't care.

"Hold on!" I yell to Kathy as the Australian beau steps on the gas. The toy-sized Jeep peels out with a small jerk. We hold on tightly. Part of my buttocks are suspended over the edge of the metal, and I'm sure the same is true for Kathy. The two of us are flying free in the back with nothing but air beneath our shoes.

"Look at the view!" The wind whips Kathy's voice through the air as she laughs. "This is beyond description."

"You haven't seen anything yet. Just wait until you see the view with the steep stairway coiling around the mysterious rock from the sea. And we're nearly there!" I bellow back with my voice stretched to the frequency of a high soprano operetta singer.

Elevated high above the turquoise water, we sway through the sharp curves on the road with our arms wrapped around the metal sidebars, screaming with excitement and the thrill of the moment.

"We're here! Look to the sea. It's the chapel." Unexplainable exhilaration strikes like lightning and races throughout my body, causing my arms to fly and my heart to explode. It's the movie screen coming to life. My legs kick higher in the wind that rushes past the back of the Jeep. I get to see the *Mamma Mia!* chapel once again and be overwhelmed by its beauty.

"There it is! Oh, it's *Mamma Mia!*" Kathy Murphy shrieks in delight. Her legs churn the air with nothing but pavement far below. Her eyes widen as she sees the magnificence and grandeur of the storybook setting and the impressive sphere that rises two hundred steps from the sea to the top.

"Can you believe this sight? It's better than the photographs. Better than the movie." Kathy's words tumble from her lips.

Hearing the *oohs* and *aahs* from inside the Jeep escalates my level of excitement as we slow to a snail's crawl around the sharp hairpin loop. The last twisting turn takes me into hysterical excitement with adrenaline rushing from my head to toe.

"We're here! We're here!" The words continue to fly from my mouth as the Jeep comes to a sudden stop, bringing us face-to-face with the magnificent sphere, and the rocky mountain that upholds the chapel.

We jump off, and our shoes slap the pavement just as the four vehicle doors blast open. The passengers pop out like the contents of a pressurized can.

We are enthralled as we stand in a babbling frenzy, seeing a genuine fairy-tale before us. The little chapel is erected upon a giant rock like a wedding topper perched proudly on the tallest cake ever.

My gaze starts at the top. I see the magnificence of the tiny church with its whiteness shining in the spotlight of the glistening Greek sunlight, manifesting its likeness to the Statute of Liberty and Michelangelo's David—a true sight to behold. The Americans dissolve into animated happiness.

Below its rising grace and beauty, beneath the platform that supports its creation from the sea, is the fabric of marbleized blues all swirled together as if an artist arrived ahead of us and swept a watercolor paintbrush across the crystal clear waves.

"This is an alcohol ink painting before us from God's own hands. The swirl of color swimming throughout the magnificence of our God's imaginative ways." Kathy Murphy, also an artist, holds her hands in the air to allow the warm breeze to whip her colorful shawl in the wind.

After many hugs and kisses to our knights in shining motorized armor, we bid them farewell. Looking back over my shoulder, I snap a quick photo of the dashing Australian hugging Jeana and wishing her many blessings for her matrimony bliss.

Standing patiently nearby are the two dynamos, Kathy Ray and Jan, with huge smiles on their faces.

"Thank you for the ride," they say in unison. They reach up with open arms and stretch on tiptoes to smack a kiss on each side of his sun-bronzed cheeks. The Aussie bends down, happily embracing the attention of two beautiful American ladies. Jan leans her head on his shoulder, batting her blueberry eyes at him. It's a spontaneous moment of fun for both of them. Kathy and Jan are two peas in a pod, like Lucy and Ethel.

"Looks like the Aussie beau is staying with us," Dorthia grins with her hands still full of flowers. Her other sister, Bonnie, snaps a quick photo of the final embrace of the Australian who is bewitched by her little sister's magnetic charm.

Simultaneously, Kathy and Jan release their arms held stretched around his back.

"We better let you go so we can catch up with the others," Jan and Kathy practically speak in unison, both of them talking over each other.

"The three couples over there are renewing their wedding vows as soon as we climb the rock." Jan dazzles him with another ray of sunshine from her sparkling eyes.

"Yes, we've got to go." Kathy pulls again from the Aussie.

Both women laugh like they always do. Jan slips a few euros into his hand to thank him for his kindness and refuses to accept it back even though he tries to decline.

"Take your beautiful wife for a cocktail. Just a little token of our appreciation." Jan backs away and turns toward Kathy Ray, who has already joined Kathy Murphy and the others on the rocky steps.

"Come on, Jan," Bonnie hollers at her little sister as she waits by the edge of the water with their other sibling, Dorthia. Her feet are firmly planted on the rocks.

"I'm on my way." Jan grabs the Aussie's wife and kisses her cheek with full southern charm.

"Where else would we experience such an adventure?" Amy, one of the brides from Texas, catches Jan's attention, and they walk toward the others who are huddled together, ready for another photo.

"This is a movie unreeling before us—history in the making. We are movie stars with no script to memorize, just raw reality television. Unbelievable." Amy accelerates to a gentle jog and leaves us all behind.

Mamma Mia! Sinners, Saints & Escapades! - Hair-Raising Adventures in Italy & Greece

Stephanie Chance is the International Bestselling Author of the *Mamma Mia!* series and an award-winning pick of the largest book club in the world, The Pulpwood Queen's International Book Club, receiving the official seal of approval for her *Mamma Mia!* trilogy of hair-raising adventures. Stephanie is beloved by millions of readers around the world for her 'tell-all' truths of the hilarious situations that Americans get in with her abroad; she's a comical, outgoing Italy tour guide with European genes stretching across the pond, leading Americans on two and three adventurous tours every year since May 2000.

As a paralegal, she worked twenty years beside a renowned attorney in East Texas. Then, in a blink of an eye, she launched a "one-of-a-kind" shop unlike any other in the world, Decorate Ornate. This store is packed floor to ceiling with gorgeous home decor from remote places in Europe. In between her European tours, Stephanie returns to Europe in search of castle doors, religious relics, and fabulous finds. This May marks her 22nd year zigzagging all over Italy and beyond in their Mercedes-Benz coach with the Americans hanging on tightly as she takes them to fairy-tale places. Stephanie has been featured throughout Europe and the USA via television, radio, and magazine, and keynote speaker around the globe. When not in Italy, you will find Stephanie in her treasure-chest shop Decorate Ornate, located on Main Street in Gladewater, the Antique Capital of East Texas.

Encounter

Francine Rodriguez

The teddy bear looked like it probably was once pink or some shade of pastel. The torn bow around its neck still had some color, but the bear was ripped at the neck, shedding stuffing as it slept at the freeway exit. The glass containers holding the half-burned candles were clouded with oil and dust and were cracked and broken in places. The bouquets of flowers had long since dried out and crumpled, caught in the green ribbon that was tied around their dark brown stems. Mostly it was the bear with only one black, beady button eye that caught your attention as you came to a stop before getting off the freeway. You had to wait out the light and so you stared and tried to read the small inscription written on the water-damaged cardboard. The name was almost impossible to read because the marker had run down from the top of the cardboard, but the date still showed, "2016-2020." Your eyes were always pulled to the left to look at it even if you didn't stop but kept driving through the exit ramp.

She saw it every day because she had to walk by there on her way to the bus stop. She'd sold the car two years ago. The social worker at the welfare office said she couldn't have a car worth more than $1500. The Audi was old, but it was still worth more than they allowed. The neighbors stared at it when she parked it in front of the apartment complex with the black iron-barred doors and cracked cement walkway. She worried that somebody would steal it when she was inside. The insurance had lapsed a long time ago, but it seemed that nobody knew what kind of car it was or else they weren't interested because it wasn't a Honda that could be sold quickly for parts around here.

As she approached the corner, she took a deep breath and tried to pretend it wasn't there or she was someone else who didn't know the reason the old bear was propped up against the stop sign. Sometimes it almost worked if she didn't look back across the street at the last minute and imagine that she saw the little girl running across, chasing after the stray matted dog running across the street. The dog hung around the apartment house, always hungry, scratching at missing patches of fur, its tongue lolling. Her daughter couldn't take her eyes off it. She trailed after it on the cement walk, reaching out to stroke it. The dog was wary, letting her get just so close, before running away. Her grandmother would grab her up and take her inside the screen door locking it. Until the one time she forgot.

It was the bear that needed replacing, she told herself. Looking all ragged like that, it was such a poor memorial, but she couldn't stand to go near it. She didn't want to put her hands on the same places her daughter had touched, to somehow erase the imprint of the little hands. No, the bear would have to stay the way it was. She looked down the street as she crossed over to the bus stop. The cars slogged along at this time of morning, making their way half-heartedly up to the on-ramp where they would sit again in another line that crawled along hesitantly. You could walk in the roadway, between and alongside the cars right now if you wanted. You would be perfectly safe since they moved only a matter of inches it seemed. But it was different in the middle of the day when all of the traffic had already disappeared somewhere else, and the street was deserted except for lone cars like large jungle animals separated from their herd that picked up speed at the light two blocks away and sped through the intersection as if they were chasing down their prey.

In the police report the car that hit her was listed under the column, "Party One," a 2019 SUV. Still new, it carried paper plates. Massive and hulking, you would wonder what a new vehicle like that was doing driving down this street where most of the residents drove rolling totals with crashed bumpers and chipped paint that had given up hanging onto better days a long time ago. It seemed that the driver of this vehicle was a contractor out to write a bid on a city job that involved road improvements. It was a side job that his company didn't know about. After unloading his packed van in the sticky heat of the Central Valley and driving for eighteen hours straight, he took a detour to make the estimate. On the way he finished all the black coffee in his thermos and snorted up a string of thin white lines laid out as straight as field sentries before he turned on to the roadway.

He thought he hit a dog at first, a skinny black dog with long flopping ears that blew straight back in the humid smog-scented breeze gusting in spurts across the asphalt. He realized it wasn't a dog at all when he saw the dog sprinting past his truck and reach the other side of the road. By the time he saw the little girl running in the center of the street, her sole focus on the elusive dog, just one step ahead, waiting for her she was sure, he was on her. She galloped toward her death without stopping. Every molecule of air froze. It was too late.

She wiped her forehead and looked over across the freeway entrance to the other side of the street. The man was still there sitting. He was always there, she thought. Sitting in his wheelchair holding his sign written on white cardboard with black magic marker. "Homeless. Will work for food." She wondered what kind of work he could do. The stumps of his legs that looked like they were wrapped in dirty white bandages ended at the edge of the seat of his wheelchair. He wheeled himself back and forth a few feet into the entrance to the freeway, breathing heavily as his arms spun the wheels of his chair forward and then turned around and started over, holding down his floppy green canvas hat with one hand and extending his sign toward the drivers, shouting something she couldn't really hear. He stationed himself there daily except when it rained, and then he pulled under the freeway underpass where he kept his shopping cart filled with dirty rags and broken objects he'd scavenged from the trash. Once when she returned on the bus after dark she saw him stretched out on the bus bench, his wheelchair tied to the bus sign with a length of clothesline. She wondered how he moved himself from the chair to the bench and tried to imagine it until she arrived home.

Today he had competition for the traffic stopped at the exit. A fortyish looking woman, probably indigenous she thought, with dark brown skin cast reddish from the sun, her deep-set slanted eyes squinting in the light, sauntered toward the stopped cars thrusting a bouquet of wilted carnations toward the drivers. Several bags of oranges lie on the ground near her. Nobody seemed to be buying the flowers or the oranges. But a few drivers handed her something out of their car window and she quickly tucked it into the pocket of her apron hanging below the long red dress that reached her ankles. She was barefoot and you could see that the bottoms of her feet were stained black from walking on the filthy asphalt covered with the grime churned up from the roadway.

The woman holding the flowers was trying to ignore the man in the wheelchair as he wheeled back and forth toward the traffic, shaking her long black frizzy braid over her shoulders, and turning in the opposite direction. They were in competition today. A small war of wills and endurance. Remaining soldiers in a lone battlefield where the struggle to survive another day depended on the support of the occupants of passing cars who usually stared at them curious or disgusted and kept on driving.

Her eyes drifted over to the teddy bear in spite of herself. Carmela was the child everybody loved. That special kind of light that some are born with burned inside of her. It blinded you when she entered the room, made you stop and watch her, wanting to absorb the rays she willingly shared. That light pulsed for the first time when the doctor pulled her out with his forceps, silent, eyes wide open, staring directly at the doctor and the midwife, challenging the forces that had removed her from the warmth and safety of her sanctuary for all these months, and pushed her into the chilly air conditioned abyss where distorted faces peered at her through a glass encasing.

If she could have seen ahead a few years, seen her daughter's tiny form huddled on a gurney, blood leaking through the white bandages, soaking her dark curls. Plastic bags containing liquids hanging from poles that connected to tubes attached to every inch of her pale skin, and all of the places she'd kissed on her baby's body. The sharp smells of alcohol and disinfectants. If she could have seen ahead, how far back could she have gone to stop it?

Maybe she shouldn't have let her mother watch Carmela. Didn't her mother sometimes forget to feed Carmela lunch or take her to the liquor store instead where she bought them both chocolate bars and potato chips. It hadn't seemed like much at the time. Grandmothers liked to spoil the little ones. But hadn't her mother locked herself out of her apartment more than once, so she had to wait with Carmela, huddled under the torn canvas awning in the back by the dumpster in the pouring rain for the manager to come and unlock the door? When Carmela was younger didn't her mother leave her alone in the bathtub until the water turned cold and rust leaked out of the faucet while Carmela shook with chills, sobbing, as she watched the faucet drip.

"It leaked blood, Mama! I kept yelling for her to come but she didn't hear. She forgot I was in the bathtub. She went to sleep."

She felt her eyes begin to tear. The terrible hollow in her heart exploding. She could blame her mother, but she was the one who left Carmela with her in that small single apartment where fifteen years of odor from frying meat had burrowed into the walls and coated the cracked tile in the kitchen with a fine layer of grease. Her mother, an unpaid babysitter, the only kind she could afford.

She still woke every day, momentarily forgetting, looking around at the space that Carmela's bed used to occupy before she remembered. Fighting the longing to slip into the darkness under the covers was the hardest. As she unfolded her body and placed her feet on the cold floor tiles she looked out the window toward the sky. They said Carmela's soul was floating up there waiting to be reborn. She whispered this to herself over and over during the day, each time someone asked her how she was doing, and she told them "fine." She wasn't "fine." She would never be "fine" again. It was a lie. Only what they expected to hear since time had passed. Her memories of life before Carmela were growing fainter, blurring. Carmela had only been around for four years. But her memories of her were sharper than ever, images that grew bolder when she saw another little girl or smelled the softly scented baby shampoo that she'd used for Carmela's hair.

She still kept a small pink barrette shaped like a duck in the pocket of her jeans and rubbed her fingers over the smooth plastic most of the day. Once when the barrette slipped off the bathroom counter and lodged behind the sink her heart started to pound and a cold sweat began beading at her neck and crawled down her back. Her hands shook and she could feel a beat pulsing in her head. The manager in her building was finally able to locate the barrette by sticking a long piece of scrap metal behind the sink and pushing it out to the other side. She hadn't lost a part of Carmela the way she feared.

Stepping slowly, looking ahead for the bus, she wondered if she should skip work today, call in sick again. Yesterday, she'd called in. Her eyes were scalded from crying, and her head throbbed. She only cried when she was sure everybody else was asleep and couldn't hear. They were the same people who would ask her anxiously, "Are you all right?"

Yesterday the heavy numbing weight that soaked into all of her cells found its way to her feet, settling in and overtaking her steps toward the bus, directing them to turn around and walk back across the street. She walked numbly for three blocks and finally boarded a bus southbound for the mall where she sat outside Macy's and waited for the doors to open.

The first customer of the day, she walked blindly to the second floor where women's clothes were sold. Slowly she wandered through the aisles, her hands grasping at garments hanging on display, closing her eyes and rubbing the fabric between her fingers. Rough wool, silky polyesters, and coarse linen weaves. For a few moments she let the sensations travel from her fingers and fill her head before pushing the garments back. Clothes she could look at and touch but not buy.

Today the thought of riding downtown to Merkinder's, sitting in the freezing back office, and entering strings of numbers and letters into the computer made her slow her steps again. There was nowhere else to go.

"Hey lady, can you spare some change for a homeless vet?" The man in the wheelchair was heading toward her, his right hand wrapped around the wheels of his chair moving in circles as he scurried across the pavement.

She backed up startled. He was older than he looked from far away. She could see that now. Wild gray hair in tight springs stuffed under a floppy cloth hat that looked as if the sides had been chewed. A blanket covered his lap falling short where the stumps of his legs peeked out. His eyes were bloodshot, and he wasn't holding his "Homeless Vet," sign up on his lap. Today his free hand was wrapped around a bottle. She noticed that it was more than half empty.

"So, what do you say? Can you give me a little somethin, somethin?"

He tried to give her a half smile, but his eyes gave him away. They'd lost their light and looked past her down the street at something only he could see. She watched him lift the bottle with a shaking hand and wrap his thumb and forefinger around the base. The rest of his fingers were missing. Her eyes were rivetted to the stubs of his fingers. So unsettling.

She didn't see the car pull into the empty church parking lot next to the bus stop. Not at first. She was still staring at the man's hand holding the bottle. She didn't look up until she heard the car door slam and the driver yell across at the woman selling the flowers. She couldn't hear what he yelled, but she saw the woman back up and look around, her eyes frantic. The man who got out of the car took a few long strides and reached the woman selling flowers in seconds. He grabbed her by the shoulders and shook her. Her small frame collapsed, and he dragged her a foot or two and pulled off her apron, digging his hands deep into the pocket before he threw it in the road. The woman curled up on the curb crying.

She watched in disbelief. It was like something she'd seen on television. One of those police shows, where the police cars pulled up at the last minute and surrounded the bad guy, stopping him in his tracks. But there was no police car and no police. The man stuffed whatever he'd taken from the apron into his pocket and looked up for the first time. His head was shaved, and half of his face was covered with tattoos. In the light of the beating sun, you could see that once the angry slash marks shaped like letters across his cheek bones had been black but were now faded to a sickly greenish cast.

"What you looking at bitch?"

Her eyes moved to his lips, narrow and drawn, over grayish teeth. *Crack,* she thought. The woman across from her still sat at the curb, her body folded in half, rocking, and sobbing, her head buried in her lap.

She swallowed hard and looked around. She couldn't move past the man coming toward her, sweat beading on his bald head. He was blocking the street. She could run to the church, but it was closed. He started his long stride, moving closer. She thought she remembered him from another time, holding a shotgun, standing at the door, and pointing it at a neighbor, threatening to kill the old man if he didn't hand over his wallet. No, that was her uncle, she remembered. He wasn't bald and he wore his long greasy hair pulled back in a ponytail. She'd lived with him when she was pregnant. He was doing time now. Away, locked up, where he couldn't point a gun.

"I said, answer me! What are you looking at?"

His voice jolted her to the pit of her stomach. She clutched her small brown vinyl purse to her chest. She had enough money for the bus, and a twenty-dollar bill set aside to pay a part of this month's gas at *CVS Y Mas*, after work because they recently started taking payments. The man was just a few feet away. She could smell his sweat. The sides of his thin discolored beige shirt were soaked and sticking to his body drawing her eyes to his ribs, sharp and protruding, like something she'd seen hanging in an open meat locker in the *carniceria.*

"Give me your purse bitch or I'll cut you!" His right arm dropped suddenly, and he reached down into his pocket, pulling out a small knife. He waved it eagerly as he walked. "Do you hear me? Don't look at me. Just give me your purse and I won't hurt you!"

She stared, not moving, her feet turning to liquid, melting into the sidewalk.

"Hey over here!" The man in the wheelchair was wheeling forward, his arms churning in circles as he spun his chair away from the underpass and headed straight toward the bald man holding the knife. Moving his wheelchair closer, he swung his arm back and pitched a large rock at him. The man holding the knife lowered his arm, shrieking in pain as the rock struck his forehead and blood began to run down his face. "God damn you!" he yelled, doubled over, trying to shield his eyes.

She looked back to the man in the wheelchair. He was pulling out something from under the blanket in his lap and pointing it in the direction of the man holding the knife. "Drop that lady's money you just took and get the hell out of here before I shoot your dumb ass! You hear me?"

The man with the knife looked up, his mouth dropping open in surprise as he squinted in the sun. He seemed to forget about the blood running down his face and stepped forward again. The man in the wheelchair raised the gun higher and she heard a clicking sound.

"Motherfucker's ready? Youngblood! I feel the need for some killing today. Might as well be you." The man in the wheelchair chuckled a little.

The man with the knife looked around. Hesitated.

"Let go of that knife, I said, and drop that shitty little purse you took offa her! Drop them now!"

"Hell no!" The man with the knife looked down at his torn cargo pants as if he just remembered stashing something there. He swiped at the blood trickling from his forehead with his free arm, smearing it across his face and onto his neck where it ran onto his shirt. His right eye was swollen and ballooned out, like a ripe grape-colored pod rising from its socket.

The man in the wheelchair moved closer, raising the gun higher. The sunlight struck the metal giving it a dark blue glow. The gun looked like a sculpture, a piece of deadly art. The man with the knife watched it rise until it was pointed at his head. He turned to glance at the woman sitting at the curb and then cut his eyes back toward his car. He licked his lips and wiped a broad streak of blood from his forehead.

"I ain't tellin you again." The man in the wheelchair raised the gun higher and kept it pointed at the bald man's head.

She could see the bald man staring at her with his right eye, the one that hadn't been hit. He was considering what to do next. She looked away at the battered bear. She could feel her daughter so close, growing deep in her body where she carried her. Things that happened could not be undone. She looked into the eyes of the man with the knife and pulled her cell phone out of her purse, holding her gaze on his hand that held the knife, and randomly started pressing buttons.

"You see," she yelled, "I just called the police. They shoot on sight here. You should know that!" The sound of her own voice made her quiver. The phone was dead for the last week. Shut off because she hadn't paid the deposit.

"You hear that asshole?" The man in the wheelchair reached into his lap with his free hand and held up another large rock. "I throw real good with my left hand. Pitched in minor league when I still had my legs. Shoot good too. Killed me a mess of son-of-a-bitches when I was over there. Got me a medal for it. Used to hang on my dresser when I had a place to stay." He started wheeling forward. "Be glad to take out your other eye while I'm on this earth."

The bald man threw his knife in front of him and ran the few feet to his car, clutching his bloody face. He started the engine with the driver's door still hanging open and pounded on the gas. Black fumes poured from the tailpipe. The car bucked and sprang forward. The sound of metal grinding on metal filled the air with a shrill screech as it drove over the curb and onto the road toward the entrance to the freeway.

The street was suddenly hushed. The traffic had passed, and the only sound was the warbling of a small brown bird perched on the overhanging branch of the live oak tree that remained on the gravel-covered yard in front of the church.

The man in the wheelchair lowered his gun and tucked it under the blanket that was folded across his lap. "Guess he's gone now. How about grabbing that purse and the knife?"

She found herself numbly bending down and picking up the small vinyl purse. It was torn at the corner and she could see a couple of folded bills below the tear. Her hand closed carefully around the knife handle.

"Don't want the purse. Give it back to her. Just give me the knife."

She walked over to the woman on the other side of the roadway and tapped her on the shoulder. She was still sitting on the curb, crying into her hands. When she looked up tears ran down her dirt-streaked face, leaving cleaner patches of skin, stark, against the deep copper stain that came from years of standing in the bright overhead sun. She reached up and took the small purse, hiding it quickly inside her clothes.

The man in the wheelchair wheeled himself over and reached for the small knife. "I see you most days taking the bus over there." He gestured toward the corner.

"I take it to work," she hesitated. Up close he gave off a sickly-sweet smell. Unwashed, she thought. "Thank you," she added, her voice flattened. She was still shaking, looking off in the direction where the bald man had driven. The man in the wheelchair saved her from having to give up her money; the twenty dollars she had in her purse. Maybe he saved her life too. She wondered if the bald man would have used his knife. She'd had her apartment broken into before. More than once, everybody here had, and one time a young guy wearing a Halloween face mask and carrying a handgun held up everybody in the laundromat. She knew it was a mistake to go there so late at night, but it was hard to find someone to watch a six-month-old baby. Today was different. She shivered in the bright sunlight, wishing she could hold Carmela again.

The man in the wheelchair wheeled back a little and studied her face. "I know you really didn't call the cops. Good move, though," he smiled, his mouth cavernous, dark. "It ain't your time yet. Homeboy was only trying to scare you. Just gonna take your money, like he did to her." He pointed at the dark-skinned woman who resumed standing at the corner. "But you can't let em get away with it you know. When the apocalypse comes, all that's gonna be left on this earth are those thugs. They'll survive everybody else one way or the other."

He patted his lap where he'd stashed the gun and met her eyes. "I see you lookin at that little memorial all the time. What's the story there?"

"It's for my daughter," her voice choked. "She got killed right here. A car ran her over." She felt herself tear up the way she always did when she talked about Carmela.

"Sorry lady. Sorry you have to see it every day. If you don't mind me asking, can't you go to work a different way or something? I mean...."

"No." Her voice was resolute. "That would be leaving the last place she was alive. Like trying to forget her. I'd never do that."

"Oh." He tilted his head back and seemed to be considering what he heard. "Sorry for your loss. I've seen a lot of people die too. Some of em on the street. Downtown. I used to stay there. I used to have me a home too. Not now. Not anymore."

Her eyes rested on the corner of the blanket that partially covered the stumps of his legs. She could read the words "U.S. Army" on the border, stamped in green. "You were in the service?"

400

"Yes sir! Stayed as long as I could too." He reached under his blanket and pulled out the bottle she'd seen earlier. "Life's hard on the outside. Hard to figure out what to do. Not like in the service. I knew what to do then. Saved a lot of lives myself." He tilted his head back and took a long drink.

She nodded weakly, knowing somehow that was probably true. "Anyway, Thank you again." She heard her voice like a whisper as she looked down the roadway. The bus stop seemed so far off now. "My little girl was only four years old you know. Just four. She was following a dog across the road."

The man in the wheelchair shook his head. "No ma' am, she was following Jesus. The lord was calling her. She's with him now."

She stared at the man, confused. She'd heard all of those words before. Those words that were supposed to ease the pain, make her feel better because her daughter had answered a higher calling. "But she was so young!" She could hear her voice rising as she answered, her heart beginning to beat faster, her skin beginning to feel damp and clammy. She closed her eyes for a moment, and she could see the man holding the knife, coming toward her. Why was she alive and her daughter wasn't? How did he pick the ones he wanted to take out of this world? She took a deep breath. "What's your name? I'm Carol Porter."

"Roland, Roland Matthews. Pleased to meet you."

"Look," she began. "I never stopped to give you anything when I passed by in the morning. I never give any money to people in the street. I figure they should get a job, not beg. But I guess it's hard living out here like this. It's hard living where I am too," she added, looking down embarrassed, wanting to ask the man how he ended up in the street. He wasn't just part of the nameless, homeless. He seemed more caring, more understanding, than most of the people she knew. Why did he just give up then? She looked across at the small memorial for her daughter and thought maybe she understood. Life was divided now. There was the "Before," when Carmela was alive, and the "After," when she wasn't. Living in the "After," was harder every day.

This was his life, "After."

Roland watched her face closely, "You can't, you know. End up like me, chickenshit, scared, hiding with my bottle, This ain't no life. Just waiting to die out here. You're too young for that. You got life ahead, people you're gonna meet and all, if you don't push your life away, like me."

"No." Her voice choked. "I can't anymore."

"Bullshit! There's so much time left. That little girl deserves a mother who appreciates that she's breathing, healthy and alive. You're letting her down, you know, hiding, running away from the land of the living."

Carol stared at the memorial and thought she could hear Carmela giggling, running toward her, her eyes shining, her lips pink and puckered. She was all smiles, focused on what she would see forever. Eternally happy in the "After." Carol wiped her eyes and reached into her purse removing the twenty dollars. "Here. It's not much, but at least... You saved my life."

Roland waved the bill away and pointed to the dark-skinned woman standing at the freeway entrance, walking up to the cars stopped at the light. "Go and give it to her. She's illegal here. Stays one step ahead of the cops. She's got a few kids she told me once. Worse off than me. I bet she doesn't want to live like this, but she's got guts. Keeps going."

Carol looked at the woman and nodded her head in agreement. She started to walk away and turned back. "I'll see you tomorrow."

The man in the wheelchair threw back his head and laughed. "Same time. Same place. If I'm not here you know I won the lottery, or I walked through a door and all my problems disappeared. Healthy and happy again." He chuckled a little to himself.

She walked away without looking for that dark quiet place to hide. Just for today, she told herself. For Roland, and Carmela.

Encounter was inspired when a gang member jumped out of a car at the freeway entrance near where I live and robbed a woman who sold oranges there almost every day.

I wasn't quick enough on the scene to stop the "grab and run," but I recognized the woman and spoke with her after buying up her oranges. She made very little money. This was mostly her story and the story of the child she lost. She had dreams of getting a better job, but her undocumented status and lack of any skills, education, and language barriers precluded this. (You might want to read *A Fortunate Accident*, my first novel, that deals extensively with the life and victimization of undocumented aliens and encompasses the lives of people I knew well). Also at this corner near the freeway, a wheelchair-bound man came every day to beg motorists for spare change. I talked to him occasionally when I had some money to give. He was an alcoholic veteran. and usually drunk or high on heroin. He proclaimed to have a purple heart. He sometimes carried a small handgun that he used to ward off Cholos. Both of these individuals respected each other's space and stationed themselves at opposite sides of the freeway entrance so they wouldn't be in competition. The wheelchair-bound man felt badly for the woman selling oranges because she was undocumented. He always said, 'I may be Black and treated like crap, but they treat them Mexicans worse."

I started my writing endeavor approximately six years ago. Prior to that time, I worked in the fields of law and psychology. I have worked as a criminal lawyer, a Federal Mediator, a Federal Civil Rights Investigator, a criminal reform lobbyist, an ADA Compliance Grant Manager, and a substance abuse counselor for pregnant HIV teenagers.

I grew up near downtown Los Angeles, close to the skid row area. Much of my writing is influenced by that area and the people living there. I write about over-looked women, primarily Latinas, whom I feel have not yet had a voice in published literature. These women's stories often speak to isolation, confusion, and bitterness. They deal with struggles pushed to the extreme and the continuing impact of trauma. These stories allow us to see the world through someone else's eyes.

I have two previously published novels, *The Fortunate Accident*, and *A Woman Like Me*. *Smiley and Laughing Girl*, one of the stories in my anthology, was published in *Fleas On the Dog* in 2020, *Finding My Father,* was published by Literary Yard in 2020, and *I Still Like Pink* was published in Taboos and Transgressions in 2020.

I am currently a finalist for the International Latino Book Awards.

Francine Rodriguez try.mediation@gmail.com
www. Francinerodriguezauthor.com

Slice of Suburbia

Joanne Kukanza Easley

As I boarded the train at Grand Central Station on the way to visit my friend Milly, I thought back to our goodbye luncheon five years ago, just before Pearl Harbor. At the time, she was newly married and already pregnant, ecstatic about her new home in Scarsdale. On the other hand, I was about to flee Manhattan for Dallas because of the ruination of my reputation after word got out I'd born a child out of wedlock. In shame, I had cut all ties with all my old modeling friends—except Milly.

To tell the truth, I was apprehensive about the trip to Scarsdale, and it had nothing to do with my friend. How would I react to her children? I reviewed the details of her brood: her eldest, Martin Junior, was four. Milly had been pregnant with him when I moved to Dallas. Priscilla came shortly after, then Teddy, who had just started walking. The contrast of Milly's pre-marriage life to her current one was stark. The contrast to her family and my lack of one, equally so.

I got off the train at Scarsdale and noted the Tudor style of the station. Milly had gone into rhapsodies about the Tudor architecture of her Scarsdale home. As I followed the directions to Milly's—it was only a short walk—I had more than my fill of the style. Strolling up the drive, I saw a tricycle on its side among assorted playthings. I glanced at the door and noticed three little faces and six pudgy hands pressed against the sidelights. Good grief. The children disappeared, and moments later, a flustered Milly, dressed in a chenille bathrobe, opened the door. Her face was shiny with cold cream, and her hair was in rollers.

"Oh, Lauren, you look like you just stepped off the runway. I love your suit. Lilac is the color this spring! And purple suede pumps and a matching hat. Gorgeous! Come on in."

I did so gingerly. As three tots circled me like I was prey, I forced a smile and stated the obvious. "You're not ready. What about lunch? Did you make a reservation?"

"Yes. No. It's a long story. My sitter canceled."

"Find another one."

"Easier said than done. Come into the kitchen. I'll give the kids a snack and see if I can scare up someone."

As soon as the snack was consumed, sibling rivalry—at least that's what I think it was—reared its head. Two minutes of the screaming, crying, and fighting children was enough. I quickly hatched a plan to give Milly some quiet to make her calls.

"Children, I've got a marvelous idea. Why don't you show me your rooms?"

As if someone had put a cork in their mouths, they stopped yelling. I walked to the stairs, and they followed me like a pack of jackals.

Each child had their own room decorated with a charming—and no doubt expensive—theme. We decided it was only fair to tour the rooms in the order of age. Martin's nautical room, with a bed shaped like a boat, was first, then Priscilla's princess-inspired room with its canopied bed and a floor littered with pink toys, and then Teddy's domain, cowboy-themed. His room had bunk beds made from rustic timber and shelves holding a collection of horse figurines. As we progressed down the hall to each chamber, I relaxed a little and managed to mouth appropriately worded compliments on each child's treasures.

As we descended the stairs, Milly came charging up. "I found someone! Marge, my next-door neighbor, agreed to bring her baby over for a couple of hours. Willya take the kids to the playroom while I get ready?"

Five minutes later, she came back in a too-tight matronly suit in an awful maroon shade and crooked lipstick. I didn't say a word, but I felt bad for her. Thinking back to her at age eighteen, I gasped when I realized she was only twenty-four. She looked at least thirty, a tired and pudgy thirty.

"Something wrong, Lauren?"

"Oh, no. I was just thinking how hungry I am."

The front door opened. "Yoo-hoo! Where are you, Milly?" Marge had arrived, and during quick introductions, we helped with her stroller and a huge bag of baby things. She had packed like she was staying a week.

"You're a lifesaver, Marge." Milly hugged her and promised to sit for the baby in return. She turned to me and practically shoved me through the door. "Let's go! It's only a couple of blocks."

As we strolled to the lunch spot, Milly gave me the lowdown on her neighbors and their palatial homes, how many bedrooms and baths—and how many children. I struggled not to cross my eyes in boredom. Couldn't she see I had no interest in that kind of life? I hoped we'd share some girl talk in the restaurant. On arrival, the maître d' seated us in a sumptuous leather booth where we had a great view of all the Scarsdale matrons.

First things first. We ordered Martinis with extra olives and a dozen oysters on the half shell.

Milly took a dainty sip of her drink and said, "I've got some juicy gossip about our former colleagues, the gals you called the Philly fillies."

"Do tell." I had always thought there was something a little hinky about Francine and Fiona.

"They were kicked out of the Barbizon for 'unholy relations.'"

"What?" My eyes almost popped out of my head.

"Yeah, they're a couple. Always were, it turns out."

"But they dated men."

"So what? Did you ever hear them rave about how much in love they were with whomever? Did they ever have a beau or even date the same man twice?

"Now that you mention it, no."

"Ever hear of a beard?

I didn't think she meant a man's facial hair. "Beard?"

"It's a term for a fake relationship, someone to hide behind when one has an illicit relationship."

"Oh."

"Yeah." Milly ordered another Martini. When I raised my eyebrows, she frowned and said, "Don't judge me. I'm not driving."

"No judgment." After having an illegitimate child and rampaging through the men returning from the war, who was I to judge? Not to mention my own periodic indulgences, but that day, I restricted myself to one martini. While Milly wasn't driving, I wasn't sure she'd be capable of walking if she kept up her intake of gin and vermouth.

The oysters arrived along with Milly's second drink. "Ooh, they're so fresh!" My friend slurped her way through three before I could serve myself. "Katherine and Eleanor are still modeling, although they're looking to get jobs either at Powers or the new Ford agency as instructors. John Roberts Powers isn't the only name in modeling any longer. He's got serious competition. Ford is advancing money to their models based on their . Let me tell you, they're cutting a swath through the scene." Milly held up her empty glass to signal for a refill.

"Interesting." It hadn't occurred to me to become an instructor at an agency. Maybe I should look into it since I wasn't certain how I'd like my new job at Bergdorf Goodman.

On the waiter's recommendation, we ordered shrimp salad and returned to our Martinis. The olives made a nice contrast to the oysters.

Our waiter returned with the salads. By the time we finished,

Milly had drained her third drink and plucked out the olive, which she popped into her mouth, nearly missing. I was starting to wonder if her storybook, happily-ever-after life hadn't turned out the way she imagined.

Milly bit her lip, then blurted, "Martin is having an affair. At least, I'm pretty sure he is. I'm mortified." Milly rummaged through her bag for a hanky. With tears streaming down her cheeks, she asked if I had one.

I handed her mine and asked, "Are you sure, hon? As I recall, Martin seemed totally in the palm of your hand, enamored like I've seldom seen."

Milly sniffed and patted her nose. "Maybe three kids and fifteen pounds ago." Her face crumpled, and the tears returned.

I ordered two coffees and listened to Milly's tale of woe. The late nights at the office. Detecting a perfume other than the Arpège she wore on his clothing. The way he moved all his expense account records to the office. It seemed she had plenty of reason to be worried, but I didn't want to fan her fears.

When the waiter came with the check, I asked for more coffee and insisted on paying. How could I help her? I racked my brain for ideas and finally hit on Joe Pilates' Contrology.

Setting down my coffee cup, I said, "I've been thinking about going back to see Joe and Clara at their studio."

"Who're they?"

"The Pilates. Before I moved to Dallas, I took instruction at their studio on Eighth Avenue and even taught a few classes."

"When was this?"

"After, you know…the baby." As I felt my cheeks burn, I wondered if I'd ever get over the shame.

Light dawned in her eyes. "Yeah, I remember now. You really whipped yourself into shape. Maybe I should give it a try."

"I recommend it. In fact, I've been doing the floor exercises at home."

Milly smiled, and I caught a glimpse of the fresh girl I met six years ago. We walked back to Milly's place. Since she was a little unsteady, I kept a death grip on her elbow. At the door, I declined an invitation to stay awhile. "Got a train to catch. It was so good to see you." After a quick hug, I turned and hustled away from Milly, her troubles, and suburbia.

My story, *Slice of Suburbia*, is from Chapter Five, Another Bite of the Apple, in my work-in-progress, *I'll Be Seeing You.* The year is 1946. Lauren has returned to Manhattan five years after having a child out of wedlock and fleeing to Dallas. When her life spirals down due to budding alcoholism and promiscuity, she returns to New York City. She finds that nothing is the same.

Joanne Kukanza Easley lives in the Texas Hill Country on a small ranch with her husband, three rescue terriers, and abundant wildlife. Retired from a career in nursing—with dual specialties in the cold, clinical operating room, and the intense, emotional world of psychiatric nursing, she devotes her time to writing fiction. Her debut novel *Sweet Jane* received several honors, including being named the 2020 winner in adult fiction at the Texas Author Project. *Just One Look*, her second book, was released on June 24, 2021, and is set in her native Chicago, Illinois. Her current project, *I'll Be Seeing You,* is based on a character in *Sweet Jane.*

The Book Of Fairfax

E. V. Svetova

665 A.D., Spring
Northumbria

Ever since he was a child, Yaret was in the habit of sleeping in
Caireann's bed. Her arm around him, his head on her shoulder—it was
the closest the boy knew to the comfort of a mother's embrace. He
enjoyed nothing more than slow winter mornings, when Caireann
lingered under the wolf skin till sunrise, holding him tight to her side,
the strands of his fair hair tangled in with her dark tresses. Her cat
purred at their feet as they told each other their dreams and then
unraveled their meaning together. She would tickle him, pull his ears,
sending him into fits of wild giddiness. He would then laugh at her,
tease her for her fear of the cold, brag about his own great power to
withstand it, show off his magic skill by starting a fire without getting
out of the bed. And his glow always shined brightest at times like this,
when she looked at him, appraisingly, approvingly, a touch of
motherly pride in her eyes.

Since last summer, however, Caireann the wicce was finding reasons for him to either sleep in the shack outside or leave for the night altogether. It was as if she changed. She hardly slapped him anymore—that he attributed to his improved skills at herbs and healing. But she no longer smothered him with kisses either, and that he missed. Now he cherished each little moment of closeness, like when they watched the sunset from the cliff above Caireann's house, her plaid shawl wrapped around them, as though he was still her little boy.

As Yaret hopelessly pondered possible reasons for Caireann's aloofness, he began to blame his peculiar nature. While he shot up quicker than an ordinary youth, by his fifteenth year he was as fully matured as he was ever going to be. He jealously watched boys grow sturdier and brawnier. Although his legs were strong from riding, as his shoulders from swordplay, still he remained reed-thin. Others grew a shadow above their upper lips, sprouted coarse hairs inside the armpits and on their shins, but his skin remained as hairless as the day he was born, untanned after days in the sun. Embarrassed, he began to shy away from baring his body in front of other men, like a pious monk.

Suddenly, one who never cared to be a part of the human race wished he was more of a man. While he was swifter than anyone, and a better swordsman than most, after he found himself pinned down in one wrestling match after another by the blacksmith's son, a boy two years his junior, Yaret realized his physical prowess was far from exceptional; but the prohibition against battle magic had been already firmly ingrained into him.

"In battle, blood boils up and obscures sight. It is too easy to make a mistake and slay an innocent. The moment you harm an innocent you defile your light. When your light dies, you die," Caireann would repeat time and again.

As if to mock him, chances to prove himself were being presented left and right. The Roman party was victorious and the Easter of the year Six Hundred and Sixty Five was the first to be celebrated throughout the whole of Northumbria on a single day. The Bright Week was especially festive this year. Yaret's uncle, Prior Alric, took the opportunity to recruit more men to accompany him on his pilgrimage.

Now these warriors sauntered about Yaret's homestead village of Lynton in their rich Welsh-made armor decorated with knotwork of Christian crosses, challenging other men to matches. Competitions and tournaments were held all over the shire, and all young lord Yaret Fairfax could do was repair dislocated shoulders and cracked ribs with his medicinal lǣcecraft.

"How unfair! I know none of them is a match for me if we battled on my terms," Yaret was saying to Caireann as they sat on a log in front of her hut. With Alric spending weeks at a time at home, it was harder and harder for Yaret, who wasn't keen on lying, to come up with reasonable excuses for leaving the village. After successfully concealing his relations with the wicce for six years, Yaret did not dare risk exposing Caireann to Alric's wrath, and the loyal Cœnred was willing to lie for his young lord only so often.

Today, Yaret managed to sneak out from Lynton to see her for the afternoon. He was angry with himself for wasting their precious time complaining, but here she was, certain, all-knowing, and under the calm gaze of her dark grey eyes he couldn't help but pour out his heart, just as when he was a child.

"I could have charmed him into submission. I could have incinerated him, or—not that I would—I could have turned him into a pile of steaming meat..."

"But you know better than to use your power unrighteously..."

"Yeah," he yawned, "I know better. Must you turn every conversation into a lesson? Sometimes, I swear, you're no different from my uncle."

"The day you harm or force an innocent will be the day you die."

"Unfair! You don't hesitate to sell a womb-unbinding brew to a woman, or a love potion to a vengeful lover. You charm merchants into giving their wares to you for free. You force innocents, curse strangers, and don't think twice. Yet, you wouldn't even teach me a single battle spell. Why are you allowed it and not I?"

"A snowflake can't feel cold, but leave a green leaf out in a blizzard and see what happens. You and I are not the same. You lose light—you lose love. You lose love—you lose power. How many times have I told you?"

"Too many!"

"I wouldn't have to, if you paid attention!" She pretended to swing at him, and he cowered playfully. "Magic hinges on focus. Whatever you do, be in love with it, breathe each breath like your last…"

"I've seen people in love. They breathe only for each other."

"People in love… what do they know? What mortal men call love is but a pale shadow of the true force behind it all. Why are you staring with those doe eyes? Pay attention, child!"

"Much good does it do me." With a deep sigh, Yaret leaned back on his elbows, letting the last rays of the evening sun caress his smooth face. "Oh, Caireann, sometimes I wonder if my power is anything more than attention—after all, can't a mother anticipate the thoughts of her child, or a lover share the moods of his beloved? My gift of beast-charming is not unique either—horse whisperers and gifted falconers aren't that rare. I have a sense for medicinal arts, but so does any village wisewoman. I can see in the dark, but so can many hunters. I am a quick learner, but so are some of the humble monks at my uncle's priory. They say I am beautiful, but in the market square I've seen plainer youths draw more interest with nothing but a practiced sway of their hips…"

"Measuring up to harlots, aren't we? Silly boy. Let me remind you of Lugh, when he, as a young man, sought to join the court of King Nuada of the Tuatha Dé Danann."

"I remember. He asked to be let into Tara, but the doorkeeper wouldn't let him in unless he could prove useful to the King. So, he offered his services as a smith, a scribe, a swordsman, a healer, a craftsman, except no matter what he said, the Tuatha Dé already had somebody with that skill."

"And then, what did Lugh do?"

"He asked if there was anyone who had all those skills at the same time."

"And he was admitted. See, no single human has all your gifts. Moreover, no one sees the world as you see it, no one loves it as you do. And they don't glow," she added with a smile, stroking his fair head. "I've seen your light."

"I see it every day, but what good is the light if all it illuminates is doubt?"

"Now you listen to me." She locked her hard fingers around his narrow jaw, shaking him a little as she spoke. "You may doubt the world around you, and you may doubt people. Doubt me, if you will, but you must never doubt yourself. The light within you is the only truth worth knowing." Her holding his chin sent warm waves down his spine; he closed his eyes, no longer hearing her voice, instead listening only to the beating of his heart.

"Ah!" She smirked, letting go of his face. "I should know by now to keep my hands off your little muzzle…"

"No, please keep your hands on my little muzzle," Yaret whined, grasping her hands and pressing them to his cheeks.

"Let go now!" She laughed, feigning struggle, then hugged him, and kissed him on the forehead before pushing him away. "Enough, pet. It's late. Come, let's ready your horse." She rose.

"Why can't I sleep with you tonight?"

Caireann frowned. "Go home, Yaret."

"You never let me spend the night anymore."

"Don't be foolish. You spent the night on the last full moon, when we cut young mugwort, remember?"

"It's not like it used to be." He sulked. "We used to share your bed, you used to hold me through the night, and tell me your dreams upon waking. It's been ten full moons since you held me, Caireann."

"Didn't know you were keeping score…"

"Have you taken a lover?" He rose to face her, looking her in the eye with a mix of timidity and defiance. When had he grown to be taller than her?

"How dare you…"

"Is it unheard of? You are no nun, you must've had lovers before you took me in. You've given a child all your time for years. I know, someday you will want a man by your side."

"You know nothing!"

"I can see you through and through, Caireann. You are the one who taught me how. I can see it here…" he touched his fingers between the woman's breasts, "…and here," he brushed her stomach. "There is a disturbance in your life force, your hælu is like a swirl of whitewater. You aren't ill, and it isn't your monthlies. So, there must be an unfulfilled desire you're concealing. What troubles you? Do you fear I am too young to understand? Fear not. I am no longer a child."

"That's what troubles me," she muttered so quietly he almost missed it, though hardly anything got past his sensitive ears. Seeing his puzzled expression, she sighed. "You've always honored me with your obedience. Do as I say. Go home."

He departed in a worse mood than when he arrived. If there was one thing he could understand about people, it was when they lied. So, she grew tired of the boy, and now wanted a man in her life. But who? Old Cœnred had a soft spot for Caireann, Yaret could sense his affection. For years he helped mend her house, brought her gifts from the market, all while claiming it was in payment for the training she offered to his young lord. But Cœnred was so fatherly to her—no, it couldn't be him. Who of the village men had business with the wicce? The blacksmith? He was the strongest man in Lynton, knowledgeable at his craft, a runemaster, nearly a wicca himself. But the blacksmith loved his wife, Yaret had felt the true bond between them. No, Caireann wouldn't care for another woman's husband. Some stranger from over the Wall? A traveling scop? She distrusted musicians and storytellers. One of their neighbor's warriors? A monk from the priory? Now, that was insane… perhaps it wasn't a man at all, but a woman! From the little she reluctantly revealed about her life before banishment from the sisterhood, Yaret knew that sisters were not above using each other's bodies to replenish their magical powers, as well as for pure pleasure. Perhaps, she was so eager to be rid of him because she expected a secret visitor.

"Ah!" he cried out loud, spooking his horse. He had to know, even if he had to stoop to spying. He reined in and turned back. As much as he suffered from jealousy and doubt, it never occurred to him he could simply force his way into her soul—the wicce had her boy trained well, like a giant wolfhound who meekly licks the hand of the houndmaster when it could easily sever it with one bite of the mighty jaws.

It was near midnight when he returned to Caireann's. The moon had risen, and cast an even light over the glen. Yaret dismounted and walked his horse in the shadow of the trees, then tied it far enough from the house. A simple charm quieted the animal, and another, more complex, made it undetectable to forest predators.

He didn't need to look in to know the house was empty. He shut his eyes, and stood motionless, inviting the night to whisper in his ears until he knew what to do; then with light, silent steps he strode into the forest, following the invisible trace Caireann left. With his true sight he could see she'd taken her mushroom potion which enabled the old magic Yaret possessed innately by the virtue of his blood. The potion never failed, but after using it the wicce would get ill for days with Yaret caring for her; and it bothered him that she was using strong magic in his absence. There was nothing he wouldn't do for her, and she was keeping secrets from him. As he walked on, he quickly executed a spell veiling him from the eyes, physical or magical: unless Caireann or her lover looked at Yaret directly, all they would notice was a shadow among the trees.

His true sight led him towards a light, which grew in brightness as he approached. It was a round patch, overgrown with bracken. Yaret crouched behind an uprooted tree, trying to quiet his heart. He was wrong to think she'd bother sneaking into the woods for a secret meeting. Caireann was alone. It looked like she was already traveling, eyes rolled up, her unseeing gaze turned towards other dimensions.

Skyclad, she was floating several feet above ground, over the fern canopy, her toes brushing fronds. Her arms outstretched, palms upward, she was rotating sunwise ever so slowly. Illuminated by the light of magic, a sanctified space surrounded her—an invisible chapel walled by high trees, roofed by the starry sky. Her body was a fine white candle, breasts and buttocks - droplets of melting wax, and her hair—a dark flame around her head; her skin glowed except for darkness hiding in the triangular spot between her thighs, but as he took in the vision, he realized it wasn't darkness at all but rather a different kind of light—the unapproachable light of the Otherworld.

He had stood naked in front of her countless times, she'd bathed him as a child, and later, taught him rites requiring him to be exposed to the elements, yet he had never seen her unclothed. Now, he hardly recognized the woman he knew. He always thought of her as high, towering over him, and ample, with an embrace to sink in. But in front of him was a small woman, so slim he could count the ribs above her narrow waist. Her heavy breasts seemed out of place on her fragile frame; the sight made him think of a brittle apple branch burdened with ripe fruit. Her narrow ribcage was offset by the smooth curves of her hips; her round thighs by sharp knees. Her body seemed impossibly soft and hard at the same time, and it was the image of her essence he so adored.

No longer able to contain himself, he opened up and took in the rocks, the water under and the soil over, the moss, the ferns, the trees, the fog between the trees, all the living creatures in all the hollows and crevices, and the woman at the center of it all. At that moment he knew her, penetrating her being in a way that made the physical joining of human intercourse just a pale shadow. A wave of unbearable pleasure knocked his feet from under him, and he collapsed on the forest floor.

So, this is how it is, he thought, choking on sobs, pressing palms against his mouth to keep quiet. Although a distance away, he was inside of her, seeing what she saw, feeling what she felt. The ice-cold, red-hot sword piercing through your chest. The feeling of emptiness when you jump in the lake from a swinging rope. The sweet nausea of being filled to the brim after gulping too much honey. The excruciating hunger for something you must consume, or you die. It was the same intoxicating clarity he felt when executing a spell, opening his heart to the universe, ordering it to change its properties. Oh, he knew exactly what it was: the elusive yet ever-present true love, the ultimate subject and object of magic. Except this time all its force was pointed at him— blinding as a searchlight in the eyes, undeniable as the fact that he'd been a fool. Her true love was for him!

Suddenly he heard her voice. In the language of the ancients, Caireann was singing something into the physical plane. As the unfamiliar spell unfolded, it began to manifest around her, beautiful and repulsive at the same time: a spider web. The wicce was slowly turning in the air, weaving a gleaming web into existence, and she was both weaver and prey caught. Suddenly, a dark ornament appeared on her skin right above her heart, developing like an inkblot through the pounce dust. From his shelter, Yaret strained his eyes: a snake circled around the tip of her left breast, its mouth open, about to swallow its own tail. He recognized the World Serpent of Middangeard, except the familiar image was disturbingly altered. Instead of the serpent's tail fitting into its mouth both the tail and the head were grasped and spread apart by the legs of a small black spider, as if the spider was breaking into the circle of power, preventing the World Serpent from completing its cycle. As the ornament took shape, Caireann's body quivered in pain, and Yaret, who felt what she felt, noted that the pain was habitual.

For a moment she stopped in the air, then resumed the rotation widdershins. She started an unbinding spell, and for one heartbeat Yaret was horrified that it was the bond between them she was trying to break. But he was wrong again. With all the power of her true love, with all the force of her desire, Caireann cut at the spider web, striking from the center at each glimmering strand at once. A shockwave rolled across the web, and it rang with a thousand strings. Yaret covered his ears, only to be reminded that the web was resonating on a higher plane of reality—there was no escape from the sound, just like shutting his eyes didn't clear the net's imprint from his mind. A dreadful echo reverberated through his body, making him nauseous. Caireann hit again, then once more. The web shook violently but didn't release her; instead it seemed to grow, sucking into the woman's veins, draining her life force. She struck three more times, and then three more, all in vain. Yaret saw Caireann convulse in the air as if a thousand strings were a thousand needles piercing her sides.

With the irrational clarity made possible by otherworldly magic, Yaret realized that the spider on her breast bound her to the web in a slave-like bond. Being a vital part of her, the spider made it impossible to tear free, even tapping into the power of true love would not sever the connection. The spider web began to demanifest undamaged. Caireann had failed to effect the spell.

The rotation stopped and her fading body jerked in the air, as though the heavenly thread she was suspended on was torn abruptly. She dropped her arms, and crashed into the bracken with a pained cry. Yaret had never seen her fail at magic before. His impeccable Caireann, who mocked him for the slightest show of weakness, who could turn any botched exercise into an occasion for learning, had failed.

It was a shock, but in his heart surprise gave way to tenderness, her failure endearing her to him in a new, yet bittersweet way. He wished he could run to her, comfort her, offer help, but by spying on a secret rite he already had committed an unforgivable offense. To dull the ache he curled into a ball, and buried his burning face in the damp moss.

He didn't know how long he lay on the forest floor. When he got to his feet, the woman was long gone, the stars pale, and the universe irrevocably re-ordered. Although she hadn't been truthful with him, it was him she loved. There was a mysterious terrible power reaching for her from her past. She tried to use her love for him to fight her enemy and failed. Her love. Her love for him. She loved him. Nothing else mattered.

"In the beginning there was her love, and her love was towards me, and her love was me," he sang at the fading stars, and laughed at his own sacrilegious recitation, frightened and emboldened at once.

His own feelings he never questioned. Despite his Alvan insight, or perhaps due to it, Yaret was not introspective by nature. While he was familiar with a variety of human passions, he himself knew only two: the ecstasy of attachment, and the agony of separation. Harmony was pleasure, discord was pain; so he was either glad or sad, laughed or wept. It was as if the intricately woven fabric of his existence contained only white and black threads.

Since the day Caireann snatched him in her arms, he was bound to her with the dumb devotion of a foundling pup; an invisible tether tugged at his heart at all times. The monochrome yarn of his destiny became entwined with her brightly colored threads, creating an exquisite tapestry. More than the harmony of attachment, she brought meaning to his world. Was there anything else to ask for?

Suddenly, there was. She had true love for him, and now he wanted it.

The Book Of Fairfax, the third in *The Green Hills* trilogy, is a Dark Ages Britain historic fantasy where the grim authenticity of the *Anglo-Saxon Chronicle* meets the intimate lyricism of *This Side of Paradise*.

As Roman Christianity and the Old Ways clash in the 7th Century Britain, a young Angle warrior struggles to reconcile his humanity with his mystical origins. Woven into the fabric of a greater historical and an even greater metaphysical reality, one eccentric boy's coming of age story unfolds as an intensely personal, yet universally human quest for love, faith and belonging.

E. V. Svetova was born in Moscow when it was the capital of a now extinct empire, and she had a chance to experience both the security and the subjugation of the totalitarian state. In retrospect, it was a winning combination of a happy childhood and a subversive youth. When the country she knew disintegrated like planet Krypton in front of her eyes, the shockwave of that explosion blew her across the world. She has landed on the island of Manhattan and has considered herself a New Yorker ever since. These days, she lives at the edge of the last natural forest on the island with her artist husband, sharing their old apartment with an ever-expanding library and a spoiled English bulldog. Her creative nonfiction was published in a few magazines; her novels *Print In The Snow* and *Over The Hills Of Green* have won multiple literary awards.

https://evsvetova.com/
https://www.facebook.com/evsvetovawriting
https://www.instagram.com/an_urban_elf/

Those Who Live by the Sword Should Die by the Sword

Mickey Dubrow

Chinese Water Torture. That's what it was, but instead of water steadily dripping on her skull, Skeeter's steady drip of stupidity was driving Nell insane.

"Let me write it down," Nell said.

"No need for that," Skeeter said. "I'll remember everything."

They were in the cab of Skeeter's truck which sat in the far corner of a Walmart parking lot in Trinidad, Colorado. A CannaCo Recreational Marijuana was on one side of the store and a LaQuinta Inn & Suites was on the other. They could see Fishers Peak in the distance.

Arguing with Skeeter had grown so tiresome that Nell was tempted to get some weed at the weed store, some munchies at Walmart, and a room at the hotel. She could get high, eat junk food, and watch cable TV. But no, she was stuck here trying to reason with an idiot.

"Okay, don't write it down," Nell said. "Tell me what you're going to get."

"Jugs of water. Dried fruit. Instant coffee. Corn chips. Sodas,"

Skeeter said.

"I mean for me. Damn it, Skeeter, I gave you cash for my things."

Skeeter pouted which was very unattractive on a man of his advanced years.

"Hair dye. Scissors. Garbage bags." He squeezed his eyes shut. "Gloves. T-shirt. Pencil" He opened his eyes and smiled, obviously pleased with himself.

"What kind of pencil?" Nell said.

"What difference does it make? A pencil is a pencil."

"No, it's not. I need an eyebrow pencil."

"Eyebrow pencil. Got it."

"And what about the rest?"

"The rest?"

Nell counted off items on her fingers.

"Towels, shower cap, plastic bowl, lip balm, make up wipes, color brush. Do I have to go in there and get it myself?"

"Hell, no! It's too dangerous."

Of course, it was too dangerous. Every law enforcement agency in the country was looking for Nell. But Skeeter was so thick in the head, she was almost willing to risk exposure.

"Let me write it down," Nell said.

"Okay, okay."

Skeeter opened the glove compartment and took out a battered driver logbook and a ball point pen with Friou Trucking Service on the side. He handed them to Nell. She tore off a clean sheet and wrote on the back. She made sure she printed clearly so that Skeeter couldn't claim that he couldn't read her handwriting. Dad used that excuse with Mom every time he came back from the store without something on her grocery list. When Nell was done, she handed the list to Skeeter.

"And get exactly what's on the list," she said.

"What if they don't have something on here?"

"They'll have it. Walmart has everything."

Skeeter folded the list and stuck it in the breast pocket of his flannel shirt. He slipped on a denim jacket.

"Don't do anything crazy while I'm gone," he said.

"I'm not making any promises," Nell said.

Skeeter left the truck. He jammed his hands in his jacket pockets as he walked toward the store. It was before noon and the parking lot was more than half full. Nell wondered why there were so many shoppers. She'd been on the run for so long that she'd lost track of the days of the week. Either this was a Saturday, or it was this busy every day because there was nothing else to do in Trinidad, Colorado except go to Walmart.

Nell sat back in the passenger seat and twirled a strand of hair around her finger. She'd always had her hair to her shoulders or longer. During ninth grade, she grew it down to her waist, but it required too much maintenance, so she had it cut back to her shoulders. Nell looked at her reflection in the rear-view mirror and wondered if she was going to look good with short hair.

"Doesn't matter," she told her reflection. "As long as I don't look like I do now."

Nell took a paperback from the passenger door side pocket and opened the book to a dog-eared page. It was a romance novel title *Gators and Garters*. There were no gators or garters on the cover. Instead there was a shirtless man in skintight jeans with huge muscles, a rough beard, and a straw cowboy hat holding a busty woman with flowing red hair, a torn top, and cut-off jean shorts. As Nell read the story of how a Cajun alligator wrangler and an advertising executive from New York City meet and eventually fall in love, she thought about Skeeter. Not in a remotely romantic way. He had given her the book which proved that despite being a major pain in the ass, Skeeter wasn't a bad guy.

The day before, they had stopped at a truck stop that had a laundry room. As Skeeter gathered his dirty clothes, he offered to clean Nell's clothes as well.

"All I have are the clothes on my back," Nell said.

"Which are starting to get pretty rank," Skeeter said.

"You're not freaked out about having to handle my unmentionables?"

"You mean your bra and panties? I used to do laundry when I was married to Edie. Underwear is just part of the job."

Nell had covered herself with a blanket before stripping off her stinky sweat-stained clothes. She hadn't cared if Skeeter had seen her naked. She could have easily broken his arm if he tried to touch her. But there was no reason to give him any ideas.

Skeeter was only gone for ten minutes when he returned to the truck.

"You done already?" Nell said.

"Just got the clothes in the washing machine," Skeeter said. "I found this in the laundry room." He handed her *Gators and Garters.* "There's nobody in there so it was probably left behind. I thought you might want it. To help pass the time."

"Thank you, Skeeter. That was mighty thoughtful of you."

"It's just a book."

Skeeter left and returned later with their laundered clothes.

Nell didn't care that he hadn't bother to fold them. She was way too thrilled by the wonderful sensation of putting on clean clothes that were still warm from the dryer.

Nell was enjoying her book, but she started to get drowsy. She was considering getting into the sleeper for a nap when she heard a loud rumbling. A black Ford F150 with oversize tires drove past. On the rear bumper was an NRA sticker and a sticker that read IF BABIES HAD GUNS, THEY WOULDN'T BE ABORTED. It straddled two parking spaces as it parked near Skeeter's truck.

A woman wearing a pink hoodie got out on the passenger side. A large man with a cowboy hat and a black T-shirt that read PRO-LIFE, PRO-GOD, PRO-GUN got out of the driver side. His big loud truck and his asshole parking technique was all the proof Nell needed to determine that the large man had a thumb dick. Not that Nell gave a shit, but she did feel sorry for the woman in the pink hoodie who was probably Mrs. Thumb Dick.

Mr. Thumb Dick lifted a semi-automatic rifle out of his truck's back seat. Seeing the weapon ignited a flare of anger in Nell that set her teeth on edge. It was the same rifle that her brother Carson used to kill twenty children. Mr. Thumb Dick slung the strap over his shoulder so that the rifle hung across his back with the barrel pointed toward the ground. He strutted behind the woman in the light blue hoodie as they headed toward the store.

There was no question about it. Mr. Thumb Dick had to die. After all, her mission in life now was to intimidate the intimidators, attack the soldier cosplayers, and put the fear of God into the gun toting fearmongers.

She studied the clock in the truck's dashboard. Skeeter had been gone for thirty minutes. Maybe if she hurried, Nell could do what she needed to do and get back to the truck before Skeeter was done shopping. She folded the corner of the page she was on and slid the paperback into the door pocket. After putting on her cowboy hat, Nell climbed out of the truck.

Skeeter had parked at the far end of the lot next to a batch of tall bushes. The greenery appeared to be a half-hearted attempt at landscaping. Nell slipped from the truck to the bushes. It was a cold day and she rubbed her bare arms to generate some warmth. Staying low, Nell moved between cars toward the beige and brown store. The Walmart sign's blue background with white letters mirrored the blue sky and white fluffy clouds over it.

When Nell reached the store, she straightened up and walked in like a regular customer and not a stalker. A blast of warm air welcomed her. Looking around at the vast interior reminded her that Walmart stores were freaking huge warehouses of consumer goods. There were rows and rows of every damn thing a person could possibly desire.

After stalking the aisles for five minutes, Nell found Mr. and Mrs. Thumb Dick in the grocery section. She pushed a grocery cart while he preened behind her with his big gun. Nell pretended to be checking out the fruits and vegetables as she worked her way toward them. So far, no one had recognized her as the Las Vegas shooter. She was just another customer doing a little Saturday shopping.

Nell sauntered over to a produce island and ran her fingers over the rows of plastic bags filled with oranges, apples, and grapefruits. Nell picked up bags to test their weight and selected one filled with Granny Smith green apples. It felt heavy enough for her purpose and she liked the solidness of the apples.

A tingling feeling of anticipation spread through Nell as she maneuvered behind the couple. As Mr. Thumb Dick waited for Mrs. Thumb Dick to stuff ears of corn into a clear plastic bag, Nell rushed up behind him and whacked the back of his head with the Granny Smith apples. The impact caused the bag to rip open. Apples spilled out and rolled in all directions. Mr. Thumb Dick fell to the floor like a dead tree.

Mrs. Thumb Dick gasped. People glanced and then quickly moved away. Maybe they were afraid that this was either a family argument or a love triangle gone bad and they wanted no part of it. While Mr. Thumb Dick was stunned, Nell grabbed his rifle and yanked it away from him. She checked to see if there was a cartridge in the barrel and the magazine was loaded. Pulling the charging handle, the rifle was ready to fire. She aimed it at Mr. Thumb Dick.

"Those who live by the sword should die by the sword," Nell said.

Mr. Thumb Dick moaned and crawled slowly to the island. He tried to hoist himself up but slid back down. He settled for sitting on the floor with his back against the island. He took off his cowboy hat and rubbed his head.

Nell didn't mean for him to be this dazed. In all the excitement, she'd forgotten that she was super strong. She shouldn't have swung the bag as hard as she did. Hopefully, he didn't have brain damage. Nell wanted Mr. Thumb Dick to be fully aware of why she killed him.

"What the hell do you need a semi-automatic rifle for in a grocery store?" Nell said.

Mr. Thumb Dick narrowed his eyes at her. "Protection," he said.

"From what? Broccoli?"

Holding the rifle close to her face, Nell picked up a scent she knew well. Hoppe's 9 gun cleaner smelled similar to gasoline. On the days Peggy cleaned her arsenal, the whole house would stink of it. It would seem Mr. Thumb Dick cleaned his weapon recently. Wouldn't want to go to Walmart with a dirty gun. What would the neighbors say?

Mrs. Thumb Dick kneeled next to Mr. Thumb Dick and inspected his head. She gave Nell the stink eye before looking about for help.

"Somebody call 9-1-1!" she shouted.

"Give me back my gun before you hurt yourself," Mr. Thumb Dick said as he reached out his hand.

"I'm just borrowing it long enough to blow your brains out," Nell said.

A security guard arrived, observed the situation, and took his weapon out. He kept a safe distance away.

"Put the gun down!" the guard shouted.

"Shoot me, and I shoot him," Nell said. She was going to shoot Mr. Thumb Dick anyway, but the guard didn't know that.

Earlier, People had avoided Nell's kerfuffle with the Thumb Dicks. But now that the security guard was involved, people started to form a circle around them. Nell was no longer blending in with the other shoppers. They held up their phones to videotape the moment for prosperity.

"Give me my rifle back!" Mr. Thumb Dick shouted.

He wasn't bad looking, almost handsome with only a slight beer belly. Around these parts he was probably considered a good catch.

"You brought your big ass rifle here to scare people," Nell said.

"You don't know what you're talking about," Mr. Thumb Dick said. "People with guns respect each other."

"The only way people will respect each other is if they know the other guy is packing heat and could kill them at any moment? That's not respect. That's fear."

"It's a dangerous world."

The security guard tried again to get Nell to behave. "Put your weapon down!" he said.

"This doesn't concern you," Nell said. "This is between me and Mr. Thumb Dick."

"That's not my name," Mr. Thumb Dick said.

Mrs. Thumb Dick put her arm around Mr. Thumb Dick's shoulder.

"What are you going to do?" Mrs. Thumb Dick said.

She wasn't bad looking either. Maybe they had been King and Queen of their high school prom.

"Those who live by the sword should die by the sword," Nell said.

She put her finger on the trigger but before she could squeeze it, Mrs. Thumb Dick stood between Nell and Mr. Thumb Dick.

"Please, don't kill him," Mrs. Thumb Dick said. "He's a good man."

"He brought his big ass gun to a public place to scare people," Nell said.

"He's a good husband and a good father. He goes to church every Sunday."

"How many kids do you have?"

"Two. Chad is nine. Jerica is six."

"There are kids in this store. Was he trying to scare them too?"

Nell wasn't sure what annoyed her more, the fact that Mrs. Thumb Dick was willing to sacrifice herself for her man or the fact that Mr. Thumb Dick didn't try to stop her.

"I'm begging you. Don't shoot him."

"Get out of the way."

"If you kill him, then you're going to have to kill me first."

Nell groaned. If Mr. Thumb Dick was a father, then it stood to reason that Mrs. Thumb Dick was a mother. Nell could never shoot a mother. That wasn't true. There was a good chance that some of the women she had killed in the convention center were mothers. But this was different. She was looking right into this mother's eyes. Nell couldn't shoot this mother. And that meant she couldn't shoot Mr. Thumb Dick.

As Nell worked on an exit strategy, she scanned the crowd to see if Skeeter was among them. She didn't see him.

Hopefully, he had gotten his shopping done before she attacked Mr. Thumb Dick. It was a good bet that the registers were closed right now due to the armed stand-off in the produce department.

Nell pointed the barrel at the floor and took a step back.

Two state troopers and two policemen pushed their way through the crowd. They ordered the crowd to get out of harm's way. The security guard lowered his gun and moved aside. One of the policemen approached Nell.

"Put the rifle down," he said.

Glancing around, Nell could see that nobody was near one of the fruit islands. She grinned at the officer.

"See you later, fornicators," she said.

Nell fired numerous rounds at the fruit island. Oranges, pineapples, mangoes, grapefruits, and cantaloupes exploded, spewing their mushy innards everywhere. Shoppers screamed and ran. Nell dropped the rifle and joined the panicked shoppers. They stampeded through the store, knocking over displays and crashing into shelves. The floor was quickly covered in cereal, dog food, coffee grounds, and laundry detergent. The people that slid and fell were quickly trampled.

An elderly Hispanic woman as tall as she was wide was among the unfortunate ones that fell to the floor. Before anyone could stomp her, Nell helped her to her feet. The woman stared in horror at Nell.

"Don't shoot me," she said. "Don't shoot me."

"Don't worry," Nell said. "I don't shoot abuelitas."

Nell left the woman in the health and beauty aisle and rejoined the crowd as they rolled through the exits. Outside there was a line of police and trooper patrol cars with their lights flashing. The fleeing customers flowed past the law enforcement vehicles and spread out through the parking lot. The policemen and troopers tried in vain to contain the mayhem. Nell dashed between rows of cars to the bushes that marked the entrances to the parking lot. Using the bushes as cover, she worked her way back to the truck. Her heart raced and she sweated like a pig.

Nell climbed into the truck, scaring the bejesus out of Skeeter.

"Where the hell have you been?" he asked.

"Did you get everything on my list?" she asked.

"Hell, yeah. Did you have anything to do with all them people running out of the store like their asses were on fire?"

"Maybe a little bit. We should probably go now."

This is a deleted chapter from my novel *Bulletproof.*

After surviving a mass shooting, Nell Slagle's life falls apart. She blames gun culture for her misfortune and goes on a cross country killing spree in which she targets gun shows.

Along the way, Nell makes a deal with a truck driver named Skeeter. Nell agrees to kill Skeeter's ex-wife's lover in exchange for hiding her from the authorities.

In this chapter, Nell is enraged when she sees a man take his semi-automatic rifle into a Walmart and decides to kill him. Since Nell sees herself as an avenging angel for people victimized by gun culture, her extreme reaction makes sense to her.

I came up with this idea because I too get enraged whenever I see someone in a grocery store with a huge rifle slung over their shoulder. I don't react as violently as Nell but I do wonder if they really feel the weapon is necessary or if they're just trying to make a statement. I suspect the latter.

They want a reaction, and they hope to intimidate people who don't own guns. This is unfortunate. It makes gun ownership seem petty and mean and not for the purpose of protection.

I deleted this chapter because my manuscript was too long. The maximum word count for a novel is around 100 thousand words. I had written 133 thousand. This required killing many of my darlings and this was chapter was one of them. I hope y'all enjoy reading it as much as I enjoyed writing it.

Mickey Dubrow is the author of *American Judas,* a Finalist for the 2020 Georgia Author of the Year Award in the category of First Novel. For more than thirty years, he wrote award winning television promos, marketing presentations, and scripts for various clients including Cartoon Network, TNT Latin America, HGTV, and CNN. He teaches classes on humor writing and often address book clubs. His personal essays and short stories have appeared in *Prime Number Magazine, The Good Men Project, The Signal Mountain Review, Full Grown People, Supernatural Streets,* and *McSweeney's Internet Tendency.*

Immortalizing Hudson

Joe Formichella

"Waters that are never still"

So the fabled Mohicans knew her, Muhhekunntuk. But you have always known her. She has always been there, the low tickle at the periphery of conscience, the heady pool after the falls. Cool wash, instant inundation, she was there. You have known her.

She was that shy little girl in class sitting mid-row who rarely raised her hand; the budding adolescent eager for cautious adventure, quick to giggle, quicker to blush; the blossomed beauty at a loss to fully explain all the newfound attention; the seasoned matron willing to lend a hand or hold a hand, whichever was most needed, mostly in the background, but always there.

She is the sound of endless and returning harmony, the soloist lulling sleep and the reawakening whisperer, the spirit of those dreams, the muse of inspiration, the welcoming discourse, the summation of fullness. She buoys and moves, carries away and mesmerizes, all at the same time.

She has been called many names—Cahohatatea, Noortrivier, Manhattes, Groote—but has only one origin, for she is the first: the first explorers encountered upon arrival to the New World, the first to lead those explorers to that world's vast and wild interior; the first line of Revolutionary defense and two centuries later the first environmental battleground. She motivated the first writers and excited the first painters. She is the cord that weaves through the entirety of the fabric of America. She is, to quote but one of her biographers, "unchangeable in [her] presence, yet always changing." She is, to quote another, "perfection in all parts."

She has been characterized as a great palimpsest, a great parchment upon which her varied stories have been written and rewritten for over a billion years. The earliest etchings of her story reach all the way back to the Grenville orogeny, the oldest mountain-raising epoch. Evidence remains across those centuries in the ancient Precambrian rocks of her highest peaks. Under those rocks and through those rocks she gurgles, and speaks.

One-point-three billion years ago those rocks emerged amidst the tectonic dance of the North American, African, and European continents. Those plates slowly and repeatedly collided and separated, pushing the rocks ever higher with the former, the sea washing in sediment with the latter. Two hundred million years ago, the plates separated one last time to create the Atlantic Ocean and continental outlines we now recognize. And 75 million years ago, a final push raised those ancient rocks into the Adirondacks of today.

On the slopes of those mountains cascading streams carved channels through the sedimentary rock, the Hudson among them. Twenty million years ago, the climate changed and what we call the Hudson Valley was buried under a thick sheet of ice. With each advance and retreat of the glacier the landscape was sequentially sculpted. The last ice flow, the Wisconsin, lent its final signature to the land about 20,000 years ago. As the Wisconsin receded the ice created a terminal moraine of sand and gravel we call Long Island, as well as Glacial Lake Hudson, an immense body of water that spilled into present-day New Jersey for thousands of years until the force of that water finally cut through the moraine to gain access to the Atlantic through what we know today as The Narrows.

But that wasn't the terminus of the original Hudson. The river and its geological story continued. Its waters channeled hundreds of miles to the southeast before dropping into the "Hudson Canyon," some ten thousand feet below the surface of the ocean. Halfway to Bermuda, at a feature called the "Abyssal Plain," the Hudson ends its nearly 900-

mile journey.

Each of these developmental moments is written into the river, the shudder of tectonic grinding and whisper of glacial recycling. And each successive inhabitant within its vast breadth has both read of those stories and left a postscript of their own, from fossilized plankton that left immutable engravings to the first natives who passed down their stories through mnemonic devices like beads on a string – their precious sewan – to European explorers who believed she held the secret to a fabled northwest passage. Each, in their own way, was drawn by her unspeakable beauty. And later they were witness to her crying out in pain from the damage they had wrought. Throughout it all, she has always been there, you have always known her. She anchors and envelopes and contains the tales of generations, holding them, telling and retelling them.

Immortalizing Hudson is a novel in stories, and is set up and down the Hudson River, moving back and forth in time.

Joe Formichella (joe_formichella@yahoo.com) is a multiple literary award winner, including a Hackney Literary Award (short fiction) and a Foreword magazine nonfiction book of the year (Murder Creek). He was also a finalist for a national IPPY award for true crime (Murder Creek), a finalist for a New Letters Literary Prize, and a Pushcart Prize nominee. His nonfiction *A Condition of Freedom*, a Pulpwood Queen International Book Club pick, was installed in the both the National Baseball Hall of Fame and the Negro Leagues Hall of Fame. He is the author of the novels *Waffle House Rules* (an AL 200 Bicentennial pick for county-wide read and a Pulpwood Queen International Book Club pick) and 2020's *Lumpers, Longnecks and One-Eyed Jacks* (an Indie Book Awards national finalist for best regional [northeast] fiction). Another new novel, *Caduceus* (an Alabama Writers Conclave award winner for best first chapter of a novel), is a work in progress, along with *Immortalizing Hudson*. He lives near Fairhope, Alabama, at Waterhole Branch Productions, with his wife, author Suzanne Hudson.

Hiding out with Holden Caulfield

Suzanne Hudson

Some lawyers are fond of saying that they keep secrets for a living. I am not a lawyer, but I do a whole lot of observing, listening, and keeping my mouth shut—except when I am required to open it. So I'm part spy, part Catholic priest, and sometime tattletale. The workaday world I navigate involves being thoroughly entertained, hearing all stripes of stories, and, for all the toil of it, has a big red cherry on top: staying in touch, on a daily basis, with my inner Holden Caulfield. Neither Holden nor I ever did really want to grow up. Lucky him, with his red hunting hat, to be frozen in fiction as THE adolescent of the twentieth century, commenting on the quality of farts at prep school assemblies and such. Lucky me, to have this job, where farts abide and never fail to amuse or humiliate. I am a grateful and wounded resident of middle school world, having come to the land of public education in a roundabout way.

It went down like this: The not-so-sad fact is that, like Dobie Gillis's buddy Maynard G. Krebs, I was never much of a fan of work and, at college in the 1970s, felt my true calling was to be a professional student and world-famous author—fairly effortlessly, of course. Screw a life of real work and the burgeoning societal desire for the acquisition of all that stuff the Mad Men of the '50s had foisted upon a generation. I was above all that, all the "phonies" Holden and I hold in disdain. I was an artiste with no bra and the armpit hair to by God prove it; I would live the good bohemian life, thank you very much. However, my parents, the funders of my educational adventure, did not concur, even though I'd actually had some success getting a couple of stories published and winning a writing contest or two. The minor Armageddon that ensued led to that time-honored, age-old question: What the hell do you actually do with an English degree? Answer: get certified to teach, a prospect that kind of turned my stomach, having denigrated education degrees as not very, shall we say, "challenging." Ultimately, though, the humbling of my academic snootiness turned out to be my salvation and made any other job I've held seem like a Dickensian tale of woe and cold gruel.

Having done tours of duty as a cuff clipper on a textile assembly line, a waitress in a college beer joint, a brief graduate assistantship in an English department followed by a year of teaching high school seniors (I wasn't paid nearly enough to give up my personal life for the honor of grading really bad term papers), I finally landed in a place where I truly, truly belonged—a place riddled with stories and peccadilloes and royal fuck-ups to be observed and filed away in my one-day-to-be-a-writer-again brain. Middle school was a land of double-dealing and plotting and subterfuge and intrigue, crawling with denizens eager to engage in all manner of posturing and preening on one end—and slinking away and fading into the background on the other. These beings were unpredictable, impulsive, and irrational, which led to all manner of grand entertainment for me. They also harbored a deep fascination with bodily functions. Old people were gross and anything that was annoying was "gay." I was surrounded by crude, tasteless, base immaturity. I was home. And, over the years, as the job evolved into a career (with four books published, I never quit this, my day job), I gained all sorts of insights—into these hormonally challenged little beings, and into myself. The latter ultimately made it possible for me to write again.

Most sane adult folk see the (sub)human creatures in grades seven and eight as unbearable at best and torturous at worst. And they are correct. Drop an untrained adult into a middle school and its citizens catch the scent of fear very quickly, subsequently gauging where the weak spots are, picking, grinning, circling, and feasting like vultures upon the kill. I've seen many a cocky substitute teacher from civilian world reduced to a tearful, quivering mass of Inner Child by twelve-year-olds who cut their teeth on subs. This pack mentality—even including the onlookers who are too sweet or too shy to join in—is an ugly thing to witness but certainly goes with the territory.

No amount of university schooling can prepare one for the land of the adolescent. Perhaps it is because so many of us have blocked out those traumatic memories of the days when we were tormented by bullies, by the onset of our menstrual periods or our impromptu erections, by our imagined imperfections, or by just the god-awful uncertainty of it all. (When I try to coax memories of my junior high days they become a blur of Clearasil, Kotex and the attendant elastic belts, awkward penny walks and bottles spinning, slam books, crushes on teachers, the Beatles, both yearning for and fearing success at getting a boyfriend—because, hey, then what?— Midnight Sun hair coloring, tent dresses, whispered judgments, snapped bras, and Yardley cosmetics.)

Once certificated and supposedly ready to be a Giver of Knowledge, I attempted to get my students to be amazed by the wonderful, intricate, scintillatingly complex world of . . . grammar. I was the English Teacher. (I would become the secret-keeping guidance counselor later, like ten years.) Painfully, I learned that no middle school teacher should ever use an outdated film that refers to "grammatical boners"—not ever. "Don't forget your period," an English teacher might sing out as a reminder to punctuate. Not in middle school. And no way in hell could we conjugate the verb "to come." When it came to literature, the "climax" of a plot was territory fraught with snickers, as were any mentions of a "nut" or a "ball." And God forbid that an author of a classic poem or story might have used the words "queer," "gay," or "breast" in some sort of confusing context. Even a seemingly safe vocabulary word like "flagellation" would bring gasps and giggles. In middle school there is not much that is not about sex.

Or about self. And how best to hide that real self.

I accepted that grammar, when held alongside sex, is pretty boring. I began to wish that I had minored in theater since it was becoming clearer all the time that I was going to have to be a goddamned actor/entertainer if I wanted them to take an interest in appositives or infinitives or the subjunctive mood. So I mugged and strutted. I did dialects. I did the hambone, for Christ sake. And I maintain that the fact that I succeeded to take their minds, fairly often, away from the teeny-bopper drama du jour qualifies me for an Academy Award.

But it was not the parsing of the language that brought me the most joy to impart; it was the smithing of the words that was heady and rewarding. And royally amusing. For middle schoolers do not possess the filters of their older brethren; middle schoolers will write or say anything. Any parental unit who thinks his/her child will be either tasteful or discreet is in a mighty state of denial. For example, ask for an expository or a narrative essay and one might get informed about how Aunt Marcy's toxic farts are known to be akin in stench level to those passed by Spence, the family dog; or told the story of how grandmaw got loose last Saturday and went running the streets nekkid, stopping only to hump light poles and parking meters; or how Cousin Eddie got arrested the other day when he showed his pecker to the little kids on the First Baptist Church playground.

In spite of the great stories, after about a decade spent observing a deteriorating state of parenting, a growing tolerance for disrespectful students, an element of pettiness and small-mindedness among teachers, and an overall system of inflationary grading along with the elevation of mediocre standards, I was burning out. The peripheral shit had sucked the spit and energy from my classroom persona. Holden's exterior world was becoming stale with superficiality while his terrified inner one was beckoning like the Grim Reaper.

And so it was that into the 1990s I marched with a Master's degree in school counseling. I set up shop, determined to listen, nod, question, nod, listen, reflect, nod, empathize, etc. No longer was I in the role of taskmaster, Nazi rule-maker, enforcer of learning and discipline. All of a sudden I was that which only the most egregious of teachers dare attempt to be: the "good guy." Now I got a more up-close look at farting aunts, nekkid grandmaws, and pervertoids like Cousin Eddie—not to mention abusive stepdads, cancer-ridden uncles, evil best friends, bipolar moms, meth-head dads, tormenting older sisters, a cast of thousands. Kids used for Internet porn, rape victims, cutters, children who served as weapons for their warring parents or who had been abandoned or were doing drugs because Mom shared with them. Those stories took on a wash of darkness that had not shown itself so boldly in the classroom and it was beyond disturbing. And of course it was only the tip of the iceberg, too, since the messy, silly, nanny-nanny-boo-boo trivialities played out most of the time—locker room bullies, girlie-girl dramas, and my-teacher-hates-me delusions. Still, all their stories, whether dark and disturbing or shallow, silly, and trivial, trickled down to the storyteller at my core. I began to miss the writing, and more than just the exercises I once did along with my students in class. I began to feel a need to reach out to that part of me that was twin to my middle schoolers. Writing was the only way I knew.

And then, out of nowhere, the stories took a turn, inside out. An eighth-grade girl defied statistics, put a gun to her head, and pulled the trigger. One of my children committed suicide. Not a girl who was neglected by her parents, or afraid of academic failure, or criticized by her teachers. This was a bright, beautiful young person, a leader among her peers, with a loving family and a constant smile for everyone. The utter tragic dissonance of it all snatched me into the real reason for Mr. Caulfield's tale and how much the surface is such the mirage, especially at an age when you're a chameleon, with the undeveloped brain of a lizard that eats its own tail. It's the flip side of Holden's funny, sarcastic musings. He is, after all, trying to hold together in the face of the most traumatic event of his life: his brother Allie's death. He also has the specter of a former classmate's likely suicide breathing down his neck. He occupies that place where self-destruction and self-awareness cleave, running scared from the truth of his own flawed reality. And that is what we have to always wonder about Holden. Does he make it? Or does he fold in on himself, like my dead student, collapsing under the weight of that youthfully false perception of hopelessness?

Adolescents hide. That is a given, of course, but I mean they really, really hide. They change personas sometimes in the space of a day. They only show a few of their cards to that one or those few who are trusted—or to no one. They hide from every shred of humanity for which they can maintain denial. Sure, some of it pops out—in some children quite frequently. But stripping emotionally naked is not something an eighth grader is likely to do, even behind the closed door of the guidance office.

I had lost other students to tragic accidents, but none self-inflicted, none so accusatory, defiant, and guilt-wrenching as that. It was a death that demanded answers, for the sake of those who might visit and revisit such a choice. Thus began the second-guessing, the what-iffing, the retracing of steps to try to find the moment when such an unthinkable act could have been prevented. But there was no comprehending. The full-bore, scorching sadness dug into me in a way I had never expected—could never have expected—yet, surprisingly but slowly—trudgingly slow—it began to dig me out of the hole that, I was discovering, had been my residence for too long.

I'm sure it's no coincidence that this was around the time I was also in the midst of a fallen-over-the-cliff, smashed-up, twenty-something-year relationship. I had scores to settle, even though I've never looked kindly on the settling of scores. There was a flux of mish-mashed karma riding the ether—a confluence of events coaxing me from that camouflaged perch occupied by the school marm/guidance counselor personas. It began to dawn on me that, like these kids to whom I was drawn, I had been hiding from my own expression, that I had spent a couple of decades as an adolescent. Literally.

But now I set about re-emerging as an author after the long hiatus from word-working. I took a deep breath and "came out," spending two class periods a day, back to back, with one group of students for both English and literature. We called ourselves "The Writers' Block." We read. We wrote. We scorned grammar drills in which students picked out prepositions for an hour and then picked out more for homework. We sneered at templates for formulaic paragraphs that cookie-cuttered the mainstream into an imitation of style. Instead, we masterfully dissected one sentence per day—obliterated it—went grammatically medieval on its ass—then got down to the really important business of books and words. Those were the most delightful years in my teaching career—when I re-birthed myself and was surrounded by some amazing students who were much braver than their peers in what they shared on the page. A few in the bunch even put me in mind of Holden C., and I put a copy of *Catcher in the Rye* in their hands, even though it was probably on some "banned" list or another in this conservative county where I toil against the tide. Of course, no student to whom I ever gave that book did not love it.

I don't do The Writers' Block anymore. I'm winding down,

hopefully into full-time writing mode. A year or so away from retirement, it feels lucky and right and symmetrical that these adolescents, who would rather die than reveal themselves for who they really are, have actually taught me that it's fairly safe to show myself, through the writing. Interesting little critters, these acne-fearing, angst-ridden troubadours, who have told their stories to me and trusted me to really listen. Sure, some of them have been a pain in the ass—some downright disturbing in their skewed sense of reality—and one in particular has become the ghost-voice in my head that begs me to give them all the benefit of the doubt, because the overwhelming abundance of them truly do want to become human, to become themselves.

It has been a dozen years since that ghost-voice was born of a gunshot, and as I write this it is only days since another young lady, a local high school student, died under similar circumstances, but in a murkier atmosphere. In a freakish clustering of events, she was preceded in death this academic year by the suicides of two teachers at her school within the span of a few months, teachers who laid out the blueprint for her and possibly for others. And now comes the collateral damage, the ruined families, the emotional fallout further scattering across the entire community, trickling down to my middle school charges, picking at my own squelched-down guilt and inciting the kind of rage that senseless death taunts out of us. Hearing about such a thing makes the heart of any parent go numb with the sudden severing of possibilities and a story incomplete, unwritten, cut off in a second's worth of irrational role-playing that has no do-over.

We have to think deep and dark, even as we enjoy our inward snickers at the shallow goings-on in 'tween and teen world, grown ever meaner with the folding in of texting, sexting, online communities, and the viral exposure of images and self-expressions that once were deeply private and respected as such. As for Mr. Caulfield: not so lucky after all, to be character-frozen at that point of cleavage between innocence and despair, between humanity and isolation, between protector of children and conspicuously consuming adult. That crazy red hunting hat, with its Elmer Fudd earflaps. That whole '50s vibe of dry martinis and materialistic myopia. Juxtaposed with the electronic age, Holden Caulfield is so very post-World War II, so twentieth century. But his outward bravado and inner uncertainty transcend the subsequent decades since his creation, to expose the sometimes brittle fragility of adolescents everywhere, who, like yours truly, fight to defy the hiding.

This is from *Don't Quit Your Day Job: Acclaimed Authors and the Day Jobs They Quit;* edited by Sonny Brewer; MP Publishing Limited, Douglas, Isle of Man; 2010

Suzanne Hudson (rps.hudson@gmail.com) is the internationally prize-winning author of three novels (one, *In the Dark of the Moon*, submitted by the publisher for a National Book Award and a Pulpwood Queen International Book Club pick) and two collections of short stories (the first, *Opposable Thumbs,* a John Gardner Fiction Book Award finalist). Her short fiction and essays have been widely anthologized. Her 2019 "fictional-ish memoir," *Shoe Burnin' Season: A Womanifesto,* was a Pulpwood Queen International Book Club bonus pick; and her comic novel, *The Fall of the Nixon Administration,* was released in the spring of 2020. Hudson lives near Fairhope, Alabama, at Waterhole Branch Productions, with her husband, author Joe Formichella.

In That Quiet Earth

Robert Gwaltney

Good Hope (Georgia Barrier Island)
November 1931

Chapter 1

The autumn wind has gone mad.

It blows colder and wilder than it ought, swaddling desolate echoes, rippling the moonlit river with despair. In waves, the howls come again. The commotion: nascent—a bairn freshly spanked and smarting. The cacophony shreds me to ribbons, my spectral edges fraying and snagging silvery upon the palmetto.

John Keats lifts a paw from the ground. Stock still, he points gracile across the Acheron out Abraham Bluff's way. We make busy. I, collecting tatters, stitching myself back anew. And poor John Keats sniffing the brackish air. Together, my old friend and I fret, waiting to greet the newborn haint, still too far from the river's bank to be seen.

This moment. *Always, I fall to pieces*. The cruel burgeon of expectancy that fate might turn kind. That this wretched soul might travel across the Acheron to stay—another of my ilk with whom to pass the slow tumble of Good Hope days. *I am but a lonesome ghost beneath the moon.*

A feeble voice manages my name. "Samuel."

Avery. I am taken aback he has followed after me. Nightfall and the moon, he fears them both. Without John Keats in tow, I might hold myself quiet, gambling he cannot see me, for I have long since faded like the rings from the tail of a baby alligator. This is the misfortune of aging ghosts, or least I suspect this to be our dole. Never have I known the *good glory-glory* of a ghost old as I.

"I know you are here," he says. "I can smell you."

I shall never forgive Eulalee Skye this eternal indignity, the forever-stink of that damned pepper sauce flask.

"Rebecca has been unkind," he says, a quiver in his voice.

I think if I do not acknowledge him, he might go away. But this ghost, I have grown wise. And a thing I know: Avery McKinley Longwood is relentless.

From the swirling shadows, Avery emerges. He wears Rebecca's ball gown, a relic of green velvet and silver moire, a Parisian creation from the House of Worth. Like his sister's happiness, Avery has commandeered and squandered her abandoned trousseau.

Amusingly, he has chosen a parasol of white tussore silk to keep the moon and monsters at bay. Rarely, if ever, has the Fiddler Crab held regard for practicality. As is his custom, his greatest treasure, a leather bound journal he calls *Memoir* is tucked beneath his brittle arm.

Upon the matter of Rebecca's mood, there is no need for explanation. No doubt my Blue Heron has refused to play their childhood game of Looking Glass.

The wind riles, fluttering Avery's threadbare edges, undermining the old bird dog's worn-out hips. Unraveling my hem. *Avery, John Keats, and I—we have all come apart.*

Avery sways, wrestling his parasol above his balding head. "Are you not going to pay me any mind?" he says, his sateen slippers sinking into sand. "You and that mongrel out galavanting the midnight hour. Chasing good-for-nothing haints. Pathetic."

John Keats lifted paw trembles with age, but he remains steadfast, sniffing and pointing precariously, leaning against the "Keep Away" sign to hold his balance on three legs. His tail, he keeps taut as a clothesline.

Before I can speak, Avery takes notice of himself, the creep of light through salt-pruned branches of the Live Oak. He is besotted, charmed by the scatter and waltz of moon lace upon the ground. I, too, am taken aback by the queer, lovely sight of it. Avery: a tableau vivant.

The generosity of white tussore silk absorbs moon glow. The effect: the stroke of an Egbert brush lifting the sag of his jowl. Dimming the constellation of liver spots sprawling his temples. I am reminded of our long-ago selves. Avery—doe-eyed and seraphic. And I—*a plume of wintry breath. Shades of evergreen roiling at my edges.*

Across the Acheron, the poor soul wails once more, the mournful sound closer—the sudden thrill sending shivers.

"Good boy, John Keats," I say, admiring his tenacity. Grateful the old bird dog has not toppled over with Avery there to mock him.

From the forest, the snapping of a branch and then another. Overhead, beyond the shimmy of Spanish moss, the canopy comes alive. A frenzy of bird and squirrel. The approaching haint and footfall upon the understory unmoor Avery from his trance and John Keats from his chore. The sound, it is not the tread of a white-tail deer.

The smell of rot, a stench unlike the life-giving marsh, is fast upon us, stirred into the air by the rising gale and yowling ghost traveling the river. Disoriented, John Keats turns from the bank. He growls low and steady at tufts of resurrection fern and sparklberry. Avery, possessing the poise of a tightrope walker, steadies himself in the turbulence, his parasol raised above his head.

From the forest, into a slant of moonbeam, a naked man limps, a billhook gripped at his side. Leaves crunch beneath and cling to the cuts on his bare feet. The putrid smell grows stronger.

Avery winces, the stink and gruesome sight of the sore-riddled man startling him. There is no need inquiring with the interloper the nature of his visit. He seeks what all trespassers upon Good Hope crave. But Avery asks just the same. "Your business, sir?" he says, paying careful mind to the curve of blade the man holds.

The man takes a few steps closer. He stops, opening a sore on his cheek with his filthy fingernail. I count the starving man's ribs. One side and then the other. *How long before he whittles himself to the bone?*

A sound travels, as if pulled deep from a well gone dry. Fraying rope working rusted pulley. The man opens his mouth. Chapped skin pulls and tears.

"Redemption," he says, tapping the billhook against his knee.

Avery tilts back his parasol. "That is a commodity free to no man or woman traveling here to Good Hope. And you are without even a pocket or coin purse to boot."

I marvel at the Fiddler Crab. He has turned Blue Heron, speaking calm and cool as the root cellar floor.

The man wiggles loose an incisor between his thumb and index finger until it comes free, leaving his tongue orphaned in a toothless, gruesome grin. "Want Leontyne," he says, holding the rotten tooth out for Avery to spy. A smatter of blood and drool travels the grime on his chin.

"The Great Redeemer," I say. "She does not barter in teeth."

Upon hearing me speak, Leontyne's Sinner takes notice. He is perplexed, possessing no mastery of this stridulous language of ghosts. My voice is not a human one; it is falsetto—a chorus of cicada and cricket. Part stutter of a Laughing Gull.

"Mercy," the Sinner says, holding out the tooth for me to take.

He, like all other Sinners, is not undone by the look of me. Perhaps they think me a hallucination. Regardless, there are far more terrifying things laying in wait than ghosts. There is Leontyne. And Avery McKinley Longwood. And Good Hope.

"Mercy," Avery says. "This I give you for free." The illusion of white tussore silk plays more parlor tricks. Lifting his cheekbones and accentuating his once full lips.

The Sinner's eyes seem to ease from the darkness of the forest, settling into focus upon Avery in the moon bright clearing. He speaks slowly, pausing between each word, taking in the creature shimmering in a ballgown before him.

"What. Are. You?" the Sinner asks.

Avery turns in a circle, the hem of his gown sweeping the sand. "A drop of Redemption," he says. "Placed beneath your tongue."

A moan escapes the Sinner's lips, longing traveling that dark empty well, trailing the path of that first word he spoke. He steps forward and John Keats lets loose a howl.

"There now, John Keats," I say. "Heel." Leaning back upon his rear haunches, the bird dog rests, the argentine light turning his green eyes eerie.

Beneath his parasol, Avery gleams. His dark eyes wander. I know this look, the cusp of undoing should he notice his own fleeting dazzle.

"Looking Glass. Looking Glass," I say.

Avery's eyes regain focus.

Raising the billhook, the Sinner speaks. "Please..."

John Keats and I focus upon the drag and hiss of Avery's velvety hem. He steps backwards from the path. Sure footed, he takes wide berth around a Live Oak stump.

"Just a drop," Avery says, opening his mouth curling back his tongue.

Between the jagged slash of the Sinner's hip bones, beneath the dark thatch of hair, there is a stir. He groans, stepping off the path. He does not follow Avery's course.

"Mercy..."

I am desperate to look away, only I cannot. Not even my green-eyed John Keats can resist.

"Your name?" Avery says.

The Sinner regards the rotten tooth in his hand, as though contemplating a thing long lost and forgotten. He pumps his jaw, right cheek and eye twitching. "Ewell Day Higgs," he says, his voice oxidized and grating.

A glint of childhood wonder passes across the Sinner's ruined face, a scrap of boy clinging precariously like a leaf at the arch of his bloody foot. *Turn away*, I want to say, but the moment is fleeting. His face turns grim and hungry—grip tightening about the blade's handle. And I know there is no saving him.

Avery revolves, walking a few steps away, the silver moiré of his gown beckoning the Sinner. "Ewell Day Higgs," he says, turning, then curling back his tongue.

Redemption. Just a single drop.

Ewell Day Higgs, below that black thatch of hair, comes fully alive, the stink of him rising up along side. He steps forward, tongue thrusting from his mouth. "What. Are. You?"

A great cracking and splintering erupts beneath the Sinner's feet. Then a *whoosh*. And Ewell Day Higgs is gone. Rotten tooth and billhook gobbled up by the earth.

John Keats howls, only Ewell Day Higgs is not fully dead, only more dead than before there at the bottom of Leontyne's pit. Wooden stakes slicing through ligament and gristle. I feel the urge to count his ribs again. Up one side and down the other, only I lack the courage to look.

I take note of Avery peacocking in the height of the moon's glory, fresh from murder and unmoved by the Sinner's keening below.

What are you? There now, Ewell Day Higgs, you have your answer.

Avery cradles *Memoir* with one arm, hugging it beneath his chin. Within this journal, handwritten poems: stanzas of Bryon, Shelley, Keats, and verses of his own—fashioned and wielded as psalms and spells. This is his own derivation of Contrivance, a sort of poetic conjure inspired by Eulalee Skye.

Sometimes Avery Longwood takes things. Sometimes he lies.

The wind roars. Ewell Day Higgs moans. And my hatchling haint screeches, riding the tail of a fast-rising storm. John Keats hurries back to his spot on the riverbank, pointing and leaning himself against the sign. In the chaos of trespass and butchery, I nearly forgot my ghost come to call.

I smell the brim of tears in Avery's eyes and turn back to look. For a moment, I think it is the Sinner he mourns, but then he speaks.

They fell and faded—and the crackling trunks
Extinguish'd with a crash—and all was black.

I know now Avery thinks of Fuller Barton, the boy he once loved and lost. In the bleakest of moods, when memory of the auburn-haired boy is fast upon him, the Fiddler Crab invokes Byron's "Darkness". A spell of sadness meant to assuage sadness.

"I can see him," I say, spying a tizzy of pearly phosphorescence in the distance.

"What shall he be called?"

What he means to ask is if I shall christen this ghost, Fuller Barton. Know this: never in the passing of a million moons and star-smattered skies would I bestow such a millstone upon another. Especially a kindred specter sensitive as I. *Fuller Barton*, indeed.

"When I meet him, I shall know," I say.

"Why do you even bother. You know there is no saving him from the bottle tree."

I am desperate for Avery to leave me be. To leave me alone with the hatchling haint. "Perhaps," I say. "But today might be different than yesterday. And different than the day before."

"Optimism is an extravagance the likes of you can hardly afford."
The likes of me. The living can be cruel.

Our visitor is quick upon us, grumbling, a building roll of thunder. He rises slowly, scintillating in time with his own rumbling. John Keats growls, and Avery hurries around the pit down the path to the riverbank.

"Shoo, shoo," Avery calls out to the haint, jealous always of anyone's prospect for happiness other than his own.

I am struck by the look of the hatchling: pearlescent streamers reflecting and seething upon the river. This specter, three bushels big, is larger and more dazzling than most. And I can tell from the Fiddler Crab's breathing he is of equal impression.

At once I am self-conscious of my malodor and opacity. I attempt to tidy myself, trying my best to glow—to be seen. *I am a relic, ancient and dim.* He drifts closer in my direction. Perhaps he feels me in vibrations or has detected a paltry glimpse of me. Perhaps he will be different than the rest. *Perhaps he is meant to stay.*

Avery clears his throat. "Heaven," he says, drawing out the word, turning it ridiculous. casting it out like shrimp bait upon a hook. "Did not seem to be my home."

Wuthering Heights. That Jezebel quotes our favorite book, enticing my caller to drift and weep across the bank to Avery who still shimmers in a moon lace shower.

Never disoriented from his best angles, Avery adjusts his parasol, tilting it back just so, glancing through the memory of his once dark, curling lashes. I mean to beat my old friend at his game, but before I can speak, he lilts. "And I broke my heart with weeping to come back to earth; and the angels were so angry that they flung me out into the middle of the heath on the top of Wuthering Heights."

Tears welling in his eyes, Avery reaches out his right hand as if to caress my visitor, his slender, elegant fingers trembling. I know this look. He is transfixed by the memory of Fuller Barton and lustful for the stunning ghost before him. Forever has Avery been in want for things not meant for him.

The ghost purrs. Avery weeps. And I am jealous. I do not care for this familiar and unwelcomed emotion. I propel myself forward, the way made easier in the breeze. "He does not belong to you," I say. *He is mine.* Immediately I regret my cuckold rant. But they pay me no mind. I should be relieved, but I am not.

Now there is a greater thing I regret, not having spoken more loudly. And I am furious to be ignored, to be passed by. Always am I spying through windows and over shoulders. I do not want to be unseen. I do not want to be shipwrecked here with only the living to pass the time. *The living*—they think mostly of themselves. And of us specters—when moods turn bleak.

"My name is Avery Longwood," the Fiddler Crab says, looking wantonly up at my caller. Avery's charms have worn thin as the soles of his sateen slippers, only the ghost fails to notice. He is naïve and susceptible to the tricks played by moonlight and duplicitous men grown old.

I wedge myself between Avery and the ghost. "I am Samuel." I am embarrassed I have no surname. If ever I possessed one, I cannot remember. My memories, they do not proceed Eulalee's pepper sauce flask. *A ghost is all I can ever remember being.*

My guest simmers to a mewl, and I am now so close to him, I revel in awe. That the dead can be vibrant and beautiful and sad as the living.

Then. That dreaded, stunning sound off in the distance from the marsh. Of fingers fondling crystal lips of half-full glasses. First, faint. Swelling and soaring celestial over the place.

Avery's lips tremble. Like me, he hears the siren call of Leontyne's haint-trap tree. The newborn ghost takes notice, his glow pulsing rhythmic to the bottles' vibrations. The ghost passes through us, a rapture of prickles and quivers. A moan escapes Avery, a private sound liberated from dark, neglected places.

The ghost is quick, a hound on the tail of a fox. I collect myself, shaking off oblivion. John Keats and I hurry down the Live Oak path behind him. In the kick of rising wind, Avery's weeping presses. *Fuller Barton. Fuller Barton.* I glance back to find him quelled in moonlit puddles staring out over the river with his Fuller Barton, and rancid last breath of Ewell Day Higgs.

The rhapsody of the haint-trap tree possesses the timbre of a harp. Cascading and mildly metallic. The sound captivates, hastening the ghost to a pace John Keats and I can hardly match. If I am not quick, the marsh, the tree, and Leontyne Skye shall have their way.

"So many things I can teach you," I say. That the clear blue of the sky turns us dizzy. That we are safest in the nook and cranny of the nighttime hour. That we cannot cross back across the river. That we are here to stay.

At the edge of the marsh, a naked creature rises before us from cordgrass and muck, a male human form posed in a macabre arabesque. His skin, gray in the moon glow, is the texture of bark. His hands lift and reach for the star-splintered sky.

The ghost trembles and yawps.

"Do not be afraid," I say. "It is only Matthew."

"Maaaa," the ghost bleats. "Maaaa tooo."

"Matthew," I repeat slowly, so he might better form his first spoken word. "Rebecca made him," I say. "A man she carved from algae, cordgrass, and mud. He is a sculpture. A statue." How I envy Matthew his chicken wire frame. A skeleton to hold himself together. I am but ether. *A pepper sauce breeze.* "You will like Rebecca." *If only you will stay.*

Of course, I shall not tell my caller that a statue soon may bear his likeness. That I might describe to my dearest Rebecca Longwood, how I imagine him to appear in the form of a fully grown man. That he is tall and handsome with a Romanesque nose. This is our vocation, Rebecca's and mine, a way to pass the hours. Me, describing all the gone-away haints, and she and I conceiving them with the marsh.

"Maaa tooo."

"Very good," I say. "And there, across the way. That is Hindley Earnshaw. And over there, that is Edgar Linton. He is well-mannered and kind." I do not bother to explain these are names of two characters from *Wuthering Heights.* That there are so many more of them tangled in cordgrass and darkness that they cannot all be seen. *Should you escape Leontyne's bottle, there will be time enough for that.* Mile upon mile of Good Hope days.

The haint-trap tree grows louder, the music more intoxicating. My caller starts to drift. He is stupefied, his movements inebriated from the sound. I might concede, allow him the comfort of a bottle. But this ghost, he seems different than the others, and I am desperate for him to stay. "I have a secret," I say. "A thing never spoken aloud."

My caller seems to snag upon my words, bobbing and weaving in place. "Ssssss," he says. The sibilant sound is salacious. It carries a thrill.

"How quick you are," I say. "Yes, a secret." He is smart and savvy a ghost as ever I have known.

I glimpse the wetland walk behind me and ahead. There is no one but the ghost and me, Matthew, Edgar, and Hindley—the others lurking in the dark.

In the creep of tide and sulfurous stink of marsh, I whisper to my caller. "I do not believe I am a regular sort of haint." Only I do not know what other sort of haint I might be. It is a suspicion, a thing I have felt these last lolling years. And I am struck with the arrogance of speaking such a thing aloud.

Wind blows cold from across the river, contradicted from the other direction by the warm, sea island breeze. In chorus with the marsh, my caller hisses and glints. "Sssss . . ."

The bottle tree plays its sweet harp music, the bright, penetrating notes replaced with a middle register. A warm, otherworldly melody.

My caller is a somnambulist once more, an acolyte, and I am not entirely immune from the thrall of Leontyne's subterfuge. Together, we meander above the wetland walk, light and burdenless as leaves afloat down a stream.

Leontyne's singing. It is the thing that rouses me.

Oh, don't you want to go,
To the Gospel feast;
That Promised Land,
Where all is peace?

Beyond her shanty, Leonytne stands, a kerosene lamp at her feet. The light tosses shadows, outlining her riotous tumble of Spanish moss hair. Giddy with my secret and the witchery of that haint-trap tree, the caller brushes against me reducing me to prickles and bliss.

"What is your name?" she says.

"Leave him be, Leontyne, I have not named him."

Leontyne steps forward, the kerosene light twitching and jigging behind her, the cloying smell of Redemption cooking in her still in the shed. "A lowly thing it is to bear no name," she says.

My caller bobs past and billows in time to the musical spell. "Please stop," I say. "Don't go." The haint-trap tree is set off in the darkness, and I can barely glean its blurry edges. And no further may I go beyond where I rest for fear Leonytne's bottles might snare me.

Leontyne sings again. The prettiness of her voice has long since faded, left in the sun all these years to harden and crack.

Oh, don't you want to go,
To the Gospel feast;

"He is not like the others," I say. "Please let this one stay." I watch my ghost stretch and swell, his movements turning provocative. I have nothing to offer, nothing to bribe, not even a rotten tooth pulled from my own mouth.

"What a cruelty it is to allow a lost soul to wander," Leontyne says, words she has spoken a thousand times before.

Leontyne means to punish me, to make me suffer. She is forever after me, wielding her stinking bottles. She will not be satisfied until she has ruined me. Until there is nothing left of me but vapor in a glass.

"I am no more lost than you," I say. She has never forgiven me the crossroads, the decision I made that day. For choosing Rebecca and Avery. For traveling off Longwood way.

"There is not much time," she says. "If you are to name him, it must be now." She shakes Eulalee's oyster shell necklace.

My caller undulates, drifting further away, and I am near mad from desire. And then, a wicked thought. A scheme: Leontyne's long dead child, a fatherless boy. How she longs for him. Oh, how she broods.

"Good glory-glory," I holler. "This haint. His name be Journey Skye." *Dear Lord I have done it.* I have given Leontyne's dead child's name to a haint. Immediately, I feel the weight of the thing I have done, my spectral hem turned heavy. Leontyne has gone still, the kerosene flame in hysterics.

My Journey Skye still drifts, but his attention is fast upon me. "Sssss crit," he hisses.

Leontyne steps back slowly until she is behind the lantern, the wash of light turning her ghoulish. I wonder if she can bear to lose her son a second time. If she might run and smash all her bottles. But she does not move. She does not twitch. She does not shake at her oyster shell charm.

Sssss crit.

Journey, he is adrift, and there is no calling him back to me. Slowly, I recede, leaving John Keats to keep watch. I hurry back to my Matthew, to Edgar, and my Hindley. I follow their gaze—their crackled, reaching hands.

"It is alright," I say, consoling my chicken wire friends.

We are all lonesome here beneath the moon.

My work in progress is a novel titled, *In That Quiet Earth*, a piece of Southern fiction in the Gothic tradition. The following is a summary.

Samuel, an aging ghost in existential crisis, alongside three living companions from childhood remain the only four residents upon Good Hope, eeking out their days in a stupor of ill-spent youth, unrequited love, and resentment.

The subsequent death of a baby boy mysteriously abandoned at the base of Good Hope's bell tower shakes Samuel and the others from their tedium, seemingly setting off a miraculous change in Samuel and the others, restoring them to their youthful selves, leaving them ravenous for second chances.

In the chaotic aftermath of this inexplicable transformation, with uncanny timing, Rowen Sparrow, a young, charismatic wanderer arrives seeking shelter and work, unmooring long-repressed passions and provoking fierce rivalries as they vie for Rowen's affection, driving Samuel to devise a murderous plot to keep the young man to himself.

Raised alongside three feral, younger brothers in the rash-inducing, subtropical climate of Cairo, Georgia, Robert Gwaltney is a lifelong resident of the South – a circumstance that leaves an indelible mark upon his voice as a writer.

A graduate of Florida State University, he presently resides in Atlanta, Georgia with his partner. By day, he serves as Vice President of Easter Seals North Georgia, Inc., a non-profit organization that strengthens children and their families during the most critical times in their development. Through his non-profit work, he is a champion for early childhood literacy. In all the hours between, he writes. *The Cicada Tree*, Gwaltney's debut novel, will be released February 22, 2022.

A Hollow Light

Heather Frese

Chapter One

My hands were bleeding when I saw Nate for the first time since I'd arrived at the inn, when he glided his kayak across the Pamlico and pushed up beside me on the dock. I reached out to grab the paddle as Nate pulled the kayak up. Tiny red rivulets ran down my wrists and dripped on the pier, the bright crimson out of place on this dimly bruised January day. A sharp wind kicked up whitecaps, ruffling the muted reeds until they bent their heads low.

Nate grabbed my right hand, cold beads dripping off his arm and landing on my own. He brushed at the red, saw that it was a thin scratch. "Stigmata?" he asked lightly, wiping the blood away.

The old me, the one standing in front of the dividing line of my father's death, would've laughed and made devil horns instead of vaguely recognizing that Nate's question ought to be lighthearted. The water lapped against the dock, and I closed my eyes.

"Charlotte?" Nate asked, his voice soft. "Are you okay?" He pulled my hand closer to his chest.

I opened my eyes and turned away. Back at the inn a light flicked on, illuminating a second story window. I nodded. "Fine," I said, through the tightness in my throat. I pulled my hand away. "How was kayaking?"

Nate shrugged. "Chilly, but I needed some water time after being stuck on the mainland." I'd been here for three days, but Nate had been visiting friends in Raleigh the whole time.

The breeze kicked up, damp and fishsmelling. I knew I should ask about his trip, force a smile and listen with interest, but the prospect exhausted me. "I'm going to go back and help with dinner," I said. The wind lashed my cheeks as I walked down the boardwalk, heading toward the light.

The Pamlico Inn was the only thing keeping me steady. The inn and the water. I was otherwise loose, untethered and distant from my brother, James, and my mother. I couldn't stand to be with them now that our family was only three. At home, I'd been constantly aware of the friction caused by my father's absence, the space where he should have been—my father, stable and strong and reassuring. A beacon. He'd been gone for six months now.

Gone.

Nine years ago, when I was ten years old, the National Park Service moved the Cape Hatteras lighthouse. I thought it would crumble and fall, afraid its solid, striped body, the steady golden sweep of its beam across the night, would be gone. The Park Service was moving the lighthouse away from the pounding waves and eroding ocean. But I imagined the black and white spirals, all two hundred and eight feet of them, swaying, rocking, left, right, catching momentum, crashing to the sand. Piles of black and white bricks. Dust. Everywhere dust, rising and billowing and choking me with grit. Days later I would still be spitting out rogue grains when I brushed my teeth.

But the lighthouse didn't fall. It just moved, the glimpse of black-and-white spirals no longer visible from Lighthouse View Road, the rotating beam now illuminating maritime forest instead of dunes and beach and frothy waves. Still, what once was can haunt a person, can make them run away from home, and this is where I ran, where I landed, this great gray seashell of an inn tumbled onto the shore. And I was still running.

I ran away from Nate, up the boardwalk and toward the inn, the cuts on my palms stinging against the salty breeze. The inn had three stories, with ramps along the outside connecting the new addition to the original, lace curtains fringing the windows of rooms named after

North Carolina wildflowers. My best friend Evie Austin's parents owned it. The inn closed for the month of January, so the Austins let me choose whichever room I wanted. I picked a small, yellow room overlooking the Sound, The Primrose Room, in the old part of the inn. I liked it because of its coziness, and I liked being close to the family quarters. Mr. and Mrs. Austin had a bedroom tucked behind the office in the original part of the inn, along with a living space, and Evie and Nate had rooms overlooking the garden, since tourists wanted a water view.

Once I was inside the inn, I went upstairs, hid in the Primrose Room and let myself cry about my dad. I felt so stupid getting upset in front of other people, hated the way the grief still rose in my throat unexpectedly. It'd been six months now. Six months and eighteen days.

Someone knocked on my door and I wiped my face with my bleeding hands. "Charlotte," Evie said. "I'm coming in."

"Don't," I said.

"You better have pants on," she said, pushing the door open. Evie stood with a hand on her hip, her eyes shadowed. Then she rushed forward, touched my face and pulled back, her fingers damp, red. "Why the hell is your face all bloody?" Evie asked. She pulled a tissue from the side table and rubbed my cheeks.

I showed her my hands. "Tin foil," I said, turning to rifle through my suitcase for Band-Aids, turning away from her. "I cut myself while ripping out tin foil." I'd cut myself while ripping out tin foil, and at first I didn't even notice. And then I didn't care. And then it hurt, and the hurt felt like something I could anchor myself to, and I'd cut myself again and ran down to the water to watch myself bleed until Nate found me.

Evie took the Band-Aids and applied them to my palms. I swallowed hard, swallowed again, stared at Evie as her dark hair fell forward, shiny and straight and long. She threw away the wrappers and I sat down on my bed.

"When are you going to unpack?" Evie asked, pulling a pair of pink socks out of my bag and tossing them at me. "You're home."

I shrugged, let the socks fall. I didn't bother telling her that nothing was permanent, not even home, especially not home. That I'd watched my father die, packed my bags, and left for my first semester of college, because he'd wanted me to go. Because everyone said it would take my mind off it. Him. September, October, November, I did everything but think about it. Him. I unpacked my luggage, decorated my dorm. And then, in December, Evie called to tell me she was pregnant, mingled notes of apology and terror in her voice. Two weeks before finals, I took a leave of absence from school. The form I filled out asked the reason for my departure. Life and death, I wrote. Melodramatic, yes, but that's how I was feeling at the time. And I left the solid Midwest and came down here to the Outer Banks, to this improbable strip of islands, this narrow, shifting place, more water than land, to be with my friend. To stare at the water and make everything go away.

Evie sat down on the edge of the bed beside me, tossing the pink socks up and down in one hand. "Did I ever tell you about the time my parents tried to make me wear a pink dress?" she asked.

I shook my head no, tried to smile, but really, I just wanted to be alone. Please leave.

Evie went on. "It was some awful Easter dress or something," she said. "I think I was seven. I was in my sherpa phase. No way was that dress going on my body."

"Your sherpa phase?" I blew my nose. Please leave. Please leave. Please leave.

"I was obsessed with climbing Mount Everest," Evie said. "You know, like a sherpa." She got up and placed the socks in a dresser drawer. "I still think sherpas are kind of sexy," she said.

"What's not to love?" I said.

A phone rang downstairs in the office. "I'll get it," Evie said. She walked to the door and paused with her hand on the frame. "I'll see you at dinner."

I went to the bathroom and washed my face, soaking my Band-Aids, then wandered over to the Sea Oats room to look out the window, relieved to be alone. Pampas grass shook and swayed in the wind around the curved gravel driveway. Winters on Cape Hatteras were more desolate and more compelling than I'd imagined. There was a quietness, a muted rhythm that made summer seem like a carnival of color and life. Ice cream stands, putt-putt courses, bright T-shirts flying from shop windows, all these furled in on themselves in winter. The island, extended and curved like a ballerina's arm, elegantly jutted people away in these windy, chilly months. I loved it both ways, winter and summer. My parents had only seen the summer months, had planned to see winter when they retired. My dad would never see a Hatteras winter. Before the grief behind my eyes could transition from a prickle to a tidal rush, I got up and walked downstairs, hoping the motion would distract me. I picked at my left palm. Outside a tall, sliding glass door, an egret swooped down, landing in the marsh grass. The sun peeked above the rim of a streaky, gray cloud, reflecting on the stillness of the shallow bowl of water that was the Pamlico Sound.

I stepped outside, the breeze fresh on my face, and breathed. Then I got out my phone and sent my mom a text message about the egret. I hadn't been able to talk to her since I'd left, too tired and griefworn to withstand her asking me to come home. I put my phone back in my pocket and walked downstairs to the kitchen, running my fingers over the carved sign that said Galley, breathing in the onion and potato smell of clam chowder preparations. Inside, Evie and Nate bickered back and forth, and then Evie said something about dying and I didn't want to hear them talk about my dad, so I went in. Nate blushed and bent down to the sink, tall and lanky with his wetsuit peeled half off. Before I could say anything, Evie grabbed a handful of silverware in one hand and me by the other and spun me out the door. We went upstairs to the inn's dining room, which the family used as their own space in the off season and started setting out plates and cups and napkins for dinner.

"He's okay with it," Evie said. Her fingers flitted down forks, hummingbird quick.

"What?"

"Stephen," she said. "He's okay with the baby."

"I didn't know you told him." I passed Evie saucers. A gust of wind shook the inn, rattling the window-lined dining room. I was still getting used to the wind in winter, to the chill and the damp. "Did you tell your parents, too?"

Evie walked around the table. "Not them yet. Nate knows. I told Stephen last night. He freaked out but then he rallied." She jostled the table with her leg and reached forward to steady a pitcher.

I stopped straightening the linen and looked at her, trying to peer past her veneer to see if she was actually upset. "He freaked out?"

"You know, whatever. 'How could you,' blah blah blah." Evie

fluttered her hands in the air and rolled her eyes at the ceiling. A ray of sun shot through the window and danced across the table. "I mean, we haven't exactly talked about what we're going to do. But the point is, he's not mad anymore, and he's coming to dinner tonight. That was him on the phone."

Stephen Oden. I walked over to the other side of the table to a window overlooking the dock. At Thanksgiving, he'd taken Evie on the ferry to Ocracoke, got drunk, and left without her. It was his way of ending their relationship. She called me from the terminal as the last boat was pulling out. They'd been broken up for a few weeks then gotten back together, then Evie realized she was pregnant.

I turned and Evie was staring at me with round, dark eyes. "Okay," I tried to sound cheery. "Hey, I'll give him a chance." I smiled and my face felt like it was cracking.

At the beginning of Chapter One of the novel *A Hollow Light*, we meet Charlotte McConnell, who has left college to stay at an inn on Hatteras Island, North Carolina, while she grieves the death of her father. Charlotte's friend Evie's family own the inn and Evie has recently discovered that she's pregnant. The novel follows the nine months that ensue as Charlotte finds a way to deal with her grief as Evie manages this new and unexpected twist in her life.

Heather Frese is the author of the novel *The Baddest Girl on the Planet,* winner of the Lee Smith Novel Prize. She has published numerous short stories, essays, and the occasional poem. Her work has appeared in *Michigan Quarterly Review, the Los Angeles Review, Front Porch, the Barely South Review, Switchback*, and elsewhere, earning notable mention in the *Pushcart Prize Anthology* and *Best American Essays.*

Heather received her M.F.A. from West Virginia University and has a master's degree from Ohio University. Coastal North Carolina is her longtime love and source of inspiration, her writing deeply influenced by the wild magic and history of the Outer Banks. A native Ohioan, she currently writes, edits, and wrangles three small children in Raleigh, North Carolina. You can follow her on social media @Heatherkfrese.

They Walk Among Us: A Mini-Memoir
Grace Sammon

It was another all-too-hot Florida morning. Covid had kept –for
the most part – the need to dress up and show up to a minimum. Now,
uncomfortable in heels and a dress that had somehow grown smaller as
my waist expanded during the pandemic, I was on my way to the
Florida Broadcasters' Club. I was going to be inducted as a result of
the launch of my new radio show, "The Storytellers." My discomfort
was not limited to my outfit. That feeling was lodged solidly in my
chest as I questioned, not for the first time, what I was doing launching
yet another venture at the age of sixty-eight.

It had been easy to say yes to the station owner. Sure, I could
launch a radio show, after all, I grew up listening to the countless
stories of my Dad going to work at CBS Radio as a Page Boy, moving
into studio engineering, and ultimately serving as the sound engineer
for many of the most famous radio shows of the 1930's and '40s.
Besides, I told myself, I was no stranger to the microphone. I had
done my own two-year stint at The Washington Ear Radio Network
with my own show, "A Second Cup of Coffee." This radio stuff must
run in my blood, right?

No, not so much. Heading into the Broadcasters' lunch, with a
solid lump of imposter syndrome tucked into my pocket, I wanted the
comfort and reassurance of chatting with my Mother, my forever
champion. I opined about how great it would be to talk to my Dad and
ask him if he would want to be a guest on my show to talk about early

radio. I wanted to tell him how important I thought it was that he got to tell that story and so much more. He helped make the Columbia Broadcasting System (CBS) grow from a small radio network into one of the foremost radio and television network operations in the United States. He worked with the renowned Edward R. Morrow and directed his famous show "Person To Person." I wanted him to be recognized for his invention of the wireless microphone and the first shoulder television camera, both born from the necessity of rapidly advancing broadcast technologies. I wanted to once again hear his CBS stories as well as those about helping start the news bureaus over at ABC TV. I wanted to hear him, once again, recount stories of the legendary, at least to my family, Bill Paley and Leonard Goldenson network presidents.

Hearing those stories was not to be. So, armed only with those memories, I entered the luncheon and did what my mother so well ingrained in me to do – mingle, introduce yourself, be more interested in others than you are in yourself, and seek out those that might not be talking with anyone else. A very elderly man in a wheel chair, with an attendant, was such a person. I introduced myself to Jim Duffy all too quickly, moving on to take my seat as the program began. A stunning older woman, perhaps in her eighties, complete with Hermes scarf at her neck, made some announcements. Then, unexpectedly, Jim Duffy was invited to the podium to receive the "Life Time Achievement Award." Jim recounted his early days at CBS radio and how, often, necessity was the mother of invention in developing broadcast technologies. He talked about his involvement with Bill Paley and Edward R Murrow and Leonard Goldenson. He spoke of starting news bureau at ABC where he eventually became president.

My heart raced and my eyes brimmed with tears.

Immediately following his presentation, I raced to his side and said, "Mr. Duffy, I think you must have known my Dad, Bob Sammon."

His eyes softened as he said, "How is Bob? He is one of the smartest and nicest men I ever knew." The tears spilled from my eyes as I told him Dad had died ten years ago. Jim turned to the stunning older woman, calling her over to us. He introduced Kay Wight, former Vice President for CBS Sports, and said, "Kay, this is Bob Sammon's daughter."

Kay grinned broadly, took my hand, and shared that she knew my Dad through Ed Murrow. "Bob Sammon," she beamed, "simply the handsomest and kindest man I ever met. Welcome to being a broadcaster, Grace." And, with that, tears turned to gasps and gulps.

Dad was in that room as sure as I was.

It was hard to leave that moment and go to an assignment to interview an elderly couple getting ready to move into assisted living. Afterall, what more could I be given this day than the gift of knowing I was in the right place at the right time? I resolved simply to interview the couple for "just a few minutes," gather some quotes and reflections, talk about the husband's love of photography, and write a nice story for the community newspaper.

Suffice it to say, Ray and Beverly had stories to tell! Ray is ninety-two now, Beverly just ninety. They met when he was thirteen. Beverly girlishly points out that she was just eleven, eleven and a half when they met. He likes to say she was his Bar Mitsvah present. The decades fall away from them before my eyes as they tell how they met on a day-trip to Bear Mountain in New York's Hudson Valley. Ray was standing at the rail and she poked him in the back of his knees so she could get a better view. The rest, as they say, is history. And what a history! Ray and Beverly dated, they dated in groups. Ray will tell you there were three "Beverlys," tall Beverly, short Beverly, and "just right" Beverly.

While she was on a vacation in the Catskills "necking" with a boy, an announcement came over the loud speaker notifying her she had a long-distance phone call. She took the call. Afterwards, she went back to the boy and said "no more kissing, I just got engaged."

Seventy years of marriage, four daughters, wonderful grandchildren, piles of newspaper and magazine articles written about them at the ready, a home filled with great art, and a dining room table that easily holds twenty four, all speaks volumes about a life filled with love, hard work, ingenuity and family.

I patiently waited through their stories. I should have known better than to think you could rush a nonagenarian telling tales. Ray recounted that early in his career he sold camera equipment to every camera store in the New York area. I asked if he had ever visited Valente's Camera in Bay Ridge. He corrected me and said Valente's was not a camera store but rather a drug store with a large camera department because the pharmacist, Charles Valente, loved cameras.

What?

"Wait," I said. "Uncle Charlie was a pharmacist? You knew my Uncle Charlie?" Ray did indeed. He also remembered that it was unusual that back in that day the camera department was managed by a woman. A beautiful, gracious, creative, Italian woman with startling blue eyes, he recalled, a woman who always seemed more interested in others than herself.

My mother.

I went to meet with Ray and Beverly to do a kind thing, to write a story that recognized that their being in the community matters. However, the gift of writing their story was all mine. There is a Yiddish word I've learned from friends, "beshert." It means "destiny." It was beshert that Ray and Beverly would meet on that boat ride to Bear Mountain. It was beshert that I would find my way to a broadcasters' lunch and come face-to-face with my dad. And, it was beshert that I would meet Ray and Beverly and bask in the glow of an unexpected story about my uncle and mother.

Jim Duffy passed away just three weeks after he and I met. Ray and Beverly have moved away. At this point in my life, I have come to believe that things happen for a reason. I believe doors open for a purpose and you walk through them – ready, or not. Recently, I've learned to slow down on my way through the door because there is magic in the journey and there are unexpected storytellers walking among us.

The difference between an autobiography and a memoir, as told to me by Leslie Lehr, is that a memoir is a snippet, a segment, an aspect of the writer's life. It is not, decidedly, the sum of the parts, rather simply a portion of a life worth memorializing. As I age, change, and reflect on the sum of my parts, I cannot help but be aware of those that walked before me – those I paid attention to and, quite honestly, those that I did not. My fourth book, and debut novel, *The Eves*, the importance of our stories – both in the listening and the telling. It touches on the conversations we wish we could have with our parents if they were still alive and those, we wish we could have with our children, if they were ready to listen. Recently, due to the advent of my new radio show, "The Storytellers," I was invited to join the Florida Broadcasters Club. Separately, I was also asked to interview a ninety-year-old couple getting ready to move into assisted living. Preparing for the day, I could not help but think that my parents would be far better at both of these events than I. I wished I could see them again, hear their voices, and know that they still walk among us. In fact, as my submission shows, they still do.

Grace Sammon is recognized in "Who's Who in Education" and "Who's Who in Literature," Grace is utilizing skills built up over decades as she re-invents herself with her award-winning fourth book and debut novel, *The Eves.*

The Eves is an intergenerational story about lives lived well and lives in transition. It is a novel that challenges each of us to ask who we want to be in the world, regardless of our age. Grace brings that quest for a good story, and a drive to keep contributing, to her new radio show, "The Storytellers." Each episode captures the stories of authors and others who leave their mark on the world through the art of story. Grace grew up on Long Island, NY and spent most of her life in the Washington, DC area. She currently lives on Florida's west coast with her husband and a small herd of imaginary llamas. You can reach Grace via email at grace@gracesammon.net and follow her on Facebook and Instagram at GraceSammonWrites.

Gowns and Crowns

Beverly Willett

I'm not rich, and I'm way too old to compete in beauty pageants. But I do love gowns, though I never thought I'd have a chance to wear one again. As for crowns, not a sliver of hope. But after I moved to Georgia in my fifties, all that changed.

When I lived in Brooklyn, for years I'd pass an old woman on the sidewalk, all decked out in the middle of the day. She always wore a fancy dress or suit and high heels, and carried a pocketbook with a handle – attire more appropriate for a night on the town than an afternoon stroll. Sometimes she even wore a Sunday morning church hat. She had a full face of make-up on too, with bright red lipstick and blue eyeshadow. Weathered and lined, she was easily the oldest woman out and about. I'm a terrible judge of age, but I'd guess she was in her late eighties.

Where was she was going all dressed up like that? To the supermarket, diner or nearby senior center? She bore a contented expression, sometimes a smile. Could she have dementia, parading about town looking like Queen Elizabeth? How I wish that I'd stopped to talk to her to find out about her life. I feel guilty now for making unkind assumptions, especially since the older I get, the more of my positive self I see in her.

The first time I saw a "real" queen was probably on the 1960s' network game show my mother watched, *Queen for a Day*. Each week, housewives vied for the title with tearful confessions of financial hardship or unfulfilled wishes. Audience members–all female –voted with applause, and the winner received her own customized dream prize–a long-awaited honeymoon or the latest household appliance, for instance. Then she was crowned, cloaked in a red velvet robe, and presented with a bouquet of long-stemmed, red roses.

As a young girl, I dreamt of wearing real-life gowns and crowns. Out in our garage, I waddled about in a long dress and my mother's high heels and fox stole, wearing a plastic dime-store tiara. A black and white childhood photo of me and my neighborhood friends Darlene and Debbie, all dressed up, is burned into my memory. We wore somber expressions–being a queen was serious business.

In high school, I vied for the titles of prom, homecoming and county fair queen, as well as the county Junior Miss. Although I never won, I still got to wear those long dresses.

At seventeen, I was finally crowned Buddy Poppy Queen by the local VFW. I won the state contest too and felt proud to represent disabled veterans who made plastic "Buddy Poppy" flowers to finance the costs of their rehabilitation and other veterans' programs.

I was indescribably giddy that I got to wear a crown, sash and red gown, and ride in convertibles alongside good-looking military men in starched uniforms.

In recent years, there's been a backlash against beauty pageants amid claims they're sexist. It never occurred to me–in my day or now –that I need to apologize for having so much fun. Being regal doesn't diminish me as a liberated woman. (The swimsuit part I get!)

In college, I joined a sorority. While the goals of sisterhood and service mattered, some of the allure revolved around the social opportunities sorority membership afforded, especially those all-important pledge and fraternity formals.

In 2016, after my mother died, I found my high school and college gowns in the back of her closet, perfectly preserved in long garment bags. The gowns weren't expensive – we couldn't afford such things. I had made several; the rest were bargain purchases. But they were beautiful, and I'd felt beautiful in them.

"I married the Buddy Poppy Queen!" In the early years of our marriage, that's how my then husband introduced me during cocktail hour at gatherings where we hobnobbed with Ivy League lawyers. I was mortified not only by the revelation of my small-town origins, but at the prospect of appearing foolish and frivolous.

"Cut it out," I'd whisper, shushing him before turning back to change the subject and trying to wow our colleagues with my brains. Petrified I'd wreck my law career by being labeled an airhead when I'd actually graduated near the top of my class.

"Where's your sense of humor?" my husband would ask.

I was unsure of myself back then. How could a woman from the sticks, however smart, compete in the male-dominated professional world of New York City? I couldn't risk being thought of as a girl who liked to play dress-up.

I wouldn't have been caught dead in a crown unless I was attending a Halloween party or playing with my children. So I packed the playroom closet with fancy dresses for them. And jewelry, high heels, and fake crowns. Old cocktail dresses of mine became floor-length gowns for them. And when confirmation dresses went on sale in my Italian neighborhood at the end of the season, I snatched them up. We played the board game "Pretty Pretty Princess" and while I often tried to lose so my children could win, I occasionally allowed myself to enjoy the denouement when the winner wears the crown.

A few years ago I transferred our home movies from VHS to DVDs and binge-watched them with my then twenty-two-year old. She'd never seen them. "Who are you?" I asked her in one of the videos. I'd discovered her all dressed one morning in an old white nightgown of mine with a makeshift crown on her head and a boa. Her little red curls grazed her neck.

"I'm a princess," she said, nearly tripping on the hem of my nightgown. Even at two, she knew the transformational power of make-believe.

After my husband became a partner at a New York City law firm, we were invited to a law gala at the Waldorf Astoria, Manhattan's Art Deco landmark and luxury hotel on Park Avenue. I'd been to the hotel once or twice for drinks, but 1998 was my first black-tie event at the world-famous hotel known for hosting the rich and famous, of which we were neither. But I was excited: I needed a gown. It had been fifteen years since I'd worn one – when I was a bridesmaid.

We'd bought a house the year before the gala, so I decided against splurging on a dress I'd undoubtedly never wear again. On the day of the big event, I slipped drycleaner plastic over a long grey skirt and lime green beaded sweater set and headed to the hairdresser's. After that, I planned on changing in the department store's salon bathroom then head straight to the party.

My colorist finished early, leaving me plenty of time to browse formalwear downstairs. It never hurt just to look.

I flipped past hordes of designer gowns that cost more than our mortgage payment. And then my fingers landed on a sleeveless black sheath, a long column of a dress with a V-neck, V-back, and a slit to the knee on the left side. The dress was covered in tiny flowers made of white beads. And came with two wispy black and white chiffon scarves. After two babies, I wasn't the thinnest I'd ever been, but the size 10 looked like it would fit. I gasped at the price tag. A tad over $300 with no extra zero like most of the others.

No harm in trying it on. I carried it to an attendant who took the gown from my arms and led me to a fitting room with 360-degree view mirrors and a pedestal. The label said Huey Waltzer for Saks Fifth Avenue. I'd never heard of the designer, but like other high-end department stores, Saks had been selling less expensive clothes under private labels for years. Except for my wedding dress, which wasn't expensive even in its day, I'd never spent that much money on an outfit. But the black beaded gown was a great buy, even if I couldn't imagine where I'd wear it again. And, it fit me perfectly, no Spanx required. (Did they make Spanx back then?) I'd never looked classier.

It wouldn't hurt to make such a purchase, just this once, I thought. Especially when I was paying for it out of my own savings from the years I'd toiled away before taking time off to raise the children full-time. For the first time in my life, I'd found a dress I just had to have.

"How do you like it?" the dressing room attendant asked.

"I love it," I said, unlatching the door to show her.

"You look stunning," she said, taking the scarves I'd been fiddling with. "Here, let me," she said, wrapping them around my neck, draping one down my back and letting the other float through the air in front of me as I walked.

I looked at myself in the mirror and then over at the plain grey skirt and beaded sweater set I had meant to wear. I loved that sweater set, but in contrast to that gown, it looked dowdy. I handed the sales associate my credit card, asked if she could cut off the tags, and got to work applying make-up right there in the dressing room. I felt young and giddy and a bit like Cinderella heading off to the ball. I wanted to make a good impression on my husband's new colleagues and wanted to look good next to him in his rented tux. But wearing the dress was more about how it made me feel inside – happy and hopeful and treasured by myself.

"I'll tell you later," I whispered in my then husband's ear when I met him at the elevator bank inside the Waldorf Towers for the pre-gala cocktail party. He'd raised his eyebrows as if to say "well, well!" when he saw me, registering approval.

I reappeared in the dress six months later at the 50th birthday party I threw for him in our new home. A few years after that he had an affair and left. I eventually sold our home, which I could no longer afford. If I ever wore a gown or crown again, I imagined my life would have to look a whole lot different than it had become.

But when I moved to Georgia, I carried the beaded gown with me, still packed in the grey zippered garment bag it had been in for fourteen years. I'm not sure why I kept it. By then I'd gotten rid of easily three-quarters of what I owned, including clothes.

Perhaps I'd mindlessly stashed it one of the wardrobe boxes I'd bought at the U-Haul store. Scrambling to pack, I had also grabbed the two small tiaras I'd worn as the Buddy Poppy Queen. Maybe I'll need a Halloween get-up at some point, I remember thinking.

About two years later, I found myself in a dressing room again, this time trying on a slinky red sleeveless sheath.

I'd received an invitation to a black tie gala from a magazine I freelanced for. For weeks, the invitation sat without an RSVP. I weighed about twenty pounds more than the last time I'd worn the black beaded dress. I had no date and hated the idea of going alone. But even if I went, I'd need a new gown.

About a week before the event, I found myself scanning dress racks at Dillard's department store. Somehow I drifted toward to a rack of gowns. Minutes later I found myself in the dressing room wearing a long red gown, marveling at how the Spanx I had on underneath shaved off about ten of those twenty pounds. And the dress was a third of the price of the black beaded gown I'd bought eighteen years before!

"You look stunning," the saleswoman said, the same words I'd heard at Saks. But it wasn't just the usual sales pitch. I felt stunning too. Why I was practically saving money by handing over my credit card. At least that's what I told myself.

"Can I return it if I need to?" I said, delaying my decision with the pretense that I'd pay for the gown and take it home, try it on again, and then make a one-hour round trip to return it. Really, who was I fooling? I was in mad love with the red dress. The dress perfectly matched my signature red lipstick and fiery red hair. The combination was outstanding, even with no make-up and the Savannah humidity which had made a frizz-bomb out of my locks.

I kept the gown. Without it, I was stuck in time with my black beaded one. A friend escorted me to the party, and I had a fabulous evening.

Not long after that, I found a reason to dress up whenever I wanted. I'd seen a group of grown women marching in the Savannah Christmas parade, all decked out. They were lit up like Christmas trees with lights pinned to their long green gowns, laughing and waving to the crowd. And they wore crowns. Their banner proclaimed them the Mint Julep Queens.

"Want to join us?" two of them asked.

As a matter of fact, I did. I ran over, smiled and leaned in for a photograph. I joined their group and became a queen myself. And as a Mint Julep Queen, well, now I needed a green gown!

And thus began the return to the glam days of my youth. Since then, I've made room in my closet for two more green gowns, one a $7 steal from the best Goodwill in America, just five miles from where I live.

Black, white, heavyset, skinny, young, old-er, blond, brunette, we Mint Julep Queens range in age from thirty to seventy-something. When asked who we are and what we do one of our founders says, "We don't do anything. We are." We just have fun, flounce about town, and try to spread joy wherever we go. We eat, drink, dance, pose for pictures, and march in parades.

The day I officially joined my sponsor draped a green and white satin sash across my new sparkly green gown. Then we queens walked for miles through the center of town in the St. Patrick's Day parade in our full regalia – long green gowns, sashes, tiaras and rhinestones. We waved and darted back and forth to the sidelines, draping parade-goers in multicolored throw beads. I'd even bought myself a brand-new crown – a sparkly one, five inches high.

After many years, I was back in my element, a queen once more, celebrating the enthusiasm for playing dress up that I thankfully never outgrew.

Greek philosopher Heraclitus of Ephesus is famous for saying that "No man ever steps in the same river twice." Sadly, it can sometimes seem like we do. By constantly dwelling on past memories of painful events, we often keep them alive, as fixed and seemingly unchanged in our minds as possible.

Behind the wall of pain I suffered over my divorce and the loss of the American Dream I'd worked so hard to build, however, I discovered a more ancient wellspring of joy, where I romped and played and firmly believed myself a queen destined for a happily ever after.

Beverly Willett is the author of *Disassembly Required: A Memoir of Midlife Resurrection.* (2019 Post Hill Press), a story about beginning again after the American dream implodes. Kirkus Reviews called it a "triumphant journey to new beginnings;" bestselling author Caroline Leavitt called it an "enchanting and inspiring look at how less can really be so, so much more." In 2016, Beverly gave a popular Tedx Talk entitled "How to Begin Again." Nominated for 2020 Georgia Author of the Year for her memoir, Beverly is a former NYC entertainment attorney and stay-at-home mom. Her articles have appeared in many of the nation's top newspapers and magazines, including The New York Times, USA Today, The Washington Post, Salon, AARP Magazine, Woman's Day, The Guardian, and many more. Appealing to a diverse audience, she's written on a wide variety of topics – everything from friendship, divorce, and parenting, to homelessness, midlife, and meditation, even her wild ride on a Harley on the back roads of Kentucky. "Gowns and Crowns" is taken from her book of personal essays in progress, with the working title "Return Engagements. She's been interviewed extensively on national radio and TV. Locally, she's written for *South and Savannah Magazine* and has served on the boards of the Flannery O'Connor Childhood Home Foundation (past President) and the Chatham-Savannah Authority for the Homeless (CSAH), co-producing a documentary entitled "Without a Roof" for public television. Her most important accomplishment, however, is having raised two strong daughters, women of integrity who live and work in New York City. Beverly lives in Savannah, Ga.

The Orphans
Susan Tanner

Chapter One

I've forgotten many things over my seventy-two years, some painful to lose—like the scent of my first child, light and sweet, but gone too soon. Other things, I recall too well and would rather forget. The thud of dirt against a coffin. The lonely ache of an empty bed in the long months after.

But I remember the orphans with vivid clarity, and the train. Sometimes that seems strange to me, that I should effortlessly recall a segment of my past that spanned no more than a few weeks, and those weeks over sixty long years ago. The inside of that railcar became more familiar to me than any home I've had since.

The morning they came for us is etched forever into my memory, deep at times, but never so deep that I cannot bring it forward to examine, to wonder that lives can be changed so swiftly and so completely. They promised futures we'd ceased to dream of, and they believed in their own promises. At least Caroline did.

Her image illuminates my memories of that day. Her image and her essence. I've heard it said that the nose is the most sensitive of our organs. That morning there was a new scent in the air, subtle and exotic and immediately at odds with the odors of furniture oil and that morning's porridge, of old books and young bodies. It clung to the woman as she entered the parlor, the hem of her plain serge skirt brushing the floor that Ivy had just swept. The man, with his lively step and quick smile, followed in her wake.

My immediate thought, as I peered at them from behind the heavy walnut settee in the hall, was that they had come to claim a child. Adam, most likely. He was our only baby. All of the handsome, young couples who came wanted infants, before—as I'd heard one prospective father say—they could be tainted by their proximity to the streets of Chicago. I crept closer, knowing I'd be punished for eavesdropping if caught but determined nonetheless.

If they took Adam, it would break Nell's heart. The morbidity of that thought drew me in spite of my dread.

Reverend Mac had opened the door of the orphanage himself, stepping from the room where he taught reading and writing to those of us old enough to learn. I'd followed, sneaking as close as I dared. That's what Mrs. Mac called everything I did. Sneaky. It was true enough, but I'd learned long ago that adults decided the fates of children, while the questions of children went unanswered and even punished—if asked of the wrong person. Or the right person at the wrong time.

The man did the talking at first, introducing himself as Jonathan Landreth and the woman as Caroline Markham. I thought him quite a dandy in his tight, nankeen trousers and double- breasted waistcoat with its little stand-up collar. Reverend Mac seemed fascinated by his stiffened cravat, touching his own soft, out-of-fashion neckcloth each time the dandy was forced to turn his entire upper body in order to look to the left or to the right.

Content to let the man speak, the woman sank gracefully onto the horsehair sofa, settling her skirts with a minimum of fuss, looking for all the world as if she were quite comfortable. I knew very well that she wasn't. Drawn by the elaborate scrolls of the woodwork and the delicate rose and moss green colors in the fabric, I'd once perched upon that sofa for all of five seconds before deciding the dubious pleasure of the forbidden was not worth the risk of being caught.

I stared at her, mesmerized. She reminded me of an etching I'd seen in a book and particularly liked. It had been of an elegant lady seated upon soft-looking grass at the very edge of a sunlit lake. A swan with an arched neck and satiny feathers fed from her hand. The tranquility of that scene had gripped me so strongly that, for one, futile moment, I'd wished I could step into the peace it exuded.

The man was not peaceful. He continued to stand in front of Reverend Mac, sometimes pacing in short turns as he spoke with an eloquent rise and fall of his voice until, at last, his words pulled my startled attention from the woman. They wanted, he said quite grandly, to give the children new homes. The children. Us.

"Which children?" I could hear caution in Reverend Mac's voice.

"All of them," Landreth said, waving his hand expansively.

"All of them?" The reverend's voice echoed my own disbelief.

Landreth nodded, obviously enjoying the drama of his pronouncement. Caroline Markham's expression remained serene. I was drawn to that serenity, but neither hopeful nor disturbed at this point. Whatever the man said, in the end, they would not want me. I'd been in the orphanage two years and had never come close to being forced from the haven it provided me.

It was my eyes, according to Mrs. Mac. Too large and dark, like a heathen's. "Folks don't like a child who looks sly and secretive," she would say, sometimes giving me a pinch to prove her point.

She was right. I'd seen it, that skittering away of glances when they crossed paths with mine. I didn't cause that reaction on purpose, but I wasn't sorry for it. I'd stayed safe through countless couples thinking to take on a child.

Even as I hovered uncertainly by the doorway, wondering if I should keep listening or run to warn the others, Caroline chanced to look my way. Her gaze caught and held mine, not probing or inquisitive, but intimate all the same. And her glance did not slide away in discomfort.

"Out West?" Reverend Mac almost squeaked the words, an amazing accomplishment considering his usual deep timbre.

Finally withdrawing her gaze from mine, Caroline spoke for the first time. "There are homes for these children. Wonderful opportunities for new lives with Christian families."

"We've made several such trips." Landreth hastened to re-establish his position of authority. "Placed dozens of children in God-led homes. Can't you picture it, sir?" He flung his hand outward as if pointing to the actual scene. "The train pulls in at the station and there await dozens of families eager to pick out their child!"

"Do you plan to sell these children?" Reverend Mac asked bluntly, his brows drawing together in a slashing straight line across his forehead.

"Merciful heavens, sir!" Landreth's sophisticated tone rose to an undignified bellow.

Caroline merely smiled, still unruffled. "We're members of the Christian Placement Society, a benevolent society devoted to the redemption of the lost children of this city."

"Then why are you not out gathering the lost? The streets abound with them."

If she took offense at Reverend Mac's pointed question, I couldn't tell it. "Our work is divided. There are those who have undertaken to bring the children in from the streets, and it is a difficult chore. Others of us have been given the task of gathering orphans already placed in county homes and orphanages. As we find safe homes for the children you have here, you will have room for others gathered from the alleys."

Reverend Mac sank back on his heels, his expression slightly mollified but still cautious.

The woman opened her reticule and withdrew several folds of paper. Before she could move toward the reverend, Landreth took them from her hastily and offered them in a pompous manner. "Our credentials, sir."

My heart began a slow crawl to my throat. Reverend Mac looked as if he was considering the suggestion. Surely, he wouldn't just hand us over to these strangers to pass out at random like puppies? For all their fine words, that's what it sounded like to me.

Before my dread could grow so large that I choked on it, a set of punishing fingers caught my ear and propelled me forward into the parlor. All eyes turned toward me, and I wanted to sink into the thin rug beneath my heels. Instead, I instinctively stiffened my spine at the first word from my tormentor.

"Sneaking about again, he is. Spying and eavesdropping. A lost cause this one." Mrs. Mac's voice reflected a wonderful pleasure in that final pronouncement.

A lost cause. The words hung in the air before drifting to rest at our feet. Reverend Mac shook his head in despair, as much that I'd been caught as that I'd been listening uninvited. Landreth nodded sagely. Caroline frowned. But she was frowning at Mrs. Mac.

"Ah, Henrietta, I'm glad you're home," Reverend Mac said gently.

She sniffed. "What should I do with *this* one?" Her pinch tightened on the lobe of my ear. I knew she'd be disappointed when she finally had to turn me loose.

"Send Lin back to the classroom, dear. I'll speak with him about this matter later." Reverend Mac gave me the tiniest of winks, imperceptible if I hadn't known to look for it.

Mrs. Mac harrumphed but released me. I cast one last glance at Caroline, wondering if I would see her again before she took the other children from here—if Reverend Mac allowed any of them to go.

Silence followed me from the room, and, as I crossed the hall, I saw Ivy hovering in the background as she tried to keep an eye on the two little ones and see what was going on at the same time. She knew her place too well to dare to eavesdrop, but her curiosity would be gnawing at her.

Nell and Ryan pounced on me as soon as I burst back into the classroom. I closed the door carefully behind me.

"Well?" Ryan demanded.

"What kind of child do they want?" Nell asked anxiously. "A boy?" Dread filled her voice.

Her words served to distract me from my recent humiliation at the hands of Mrs. Mac. I walked to the globe the reverend used in our lessons. Inspired by the drama of what I had to say, I placed my finger somewhere upon the western half of the continent. "They want to take us here. Out West."

"Us who?" Ryan demanded.

"All of us." But in my heart, I knew they really didn't mean to take me as well. They wouldn't have anyway, but especially not now. Not after I'd been caught eavesdropping. For the next half-hour or so I held sway. I could wax as eloquently as I pleased here in the safety of the children. Not just Nell and Ryan, but all of the children who had come and gone in the two years I'd been at the orphanage. They understood me, and whether they loved me, liked me, or merely tolerated me, they protected me. They'd all either guessed or been told my secret, and not one of them had betrayed me to the adults.

Enjoying my moment, I entertained them with actual details and sheer conjecture. I described the dandy in a less than kind manner, then told every detail I could recall of Caroline from her fashionably tiny feet and unfashionably slender form to her expressive eyes and golden-brown hair. But it was her voice that had most impressed me, and that I didn't describe at all. It was an angel's voice, I was convinced, soft and husky and warm. If I'd had a mother who loved me, I would have wanted her voice to sound like Caroline Markham's. I held the memory of that voice to me, something to treasure that I would not share.

"What do you mean she liked you?" Ryan asked belligerently at one point in my discourse. "She don't know you to like."

I didn't take offense. That was simply Ryan's response to any notion he considered typically female. And despite what the Reverend and Mrs. John MacIntosh believed me to be after two years under their roof, Ryan accepted me for the female that I was. And treated me accordingly.

"She did like me," I insisted simply. "She would like anyone, I think. Though she frowned at Mrs. Mac."

Nell snorted. "Little wonder, there, now, is it?"

Ryan had heard enough of the virtues of Caroline Markham. "I could be a cowboy!"

The excitement in his voice horrified me. "You can't want to go!"

Nell placed a hand on my arm. At thirteen, she was the oldest of us. I was twelve, but looked ten to those who thought me a boy. Ryan, my opposite with bright blue eyes, light hair, and a liberal sprinkling of pale freckles, was twelve, also, but twice my width through the shoulders, a clear promise of the man he would someday be.

"It would be exciting," Nell admitted. "A chance for a new life. As it is, none of us are going to leave here until we can hire out as laborers. At least not the three of us. There's still a chance for Rebekah."

I glared at Ryan, daring him to mention Adam and the fact that he was still a baby, still desirable for adoption. Adam was only eight months old. Prissy little blonde-ringleted Rebekah was four.

Ryan took the hint and held his tongue, but he looked as though he might choke on it.

"At least here we're together," I reminded softly.

That solemn reminder sobered them from their thoughts of adventure and things that could never happen. Being together meant something to the three of us. Something secure in an insecure world. Nell's past was so tragic, she would never talk about it. Ryan had lost a happy home and two loving parents within the same year, and me—I'd never had any kind of a home or been loved at all. As they stood staring at me, I took another turn around the room, my favorite at the orphanage. Perhaps because of its worn, rather threadbare furnishings and a fireplace that crackled and popped in the cold of winter. Or perhaps because it was here that Reverend Mac's deep voice read to us for hours at a time while Ivy, the day help, entertained Rebekah or rocked Adam. More likely, it was due to the fact that this was Reverend Mac's study, a room no one entered without express invitation, the one room Mrs. Mac almost never entered at all.

"Do you think we'll be made to go?" Ryan asked in subdued tones.

I turned, satisfied to hear the hint of hope gone from his voice. "I don't know," I answered without prevarication. "Mrs. Mac would sure like to see the last of me."

"I won't let them send you without me," Ryan said stoutly.

I smiled at him, feeling a prick of sadness. Of course, we knew we couldn't be together always. "You just want to go and be a cowboy. Besides, it's more likely they'll want to take the two of you and not me after I was caught listening and sent away in disgrace."

Nell tilted her head at my wistful tone. The knot of fiery red hair at the back of her head slipped a little further. Try as she might, Nell never managed to remain neat through an entire day. "But you don't want to go," she reminded.

"Of course, I don't." Still, I couldn't help a fleeting regret that today was all I would ever see of Caroline Markham's gentle nature. Though she was a stranger, she'd caught my imagination. Considering my circumstances, I'd long since given up hope of becoming a lady, but if I'd ever had the chance, I knew she was the kind of lady I'd want to be. But, that, I feared, was something bred, not learned.

The door squeaked a warning, and we fell silent, turning to face its slow opening. Mrs. Mac preceded the reverend into the room. She nearly preened with satisfaction, and I felt that lump grow in my throat once again.

"Children, please sit down." The reverend didn't preen. If anything, his moustache seemed to have taken on a rather sad droop.

I plopped to the rug with practiced lack of grace, drawing an immediate scowl from Mrs. Mac. I wasn't going to like this, I knew. I wasn't going to like it at all.

Nell sank down beside me while Ryan scooted up behind us.

We looked up with varying emotions. I could feel Ryan's anticipation, a silent hum at my back. He was all boy, worry as foreign to his nature as caution. I'd lived with fear too many years not to feel its resurgence now. I kept my eyes on Reverend Mac and away from Mrs. Mac. I didn't want to go, and I didn't want to stay, not without Ryan and Nell. But whichever it was to be, I knew I wouldn't be offered a choice in the matter. None of us would come to that.

"You've been given a wonderful chance, children. I've worried about you, about your futures here in the city." The words were brave, deliberately encouraging, but the sad look hadn't left Reverend Mac. "Nell, in little more than a year, you'll be past the age my congregation has established for orphans. You'll be expected to earn your own way. I've taught you all I can, but ...."

He didn't have to finish the thought. Females could marry, they could toil and toil for a few pennies a week from rich folks, or they could sell their bodies. We weren't supposed to know about the last, of course, but we all did. I better than most, perhaps.

"It isn't as if anyone will want to marry you," Mrs. Mac pointed out. "Not with that awful red hair and all those freckles."

"I can't truly agree, Henrietta. Nell has a disposition any man could wish for in a wife, but life *is* uncertain at its best." Reverend Mac smiled at Nell, obviously wishing he could take some of the sting from Mrs. Mac's words.

Mrs. Mac wasn't through with us. "It's clear you young people aren't going to be adopted around here. You've all been here too long and been passed over. Chicago is full of children needing homes, plenty of them babies. No, the three of you are much too old." Mrs. Mac folded her arms across her ample bosom, satisfied now that she'd had her say.

Reverend Mac cleared his throat. Mrs. Mac usually did have her say then she'd leave him to soften the bare facts as best he could. Somehow, I didn't think there was going to be any way to soften what was to come next.

"There are many societies—good Christian organizations—devoted to the placement of homeless children in the west. Mr. Landreth and Miss Markham belong to one of them."

"We're not homeless," I muttered in protest.

"Perhaps not completely, but an orphanage could never be considered a true home. Something much better awaits you children. Mr. Landreth has assured me that families in the West are desperate for children. So many babies are lost at birth or in the first few years."

He looked down at us expectantly. I wondered what he thought we should say, what we should feel about being sent to replace dead children. Apparently, the West wasn't a very healthy place. Did he wonder if we would die and need to be replaced in a year or two? Well, I supposed we were old enough and strong enough we'd be all right, but what about Adam and Rebekah? What would happen to them?

I knew that Nell was thinking the same. She would have no worries for herself, only for Adam. She had cared for him from the day he'd been thrust at Reverend Mac by a wild-eyed woman who'd pounded on the door of the orphanage in the middle of a wintry night. For all Adam knew, Nell was his mother, and as far as her heart was concerned, he was her baby.

"Lin, I only want what is best for you."

"You're an adult." That said enough as far as I was concerned. Though I'd come to love and trust Reverend Mac in the time I'd been at the orphanage, he was still one of them. He'd have an answer for every fear we could think to voice. Answers that would make him feel better, but wouldn't do much for us. I wouldn't waste any more of my time either speaking or listening. His mind had been made before he came in. He believed he knew what was best for us.

I turned my face from him and looked into the hearth, cold since the first day of May two weeks earlier. Ivy had swept it clean—barren of any sign of remembered warmth.

If Reverend Mac looked at me, he would see the sullenness that always saddened him and infuriated his wife, but my feelings of being betrayed were too strong. I couldn't force a smile to make him feel better even though I knew I owed him at least that much.

"Reverend?"

"Yes, Ryan?"

"When ..." Ryan cleared his throat and started again. "When are we to leave?"

While Reverend Mac paused to wipe at the moisture in his eyes, Mrs. Mac took charge. "In the morning, and we've lots to do before then. It may not be washday," she added briskly, "but I'll not have it said I sent you off with dirty clothes. Lucky, it's still early and there's a drying breeze. Nell, Ivy will need your help. Ryan, you'll fill the wash tub. It takes Lin all day to carry that much water. He can watch Adam and Rebekah while I finish my baking."

As usual, she spoke of me as if I didn't have sense enough to comprehend. If there was anything hopeful about the thought of leaving Reverend Mac and the one place I'd felt safe in my twelve years, it was the thought of leaving Mrs. Mac behind as well. She was already moving toward the door as she spoke the last sentence, and I shot a hostile look toward her back not even caring if Reverend Mac saw it.

He did. He was looking right at me when I looked up, but the only thing I read in his expression was love. "If I didn't believe this was best for you children, I would never let you go."

I knew that. Even without him saying it, I knew it. I tried, really tried to tell him so, but the tightness in my throat just got worse and worse. When I felt tears burning my eyes, I scrambled to my feet and raced from the room.

My foot was on the first step when I heard Nell tell him, "It's alright, Reverend Mac, I'll go talk to him. It'll be alright, you'll see."

But I knew Nell was wrong. It was never going to be alright again.

I began writing in the heyday of the bodice rippers. Not that what I wrote fit really well into that genre. It didn't. But, after adding the two obligatory sex scenes to each book as required by my editor, and acquiescing to covers which included the ripped bodice, or a reasonable facsimile, I became—for a few years—one of Leisure Books midlist authors in that genre. Not a bad place to be but not what I'd planned. My stories did get read and I did make money. So, there is that!

Then I wrote what I thought of as *just a story. Leisure*, an imprint of Dorchester Publishing, loved it and offered a three-book contract for it and two more young adult books to go with it. Young adult? That was how *Leisure* regarded it, much to my dismay! But—I thought in bewilderment—I don't know *how* to write young adult. After a few botched exchanges between my agent and *Leisure* and me, I walked away in frustration. Silly me.

From there I wrote two historical romances never published and two pieces of historical romances never finished. Only in the last decade have I come to realize that all four of them fit more in line with historical intrigue than historical romance. Maybe someday.

But understanding, now, where those last efforts fall in regard to genre, gave me the confidence to say, yes, when Carolyn Haines asked me to join her in The Trouble Cat Mysteries. I love those fun and witty intrigues. I love the dose of solid mystery, the light touch of romance, and our feline detective with his own point of view and a very clever way with words...er...thoughts.

But that never published *just a story*? I'm dusting it off and taking a fresh look. The poor thing was never given a proper name. I called it The Orphans. And, yes, it *is* clearly young adult. Don't tell them I said so, but agents and editors and publishers do understand marketing. My *work in progress* is the first chapter as it was written so long ago.

Susan Y. Tanner blends her passion for horses with her passion for writing. In *Trouble in Summer Valley,* she introduced readers to the rescue horses of Summer Valley Ranch where they prove their worth in therapeutic riding. *In Turning for Trouble,* her own rodeo experience brings that rough and tumble world to life. *Trouble in Action* showcases the risky profession of stunt riding while giving a glimpse into historical reenactments. A *Whisper of Trouble* provides insight into a talent practiced by few—the art of horse whispering. Her next in the series, *Trail of Trouble*, is scheduled for a January 2022 release. Published by KaliOka Press, these romantic mysteries feature a super-sleuth in the form of a black cat detective. They are part of the *Trouble Cat Detective* series written in concert with some very talented authors.

Ms. Tanner's first five historical romances—*Highland Captive, Captive* to a *Dream, Exiled Heart, Fire Across Texas, Winds Across Texas,* and *A Warm Southern Christma*s (a novella)—have been rereleased by Secret Staircase Books, an imprint of Columbine Publishing. All were previously published by Leisure Books. Her sixth historical romance, *Storm Out of Texas*, was also published by Secret Staircase Books.

When she's not at her desk, Ms. Tanner can usually be found in the barn or on a horse.

The Solace of a True Center
Linda Carrillo

"Wake up! Virgil, wake up!"

A mumble came from under the covers. He poked his head out and squinted at me in the clouded moonlight. "What? What's wrong?"

"Someone's pounding on the front door." In the next second, he heard it for himself. Pulling on my robe as I started for the stairs, I ran to catch up, grabbing the railing. Had Scott's father found the boys in the Quaker Meetinghouse and they'd run here? Nothing at this time of night boded well. I was halfway down the stairs when I heard a woman screaming.

"It's Maggie!" I yelled to Virgil.

He wrenched open the door and Maggie stood before us, doubled over, breathing hard and coughing. "Fire! Store," she gasped.

"Are you all right? Where are the children?" When she didn't answer at first, her eyes riveted on mine, I repeated, "The children? Where are Cooper and Abby?"

"Car," she motioned behind her.

"Did you call the fire department?" Virgil asked.

"Couldn't. Had to get out. Smoke."

Virgil ran to get his protective clothes and boots. Like most of the men in the area, he'd trained as a firefighter and had served on the volunteer department for several stints. "Go get the children," I instructed Maggie. "I'll call for help."

After calling the fire department, I returned to the living room with a glass of water for Maggie. She hadn't moved from the door, and I wondered if she were in shock. "Let's go get the children and bring them inside." She nodded, finished the water, and, instead of handing me the glass, uncurled her fingers, letting the glass fall to the floor and shatter.

"Oh, no!"

"Not a problem," I told her gently. "We'll clean it up in a minute. Let's go get the children." She followed me to the car. When Cooper tumbled out, dragging a blanket behind him, he asked, "Why are we here, Mama? Has Daddy come back? Why are you crying?"

Blinking her eyes hard, Maggie swiped at her face with both hands. "No, baby, it's not about your daddy. The fire scared me, that's all, but we're fine here. Mr. Virgil has gone to take care of things, and the fire trucks will be there soon."

Cooper looked dazed, and I knew it frightened him to flee his home in the middle of the night. I tried not to think about our son and his friends hiding in the Meetinghouse. They're smart and decisive, I told myself. They would have acted quickly if the fire had spread through the woods. They had to be safe; surely I would have felt something had it been otherwise, would have felt it thrumming within my bones, an urgent quickening of my pulse.

I stooped down to Cooper's level. "Until everything is taken care of at your place, why don't we have a sleepover here? And if your mama agrees, how about a cup of hot chocolate? It will make it easier for you to go back to sleep."

Skirting the broken glass, we gathered in the kitchen with Abby in Maggie's lap and Cooper counting out marshmallows on the table. By the time we'd finished the cocoa and gotten the children settled in the guest room, I heard our clock chime twice as Maggie and I returned downstairs.

"We should call Grady and Delia, though someone may have notified them already." I refilled Maggie's cup.

"No, they went away for a few days. Delia's aunt is doing poorly, so they went to Norfolk to see her. They've been calling me every day, so I can tell them later. Lordy, I hope it's not too bad. They've been so good to me. And Virgil and Grady just finished turning the upstairs into my apartment."

"Do you know how the fire started? Was something on in the store's kitchen?"

"No! Eleanor, I triple-check *everything*, every night! I check the windows, the stove burners, the oven, the lights, the doors—in the store and in my apartment—before I go to bed."

I stopped her. "I'm not blaming you. I'm simply wondering how the fire started."

She lowered her head and whispered, "Sorry. I'm not sure. I didn't see fire inside the store, only smoke. Maybe it was in the attic."

The lights of Virgil's truck flashed in the windows. As soon as he came in, before I could ask, he said, "I think they're safe." Maggie looked puzzled but didn't ask for an explanation.

Leaning against the sink, Virgil drained the glass of water I'd given him. "The fire's contained. Most of the damage was on the corner with the storeroom, and part of the roof is gone. Maggie, it affected your apartment, as well. You can stay with us as long as you need to. The children especially can't be around the smoke. I came back long enough to report in, but I need to go back out."

"Go on ahead to the truck, and I'll fill a thermos with water and bring it to you." It would give me a chance to talk to Virgil privately; he'd said he *thought* the boys were safe, not that he knew they were. After filling the thermos, I grabbed apples and bananas out of the fruit bowl on my way outside. "I'll be back in a minute, Maggie. Answer the phone if it rings, please."

I hurried down the back porch steps to the truck. Virgil took the thermos and stuffed the fruit in his pockets. "Thanks. When the fire at the store was mostly under control, Josiah and I drove to the Meetinghouse to check on the boys. It was on fire, too."

"The boys?" My mouth dried, my words becoming fragments of tangled wool.

"They weren't there. I checked every room, every closet. The fire was extensive, but they wouldn't have been trapped."

"But where are they?" I tried to keep the panic from ballooning into a recognizable shape. "Is it possible whoever set the fires . . . could Scott's father have gotten them?"

"Don't go thinking the worst. I bet they heard the commotion and bailed out the back. They know these woods inside out, so I'm sure they're at their fort, which is where I'm going next."

I gave him a quick kiss before he left, smelling the acrid smoke and soot as I stood on my tiptoes and leaned into the truck. "I'll find them, Eleanor. They weren't in the Meetinghouse."

***

I told Maggie about the second fire, and we were still in the kitchen when Virgil returned half an hour later. He gave me a thumbs-up gesture and went to take a shower. Until we were alone, his signal would have to suffice, and I unclenched my hands, lofting a silent prayer of thanksgiving.

"Wow, I feel better," he said when he returned, accepting a cup of coffee and a ham biscuit from me.

"This will tide you over until I make breakfast. What kind of damage did the Meetinghouse suffer?" The building, a Methodist church before we acquired it, was almost a century old, and I loved every board, every corner of it, the way the light suffused the room, the bubbles in the original glass panes, the pews worn into glossy smoothness.

"Could have been worse. We'll need a new entrance, front porch, and steps. The siding on the east wall and part of the roof will need to be replaced. The education wing fared better since it's brick. At least we kept the fire from extending into the woods."

"Captain Alvis was there?" I asked about our county's fire marshal.

"Yes. They called him when they realized two separate fires had been set at the same time. He'll need to wait for full daylight before figuring it out. A crew is there and at the store, keeping watch." Virgil turned to Maggie. "One of Grady and Delia's neighbors helped put out the fire. He knew they were gone to Delia's aunt's place, so he said he'd call them."

"Oh, thank goodness. I was dreading telling them."

Virgil drank more water. "Captain Alvis wants to talk to you."

"I didn't start the fire! I didn't leave anything on, I swear to you! I've been nothing but careful! I told Eleanor I triple-checked everything."

Virgil looked taken aback. "I wasn't implying you're to blame,

Maggie."

"I did it again, didn't I?" she murmured, and I realized her reactions were one of the legacies from her abusive marriage.

I tried to soothe her. "It's all right. It's been an upsetting and scary night for you."

"They were two separate fires," Virgil emphasized. "It didn't start at the store and spread through the woods to the Meetinghouse. You did a wonderful job getting you and the children to safety and alerting us. We owe you our thanks; had it not been for your fast action, we could have lost so much more. Truly, the only important thing is that you and the children are safe. Captain Alvis will want to ask you if you heard or saw anything, that's all."

Maggie looked away, and I got the strong feeling she knew something she wasn't divulging. I decided not to press her until she was less distraught. I thought of the advice the boys had received at their graduation party: Most things really do look better in the morning.

***

Maggie left to check on the children and to try to get more sleep herself. With her gone, I concentrated on Virgil and saw the weariness in his eyes. "Were they hurt?"

"No, thank God. They got out in time without inhaling much smoke. I brought them with me, and they're in the barn. When Scott heard Maggie and her children are here, he wouldn't agree to come inside. They'll be fine; I locked them in, and Morgan has a key. They're exhausted and are probably already asleep." He drew a hand over his face and shook his head.

I grasped he hadn't told me everything. "What else?"

"We found a burned cross in the front yard, as well as a couple of torches."

I felt a slithering coldness and recognized it as a personification of evil. "The KKK."

"Yes."

"Because we held a worship service with Mount Gilead?"

"I imagine so."

"All because black and white folks got together to pray and sing.

When will it end? When will people run out of hatred?" I asked.

Making sure everything was off in the kitchen, we started to our bedroom to get a few hours of sleep, although the sun was on the verge of rising. Virgil turned around and pulled a quilt and a throw pillow off the sofa. "On second thought, I'm going to sleep in the barn."

"Thank you." I reached up to hug him, comforted by his strength, by his recognition I'd feel better if he stayed with the boys. "I won't worry as much." When he left the kitchen, I locked the door behind him, realizing we'd need to make locking up a permanent habit now.

***

After driving through the night to return to Drake's Springs, Grady and Delia came by and insisted on taking Maggie and the children to their house. "Are you sure?" I asked. "They certainly can stay with us until the apartment is repaired and cleared of smoke."

"Thank you kindly," Grady said, "but we'll be fine for a few days. It'll be like campin' out. I know Delia will feel better bein' able to keep a watchful eye on her chicks." He ruffled Cooper's hair.

Putting her arm around Maggie, Delia pulled her close and reached out to clasp my hand. "We're grateful Maggie had someone she could run to. We're beholden to you."

"Not at all. Maggie saved your store and the Meetinghouse by her quick thinking. We're beyond thankful they weren't hurt. You let us know how we can help with the cleanup and rebuilding."

"Don't you worry none," Grady told me. "It won't take much to put it to rights. And we'll help with the Meetinghouse. That beautiful little church has been here forever; we're glad to hear it can be saved."

Delia guided the children outside. "Come along, my precious chickadees. We'll enjoy a big ol' breakfast together and then get to work."

When I entered the kitchen and looked out the window, I saw the boys crossing the yard from the barn. Meeting them halfway, I hugged each one, running my hands over their shoulders, down their arms. They reeked of smoke and were filthy, but I saw no worrisome signs.

"We're fine," Morgan promised, shrugging me off but giving me a smile, nonetheless.

"Go get showers. Morgan, pull together whatever clothes they need; you're about the same size. By the time you're done, I'll have breakfast on the table."

"Thanks. We're famished," Scott told me.

Before beginning breakfast I went outside and found Virgil. When he drew me to him, I once again savored his closeness, taking in his distinctive smell, feeling safely enclosed in his arms. I craned my neck back and looked at him. "Go ahead and say it: 'I told you so.' The boys were safe."

"A mother hen has the prerogative to worry about her chicks."

"You and Delia. That's what she calls Abby and Cooper, and Maggie, too, for that matter. While you were asleep, she and Grady came by for them. Come in for breakfast and we'll get the story from the boys."

Virgil tended the pancakes and started the coffee while I made bacon and eggs. The boys hadn't eaten much since lunchtime yesterday, and I wanted a breakfast to linger over.

"Slowly," I cautioned, as they began wolfing down the food. "I don't want you to get sick."

"Don't you two have to get to work?" Morgan asked. "It's getting late."

"We're both taking the day off. We didn't get much sleep last night, and I know I wouldn't be able to concentrate," I said.

Scott reached for another pancake. "You're playing hooky," he said in a singsong.

"With a breakfast like this, I could get used to it," Virgil told him.

We let them eat without asking for details until they finished. I poured more coffee all around and cleared the dishes.

"What happened?" Virgil asked. "Take your time and tell us everything."

I got up and found a pad of paper. "I'm going to take notes; it's too easy to forget the specifics later."

Scott started. "We decided to play cards in the fellowship hall since the only windows down there face the back. We tacked up an old tarp over them, anyway, and used a lamp from the office rather than put the overhead lights on."

Jacob took up the story. "I heard a sound. At first I thought it was the wind since we've been expecting a storm. Then I heard a rattle, like someone was trying to get in the door. We'd made sure all the doors and windows were locked, though, when we arrived. In fact, Scott and I had tested all the doors and Morgan checked behind us. When we heard the rattling, we didn't even stand up but crawled upstairs; Morgan knew of an out-of-the-way closet where we could hide."

"The closet in the children's room. So much stuff is in front of it that it's hard to see," Morgan explained. "But on the way there, we smelled, then saw, smoke. I'm sorry, but we didn't take the time to go back to the office to call for help. We saw flames as we ran out the back door and into the woods. I suppose we panicked."

"No, you did absolutely the right thing, exactly what we've always told you," Virgil reassured them. "Seconds count in a fire. We can always rebuild, but we cannot replace the three of you."

"How much was ruined?" Scott asked.

"We lost the entry, the front porch and steps," Virgil told them. "Some siding and part of the roof will need to be replaced. Of course, there's quite a lot of smoke and water damage inside, but we can repair or rebuild it."

"I guess the rattling we heard wasn't someone trying to break in, after all, but the fire," Scott said.

Virgil placed his dishes in the sink. "I'm sure Captain Alvis will want to question you. He was with the team that responded last night."

Morgan looked alarmed. "We were careful, Dad. We didn't use the oven in the kitchen. The lamp was the only thing on, but we turned it off when we heard the noise."

"We weren't smoking," Jacob added. "You've gotta believe us; we've kept our promise to you."

"I believe you. You're not in trouble; you had our permission to be there, and from what we've seen so far, the fire started outside the Meetinghouse." Virgil hesitated, as though weighing how much he wanted to tell them. "It was arson."

"Someone deliberately set the fire?" Scott asked.

"Yes. There was also a fire at the general store, but it didn't ruin as much as at the Meetinghouse."

Jacob asked, "Was it arson because it would have been too great a coincidence to have two fires on the same night?"

"That's part of it. The woods didn't burn between the two, so the fire didn't start at one place and spread to the other."

"Why would someone want to burn down the store and our Meetinghouse?" Morgan asked.

"Concerning the store, we don't know. As for the Meetinghouse, we suspect it's because we got together with your church, Jacob. We found a burned cross in the front yard."

"We don't have a cross at the Meetinghouse," Morgan said.

"The KKK," Jacob answered, his voice flat and resigned.

"Yes. That's what they commonly do. Did you tell anyone you'd be staying at the Meetinghouse?" Virgil looked at each one of them.

"No," Morgan replied, "I didn't even tell Jenny. Besides, after our meeting, we didn't leave, remember? None of us called anyone. Dad, you brought us items from the fort; did anyone follow you, was anyone around who saw you at the time?"

"I kept watching for someone, but no."

I collected our empty coffee cups. "Scott, obviously, you can't continue to stay at the Meetinghouse until you go to Canada. It's not safe there, not to mention the smoke and lack of electricity. We'll make other arrangements."

"Jacob, I'm going to take you home," Virgil decided. "We should have called your parents before now. Word spreads fast, so let's go. I don't want them worried. And until we know more about what's going on, I don't want you and Morgan walking or biking around. I don't think you need to be scared, but be aware of your surroundings. Make sure you're not alone, either."

The boys went to get their belongings out of the barn, but before Virgil and I could leave the kitchen, the phone rang, startling us. I whirled around to get it. It was Jacob's father.

"Good morning, Alden. I was getting ready to call you and let you know Virgil is bringing Jacob home. Look, everyone is safe, but someone set a fire at the Meetinghouse and the general store last night. The boys got out and spent the rest of the night in our barn. They weren't hurt." Virgil got up and stood next to me in order to listen in.

Alden groaned. "Ah, no, not your place, too, and the store."

"Wait a minute, are you saying there was a fire at your house? Or at Mount Gilead?"

"The church. It's in bad shape. They left a burned cross in the front yard."

Bile rose in my throat. "The KKK's favorite calling card. They left one at the Meetinghouse, as well."

"I wonder if despite all our precautions, someone saw us worshipping together yesterday. That doesn't explain the store, though. Is your fire department investigating?"

"Yes, the county's fire marshal has already been on the scene."

"Sometimes local fire departments don't look too closely or investigate too long at a black church's fire. We'll see if we become a local test case for the most recent hate crime legislation under the Civil Rights Act." I could hear a tinge of bitterness in Alden's voice.

Virgil leaned in and said, "We'll tell Captain Alvis about Mount Gilead and ask him to contact his counterpart in Nelson County. I'm on my way now with Jacob. I've cautioned the boys not to go around by themselves."

"Good advice. Thanks for making sure they were safe. Have they picked up Scott?"

"Not yet. We're going to make other arrangements for him in the meantime."

"Sure didn't take someone long," Virgil mused after I hung up the phone. "I can understand their going after the Meeting and Mount Gilead. It isn't the first time we've each been threatened, and it won't be the last. What I can't understand is why they'd go after the store. We'll see if anything shakes out of the investigation."

"Remember when we were walking home after yesterday's service, and I thought I'd heard something in the woods?"

"Yes, but we attributed it to the squirrel we saw."

"What if the squirrel was simply a coincidence, and I actually heard a person? What if someone is watching us?" Virgil gave me a startled look; he was not a man who was easily unnerved, and I felt a frisson of foreboding.

Virgil and Jacob left, and Scott and Morgan went upstairs to get more sleep. I welcomed the mundane tasks of cleaning up the kitchen and sweeping the floor, wishing I could sweep away as easily the images of burned crosses and scared boys. And Maggie, terrified and shaking, clutching her children, her eyes wild with a smoldering fear and some other emotion I couldn't quite place. All at once, I yanked a plate out of the soapy water. Anger. She was furious.

Despite the sea changes of the late 1960s—civil rights protests, antiwar demonstrations, women's liberation—the Shenandoah Valley town of Drake's Springs, Virginia, is an idyllic place. That begins to change in one night, however, when someone sets fire to the general store, the Quaker Meetinghouse, and an AME church across the mountains. The upheaval continues when the local draft board denies Virgil and Eleanor Schoenfeld's son, Morgan, conscientious objector status even though he is a Quaker. Everything begins to unravel when the events start to point to one man, just as Hurricane Camille makes an unexpected turn and heads straight for Virginia.

Linda Carrillo is a former English teacher who lives in Keller, Texas, with her husband, a merry little beagle, and a grumpy kitty. She is working on her second novel, *The Solace of a True Center,* which is set twenty years earlier than her first book, *In the Light of Silence*.

Contact information:
lcarrillo024@yahoo.com

In Less Than A Year

Barbara Conrey

Every Friday afternoon, the senior partners gathered in the smaller of the two rooms designed for staff and client meetings to discuss new assignments, who was available among the mid level and junior associates to perform the grunt work on those assignments, and the status of ongoing cases.

Yawn. Jake was there by invitation. Not that Jake was a senior partner. Not yet anyway. Two years ago, he made junior partner and was shuttled into an office with a window and a view of the brick wall on the north side of the medical office building next door. The rest of the firm only noticed Jake's change of address when they needed to pass along some grunt work beneath their pay grade. Jake, on the other hand, knew he was on his way to fulfilling his dream.

Jake daydreamed of business cards stenciled with the title Senior Partner, but at that moment, he was seated at the teak conference table by invitation to get a feel for how the big boys played.

Stephen Cranston, *the* senior partner, the only one with his name on the wall, watched as Brian, the firm's newest partner, delivered the latest in a multitude of snags with the class action suit against the emergency air transportation company, AIR FAST, a case long overdue for settlement. Just as Brian reached the meat of the matter, Stephen looked up as if someone had tapped him on the shoulder, "What time is it?"

Six arms cocked their wrists simultaneously, but the winner was Brian.

"1:15," Brian fairly yelped.

Jake almost smiled at Brian's eagerness. And then he stopped smiling. "1:15? Shit!" Pushing back his chair, he grabbed his notes and stormed out of the conference room, completely forgetting to hold the door so that it didn't slam shut on his way out.

The remaining men, somewhat startled by Jake's hasty exit, took a moment to look at each other with slight amusement in their eyes at what they clearly considered an overreaction of some sort before assuming the back-to-business position.

Stephen made a point of jotting a note to himself in his daily planner before calling the meeting to a close.

When Jake reached his office, Amy, Jake's secretary, had just placed a file on his desk as he shot past her, nearly knocking her off her feet, "Sorry," he had the decency to mutter, "I'm in a rush."

"What's wrong?"

"I don't have time right now; I'm late." Jake grabbed his briefcase, dug his hand into his pocket for his car keys, decided it would be faster to catch a cab, and practically ran Amy over again on his way out the door.

Flagging down a cab, he jerked open the door and threw himself into the back seat. "South Willard. I'm in a rush." He slammed shut the cab door, anticipating that the cabbie understood his need for speed and would quickly pull away from the curb.

Instead, the cabbie turned to look at him. "Gonna give me the rest of the address, Mr. In A Big Rush?"

"Just start driving." Plugging the name of the center into his phone, he yelled, "2544. Now move." The cabbie finally pulled away from the curb while Jake rechecked his watch, "Shit!"

It seemed like an hour, but minutes later, the cabbie pulled in front of Jake's destination while Jake flung money at him and jumped out.

"Buddy, you really need to take it easy; you know what I mean?" The cabbie breathed in deeply and let it out slowly. "Be in your moment." Then he laughed and pulled away from the curb while Jake straightened his tie and walked into the building. Muttering, "Shit!"

Jake stopped at the bank of elevators and looked at the wall plaque listing the offices on each floor: A Promise To Keep Surrogacy Center. Fifth floor, Room 502. He didn't even know what kind of place this was or why he was here; he just knew that Sophia had begged him to meet her here. And he'd agreed. He still wasn't sure why.

Pasting a smile on his face, Jake was led to an office similar to his own, except this office had a great view of a small park and Mt. Mansfield in the distance. He'd kill for this office. Jake imagined that the woman sitting behind the desk could at her leisure swivel her char around and stare into all that freedom any time she wanted.

Flashing Sophia a big smile, he swooped in for a quick kiss and slipped into the chair next to her as if he'd just stepped out for some air but was back, ready to proceed. He'd arrived just in time to hear Ms. Boden—according to the nameplate on her desk—explain surrogacy jargon, most of which Sophia apparently knew.

"Wait a minute. What is this?"

Jake knew he sounded as clueless as he felt while he waited for an explanation. Ms. Boden and Sophia looked at each other until finally, Sophia spoke.

"I want to have a baby."

Jake stood. Irritated that he'd left work—making a damn fool of himself in the process—to discuss what had been decided years ago in front of a perfect stranger. "Sophia, you know we decided we wouldn't have any more children. And I hardly think this is the place… "

For some reason that Jake couldn't fathom since this was clearly a personal conversation, Ms. Boden took it upon herself to answer for Sophia.

"I think what your wife is trying to say, Mr. Trenton, is that she wants to be a surrogate. She wants to have a baby for someone else."

Jake stood, looked from Ms. Boden to Sophia, barely understanding what he'd just heard. "Oh, for Christ's sake. I'm leaving. Are you coming?"

When Jake turned toward the door, Sophia stood, and without saying a word to each other or Ms. Boden, they walked out the door, if not in unity, at least side by side.

In Less Than A Year is my current work-in-progress; it's a two-person point-of-view story where one of the main characters is male. I thought it would be fun to create a 'flawed' man (who could I possibly model him after?) that could become a better human being after I put him through some pain and suffering.

What woman will be able to pass this up???

The connection between my two main characters, Jake and Sophia, is that they were both raised by overbearing, controlling parents.

Jake bluffs his way through life even though he is deeply stigmatized from his past. He remembers the night his brother died. But it is only as an adult that he remembers everything that happened that night. His father yelling. His brother falling to his knees. Both Jake and his brother muttering simultaneously, "Dad… "

Sophia, Jake's wife, tries her best to be the wife her mother raised and the wife Jake expects her to be. Until she can't.

Barbara Conrey is the USA Today Bestselling author of NOWHERE NEAR GOODBYE, published on August 4th, 2020, by Red Adept Publishing.

NOWHERE NEAR GOODBYE is Barbara Conrey's debut novel.

Previously, Barbara worked in the health care industry before opting for an early retirement, which lasted all of three months. She then accepted a finance position, for which she had absolutely no background, and four years later, she decided to write a book. But not about finance.

Travel is her passion, along with reading, writing, hiking, and exploring antique shops. Her greatest love is Miss Molly, her rescue beagle. There are stories to be told about beagles, and Barbara hopes to incorporate some of them into her books.

Barbara lives in Pennsylvania, close to family and friends.

Social Media Sites:

www.facebook.com/baconreywriter

www.Twitter.com/barbaraconrey

www.Instagram.com/barbara

Barbara Conrey Books - BookBub

Website: www.barbaraconreyauthor.com

Aucilla Hall Wilderness School

Claire Matturro and Penny Koepsel

The guard stuck his hand in the trash can full of water and laughed. He flicked his wet fingers at Carley, splattering her face with ice-cold droplets.

She nearly choked as the guard rubbed a long-handled scrubbing brush over his hand. This close, she could smell the rancid sweat off his body.

Carley looked away, still not convinced they were going to do this to her. As she swung her head toward the gate and the way out, she spotted Mouse hunched against the fence. His big blue eyes stared at her and his lips hung open like he was going to scream.

How's he stay alive here? And not go crazy?

How am I gonna stay alive?

A woman guard dumped more ice cubes into the trash can and turned to Carley. "Awrighty, take your clothes off."

Carley shook her head. Her mouth was too dry for her to speak. All this for backtalking a guard. Back home in the trailer park, she'd sassed Mom and Dad and all those stupid teachers, and nobody ever did anything except give her dirty looks or yell back. But here at Aucilla Hall Wilderness School for Delinquents, other kids had tried to warn her: keep your mouth shut and your eyes down.

Now they were going to dunk her in the GI bath. That's what they called this ice water and wire brush scrubbing.

The woman guard snatched the front of Carley's shirt and dragged her toward the trash can. She fought, but the woman was strong, and one of the men helped her, yanking at the zipper on Carley's jeans so hard she fell down. Once they had her naked, they threw her into the ice and water.

She peed, feeling the faint warmth of her own urine for a second or two before the cold bit into her skin. She screamed as the man took the brush and started rubbing it up and down on her back. The bristles felt like tiny razor blades ripping into her skin.

Though the water was ice cold, Carley felt like she was on fire.

***

There were no large cities close by, no civilization, no kindness.

It didn't matter. Carley was getting out of this hellhole. She shuddered as she planned her escape from Aucilla Hall.

If she made it through the busted glass bottles the guards scattered around the trailer, she'd have to climb the chain length fence with the barbed wire strung across the top. She had done that before and knew she would get cut, but that wouldn't kill her, and the guards might.

Carley sweated and shivered at the same time in the dark kitchen of the crappy old trailer. She could tell from the stars that it was well past midnight. They didn't have a clock in the whole damn trailer. The guards had taken her shoes away and hidden them after she'd tried—again—to escape and then they made her run back and forth across the compound till she fell and almost passed out. All those sandspurs and rocks and sticks. She wasn't used to going barefoot.

As Carley peered out the barred window of the trailer's only door, the moonlight shined off the shards, their jagged edges glimmering in a random, scattered pattern. But that wasn't the worst of it. Aucilla was nothing but a dump full of old house trailers out in the middle of nowhere, with Houston the nearest big city but closer to the town of Liberty. What really worried her were those miles of palmettos thickets and slash pines with nothing or nobody anywhere close by except snakes, scorpions, and coyotes. Running through that scrubland barefoot terrified her. But that was the only way she was going to get out of here.

While everyone else was at supper, Carley had ripped up her sheets and hidden them. Now, moving as quiet as she could so she didn't wake the other girls in her trailer, she pulled the cloth out from behind an old couch that smelled like puke. She wrapped her feet in the sheets and tied the thin cotton as best she could. They looked more like bandages than socks and sure weren't anything like a pair of shoes.

Carley took a few steps. The cold from the linoleum floor came through the ragged cloth. Those sheets weren't going to help much. Still, it was better than nothing.

She took out the kitchen knife she'd stolen earlier that day and pried open the jerry-rigged catch on the trailer door. *Cheap bolt.* If she ever saw her brother again, she owed him a favor for teaching her how to bust through most locks. She pushed open the door, listened to see if she could hear anybody stirring, then opened it wider. Inhaling deeply, Carley tiptoed down the steps. Cautiously, she surveyed the area before stepping on the ground. With any luck at all, she could see the shards of glass well enough in the moonlight to keep from stepping on them.

Not more than three feet from the fence, she stopped. She heard somebody running—sounded like it was coming from behind the concrete block building they pretended was a school. She eyed the trailer but didn't think she'd have time to get back inside. Anyway, the busted lock would give her away.

Caught in the open compound, Carley pulled out the kitchen knife and waited.

Fat lot of good that dinky shit knife will do against one of the guards. But there wasn't any place for her to run but across the compound to the fence and the footsteps were already too close. She waited, her throat closing up so that it was hard to breathe.

Mouse sprinted around the corner of the concrete building, partially hidden in the shadows but Carley knew it was him. He was small and quick. In a second or two, he broke out of the shadows and the moonlight practically bounced off his bald head. One of the guards had cut off his bangs, nearly yanked his chin-length hair out with dull scissors and shaved his head.

Earlier that day, Carley had warned Mouse she was leaving tonight. Now, as he ran toward her, he had something in his hands.

He's going to come with me. Carley exhaled in relief and stepped over to meet him.

"Here," he shoved a brown grocery sack into her hands. "Shoes. Shiny ones, and new. Socks too." He was huffing and she shushed him, hissing air through her dry lips and shaking her head.

Carley clasped the package against her chest, spun her head around, and looked for any other movement in the compound. She didn't see anybody else and tilted her head toward the fence, motioning for Mouse to follow her. Walking as lightly as she could, she eased over the rough soil toward the chain link fence and the barbed wire. Mouse panted right beside her. Carley glanced down. He had on a pair of socks, but no shoes.

Near the fence, she pulled Mouse to the ground behind a stunted, half-bare Chinaberry tree and scrunched up beside him. Hurrying, but trying to be quiet, she pulled the shoes out of the bag. Men's. Florsheim, wingtip oxfords. They looked huge.

"Where'd you get these?"

Mouse shrugged. Then he looked up, met her eyes in the dull light from the stars and the three-quarter moon. "From the cottage." As soon as he said it, he dropped his head and shuddered.

Carley patted his hand but didn't take the time to hug him or say how sorry she was. Instead, she tore off the stupid, useless sheets and tugged on the socks, grateful for their thickness. She crammed her feet in the shoes, laced them as tight as she could, then stuffed the heels with shreds of the sheets. Mouse kept looking around like he expected a guard to swoop down and grab him.

"I know they're too big, but that's all I could get. Least ways the socks'll help." Mouse's voice was so low Carley leaned forward to hear. "Here, take mine too." He pulled off his own socks and handed them over.

"Come with me," she said. "It's the only way you've got any kind of chance."

Mouse shook his head. "They ..the shoes…were left in …his…his bedroom. In the closet."

"Come with me, please," Carley said.

"I can't, you know I can't. My old man would just send me back here. 'Sides, how would Dana know where to find me if I leave?"

Carley didn't even think Dana was still alive. She'd disappeared a couple of weeks ago, and nobody knew anything about her. Carley figured she was buried in that pit out back behind the compound where the guards threw trash. But she'd never had the heart to say that to Mouse.

"Come with me. We'll find Dana. We won't let your parents get you."

He shook his head. "No. I promised Dana I'd stay put so she could find me again."

Carley didn't have time to argue. She stuffed Mouse's socks into her pocket, reached over and kissed him on the cheek. He was still such a sweet little kid, he hardly even looked fourteen. Maybe because he was so small, he seemed like a child. Like Dana. They'd been a real cute couple.

"Austin," she whispered. "If you change your mind and get out, come to Austin, the drag along Guadalupe Street opposite the University campus. I'll get there as quick as I can. You hear? The drag across from the campus, that's all you have to do, get there."

Carley stood up, not daring to look back at Mouse, and clambered up the chain links and bolted over the fence, tearing her blue jeans on the barbed wire. She stifled her cries as the wire sliced across her thighs and her arms, and she landed on the hard ground with a grunt. Then she took off running as fast as she could in the too-big shoes.

***

Carley groaned. She couldn't help it, her face and arms were sunburned, her body still ached from the punishment she had taken days before, and she was totally parched and starving.

Yet, she felt a kind of joy. She was out of Aucilla, out of the hellhole again. Her fifth try. This time she'd gotten further away than she ever had before. But she'd been out in the wilderness, wandering around for days. She still had those huge shoes Mouse stole for her, but the blisters were worse than just wearing socks. Half the time she carried the damn shoes.

Carley was afraid to go to Liberty, the nearest town to the school. The law would just send her back to Aucilla. She'd learned that the hard way on her second try when she made it to pavement and hitched a ride with an old farmer who dropped her right off at the Sheriff's

Department. No matter how she'd screamed, cried or begged, a deputy called Aucilla and a guard came and picked her up. Then they locked her in the cage outside in the sun for four days.

She'd been so sick from the cage it took her a while to try again. That time, she got tangled in the barb wire and cut her leg so badly she couldn't keep running. With nothing to bandage it with, it bled, and the guards tracked the blood and found her before noon.

Now, her grand plan was simple: get to a paved road that went to Austin. US 290 was the target highway, and she'd stick out her thumb. She'd be damned if she'd get in any vehicle that had a local yokel in it. No, she'd wait it out till a trucker picked her up. She'd go all the way to Austin and skedaddle it to the university campus. There'd be other kids there, and somebody would help her. But first she had to find US 290.

Carley stumbled on through the scrub lands and into the forest and pine trees called the Big Thicket. There were rumors that a hairy Bigfoot type of creature had been seen over the years in the wilderness. She'd dealt with men at Aucilla Hall who would give Bigfoot a run for his money and she didn't believe in folklore like that. Still, she kept one eye on the ground to check for snakes and scorpions—or big tracks.

She aimlessly searched for an abandoned shack, hopefully one with supplies. In those old Westerns her dad liked to watch, the outlaws always found a cabin with cans of peaches or moonshine. "Movie crap," she muttered and longed for something to eat or drink. She had the feeling she might be wandering in a circle, but, for sure, there wasn't a house or shed or well or a can of peaches anywhere in sight.

The sun was going down. At least she wouldn't be so hot and her sunburn wouldn't get any worse. She was amazed that she was still getting so sunburned with all the trees, but she walked for hours at a time.

Nights were scary. There wasn't any place for her to sleep but on the ground. She was so afraid a rattlesnake would bite her, or that she'd be attacked by a coyote or wild boar, that she couldn't do more than catch a nap. Then she'd wake, heart pounding, on the harsh, unforgiving ground.

Snakes or not, she had to find a place to hunker down for the night, and she looked for a tree tall enough for some cover. Why she wanted shade branches over her at night, she couldn't figure. Maybe because it was kind of like a roof. Who knew? If she didn't find water soon, she might die. *How long can a person live without water?*

Stepping carefully through a dense thicket of prickly things, she eyed the landscape. *Nothing helpful, just more of the same.* A few steps later, she stopped and studied the ground. There might be a faint trail. A deer trail might lead her to a creek, but if it were a coyote track, she could be in worse trouble. She squinted in the fading light and took a few steps down the narrow trace. With no other choice, she followed the path.

In what felt like an hour later, pitch black night, barely even a squirt of moon, she stumbled into a small clearing with a deer stand high up in a tree. She climbed the planks up to the stand and gingerly patted down every inch, looking for something to drink or eat. She didn't want to set her hand down too firmly in case there was a scorpion.

Just her luck the hunters who were using this were tidy. Not even a bottle of whiskey or a loose cig.

At least she was off the ground. She curled up into a tight fetal position, closed her eyes, and recited the Lord's Prayer.

In the morning, a sharp noise woke her. She jerked up and struggled to the edge of the deer stand. Looking down, she stared straight into the face of a man in a brown uniform.

***

Carley twisted around in the hospital bed to listen to the men in her room. The Liberty County sheriff, Buck Sterling was his name, had his head together with some guy in jeans and cowboy boots, but who was also wearing a black jacket over a white shirt with a red tie. They were standing in the doorway, whispering but not so quietly. Carley could hear them, but just barely.

"I never did like that smug son-a-bitch, coming in here, buying up that land on the sly, cheap like, bringing all those repo trailers, and running that school like he didn't have to answer to nobody," the guy in the cowboy boots said. "Let's get somebody out there to inspect it, rope in the state attorney and use some of his resources. We can convene a grand jury if we need to." He paused, turned to look at Carley. "Hell, let's call the attorney general and the lieutenant governor on this."

Sheriff Sterling had earlier told Carley this guy in the boots was the chief judge of the circuit, whatever that meant, but she got it that he was somebody important. Carley thought his last name was Cain, but she couldn't remember exactly. Her head was foggy, and she was weak.

Carley tugged on the IV in her arm. Before she had passed out her first day at the hospital, someone told her it was called a banana bag, full of fluids and vitamins and stuff like that. She'd been dehydrated and suffering from exposure, that's what the doctor said. Oh, and she'd snuck a peek at her chart before the nurse hooked her up to the IV— evidence of recent sexual trauma. *So, yeah, maybe somebody will believe me this time.*

Turned out the man in the brown uniform was a game warden, and a decent guy. When Carley couldn't climb down out of that deer stand, he went right up and got her. Carried her down in his arms, sped her away in his jeep to the ER.

Carley found it hard to believe there were many good adults left anywhere around Liberty, but that game warden was definitely one of them. And everybody at the hospital was super nice. The sheriff was jumping hoops to help her. *Well, yeah, he owes me that, doesn't he?* After all, he'd sent her ass back to Aucilla the first time she'd ended up in his office. He'd told her just a few minutes ago, embarrassed like, how that image of her screaming and fighting the guard who came to take her back to Aucilla had stuck with him.

Maybe that scene had bothered a lot of other people too. The game warden said he'd been at the courthouse that day and had also seen the guard dragging her across the lawn, Carley kicking and begging. He had a girl her age himself. No way, he said, was he taking Carley back to Aucilla. When she started crying in the jeep on the way back to Liberty, he'd promised her he wouldn't let the sheriff return her either.

The hospital bed sheets were sticky yet smelled like Clorox so Carley knew they had to be clean. The sores on her back from the wire brush had been greased down with some kind of antibiotic ointment. Her sunburned face and arms throbbed, despite all the Noxzema plastered on her skin. She was sleepy. Maybe she was safe for a little while, though it was hard to know. But judging from the look on the sheriff's face and the cuss words spewed out of the other guy's mouth, they weren't going to send her back to Aucilla.

Sending her home might not be much better though.

The judge guy broke away from the sheriff and came up to Carley's bed. "I'll be calling in some state officials to start looking into Aucilla. First thing, they'll look at that arrangement with the juvenile justice authorities and if all the i's aren't dotted and t's crossed, they'll shut it down. Even if that looks good, we'll convene a grand jury, send in investigators. One way or the other, I'll see to it that place is shut down. Permanently, and we'll get those guards and the owner up on all kinds of criminal charges."

"You believe me?" Carley asked, her voice slurred. Maybe they'd put some dope in that IV too. She could barely keep her eyes opened.

"Yes. I believe you." The judge guy looked right at her when he said that. "We've been hearing rumors and complaints before, but nothing we could nail down."

"He didn't believe me when I tried to tell him. Before." Carley shook herself to keep awake and glared at the sheriff.

Sheriff Sterling eased up on the other side of the bed. "I am sorry I didn't believe you the first time." He paused, looking down at her so long she turned away from his stare.

"I'm driving out there myself, soon as I leave here, taking a couple of deputies with me, going to talk to some of the other kids and the guards." The sheriff reached out as if to pat her hand but then stepped back from Carley.

"The guards'll lie, they'll just say we made it up and that we hurt each other. You know, bad kids. The crazy ones who lie." Some of those kids, maybe most, would be afraid to testify. She was too tired to explain that and closed her eyes. *Just for a minute, let me shut my eyes.*

"Leave that up to us, okay," the judge guy said. "I'll issue the warrants, we'll search the grounds, and search that place you called the cottage. Talk to …what's the boy's name? Mouse?"

"And some of the girls," Carley said, her voice almost a whisper now. "Somebody called Rose and, way back when, some girl named Dana went missing." Carley swallowed, inhaled, and licked her lips. She closed and re-opened her eyes, wanting to forget all the horrors of the school, but realizing that for the first time someone was listening to her. "They dig holes and say it's for trash, but you ought to look there. Dana…"

"Go on," Sheriff Sterling said. "What about this Dana girl?"

"Story was…story …I heard…I heard the owner killed her." Carley was so sleepy now she could hardly speak, barely understood the questions, and wanted the sheriff and the judge to just leave her the hell alone. But she kept watching them from half-closed eyes. *Do they really believe me?*

"So the girl, Dana, she disappeared?" This time it was the judge who asked.

"Yeah. And somebody named Rose, just a little girl, maybe ten or eleven."

"You get some rest." The judge guy patted her hand. "We're going to need you to testify to the Grand Jury."

The sheriff and the judge walked out of the room.

Testify! No way she was doing that - she was getting out of here. Before her parents put her someplace worse than Aucilla.

Carley rolled over and looked at the IV. *Tomorrow I can pull it out. Get some clothes. Get out of here, get out to the highway, get to Austin and hide out by the university. Lots of runaway kids go there, so I'll make out fine. After all, I'm fifteen now.*

But when she closed her eyes, she saw Mouse and Dana, walking hand in hand behind the trash bins. They'd been her first friends at Aucilla.

The sheriff believes me. The judge guy did too, and the game warden.

Nobody had before.

But now they do.

She wasn't ever going to shut up about it again. She'd damn sure tell that grand jury everything that had been done to her and others at Aucilla Hall. She wouldn't let them ignore her or throw her away. She'd make sure they believed her.

As she fell asleep, she hoped somebody would get her a decent dress to wear when she testified to the grand jury.

The story behind the story: "Aucilla Hall Wilderness School" is revised from several outtakes from the novel *Wayward Girls* (Red Adept Publishing 2021), by Penny Koepsel and Claire Matturro. The story is a fictionalized retelling of a girl who escaped from a very real Texas wilderness school known as Artesia Hall. In the true story, she was found by a game warden and was finally able to convince state authorities that she—and others—were being abused. A girl died at Artesia Hall before it was finally closed. Official accounts of the Texas wilderness school are heartbreaking, and the GI bath in this story is taken from official transcripts.

Penny Hagner Koepsel has a PhD in psychology and has provided psychological services for many years. She has been writing creatively since childhood. She has also authored and co-authored research-based articles and a dissertation. Her experiences and career in psychology are often reflected in her fiction, as she continues to be a voice for those less fortunate. She is the co-author of *Wayward Girls* (Red Adept Publishing 2021) with Claire Matturro. Penny and her husband live in Texas with their rescued fur babies.

Claire Hamner Matturro has been a newspaper reporter in Alabama, a lawyer in Florida, and a legal writing teacher at Florida State University and University of Oregon. She is the author of seven prior books including a comedic legal thriller series published by HarperCollins, and co-author of *Wayward Girls* (Red Adept Publishing 2021) with Penny Koepsel. Claire and her husband live in Florida. Claire is an associate editor at *Southern Literary Review.*

Me and my Shadow
Ruthie Landis

In Giving Me the Shadow She Showed Me the Light

I have always loved playing with my shadow, especially on the beach. I am only five feet one and a half inches in height (on a good day and a shadow can make me feel luxuriously tall and thin. I am aware that this is a way for me to play with reality and see what I want to see, as opposed to what is truly me. I suppose the Shadow, as Carl Jung explored it, does a bit of the same thing, but only because we hide these rejected parts of ourselves away, in order to allow us to only show or own how we want to perceive ourselves and how we want to be perceived by others. When those very same dismissed human traits are somehow exposed to the light, if we can learn to embrace them, we might ultimately feel relieved, more self-accepting and less self-deceiving; we may be less in need of maintaining an exhausting vigilance around our image.

Often though, when these unacceptable human qualities are revealed to us by others, shame may arise, and we might feel very defensive as we try desperately to push those shadow characteristics away, back into the hiding places of the forbidden. Yet when these shadow parts are seen with loving eyes, by someone who accepts us just as we are, uncovered perhaps with gentle humor and lightness, this can be a huge breakthrough for us. We can begin to see that we need not edit ourselves to emulate a valued societal norm, or some unreasonable expectation of our purely human self; in fact, maybe we can learn to love in ourselves even what we may deem most unseemly. And eventually, perhaps we can meet those parts with an acknowledging nod and a generous giggle.

It takes a lot of energy to keep secrets and hide our whole self from ourselves.

I feel extraordinarily blessed that in January of 1994 I met Joy, who became one of the most profound relationships of my lifetime. She died in December of 2019. Actually, we are still in relationship and always will be. I know this truth to the core of my being. I talk to her in my head or aloud throughout the day. I hear her sweet contagious laugh, (we laughed a lot!) and when I am especially fortunate, she comes to me in my dreams.

The other day, I was really missing her, and I said so to a friend, and within an hour of saying that out loud, I was digging through a cabinet to find something I had lost, and a card she sent me long ago fell into my lap. This was not a cabinet that I kept her cards in. Everything I needed to hear at that moment in time was in that card. It was encouraging and unbelievably apropos to the issues I had been struggling with.

During our very long friendship, she was my spirit sister, my emotional companion through the seesaw of life, my playmate, my marriage and parenting advisor, my shopping and home decorating buddy, my creativity pal (though she always said, as my eyes rolled, that she *wasn't* creative) and beyond all of that, she was my humble mentor and teacher. I cannot put into words the depth of love and gratitude I have for Joy. She will be with me until the end of my own life, and I am certain, beyond this life. Joy and I were committed to reciprocity in our relationship, so I sense and hope that I filled many of those roles for her too.

Joy and I were on an adventure together of shared introspection, personal growth and development, and most importantly, we had an aspiration for lessening our own suffering. Could we transform the suffering we felt into a tolerable and lovingly held pain? Pain naturally accompanies our being human. Need it be suffering? We tried to do this together through lots of learning tools, books, workshops, and jabbering away, sharing our shame-filled revelations with equanimity. We used our body-data to reveal the unseen blind spots. The body never lies. We tried our best to be personally accountable in our talks with each other, and to hold each other's feet to the fire, no matter how distasteful. As we learned to kindly recognize our hero/victim, and the "put upon" parts, we were also seeking some level of spiritual awakening. We knew we were safe with each other's love.

We held each other accountable in tenderness and mutual respect. When we weren't traveling, we spoke five days a week. I live in Chicago and Joy lived in North Carolina, and we sustained a long-distance relationship with perseverance. We maintained our own lives and families, but when we talked on the phone or visited each other, we created a timeless bubble, listening intimately, and then listening even more carefully. And together, we grew.

On the Enneagram model, which Joy introduced to me (of course!) when we first met and which is a cornerstone for this book, she identified herself as a head type number six, navigating her fears. I am a heart type number two, in case you haven't guessed by now, navigating my worthiness and shame. We saw the world and situations through the lenses clouded by our different secrets and motivations. When we were fully present with each other, we completely unmasked, trusting each other in a common language: the language of bare-naked honesty and love.

On my many healing vacations visiting Joy, we would spend hours in the tiny cathedral-like studio that her husband, Bob, had built for her. This sacred space was set in the quiet little woods behind their home in Greensboro. It had vaulted ceilings and was filled with a magical expansive energy, decorated with meaningful art and symbols. Three of its four walls were constructed of floor to ceiling windows, so light had a way of appearing and disappearing, and of course, casting many shadows, as well.

This was the place Joy had given body-centered sessions to her clients and friends. She was also a master of the work of Byron Katie. This is the holy space where she and I shared and traded sessions with each other, too. Our last day together, before she died, I gave her a final session on her table, right before leaving for the airport. It was a most intimate farewell, as she decided it was time to let go of clinging to this life and all the suffering she was experiencing from an aggressive form of Parkinson's disease. Needless to say, this was one powerful place for both of us.

Rewind back to the year 2006. One golden sunny afternoon, when I was visiting yet again, we had been talking for hours, which was how it always went with us. I guess that day she unconsciously decided to teach me about the Shadow. Joy was always bringing me more things to learn. Out of the blue, she demanded, in her adorable, lilting, soft spoken, and distinctly southern dialect: "Say - 'Ah am selfish.' Just you say those words aloud - 'Ah am selfish.' Go 'head and say it!"

What! What was she up to now? I knew she was heading into new territory, because whenever she did this kind of thing, I could feel nausea coming on and my face flash with a flushy, hot pink. Maybe even little girl tears might well up in my eyes. I also knew that to become defensive was not going to work out for me in the long run. The bigger the pit in my stomach, the greater the lesson that I was about to learn. Damn!

I didn't want to say I was selfish. Are you kidding? I am a two on the Enneagram and in those days, I used to pride myself in not being selfish. I mean, it was at the heart of my identity. Who would I be if I was selfish? I was NOT a selfish person! So, I thought.

She persisted. "Now girly girl, ah know you are a generous, loving person, but you are also selfish, ya know. We all are. Even when you eat a piece of broccoli you cut that broccoli's life short. You are selfish. You are choosing YOU over the broccoli. So, now say it! 'Ah am selfish.'"

Please, you have to understand that Joy was the gentlest and kindest of souls. Never harsh to me. Sooo loving. Her eyes were like the vast sky and her face was angelically beautiful. This tone was a new one for me, but she was relentless. During our twenty six years of living friendship, she and I had only had three or four short, difficult conversations that always led to immense healing. Why was she pushing me like this? And she seemed to be getting a real kick out of it, to boot. Hmmm, maybe a little of her own shadow was shining through that day.

She persisted. She couldn't stop herself. This was an important agenda and she wasn't about to back down.

I took a deep breath. Maybe several. I tried to say it and I gagged, literally like I was going to puke. It was reminiscent of when my mom was forcing me to eat liver for dinner when I was a child. I still gag when I smell liver.

We laughed hysterically, though she was dead serious. It wasn't a mean laughter. It was a laughter of nervousness. It was a laughter of recognition. She had metaphorically caught me with my pants down. I mean, why else would it be so hard to say?

"Ah am not letting you off of this," she said, her sides splitting and wheezing through hilarious tears. "Ah said, say it! Ah mean, what are you afraid of? Just say it."

I gave her a look, then I burbled out pathetically, "Why are you doing this to me?"

"Say it!" she repeated with funny tears running down her face. By now, both of us were gasping for air we were laughing so hard. Have you had those kinds of complex moments when comedy and humiliation and honesty just come together? She was lovingly exposing what I wanted to keep most secret.

So, I tried again. This time I almost did throw up, but I forced out the words, anyway.

"I am sssss… sssselfish." She laughed even harder. So did I. I wish someone had been videotaping this scene.

"Now say it lahk you mean it! Go on." I gave her another look, and it was not pretty.

I really felt myself wanting to cry like a baby. This really ran long and deep. I practiced it again, trying to get behind the words. I told myself to be a good human-actor, and make it believable.

At last, "I am selfish" became the truest words I had ever spoken. I repeated those three words over and over again, each time with more ease. This part of me, selfish Ruthie, that I wanted to disown so badly, became a part of me again, as I reclaimed my wholeness. I could feel the relief in my body, letting go of the energy it took to preserve a certain image of myself, by hiding an unloved and unlovable part of me. Big breaths followed. I sighed fiercely with unburdening.

"And then she took my hand, looked softly into my eyes, and said, "Well done. Good girl. Brave girl." Tears ran down my cheeks. I was so moved by the trust and that I could actually own something about myself which I had so thoroughly rejected. Selfishness can be a good thing within reason. It can help me address my own needs and avert future resentment because I am not taking good care of myself. We sat there for a very long time in complete silence. The work of Spirit had been done. I had awakened to myself in the breadth of consciousness in acceptance. It was Joy's constant unwavering love that brought that about."

That day my love of shadow work began. A series of workshops were born called *Loving the Ugly* and now you are reading this book, *Loving the Unlovable.* My publicist decided Loving the Ugly might put people off. Ya think? Ironically, however, the creative workshops were so incredible and life changing, and well attended, in spite of the name. We all know that we have our Uglies, after all, don't we?

Joy was right, as always. My selfishness is slippery. When she was in hospice, though I wanted her suffering to end and her soul to be set free again, I could not bear it. All I could think about was how could I go on without her friendship and guidance? How would I continue to grow? What would I do without her support? Me. Me. Me. Yes, selfish. Of course, I didn't tell her that. I told her how courageous she was to work so hard to let go of the life she had cherished, and leave those she loved dearly. I told her how much I admired her deep commitment to setting herself free and moving onto her next adventure.

I know, when I listen carefully, I hear her reminding me that I will go on without her physical presence and I will continue to grow. I have published three more books in the two years since she transitioned. But I will not be able to hold her hand again, see those crystal-clear sky-blue eyes, hear that dearest southern drawl, (though I did keep some recordings of it) laugh uncontrollably with her as we continuously sought out new perspectives and revealed to each other our most "unacceptable" human places. Some days I feel lost without her probing and sharing. I want her back! I am indeed selfish. And I feel more whole admitting it.

I still have times when I want to indulge my grief selfishly. I want to feel everything about her leaving us, profoundly. Deep, cutting, raw and sometimes vicious sadness will overtake me. Sometimes I don't want to feel comfort or peace. Now and then I want to sob and scream and wail. Sometimes I want to feel either dead or the excruciating pain of this lost treasure. I want to hold onto the pain, not transcend it. And my promise to her is that I will feel the pain, yet I will not suffer.

Losing relationships through death, divorce, breaking up, people moving away and beginning new lives, or unresolved disputes can be so challenging to make peace with. This kind of healing can take a very long time.

I know I would be peaceful right now if I was sitting next to Joy. If I could call up my finest hour for her, I could set aside my selfishness. I could find the deepest sense of well-being and do it for her. Enter peace, remember she is no longer suffering. She is far away, and the honest truth is that I cannot always bypass this unsettled heart ache. "I am selfish, Joy, wanting you in my life forever."

On that last visit to see her, I massaged her delicate feet, listened to her aching, shaking body with such care, acknowledging its conundrum of whether to hold on or to let go. Maybe it was time for Joy to be a little selfish and will herself to the other side. We laughed and cried together as I held her neck and her head. We were in the ethers together, floating above this all, this hard life of ours: this life I was so graced to have been given a friendship like this, the gold standard. I didn't know then that would be our last physical contact. In retrospect, I see that those last sessions opened the portal to her exit. I was holding all of her as we spoke of letting go. My dear selfishness stepped aside then, to help her let go.

As I left her, she shuffled to the back door as I climbed into the car to go to the airport. She waved at me like we were two little girls saying goodbye. That image of her is burned into my memory forever.

I know the purest light will continue to come, through me and through her. It always has as far as Joy is concerned. It will come because the light creates the shadow; the shadow was one of her many gifts to me. The light is always there in all of us, but gets obscured.

Most times these days, when I think of Joy, I just feel unbelievably exalted with moments of awe, gentle peace, and immense gratitude. I know, intuitively, that she will always be nearby. Joy and I are in a timeless relationship. I actually feel her sitting here next to me as I write this, dropping little gems my way. Our relationship is a shimmering silver thread throughout this book. The light comes and shows me the shadows, and Joy will continue to remind me to look at both, shadow and light, with acceptance and love, wherever she is.

She loved my most ugly and unlovable. And now, so can I.

In giving me the Shadow She Showed me the Light.

My intention when I write and share this content is so that you, too, may know this precious kind of connection, this kind of friendship, this kind of love. I wish I could say that all my relationships feel as winning, but that is not yet the case. I am still learning and growing. My relational teachers surround me each day, thank goodness. I want to share with you many of the things I have learned from practicing sacred rules of engagement with Joy, the ways and agreements we held dear, to maintain our exquisite connection. So, I will reference Joy throughout this book, because my friendship with Joy was my most realized relationship. I also want to share many extremely effective interventions that I have used with my clients for over two decades. I see beautiful changes and clarity unfolding with so many of my clients in their relationships using these practices. You see, we all can become Joy. We all are Joy.

Ruthie Landis believes life is an opportunity to learn and grow. She is dedicated to helping people become their own best friend, loving and accepting themselves and others better.

She is a best-selling author of *Beyond the Bookclub: We are the Books We Must Read, My Musings, Acting Lessons for Living* and its accompanying Guided Journal.

Her other professional roles include facilitating growth as a body-centered psychotherapist and coach, certified hypnotherapist, Enneagram teacher, Award winning international workshop designer, trainer, and facilitator, visual artist, actress, director, acting and presence development coach, Spiritual guide, and Reiki master.

In addition to using theatrical and psychotherapeutic tools, Ruthie uses Nature, Ritual and Ceremony, life transition directed interior design, and the Chinese Five Element theory.

It is her mission to find ways to reclaim our wholeness with gentle, insight-driven change. Her intention is to bring all these interests and skills together to co-create unique encounters of waking up, self-empowerment, and healing.

For more info visit ruthienergy.com and Ruthie Landis YouTube.

In the Sanctuary of Hell
Janet Oakley

Marcus Thatch pressed hard against the main artery in the private's thigh. Earlier, for a second time, he had taken off part of the leg, cauterizing and tying the artery as he did so. But now it was so close to the young soldier's body that he could not take up any more of the smaller arteries. When the main opened afresh a few hours later, he had been by the boy's side and plunged his thumb into a space that barely had room for it. But the bleeding had stopped. So had the cannonading. Just an hour ago.

"How long I got?" the private asked. Candlelight flickered on his sweaty face, softening the pain lines. The adamantine candle sputtered and created crooked shadows on the back of the pew behind his head.

"As long as you need, Will." Thatch shifted on the hard pew seat to avoid the cramp in his hand. He gave him a weak smile, then looked away, suppressing the rising tide of grief. He straightened his shoulders. You have to do this for him.

Thatch's steward, Clem Walker, touched his shoulder. "Can I bring you water, sir?"

"Please."

It was a miracle Thatch made it back into the church designated as the Second Divison hospital. The surgeons had gone out to view conditions at a temporary field hospital on Seminary Ridge when the

Rebs broke the Union line and twenty thousand soldiers fled through the streets of Gettysburg to the safety of Cemetery Ridge. Thatch fled with them not wishing to be caught up in the fighting and captured, but the battle followed him into the streets of the little town. Horses and men screamed and fell. Cannon and caisson tipped and clogged. Bullets flinging around his head, he made it to the Lutheran Church's steps. His companion, a chaplain from another unit, turned just briefly and had his head blown off, splattering Thatch. Not long after he was safe inside, a Reb officer came around and said they were under guard.

"Best tie something white around yur arm so's we know you's a medical man."

Thatch and the other surgeons found what they could find and then tended to the chaotic moans and cries of helpless men.

"Found some writing paper in the vespery, Dr. Thatch. I'll write, if you like."

Will laid his head back on his knapsack. The board bent as it stretched from pew to pew. Like the nearly hundred others in the sanctuary.

Thatch adjusted the wool blanket around Will's shoulders with his free hand. "Steady. Who do you want to write to first?"

"Ma." Will turned away and sniffed.

"Of course." Thatch avoided his eyes. They had only told him a few minutes ago that it was no good. The other surgeons in the church had all consulted with Thatch and agreed there was nothing they could do. Will would bleed to death once pressure on the wound stopped. And it would have to stop.

Thatch tried to think of something else, but with all the moaning and stench of the place there was no refuge from reality.

Walker licked the pencil, poised.

"Know anyone else here you want to see?" Thatch asked.

Of course, he knew.

"Cecila ain't here," Will said, his voice a harsh whisper. "Guess it's to be Gopher. He make it?"

"He made it." Thatch nodded to a soldier standing by. "I think Private Hayes is down in the basement. Could you fetch him? I think he can walk with assistance."

Someone screamed over by the stained glass windows. It was early evening, the sticky summer air full of sulphate coming through the broken wide panes. Thatch shifted his thumb to remove the ache.

"What was that you say?" Walker leaned in and wrote down the last words and testament of Thatch's youngest brother, Willard Bailey Thatch.

As assistant surgeon in a Pennsylvania regiment, Dr. Marcus Thatch saw more misery and suffering he cared to write home about. Then came Gettysburg and the heartbreaking decision he knew would end only in death. Devastated, he reluctantly takes on an assignment to find a former medical colleague and friend and thwart the man's plot to overthrow the Union in the Pacific NW. In Thatch's War, peace in heart comes only through fire.

Janet Oakley (aka J. L. Oakley) writes historical fiction with characters who stand up for something in their own place and time. The inspiration for Thatch's War came from her great-grandfather's experiences as the assistant surgeon for the 11th PA, a Union regiment right in the thick of the Battle of
Gettysburg and to the end of the war. A college trained civilian doctor, Gettysburg was his first major battle. His journals and letters led to imagining a surgeon on leave in the Washington Territory in 1864. I've always wondered if surgeons suffered from PTSD. Thatch's War won third place in historical fiction at the Pacific NW Writers Conference. Time to finish it!

www.jloakleyauthor.com

The Pulpwood Queen's Work in Progress
Kathy L. Murphy

As we come to the end of this book, I must remind you of the story. The story that began with the dream of sharing writers who had a unique story to tell. One that drove each and every one of our authors in this book to begin their journey in the writing world. To write one's thoughts and dreams takes a lifetime of missteps, detours, and frankly, getting lost to finally find their way with the words formulated from years of pondering the exact ones to convey what they had this burning desire to tell. True writers never stop lest they get broken by the arduous challenge of getting their words out into the world. My gift has been bringing these author's stories into the light of readers around the world.

I began my travels in the world of sharing our author's stories with others when I started with The Pulpwood Queens of East Texas. It eventually became (over 20 years in the making) The International Pulpwood Queens and Timber Guys Book Club Reading Nation of today. Most of my life I just ambled lost with no direction in mind. Once I discovered that I found myself in reading, I also found sure footing. I see very clearly the road ahead. All the years of sharing my author's stories, their books and dreams, I am now on a mission to see long past the seeds that were planted by the teachers who read aloud to me in my childhood classes, that reading brings a bountiful and fruitful harvest for years to come.

I have had many moments of wonderful and delightful experiences throughout our twenty one years of showcasing many first time, first book authors. I have delighted in helping authors who may have never been discovered in a big way. Kind of like a mother bird, pushing her fledglings from the nest to see them fly and soar to heights in the heavens. Great joy comes to me in all our authors' accomplishments. These stories, these 'works in progress' are shared with our book club readership and beyond to give them a taste of how different and special each one of our book club authors' words to page really are. No one truly understands just how hard it is to be a writer and become an author. Years of toil and strife in a world where everybody is writing a story. The authors in this book are very special. They hold the promise of the passion of getting the words all together in such a way that you will remember them and look forward to their next publication.

We are all 'works in progress'. One thing I have learned in my reading life is that if you devote yourself to your life's gifts and talents, it does not matter if you become successful in society's eyes, as in rich and famous. What matters is the joy in the passion of telling the story that has unfolded as a present that will keep on giving to the world.

They say that people will forget who you are, what you have accomplished, but you never forget how people make you feel. You see this book is about feelings. Our emotions are poured out for everyone to connect by the experience of the read. You have probably heard a million times that "books saved me". They did me. I escaped into the stories of authors as my life at times became simply unbearable to face. Warring parents, hidden family secrets, harsh consequences, and brutal words beat me down on me until I was looking for anything to escape.

My teachers who were also my childhood librarians showed me the world was much bigger than I ever dreamed. I have traveled the world through reading and now it is my goal in life to share even more books that take us out into the world, not hide from anything. Books are the springboard to discovering that we live in an incredible world of different cultures, people, beliefs, and pure beauty in what God, however you name your higher power, has created for us.

So, in this world of my imagination through a lifetime of reading and being out in the world of nature, I have found the balm that heals all wounds. Reading! I want my world to be perceived, figuratively and virtually, as an author, artist, booklover, one that inspires, enlightens, educates, and lets you walk in the shoes of people much different from yourself. How boring life would be if we are all the same. Through the conversation of sharing our stories with others and our authors, we can see the beauty in the world as it shows we are human. We are the only animal that shares stories. It's all about the story, yours, mine, and ours.

"Work in Progress" created and edited by the incomparable Mandy Haynes is the gift to all of you that keeps on giving. Share this book with someone you love. Now in the immortal words of Alfred, Lord Tennyson...

Ulysses
BY ALFRED, LORD TENNYSON

It little profits that an idle king,
By this still hearth, among these barren crags,
Match'd with an aged wife, I mete and dole
Unequal laws unto a savage race,
That hoard, and sleep, and feed, and know not me.
I cannot rest from travel: I will drink
Life to the lees: All times I have enjoy'd
Greatly, have suffer'd greatly, both with those
That loved me, and alone, on shore, and when
Thro' scudding drifts the rainy Hyades
Vext the dim sea: I am become a name;
For always roaming with a hungry heart
Much have I seen and known; cities of men
And manners, climates, councils, governments,
Myself not least, but honour'd of them all;
And drunk delight of battle with my peers,
Far on the ringing plains of windy Troy.
I am a part of all that I have met;
Yet all experience is an arch wherethro'
Gleams that untravell'd world whose margin fades
For ever and forever when I move.

How dull it is to pause, to make an end,
To rust unburnish'd, not to shine in use!
As tho' to breathe were life! Life piled on life
Were all too little, and of one to me
Little remains: but every hour is saved
From that eternal silence, something more,
A bringer of new things; and vile it were
For some three suns to store and hoard myself,
And this gray spirit yearning in desire
To follow knowledge like a sinking star,
Beyond the utmost bound of human thought.

This is my son, mine own Telemachus,
To whom I leave the sceptre and the isle,—
Well-loved of me, discerning to fulfil
This labour, by slow prudence to make mild
A rugged people, and thro' soft degrees
Subdue them to the useful and the good.
Most blameless is he, centred in the sphere
Of common duties, decent not to fail
In offices of tenderness, and pay
Meet adoration to my household gods,
When I am gone. He works his work, I mine.

There lies the port; the vessel puffs her sail:
There gloom the dark, broad seas. My mariners,
Souls that have toil'd, and wrought, and thought with me—
That ever with a frolic welcome took
The thunder and the sunshine, and opposed
Free hearts, free foreheads—you and I are old;
Old age hath yet his honour and his toil;
Death closes all: but something ere the end,
Some work of noble note, may yet be done,
Not unbecoming men that strove with Gods.
The lights begin to twinkle from the rocks:
The long day wanes: the slow moon climbs: the deep
Moans round with many voices. Come, my friends,
'T is not too late to seek a newer world.

Push off, and sitting well in order smite
The sounding furrows; for my purpose holds
To sail beyond the sunset, and the baths
Of all the western stars, until I die.
It may be that the gulfs will wash us down:
It may be we shall touch the Happy Isles,
And see the great Achilles, whom we knew.
Tho' much is taken, much abides; and tho'
We are not now that strength which in old days
Moved earth and heaven, that which we are, we are;
One equal temper of heroic hearts,
Made weak by time and fate, but strong in will
To strive, to seek, to find, and not to yield.

Afterword

"Try to be kind and constructive to any other writer who approaches you for help.... It is an act of courage to write anything, but is an act approaching madness to want to do this for a living."—
Pat Conroy

This collection of more than 50 works in progress from amid the pantheon of masterful writers in the orbit of the legendary Pulpwood Queens Book Club is a treasure trove for readers—an unprecedented opportunity to see stories still in the act of becoming and to be introduced to wordsmiths still ascending in the arcs of their writing lives. Kudos to editor Mandy Haynes for assembling this remarkable collection.

The profession of authorship can be a lonely, uncertain endeavor, building worlds with nothing more than words in the earnest hopes they will, in time, speak to the hearts of readers and remind us all that we are bound together in a rich tapestry of stories spanning backwards and forwards across time. The writers in this collection have shared their still-burgeoning works as acts of courage and solidarity, an invitation for readers and their fellow writers to glimpse into tales still unfolding and books still inching their way toward publication. While many of these writers are established, accomplished presences in the House of Literature, others are new arrivals, still finding their ways and being guided selflessly by their peers. But that has always been the inclusive nature of the Pulpwood Queens, where authors of many levels of experience and success are revered and bolstered by a loyal and lovable motley crew of hundreds of dedicated readers, spanning the nation (and beyond) and gathering together in celebration of the transformative power of reading.

If you've arrived here at the tail end of this keepsake volume, then you already know the value of the journey of discovery you've undertaken through these pages. Your reward is an extensive reading list of the authors included herein whose published works you can now seek out to enjoy and whose as-of-yet unpublished works in progress you can await with eager anticipation.

Thank you, dear readers, for championing these writers and accepting their invitation to preview their upcoming volumes. And thank you most of all to Kathy L. Murphy and Mandy Haynes for continuing to bring us together, readers and writers alike, in supportive camaraderie and stalwart service to one another through the Pulpwood Queens. For your tireless work and neverending progress, we are eternally grateful and in your debt.

Jonathan Haupt
Executive Director
Pat Conroy Literary Center